I0641567

Lost and Found

Endless Tempest, Volume 3

Mark Landon Jarvis

Published by Mark Landon Jarvis, 2023.

LOST AND FOUND

First edition. October 31, 2023.

Copyright © 2023 Mark Landon Jarvis.

ISBN: 979-8986701264

Written by Mark Landon Jarvis.

Also by Mark Landon Jarvis

Endless Tempest
Lost and Found

Standalone
Lightning's Hand
Bewildered

In fond memory of Kenny Ray and Steve, two of my most ardent fans.

Chapter 01: Sky

Pettijohn's voice warned, "Depressurizing," through the brass voice pipe.

A woman nearby dutifully snapped the flap shut over it. The flight team members set about their rituals.

Ashley Elizabeth Winston, their leader, watched over them, but she focused on her breathing: in through the nose, long deep belly draughts; exhale through the lips pressed together in resistance. She was very intentional about this. The other girls didn't even know they were breathing specially laced cabin air, supercharged with oxygen. They wouldn't have cared, being soldiers first. Seasoned jumpers, they trusted their respirators and Ox tanks and all the related tech that went with it.

Rituals varied, but they all focused on the gear, tracing cables and hoses. The girls did this in pairs, running fingers over the wingsuit seams and ribbing: down the back, under the arms, down the legs, between the legs. Every buckle and rivet was inspected yet again. It all had to snap into position and stay clear of the propulsion systems and parachutes. If anything were defective, a girl would be sent back inside. Live to fly another day.

Even through the methodical inspections, she saw their fears tamped down with rituals. Double tap on the helmet. Raise and lower the visor twice, for luck. Knock helmets together. Some carried tokens of their faith or superstition, giving them a final squeeze or kiss and tucking them into their wingsuits.

All the girls would look to her, just quick glances, seeking reassurance. She'd wink at one, give another a curt head bob. Some had been career military, and others had fought decades earlier in the Turncoat rebellion, but none of them matched Ashley's time in the sky.

The airship, a Nebulosus class vessel, was fighting its way into the thunderstorm. It was their final descent. This was the most unnerving, even more than diving. She had been in the Quake so many times that she expected all the things that could be frightening. The ride was so rough here, the ship gyrating so, that it cracked and creaked and popped like it was coming undone. It was common for a seal to leak, or for a bolt to ping free and roll around the floor. Recently a window shot spiderwebs, but the layered glass had held. She glanced at it, remembering that day and how rough it could get in the air.

The girls were careening, but fighting it, clutching at handholds. A few wore mag boots and did their best to stand rigid and brave, fists at their hips. Some held hands. In the privacy of their helmets, all of them were mouthing prayers and mantras and otherwise cursing every decision that had led them here.

Ashley had a favorite position at the airlock that gave her a solid purchase and purpose. She had her back to the corner, stationed for that last smile and Affectation that would send her flight team out boldly. She had done this so many times; she was part of the machine. Her right hand, grasping at an instrument cluster, was keeping her poised. Her left was working the airlock. Two at a time. Shut. Watch them exit. Wait for the green light, then two more.

She was not without ritual and superstition. After the last girls were out, she pulled down her brass aviator goggles, relics from the early days of flight. It left her face unprotected from the fierce wind and chill, but it was her thing. She liked the way the leather helmet cupped her head, and she liked the way her platinum hair flared out at her neck and trailed behind her. It was a good look for a wild ride.

Stepping over the sill and into the airlock, she whispered the same three words, four times, so quickly it was just one word: *Thisiscrazy.Thisiscrazy.Thisiscrazy.Thisiscrazy.*

Like all the others, when Ashley exited, she tapped the phrase scratched in the metal of the transom: *Free Your Mind.*

Six girls fought the wind and rain and made their spacewalk to fan out down the left wing. The other six did the same to the right. Ashley was the thirteenth girl, the Spearhead, the one with the deadliest dive. She marched aftward, past the familiar flexiglass fuselage. The helmsman saluted her as she passed. She tapped her knuckle down the side of it until she reached the place where it receded back down into the hull. From here to her jump point, it was all improvisation.

There was no fuselage to brace herself up with, should the ship lean sharply left or right. No cables or guide wires were mounted here, for this model of ship could not be bound by such things. It was an untethered walk of a hundred feet or more, toward the back lip of the ship, but not yet over the edge. She approached the tail with trepidation, watching her footing, for when there was icing, it was found here where the winds whipped around the fuselage and met. At altitude, icing was common. Cutting through storms generally melted it, but she had slipped and been tossed into the void too many times to not take it seriously.

Whoever came up with the name for her position had a wry sense of humor. The worst of the jump for the Spearhead was not being the first to jump. It was dodging the antenna and sensors that jutted out from the tail like spears. Though they pointed aftward, more than one person had been fatally tangled or impaled by them in a poorly executed dive. This was her lot as leader, and she had come to terms with it... and she was the best wingsuit pilot in the sky.

On a good day, the pilot would cram a Nebulosus between other airships, and the turbulence and storms generated by each would give them good cover and fast sky. On the best days, a pilot like Pettijohn could maneuver just above and ahead of the airships they flew with. In that case, a flight team could "drop in the seam," a strange, still air pocket of a few hundred feet, before being buffeted by the worst of the weather.

Her boots were pressing down into the rubberized skin of the airship. She felt three times as heavy as usual, and she bowed her knees just a bit to compensate. She knew from this that Pettijohn was leveling out, and that there would be no better time to jump.

She looked to her left and right, giving the nearest girls a last wave. They would pass that down the ranks. Then, the nearest girls would watch for the Spearhead jumper. When she would dive and flex out her wings, the next girl would then dive three counts later. Each girl down the wing would do the same, following the lead of the innermost jumpers.

Ashley sucked in a last deep breath, then bit down on her mouthpiece. She flexed her legs and pushed off, free-falling. This was not a drop in the seam, but a tumultuous battering of counter cross winds that smacked the breath out of her. Her wingsuit flared out like a skirt between her legs. The wings underneath her arms pressurized with rammed air. The suit buoyed her up, and she was gliding. Some of the men on the boat above called it "skydiving sideways." Others called it "squirreling," for wingsuit webbing made pilots look like flying squirrels—and only a squirrel would be so stupid.

The skin of Ashley's cheeks was flapping from the rushing wind in her face. She was clicking along at over a hundred miles an hour, and she was loving it. Her antique brass aviator goggles protected her eyes, and she immediately started scanning below.

• • • •

Any airship created within the last twenty years could skim the earth under 1000 feet above sea level. Some could ascend to 40,000 feet or more. Unfortunately, whether below radar or above conventional cruise altitudes, airships the size of a Nebulosus had nowhere to hide. They were simply too big, with a wingspan of two miles and a depth of nearly two thousand feet.

In the case of a Nebulosus, the best place to hide was in plain sight. Like its cloud namesake, a Nebulosus class airship was the most indistinctly designed veil of fog, a wispy and vague cloud cover that barely left a shadow. It was the last airship LF Winston had designed, and it was his most sophisticated. Created from a translucent and flexible skin, these vessels were commonly known as ShapeShifters.

Even had they been entirely invisible from the ground, it was not worth the risk of being spotted by instrumentation. The Eat the Rich factions had spotted too many stealthy airships and damaged them in the last few years.

Ashley Winston was through taking chances. Every ship in her fleet, now over a dozen strong, was a Nebulosus class. These unique vessels drifted above 50,000 feet, exchanging morse code communication flashes, flying silently. Hiding on the cold, dark edge of the troposphere, they haunted the heavens, waiting for the next reconnaissance opportunity.

When conditions were optimum, a Nebulosus would swoop down among other Winston Weeklies, the Rainmakers, again hiding in plain sight. Whether mistaken for a fellow airship or disregarded as a natural cloud formation, a Nebulosus was seldom challenged. It was impossible to hide an airship, but the tiny, individual squirrels—constantly rotating out into the skies to search the waters below—were undetectable to any equipment scans. The skydivers could fly low, look close, mark wreckage, and land in the water with the most promising finds.

The Eat the Rich had raided, plundered, and sunk hundreds of yachts and cruise ships, many with all hands and guests still aboard. Her teams looked for any trace of any they had missed before. Altogether, the airship teams had found and rescued over 500 survivors along coastal areas worldwide. However, often airship teams were too late, only finding traces of wreckage with only the occasional parts of corpses clinging to them. Even that had become more rare over the years. Beacons drew them farther and farther out to sea, but often all that was left was the beacon itself.

Previous, less scrupulous crews had picked the bones of these tilted cruise ships and derelict yachts, but Ashley's people had different objectives: save the victims of Steve Spexarth's insanity. Free your mind. Restore the Winston name and the Pride of the Skies. These were the rallying cries of every flight, every jump, every reconnaissance vessel that was followed by water. Even so, over the years and through the sorrow of it all, the cries had grown fainter. The objectives were considered more and more obsolete. The team, one hundred and seventy-two men and women spread among the fleet, was letting go of the dream.

Ashley knew they were well past the point of exhaustion. Beyond the limits of anyone's reasonable expectations. Long past any diminishing returns. They found fewer and fewer survivors awash on islands or stranded on strange shorelines. There were days at a time when not a single person was rescued.

The crews, however, were loyal to her. The remnants of her Water Works never gave up. Their grit won them victories beyond the lives they had saved. It had been a hard battle, but over time she and her faithful crewmembers had reclaimed fourteen airships.

Their resolve had protected them, too. They had fought hard, battled hand to hand with rival Eat the Rich airship crews that had boarded theirs and attempted to take them down by force. They endured weeks of scant rations and airsickness, altitude and aether illnesses... all for her, and all for the Winston family name.

She felt terribly guilty pushing them on and on, but there was one more goal, an unspoken mad desire that she had yet to fulfill: *find Rory Reed.*

It had been a difficult sell. Even a ship as strange and powerful as the Nebulosus was a target, and everyone knew it. Rumors were rampant that another of the fleet had been shot down, the *Aelon.* No one believed it at first, until the sightings of it were reported among Ashley's own people: one of the largest of her airships was draped over a volcanic spire on a Pacific island. Though images of it had been all over the Interface, Ashley's people knew better than to believe anything they saw in their HeadGear anymore. More and more first-hand accounts confirmed it, however, and it brought up a bitter bile in Ashley's conscience. If even airships could now be brought down, what hope was left?

She squinted to see her fellow squirrels peppering the sky, gliding the trained routes they had perfected over time. Launching shifts of a dozen women at a time, the Nebulosus squirrels could effectively search over its entire wingspan. Every daylight hour, another flight would take to the skies and zip around, to then—just a few minutes later—parachute into the ocean.

They dropped red flares if there was a survivor. Yellow if not. Speed boats would then be deployed to retrieve the squirrel scouts, and occasionally, those they found who had been victimized by the Eat the Rich rebellion, the ETR.

Though an analog, off-the grid effort, it was a sloppy system, using entirely too much fuel and too much manpower. It was riddled with risk. The squirrels knew of their fellow fliers being shot down. Some had been duped by speed boats that had been overtaken by the ETR, and they had died bobbing in the ocean, flares still burning. They had been picked off, murdered, while on a humanitarian mission.

Those incidents, and visuals of the downed airship, had two effects on the crews of Ashley's airships. Some were galvanized and angered by such atrocities. Others were struggling with fear and defeat.

Survivors of the downed airship *Aelon* told of ETR ships that descended on them, three at once, with raiders mercilessly cutting down those aboard, men, women, and children. The attackers dressed and behaved like old-time mariner marauders, calling themselves Sky Pirates. They were vicious, but also organized, slicing aether ballasts strategically at the ribbings, cutting the crosshatch cables that kept the ship intact. Before the *Aelon* could offgas, before it could even make a counter turn, it was doomed to drift down and collapse like a deflated balloon. Fortunately, the ship landed on the island, and many were able to escape their attackers.

Regardless, it had been a bloodbath, and it had made a statement. The ETR had routed yet another Winston airship.

Retaliation would be swift and equally merciless. Ashley's fleet, though vastly outnumbered, had recouped the pilots skilled from 20 years at the mast. She longed for the opportunity of revenge.

The Winston name was tarnished by *Eat the Rich*, that terrible campaign that used her Rainmakers to brainwash millions, if not billions, of people. She would keep the water flowing, keep the rain coming, save the stranded... and one by one, they would retool or destroy the ships and crews of Eat the Rich sympathizers.

Chapter 02 Airship History

The airships of Winston Water Works were designed to fly forever. They took on and exhaled atmosphere in big, graceful gulps of the sky. Aether was their fuel, oxygen, their ballast, and weather was their wake. The Rainmakers flew in braces of five, spanning over 150 miles, and along their front edge, under the right conditions, powerful storms were constantly generating rain. Regulating the amount of rain and severity of the weather was a matter of altitude and speed. Airborne for twenty-five years, the ships swooped like schools of manta rays, gliding in established patterns referred to as Swipes.

The airships averaged 100 knots per hour, and they moved in large circular patterns of over 200,000 miles per week. Tracing the same routes, they were dubbed the Winston Weeklies by their creator, L.F. (Levi Finn) Winston. These lighter than air crafts were considered the greatest single man-made contribution to the world's well-being, over vaccines, desalination, HFCS foods...

Winston had launched them with the sole intent of bringing water to even the most arid climates, and had he made more ships, or set them on longer routes, they could have distributed ample moisture all over the globe. When all 100 of them were airborne, the charts provided irrigation to arable lands that had been previously too dry for crops.

Winston's charts were unforgiving, immutable, and accurate. In a decade, the swaths of land under the weeklies turned almost entirely to high-yield cropland. In a quarter-century, population centers grew on the edges of the Weeklies' paths, for that land came to be prioritized for agriculture. Historically productive farmlands benefited from the Weeklies Swipes, even if they were not directly under them. Winston's carefully calculated routes made the most of existing weather patterns, spawning new high and low fronts on their fringes. Predictable weather was a boon for agriculture, and powerful ag magnates swept in to manage the lands. These consolidated to become ChompCorp, which came to dominate all food growth and distribution.

TransCorp airlines built their flight plans and itineraries in consideration of the routes of the Weeklies. Knowing the weather made it more efficient to work on construction and roads. Lifestyle patterns, right down to weddings and funerals, sporting events, vacations—even recess—whirled around the patterns of the Winston Weeklies. Children were taught that the Water Cycle, the natural order of the world, was influenced by the Weeklies. *The world was better with predictable weather*, Winston Water Works proclaimed.

L.F. Winston created various models of airship, each of them patterned and named after cloud forms. He was not content crafting simply functioning airships; he wanted ones that made a statement. He wowed the world at every opportunity, building Rainmakers that rivaled the scale of the clouds themselves.

He was every bit the showman as P.T. Barnum. He piloted a gigantic CumuloNimbus class vessel to land on Lake Michigan for a G12 summit. He used another Nimbus to hoist aircraft carriers aloft for a show of force. When there were only six ships in his fleet, he abruptly turned them all toward a hurricane and was able to tame it, earning him the moniker of the Typhoon Tycoon. Not long afterward, he established a specialized fleet with the express purpose of quashing tropical storms before they destroyed coastal areas.

The entire enterprise was LF's gift to mankind. He never charged for the services of his airships. Even though his contributions revived entire economies and brought whole nations back from destitution and drought, he refused compensation. Though his philanthropy touched most lives on the planet, there were many who sought to take control of his airships. They wanted to weaponize them.

The corporations that benefited from the Weeklies mounted a concerted effort to take them away. The businesses that had thrived on imbalances in food and rain were out to ruin him. LF faked his own death, and for years little thought was given to him.

In 2047, he reappeared, claiming it was time to use the ships again for the greater good, for an even higher purpose than he had set them on before. He was going to use them to distribute his philosophy. They were going to convert the conscience of man to share LF's global sensitivities. The world would at last "Put Others First." But the plan failed.

Just as his ships were being loaded with an elixir that was billed as nothing short of a compliance chemical, another faction took the reins. Winston and his empowering message were shot down, and a new philosophy was broadcast using tools gained in his acquisition of CommCorp. Every broadcast channel, every medium of communication on the planet began issuing the message that had kept the world on fire for five years—with no end in sight.

Born a downtrodden street urchin, Steve Spexarth had seen a different opportunity and took it. Always an opportunist, he rose in the ranks of the Winston family's security detail. He worked for the very people he despised the very most: the uber-wealthy. He learned of LF's scheme and sabotaged it with an alternative message, "Eat the Rich." It had been a rallying cry over the last century, damning the disparity in wealth distribution. Protests and politics had flared up from time to time with proponents of the cause.

Spexarth, however, had taken it to another level by enlisting Winston's ships and ports. Everywhere a Weekly stormed, trace elements of LF's compliance chemical rained down on the people.

Everywhere one went, the Eat the Rich edict was chanted via CommCorp. It was the first and most powerful message victims of the chemical rain were exposed to.

The substance, scopolamine, blocked the neurotransmitters in the brain specifically used for short-term memory. The victims of it, millions of people in the paths of the Weeklies, were made susceptible to suggestion and without a memory of what they had done while under its influence. Regardless of form, whether aerosol or diluted liquid, whether in the form of raindrops or fog, scopolamine lasted 24-48 hours once ingested...and once ingested, people had no resistance to suggestions posited by others.

No studies attested to how it fared in groundwater, cisterns, water reservoirs or treatment plants. Quite possibly, the side effects of the drug lasted for days. What was known, however, was that scopolamine could kill in strong doses.

When coupled with the violent bent of the Eat the Rich suggestion, side effects of the drug were chaos, anarchy, and the sure and certain murder of anyone of means.

Chapter 03 Neon

The drunk rapped the bar for another shot. He was perturbed. It wasn't like the barkeep couldn't hear him. The juke box was wailing, but otherwise, only a handful of people were still swaying on the dance floor or hunched over their drinks.

"Henny!" he called again. "Hit me."

"Dad says you're done," the bartender said when she appeared in his field of vision. She slid a bowl in front of him. "Have some peanuts." She was the pretty one Kenny Hinman usually kept in the kitchen, the one with all the mascara.

"You tell your dad," Lark pointed at her with the prosthetic on his right arm, "you tell him I'm done when I say I'm done." The mechanical fingers moved to point an index finger menacingly, if belatedly, at the young woman.

They both were transfixed by the finger.

"Your servos are gummed up with hooch, Lefty." It was Henny, behind him.

The drunk turned on his stool, and the room turned with him. "What're you talking about? I'm fine."

"Then count," Henny challenged. "Count to five."

Henny was a blocky man who looked even more immovable when he stood there like that, his arms folded over his belly, his head tucked onto shoulders that left him no neck at all.

"I don't have to count," the drunk said.

"Tell you what, you count to five, *and use your fingers*, and I'll spot you another. You fail, and you stay here for the night." Now his hands were on his hips. The big man. The proprietor.

"What if I don't?

"You close your tab and walk to your mom's place," Henny said.

"Tell you what, you get me a drink and we'll call it square."

"He's not gonna give, Mr. Fortune," the girl at the bar said.

The drunk shrugged, held up his left hand, and enumerated his five count with a broad smile. He turned back to the bar and asked the girl again for his drink. She looked past his smile to confirm with the owner, then busied herself making his drink.

"I meant the *other* fingers, and you know it," Henny grumbled, wallowing up on a stool beside him.

"Not nice making fun of the disabled," the drunk said, not bothering to look Henny directly in the eye. He was watching him in the bar mirror.

"What gives?" Henny asked.

The drunk grasped his glass with fingers and thumb. He liked the heft of the glasses at Henny's. Whether it was a shot glass, a tumbler, a pilsner or a big pint, they were all heavily made. He studied his prosthetic hand holding the glass and squeezed a little. His plastic fingers flattened out with increased pressure. *Servos gummed up*, he smirked, knowing he could pulverize that glass with just a little more grip.

"Lark. You readin' me? What's the matter? You been in here soaking up the sauce all night. Ya didn't come out back, even to say hello?"

Kenny Hinman lived above the bar, but he had offices and a lounge in back. It was a hell of a place to raise a family, but they had done okay. Three girls. Oldest at college. Youngest sweeping up behind the bar. "Where's Peg?"

"Hey. Hey." Henny was shaking his shoulder. "Are you all there, pal?"

"Why haven't I seen Peg all night?"

"You know she's got a beau and a baby, now. She's not kept bar in over a year."

"I wanna see Peg," the drunk said. "She makes me laugh."

"I'll make you laugh," the young one said.

"Gail's tellin' jokes," someone hollered nearby.

The drunk looked around. The hollering man was all smiles, pulling up close on Henny's other side. Two or three others from the dance floor were coming up. The front door slammed. Some others had left.

"I went to a zoo the other day," she started, ducking down to catch his attention. "Did you know that, Mr. Fortune? I did. I went to the—"

"There's no more zoos, kid, you know that," he slurred.

"I did though. I found one. Yeah. I went to the zoo, but I was a little disappointed."

"Why's that, Gail?" the bawdy drunk said over Henny's shoulder. He was beaming as if he knew the punchline already.

"Well, there was only just one animal there."

"Awwww," a couple of people drawled out in unison.

"Yeah, just the one dog there. It was a Shih Tzu."

Everyone laughed. The drunk smiled in spite of himself.

"One day, a fourteen-year-old weasel went down to the local dance hall," Gail said, looking the drunk right in the eye. "Bartender took one look at him and says, 'You are under-aged. I can't serve you beer.' The weasel asks, 'Well, what *can* I have?' The bartender replies, 'Well, I have bottled water, juice, energy drinks, and pop.' 'Pop!' goes the weasel."

Laughter and groans surrounded him. The drunk shook his head and repeated the punchline. "'Pop!' goes the weasel."

"Attaboy, Lark. Finish your drink and let's get your cot set up."

Lark Fortune let them lead him to the back room, off the kitchen, where they kept a cot for him by the bathrooms. The jokes were rolling out at the bar, but he didn't really care. Jokes were superficial. Band-aids. Laughter wasn't medicine at all, more like the hiccups. He found he had the hiccups.

Henny was standing by the cot, looking down at him with concern. "What's brought you here tonight, pal?"

"Hiccups," he said.

"What else?" Henny pressed, pulling up a mop bucket to sit on.

"I got the radiation," Lark said, sitting up. "Just like old lady Wiebe and the others. I got it, and it's eating me from the inside out."

"You don't have any—that was years and years ago! Don't you think it would have caught up to you by now?"

"The radiation's took out Rob Ward. *Did you know that?*" He flopped back on the cot, grasped at Henny with his real hand. "Ohhhh... Bed spins."

"He was driving right in the thick of it," Henny argued. "An' it took thirty years to catch up with him, Lefty. *Thirty years.*"

"I can feel it, Kenny. I can feel it in my stump." The drunk's eyes were wide. He shook his mechanical fist at the bar owner and whispered the curse, "Radiation."

"Now that, I could sooner believe. Want me to take a look at it?"

"I'm not a damn beer tap. Deep fryer. What do you know about my arm?"

"How many times have I tweaked—"

"A lot you know," Lark growled, but he let Henny gently remove the prosthetic and examine both it and his stump. "I'm like a lightning rod for radiation."

"You are not," Henny said without even looking up. "But you're a sponge for my liquor. Gail says you drank a fifth of Bacardi all by your lonesome."

"I think I shared a few rounds."

"You never share a few rounds."

Henny pulled a pen light from his pocket and shined it up the cuff of the prosthetic. He removed his glasses and peered inside it more closely.

"I ate my weight in nachos. There's that."

"Good thing. Otherwise, your blood alcohol would be fatal. Good thing you built up such a tolerance."

"Good thing," Lark said, watching the neon flashes in the reflection of the back window.

"Nothing's out of sorts," Henny said finally, laying the arm across Lark's chest. "Nothin' but you."

Lark willed a vile gesture from the detached hand, and it flashed it at Henny.

"What's the range on that thing, anyway?" Henny asked, "When it's off your arm like that?"

"I dunno, hundred yards maybe. Why?"

"Pranks," Henny smiled. "Halloween's coming."

"You're an idiot," Lark said, and laid back, smiling.

The front door opened and closed. The music was off. Lark could hear all the bumping and scrubbing out front. He could hear Henny wheezing.

"What are you looking at?" he asked.

"Still trying to figure you out," Henny shrugged. It was his trademark gesture. The bar should have been named *Shrugs* not *Sharts N' Grins*.

"Nothing to figure."

"Rob Ward died two years ago."

"It's the anniver—"

"It is not the anniversary of anything," Henny said more firmly. "Now why're you here tonight. What's wrong?"

"Rainmakers!" Lark sat up on the cot abruptly, so fast his mechanical hand fell to the floor and was grasping at air.

Henny groaned and bent over, grabbed the hand, and returned it to Lark. He shook his head. Another theory about the Rainmakers. They were evil. They were from another planet. They were weapons. They brainwashed people. There was never an end to his theories.

"You know they're off course. Off schedule."

"Yeah, yeah. So what?" Henny said.

"Hasn't rained in a year."

"Well, maybe—"

"It hasn't. I keep a tally. It's been 366 days since it rained here last. Nothing but a few natural showers. You know what that means?"

"You need something better to do with your time? Some Eat the Rich jackass hijacked the airships that serviced us?"

"It's a *conspiracy*, Henny. They're drying us out. Slow, so most people don't even notice it much. A shower now and then, and they're pacified. Not me though, not me!"

"*You* need drying out," Henny chuckled. He pushed Lark back down on the cot. "You get some sleep, and you can tell me all about it in the morning."

"They couldn't find me with their Rainmakers, you know....so now, they're sending drones to hunt me."

"Drones?"

"Yeah. They make them up to look like birds."

"Birds are spying on you?"

"Yeah. Drone birds. They have sophisticated camera works in 'em. That's why I came at night, you know."

"Because of spy birds?" Henny said. "It wasn't for Nacho night?"

"They don't have night vision. Not yet." Lark glanced at the windows. "You going to shut the blinds?"

"Gail, honey? Can you shut the blinds before you go up?"

"Sure," she said.

Lark listened for it. Watched her closing blinds even in the little back room.

"Drying us out. Smoking me out. I can feel it coming," he shook his stump in the air again.

"You know you're safe here," Henny said, pulling the blankets up around his friend. "The neon keeps you safe here."

"That's right," Lark said, struggling to keep his eyes open. "Neon keeps me safe."

He had a theory that the goons hated neon. Maybe it didn't exist in their time or dimension. Maybe it blocked their sensors or something. All he knew was that he had never been caught when he was at Henny's place. Not in all these years.

"Thanks for the neon," he muttered, drifting off to sleep. "Neon. On and on and on and..."

Chapter 04 Speed Reading

S tu Wiebe sat in his truck with his son, Nat.
That was the simple way to tell it.

He was sitting in his truck. He was sharing the cab with his offspring. After that, he wasn't on sure footing. Nat was Nathan to him, and always would be. Looking over at him, however, he wasn't seeing it anymore. No more Friday night lights football. No hunting trips. No cigars and strong whiskey.

Nathan identified as Nat.

Nat was neither man nor woman, not to be confined by the binary, not to be assigned a sex and a role and a predetermined place of preference in society. It was 2054, and to Nat, it was no longer a time for sad, posturing pretenses. It was a time for the individual.

That ran contrary to nearly everything Stu knew, and confused him as to what he didn't know, maybe. But what he *did* know was that this was not a boat to rock. He'd heard of men doing interventions, even of them just asking too much, and the outcome was never good. It ranged from teen suicides to drugs to runaways. Better to go with it, learn about it when the lessons were offered, and otherwise hope for the best.

At least they had one thing in common: a deep and abiding loathing for Corporations and the micromanagement they imposed. That had united father and... and Nat in doing whatever they could do to support the Eat the Rich movement when it came and went with the MagLev passenger trains through Laramie. Over the last few years—after the electricity was throttled off and the CommCorp broadcasts were all one way, after the cattle buyers from ChompCorp had all been run off and a man couldn't sell a damn thing... even to a tourist half the time—the Wiebes had made a practice of taking representatives from the Eat the Rich movement out for a steak. More often than not, Stu learned they were vegan, and that led to problems dining out in Laramie in the new world. So, he'd opened his home to wayward movers and shakers of the movement, at first out of curiosity, later out of necessity.

His wife, Rae, was a hell of a cook, and when guests were vegan, she'd cook vegan. When Nathan became Nat and Nat became vegan, Rae made that accommodation without missing a beat, every meal.

Her right-hand girl, Yadri, was about as capable as Rae herself, specializing in keeping the place open to guests when they strayed in from hitching or trudging the long thirty miles south of town. On any given day, they had a dozen wayfarers in the outbuildings to feed.

Things had gone smooth enough for too long. Stu knew it. He had learned of entropy and fiscal responsibility and the inevitability of collapse. He had lived through government shutdowns and what they called The Big Reveal—simply that government was owned by corporations and nudged around by lobbyists... and they cut out the middlemen then and tried running things themselves and then...

Then Nat had gotten old enough to get interested, just as the whole house of cards tumbled down. Thank God they were a far cry away, where it didn't much matter whose political banner was waving so long as the spring didn't dry up, the cows calved, and the grass grew. He thanked God every day, sometimes even in the stray moments like this when they were waiting for a train to pass. They had safety from the madness and mayhem and collapse of it all, and from that position of safety and strength, Stu dabbled.

When he was Nat's age he had more-than-dabbled. He had been part of a vigilante group, The Boys. Now all old men like himself, and most of the rest of them in the grave, The Boys were the men, and the men were restless.

They had relocated to Wyoming with him and his family back in the 20's, and together, they struck up with some regional posse and militia folk. When the shit went down, they were all ready. They all stood together. When the kids from the cities got all excited about fighting The Man, he encouraged it.

Now he was a regional connection for the Eat the Rich rabble. Every time he thought about taking down his shingle and living a life of quiet desperation, Nat would get excited about something.

The train was the source of Nat's current excitement.

Among the Eat the Rich, Nat had explained to him, there were some who were "subverts," which in Nat's opinion represented *the real deal*—people who would not settle for anything short of the total destruction of oppression. These men, women, and others did not abide by conventional currencies or communications. Their work was under the radar, underground, off the rails... yet surprising to Stu, very much on the rails, literally.

"Subverts use the train cars, Stu," Nat had told him some time back. (This was about the hardest part of the new Nathan, that he called his own father by his given name and not his title, but Stu rolled with it.) "I'm learning to read them."

At that time, it had been a way to spend time with Nat, but as they shared insights back with Stu, and as those insights were proven out, Stu had built more and more trust in Nat's "train reads."

Stu had caught wind of something very disturbing: ChompCorp had militarized, and they were coming across the ranch lands of the north, down from Canada and through the Midwest, "appropriating" properties. Nat had offered to look into it, so they spent many afternoons at the depot when the 4 o'clock freighter rolled through.

Nat had filled a notebook with scribbles and scratches, quick sketches of things Stu would have written off as gang signs and tags. Nat spent hours at night rewriting and juggling them around in the bedroom. Once forbidden territory, Nat had even come to invite Stu into the room to help make heads or tails of the symbols.

It was mid-October, chilly enough to sit in the truck with the windows up and yet not cold enough to run the heater. The train was just getting its magnets into position, rising off the track, just pressing silently forward. Stu took out his old HeadGear camera and hung it on the rear-view mirror, hoping to capture the train cars without getting spotted himself with Gear he and his own men had a terrible distaste for.

He glanced up and down the track. Pickups were in position. His own men were watching out for his well-being. Stu had made the assignments. Something about sitting out in the open paying such attention to coded train cars did not seem safe. Schmidt and Lowen were on the far side of the tracks, doing their damnedest to jot down and record anything they could see of the subverts' messages.

Training those buffoons, redneck kids from the high country, had been Nat's summer highlight. They had obvious misgivings and discomfort, learning from the long-haired kid with piercings and nail polish, but as time went on, they learned Nat knew what train readings were all about. They learned Nat was also a damned good teacher.

Cars were skimming by them now, and Nat was scribbling, flipping pages, scribbling more and more. "That can't be right," Nat said once. Pages were flipped back and forth for quick review, frantic arrows and stars marked the pages. "Check with them, see what they say," Nat said without so much as looking at Stu.

"AM 1420, Ranchland Radio. Anything to see? Call the station," Stu broadcast on the CB, using their practiced code.

"Some craziness in the afternoon news, Chief," Schmidt said.

"Ask him if he got anything about a raid."

"I wonder, listeners, if we should expect a storm soon?" Stu said into the mic, "Spotters got anything to report?"

There was no reply on the CB. Stu looked at Nat and shrugged.

Nat looked from the train graffiti to Stu and said, "Says they're coming from above, Stu. Tonight. On Rainmakers."

"Mr. Wiebe." It was the other kid, Lowen, panting into the mic, "We ran alongside to make sure. Better tell Nat. See if Nat saw it too, that we was—"

"Go to the spring," Stu cut in abruptly. "Get everybody to the spring. Now."

He fired up his truck and glanced at Nat for confirmation.

"Good call. If it was on both sides of the train like that, it's a sure thing."

"Nat," Stu said, dropping it into gear, "Rainmakers are one thing, but do you read anything about Lightning's Hand?"

Nat flipped through the train readings notebook, scanning each page with a hand. "Some lightning, here and there, but no, nothing coded about Lightning's Hand." Nat swallowed hard, looking out over the prairie.

They both knew the whole region was a tinder box. Lightning from natural storms caused the occasional grassland fire, but a Lightning's Hand, an airship cruising far too close to the ground, could set it all aflame and much, much worse.

. . . .

"Glad you boys brought the water trucks," Stu said, slapping the side of a hulking truck as he passed. An entourage of open range fire fighters walked with him. The Springs were teeming with dozens of farm trucks and exotic four-wheel-drive pickups, former law enforcement vehicles of every model, and too many people on horseback to count.

A marshal from the old Wyoming force put a hand on his arm and asked quietly, "Eaters think this is some kinda attack, Stu. What's your take on it?"

"I think they brought the fight here, and they knew what they were doing," Stu said. "We like a good fight."

"Rumor is, though, it ain't going to be a fair fight," the marshal looked up over the mountain range to the west.

"It never is," Stu smiled a wicked smile he'd kept in check for far too long.

Chapter 05 Blackbeard

A shley's dive confirmed a thin ribbon of smoke indeed was rising a few hundred yards into the forest. She pulled up her chin and her body followed to a near standing position, then she arced and pinioned. Her wingsuit snapped to release its form, and she slapped her palms to her hips, dropping feet-first into the ocean.

Old wingsuits were all fabric, all wings for maximum lift and glide. They would have been as dangerous as a billowing parachute in the water. These, however, were sleek and tight wet suits that supported wings with composite steel spars. When a girl dropped a ways from shore, the wetsuit wings served as broad pectoral fins, allowing them to glide underwater as gracefully as they could in the sky.

Ashley had maneuvered closer than most would dare, confident in the tide charts and her visual estimation of the seabed sand. In just a few strokes she was in the shallows and stood, wringing her leather helmet as she looked about. It had once been a beautiful, pristine beach, but it was now awash with ship wreckage that had been picked over by beach combing vagrants and barraged by the sea for years now. The nature of things would win, and eventually the beach would bear only traces of the Eat the Rich attacks.

Such detritus was of great value to her team, for it gave them direction and landmarks. This cove was familiar, though some of the wreckage was not. It could be a trick of the sun, she thought, or it could be nerves. In any case, with unfamiliar wreckage and the smoke trailing into the sky in the distance, Ashley was confident someone on her team would find survivors this morning.

She stepped lightly on the sand, alert and stealthy. Carefully, she rounded an upturned hull and peeked in a gaping hole. "Hello," she said softly. "Anyone here?"

Even this reminded her of Rory. A trained mercenary, he would have frowned at her approach. How many times had he said, "Might as well just shout out, 'Shoot me, I'm right here!'" with a bitter chuckle. All the silent landing and stealth gear would do her no good, he would chastise, if she acted like this was a seaside social.

The second hull she approached had been there a long while. She recognized it from before, having landed here four times over the years. She knew its unfortunate name, *Destiny*, even before she ran a hand over the upside-down carved letters of the name board. This time she did as he had trained her, sidling up to the broken hull, standing aside, rapping on the wood. "Come on out," she commanded, as boldly as she could muster.

Nothing.

No one.

Not a trace of recent activity inside.

Ashley walked up and back on the beach, examining it closely for any signs: an MRE wrapper, an article of clothing, even human waste. Eventually, she found her way into the forest and picked her way down a sandy trail. The farther inland she walked, the more she thought she could be seeing footprints, but she knew that might be an overly eager imagination at work.

The trail went over a sandy dune with sparse trees ahead. She was cresting the hill when she heard a sound, a human voice. She crouched, taking a knee on impulse. Her wings fanned out behind her like a cape. She took a beat to collect herself. Was that voice crying? Singing? She could not make out the words, not even the language, but it was a vocalization, and she strained to hear it more clearly over the wind in the trees.

The reconnaissance teams had learned hard lessons over these last few years. Surprising a camp could be fatal. Not all survivors wanted to be saved. Some, in fact, were more dangerous than anyone else who may have come across them. The Rich, if that line were to be drawn, tended to be more inflammatory, more trigger happy, and less stable overall. Ashley understood. They were the most poorly prepared, and without their resources, they were at the mercy of the elements and fearful of everyone who might have heard Spexarth's message.

Her team had come to terms with the danger, and they improved each day in every aspect of their operation. Pilots became ever-more adept at hiding among the other Rainmakers. Squirrels were all women, all as light as could be found for maximum airtime, but then trained in combat and field medicine as well as the intricacies of flight. They had learned morning was the most opportune time of day, when the fires were smoldering and the guard was most lax. They knew the sixth day after a passing Rainmaker was the safest, when the tainted rain and the "Eat the Rich" rant were most diluted and distant.

Listening, Ashley struggled to keep herself in check. She wanted to pop over the hill and make herself known. Taking this pause was so hard for her. She was a woman of action and impulse. She looked at the old analog watch on her wrist. It was a diver's watch, an antique model her friend Alex Gault had given her. She had only thirty minutes before the boat would sweep through the bay. The rule on this was hard and fast, even for her: be at the rendezvous site, or be left on your own for a week.

Her mind folded in on itself, and she was revisiting the most horrific of all her rescue efforts. A man in his thirties was alone in his makeshift shelter, the bones of his family and friends littered the floor. He had taken the message "Eat the Rich" far too far.

"*Can't be bad as that*," she said through gritted teeth, and then she stood, reached over her shoulders to grasp the pointed joints in the wings she wore. These were rapiers sheathed in the folds of her wingsuit, and as she extracted them, she crossed them before her and called out: "We're here to help."

The wind turned on her as she came over the crest, and with it, the stench of death. She blinked at the sand blowing in her face, and then she saw remains of a dozen or more bodies, and she retched.

Across the fire, a man was sitting in the sand, his arm around a woman at his side. He looked up at Ashley, but he did not seem to fully register her presence. The woman kept her head bowed. She was propped unnaturally against the man's shoulder. She was most likely dead.

Other corpses around the encampment had been posed as if rolling a sleeping bag, tending the fire, lying on the sand watching the heavens. A thickset man had fallen over but seemed to have been struck dead while in the midst of tying a lure on his fishing gear.

The man at the fire was humming again, disregarding Ashley.

"We're here to help," she repeated.

"You're too late," he said absently, not passing judgment, just stating a fact. He resumed his humming. She knew the tune. It was a rock song that shared Spexarth's message.

She studied him closely, looking for a gun tucked in his ragged shorts. She moved around a couple posed as if they had been dancing and fallen over together. Gradually, she moved to his side of the fire, her eyes never leaving him. He was not wounded as all the rest clearly were. He had no defensive wounds on his hands.

Standing in the midst of them all, she fought back a gag at the smell. Bugs were scuttling in and out of mouths. Ants were thick on some of the bodies. One body was face down. It moved as if something larger than a bug was burrowing inside it.

"I can take you out of this," she said, crouching near him. "We can get you somewhere... else."

"I can't leave them again," he said, feebly, squeezing the tears from the corners of his eyes.

"What do you mean?" Ashley sheathed her swords. "They're... gone."

"I left them alone, not even five minutes," he said. Tears were streaming down his face now. "Went for some wood."

She just listened. There was more, how he came back to find all nine of them dead, how he tried to revive them. How he feared the beast that had killed them would be back for him. He went on to explain that they had shared this camp for over a year. He was falling in love with the woman at his side. He couldn't be without them ever again.

"Listen," she said, as kindly as she could. "It was not an animal. It was those Eat the Rich monsters."

"How do you know?" he asked, incredulous.

"These are intentional wounds," she noticed a cut throat, a stab right through the heart, a head chopped off between vertebrae. Whomever had cut through this camp was not on a rampage. They were methodical, efficient, and expert at their tasks. "They just came and went, you say. Didn't even look for you?"

He shook his head and sobbed into his dead girlfriend's hair. He was reliving the horror, she knew. Ashley gave him space, standing again and pacing, trying to find anything upwind of the stench of death.

"We all fought with it, the periodic, serial insanity," he said, craning his neck then to look her eye to eye. "We had coping skills." He barked a little dry laugh. "The profanity! After a rain, we'd just berate one another, the most vile and hateful things. Yelled at the top of our lungs for a night and a day... but we never touched one another."

He gently laid the stiff woman on her side, then he rose to his feet. He was very tall and athletic—at least he had been before being reduced to eating coconuts and sawgrass. A twinge of alarm coursed through her, and Ashley readied an Affectation that would bring him down in a blink, if needed. What if, she realized, he had killed them all, himself? What if this crazy encampment was him dealing with the guilt of it all?

"I'm a Mennonite, miss. We all are. Were." He looked around as if he were realizing again that he was the sole survivor. "We believe in absolutes. Heaven. Hell. Good. Evil."

She nodded her head, actively listening, but also prepping to deal him a level of mental anguish that would cripple him.

"Believing is academic," he said with a sigh. "Seeing pure evil with your own eyes, now that brings absolutes to life. I don't just believe in evil now. I saw it in action. I saw him in action."

"Wait. Wait... you *saw* this happen?"

He fought back crying again, nodding his head. "I was coming up, carrying that bundle of wood when I saw him."

She looked where he pointed, and there in the grass was a little armload of branches, right where he had dropped it. "You saw the killer, but he didn't see you?"

"It was night, after the rain. He was by the fire, I was there... He looked just like that pirate from the stories—Blackbeard." The man quavered, then continued. "Bigger than me. Black hair, woolly black beard with ribbons tied in it. He was some kind of martial artist. He was so precise. Screaming 'Eat the Rich.' He was a madman! He cut them down like they weren't even people. Like they were just... just dummies or something."

"He may come back sometime. You should come with me." Ashley was looking again at the bodies. Had this man, this damaged survivor, moved them around in his bizarre coping strategy? She could not imagine how the killer had mowed through them. Ten people in just a few minutes. Ruthlessly motivated by that damn message.

His arguments never changed. He could not leave his friends. It was his fault for leaving them last time. If the man he called Blackbeard returned, this time he would confront him.

Ashley stayed as long as her watch allowed, but the boat was coming soon. She took a vial of tablets from a pocket on her inner sleeve and handed it to him. "These will save you from ever experiencing the insanity again. Give them to everybody you can."

"Pills?" he said with doubt, examining the vial.

"They contain a small dose of a virus that will take away your sense of smell and taste. It's an olfactory agent that's causing everyone to be this way. It may be effective on contact, too. We don't know, but these help. Trust me." She wrapped his hand around the vial.

"I trust my God," he said, looking heavenward, "even now. If I am attacked, so be it."

Ashley shook her head sadly as she walked out of the camp. She felt for the guy, but she understood. He wanted to be with his people. His tribe.

She was more concerned with the man who had killed them all so professionally. Everyone on this coast had reported similarly over the years. Generally, it was a free for all after a Rainmaker storm. They had all been rich, and so, they reasoned, they had all been wrong. They all must be removed, so they would set upon each other.

The killer the Mennonite described, however, worked alone, and he worked with an ugly efficiency she feared.

• • • •

S he shot off a yellow flare.

Those with red flares were picked up first and with an armed escort, traveling in groups of three inflatable speed boat rafts. She saw no red flares up or down the coast, only other yellow flares coursing through the sky just like hers, yellow smoke curling down toward the sea. Defeat.

She sat on the beach and waited. The other two girls in her drop zone returned from their searches, also with nothing to report. She wasn't going to say anything to them now, not until they were all safely back aboard the *Necromancer*. Something about the Mennonite's story of Blackbeard chilled her to the core. She had to forewarn her teams, but she didn't want to scare them away from the mission.

The boats whirled into the cove and twisted toward the beach.

Ashley saw lightning back toward the fleet of airships. Nothing new about that... but something in the shadow of the storm made her uneasy. She felt she was being watched.

Chapter 06 Warrior

"**E**at the Rich, Eat the Rich," he whispered, but when she turned her head and looked across the cove, *looked right into the shadows he hunkered in*, his whispering stopped. Fiercely beautiful, tempered with anger, steeled with self-righteousness. Her white hair flared around when she turned her head back. The Warrior was now just mouthing the words, not a sound escaping his lips.

"Eat the Rich," he forced between his teeth, growling it. It centered him, and the weakness in his core turned hard again. This was his mission. It was his only mission.

The Warrior calculated the distance to their boats, the number of armed men and women in those boats, the time it would take for him to dispatch the lot of them and have that prideful rich woman to himself.

What would he do with her then? Flay the skin from her bones while she begged for her life? Take her in his arms and whisper his mantra to her? Win her over? He slammed his fists against his head and roared—stopped to see that the boat motors had drowned him out—roared again. He groaned low and loud, moaning away this skull-splitting conundrum he faced every time he had seen her.

· · · ·

He awoke in the water. Waterborne. Water born. Born again. Born at sea.

Incessant sea and salt and storm.

He had clung to the remnants of a whale, a whale of the sky. Beached in the ocean. Sinking in the ocean in the eye of a storm. The Warrior clutched at the rubbery hide and crisscrossed ropes until his hands were numb and bloody. He looped an elbow in the ropes and dangled by it when the waves would move the mass that kept him aloft enough to catch a breath now and then and then again.

All the while, for all he knew, the message pounded at his head: Eat the Rich. Eat the Rich. As the storm spun above him, a tilt-a-whirl of wind and rain, the message droned on and on.

To stay alive, he set his breath to it.

To preserve his mind, he repeated it.

He could still hear. He could still speak.

He could still think.

Eat the Rich.

Eat the Rich.

He could remember, sometimes at first. He remembered the strange men with even stranger weapons. They passed by him like he was nothing. A bump on the ship. A dead fish to step over.

He was the Warrior, though no one cared. They were single-minded. They were after someone else, but he had closed that door. They did not begrudge him. They did not torture him. It would have wasted their time. So, they left.

He was left alone in the cold eternal storm, in the infected rain with only the ghostly, insistent voice of Steven Spexarth, the traitor, to keep him company. "Eat the Rich," the recording repeated. "Eat the Rich."

He knew it was poison, an irresistible message he had no hope but to hear and obey. When consciousness graced the Warrior, he used his teeth to tear the fabric of his tactical gear in strips and stuff his ears. When he succumbed to Spexarth, he raged across the surface of the Undulatus, screaming the words as he ran for miles in search of anyone Rich he could slaughter.

He was alone on a sinking airship hundreds of miles at sea.

When he knew himself, he would scramble together every weapon and resource from the dozen dead. These bodies that littered the core, near the waterfall, were not corpses of the rich, but fellow warriors, regardless of their side in the battle. From them, he found very little food, an energy bar, an MRE, a canteen of fresh water. He would measure and think, calculate how long the meager provisions would last.

Then, in a gush of the storm, he would devour it all, spitting it out with his screams of "Eat the Rich."

He found a trove of provisions, a watertight case of survival food, in the wreckage of a helicopter he could no longer identify by name. He rejoiced over the food, wept over the helicopter. He knew that craft was important, but not as important as his mission, Spexarth's message. "Eat the Rich," he said, trying to put it all together.

He was smart. He remembered that. He had been smart. Before the next rain, the Warrior learned to outsmart himself. He hid the food. Whenever he learned something new, he would bury it deep inside. Whenever he would have a memory of who he was and why he was there, he would hold it tightly and hope to wait out the next torrent of rain.

The bodies decomposed and washed out into the water that crept ever closer to the center of the sinking surface of the Undulatus. The food, all the food, was long gone. The salt water stung his skin, and he had only the wits remaining to try to stay out of it. The rain was bad, but the salt water would sooner or later be fatal. When the thought came to him, he crafted a rain catcher, and that water, while tainted, was otherwise fresh rain. It sustained him.

Spexarth's message rained down on him and kept him alive. He owed it to Spexarth, if he survived this, to carry out the mission like a good soldier. A Warrior's way. A code.

Eventually, even the remains of the helicopter slid off into the ocean. He was stranded on a stretch of airship rubber no bigger than a bed. All he had in the world was a collection of knives and swords and the airtight container his provisions had come in. When the airship sank away entirely, the warrior managed to strap a sword to each leg, then held onto the container and spit away the salty sea that was relentless in taking him.

He had days of respite, those days when the storm whirling overhead dissipated. After so very long, months if not years, the sun returned, and the storm was no more. He did not think he heard Spexarth's "Eat the Rich," or maybe he simply did not hear it aloud or allow himself to hear it.

Though his muscles ached and cramped, he held on. When the container bobbed free of the current of the sunken vessel, the Warrior had to fight a new battle: the tropical Sun and chilling night winds. All that time of torment, of endless rain and rant, proved to be not so bad as being alone at sea in the sweltering sun. It was baking him alive in the seawater's brine. One day, he might be a meal for a sea monster. Though he coughed and choked, the thought of such a predator brought a primal growl from his throat.

He held onto his sanity, to a scrap of it, a vital part of any warrior's calling: his mission. "Eat the Rich," he whispered with each breath. It was his pulse and purpose. It brought him back from the dead in the shallow waters of a shoreline he did not know.

Chapter 07 Be Prepared

I ce cubes were one of those things that people took for granted until they didn't have them. Henny knew that. Henny was one of those guys that really wanted his customers, even these guys here in Guthrie, to be able to come into *Sharts N' Grin's* and just forget about things for a while. The last thing he wanted them to think about was a shortage of ice.

He could have told one of the girls to do it, but he wanted to chip the ice. It was free therapy, and it was one of those things that he still enjoyed, pounding on the bricks of ice that came in on a transport now and then. He was smart enough to store some up for when the transports didn't come. He always had a quantity of ice for the evening.

Chipping ice also gave him time to think. He was thinking about the visitor that had just been in the bar. He was asking himself whether or not he should tell Lefty someone had been asking after him.

• • • •

T hey had told him there was some guy out front. Some lurker. Somebody just hanging out in Guthrie, asking a lot of questions. That surprised Henny. *Who wouldn't ask at the bar first?* If you wanted to know anything in a given town, you went to the bar, not the bank, or the law, or, of all places, to a church. This guy had been to all of those places before he ever came by *Sharts*.

He said he pulled in for juice for his transport. That fit the profile alright. People like that wanted to keep a low profile. They didn't use registered power charging stations. Ever. They would seek out a hook up like Henny's, a place that would give them anonymity. He didn't have to advertise that his hookups were anonymous. It was just expected.

The guy came in, all casual and kind and sat at the bar and made small talk with Gail. He ordered a ham melt without even looking at the menu. He asked a lot of questions about things that seemed just a little bit curious to Henny. For example, how was it that this guy from out of town knew anything about Shae Ward? Why would he want to visit with her, when she was a retired law enforcement officer and had been for a couple of years? Things just did not add up.

So, Henny took it on himself to belly up to the bar. He dried his hands and sat down. He smiled across from the guy, and just played bartender for a while. The guy didn't seem thirsty or hungry. He just seemed spooky.

He thought the guy was familiar, though he'd never heard of Alex Gault. Henny thought maybe he was somehow related to Lefty. They sounded a lot alike, and they both had similar features.

And that of course, was the first thing that set off any radar. The last time someone came through town and sounded like a Fortune, it was big trouble. That, in fact, had been the time traveling freak, Sackerson. This guy Gault was way too young. He was tall, thin, and sported a spiky haircut. That voice, though, just sounded so much like Lark when he was a kid. He sounded a lot like Sackerson, too, the way he talked. Just for good measure, Henny turned on his recorder under the counter.

The stranger said that wouldn't be necessary. Somehow, Gault switched off the recorder without so much as reaching around the bar to do so.

Henny shrugged. Small talk continued. The guy was a talker. He had lots of interesting stories to share about what was up in the world. He said it took him a week to get to Guthrie from the east coast. Bad roads. Terrible infrastructure. They bickered about whose responsibility it was to maintain roads, anyway. With the corporations in shambles, Henny thought everything had fallen on the skids. Gault told him in some places, what he called the 'dry places,' people were taking things on themselves. He said this swath of Oklahoma was a dry place.

Henny thought back to Lark's concern about just that. *No Rainmakers in a year.*

Gail was back from the store, unpacking grocery sacks of seltzer and nuts, and she took an interest in the stranger. And she, as usual, started in with the jokes. Gault had an unusual bray to his laugh. It made him that much more fun to hang with, like the hairdresser who snorted when she'd laugh. Henny liked the customers who'd just cut loose a little. Have a good laugh.

Gail's stand-up routine gave Henny a moment to study the records of the man's transport. Sure, his go-jo was an unregistered hookup, but that didn't mean that he didn't run a trace on every vehicle that tied in. He was glad he did this time. The last known destination of that vehicle was the Installation, the museum where Lark worked. The stop before that he recognized, too: it was Lark's mom's address.

The address before that was even more curious. It took Henny a bit to look it up, but it was beyond a doubt the former Oklahoma City address of Dr. Christian Fortune, Lark's dad.

Henny went back to the bar and dismissed his daughter, right in the middle of a joke. He cut to the chase. "What exactly are you looking for? Why are you here?"

"I'm just here to broker a deal," Gault said with a beaming grin.

"What kind of deal?"

"I'm here to bargain with one of your best patrons, as I hear it. Lark Fortune."

"He isn't here," Henny said. "He's off to Kansas City."

"Kansas City?" Gault said. "Does he travel much?"

Henny could tell the guy didn't believe him. He had probably already been told otherwise. In a town the size of Guthrie, people probably told this Gault guy that Lark was just there a couple nights back.

"So, he's gone, yeah. How can I help you, then?"

"Well," the man said, sliding a box of Tic Tacs between them. "You got any information where a guy can get some candy?"

Try as he might, Henny was not able to keep his eyes from flaring wide or his pulse from racing or his blood pressure from soaring. But he *did* do his best. He puffed up like the linebacker he had been in high school, and he said, "You know, you should probably leave right now before things get difficult."

Henny felt for a weapon he kept under the bar.

"Looking for this?" Gault pulled the shotgun up from his lap and laid it on the bar between them. "Gail let me have a look at it. I took the shells out for safety's sake."

Henny scanned the room. He'd get no help from two old boys eating by the jukebox. The only other patron at the moment was the cat lady, and she was already into her suds.

Gail came up with the sandwich wrapped in wax paper. "On the house," she said with a smile.

Henny looked at her hard, then returned his attention to Alex Gault, who was bending over on his bar stool. Henny grabbed the shotgun with both hands. Even unloaded it would be a good club.

Alex sat upright, smiling again. "Henny, really? I come bearing gifts."

He had picked up a black hat box, and he sat it on the counter like a magician in a show. "This! This is a Stetson... for our buddy Lark Fortune," he said, hopping off the stool. "Have him give me a call, will ya? It's on a dedicated channel. Below frequency. I think we have some things to talk about."

He grabbed up the ham melt, then fished something out of his pocket. "And this is for you, pal."

Alex Gault turned and left, whistling on his way out. Even the guy's whistle sounded familiar. The tune sounded familiar.

Henny shook his head and opened the leather pouch Gault had tossed on the bar. Inside was a fine pair of brass knuckles with a note: "Be prepared."

· · · ·

H enny stopped chiseling on the big brick of ice. He fished the brass knuckles from his apron and put them on. They were oversized and fit great. Had Gault known how ham-fisted he was? He took aim at the ice block and punched it. The ice made a satisfying crunch. Henny hit it again with his other armored fist. Then again and again, alternating punches, changing it up like he had in the gym years ago. He pulverized the block.

Breathless, he looked over at that Stetson, again, resting on the black hat box. The damn thing was worth more than his whole bar. It was a dangerous thing to even have in your possession. It was the kind of thing that nobody in Guthrie had anymore. It was a model like he had seen himself once in a museum.

And there it sat with Lark Fortune's name on it.

Chapter 08 Stormfront

S tu pulled his pocket watch out and confirmed the time. It was 6:30. The sun had just gone below the horizon. Heavy cloud cover obscured the sunset. Behind it, he heard the unnatural thunder of a low-flying airship.

It was a rumbling he had only heard once before, when Winston was demonstrating the awful potential of an airship out of control. L.F. had personally piloted a Winston Weekly low to the ground, coasting overhead at under five thousand feet. Due to electromagnetic conductivity, so the flyer read, a Weekly would ground out, much like any thunderhead, arcing lightning across the heavens. Flying lower and lower, however, increased the frequency and intensity of the lightning. Winston had dipped that ship down for less than a span of a mile to show that it produced so much lightning it left little in its wake unscathed. The land in that swath had never recovered fully.

That stunt had been done decades ago, but it was fresh in his mind now. He had encouraged area ranchers to watch vids of it from time to time. It spoke to the terrible power of technology. It was unnatural, and in his way of thinking, a brand of evil no one should mess with.

Now a similar ship, on a similar evening, not 200 miles from where that stunt had been conducted, was swooping down range and coming right for Laramie.

He removed his hat and spoke firmly over the distant rumble. "I haven't seen what that'll do to a town," he told the group at the Springs. "Some of us remember what it did to the reservation."

Heads nodded. Voices grumbled.

"The thing is, we can't stop it," Stu said over them all.

"Why the hell not?" one of them called out.

"I got an RPG," someone else offered. "Let's drop it out of the sky."

"My brother's got a chopper. Let's get up there and reroute it."

"It's got a hell of a thunderstorm at its front edge, probably terrible wind all around," a crop duster offered. "Not like you can land on a Weekly."

"Worse yet," Stu said, eyeing the strobing storm, "It's all lightning, all the time."

· · · ·

Nat was bent over a surveyor's instrument. They then looked up, to their right toward town, back to the instrument. "Warning pass," they said again.

"Not over town, then? You're sure of it?" Stu asked.

Nat shook their head. "No. I'm not sure. Since we sighted it, the storm's been coming south, southeast. Straight. If it doesn't deviate, then it will miss town. If it does change course, like soon, it could still sweep right over Laramie."

"Geometry," one of The Boys said, nodding.

"Calculus, actually," another corrected.

"I don't care if it's alchemy," Stu said. "Is there a last call on this? Too tight of a turn they can't make last minute?"

"Safest thing to do would be to evacuate everybody in town," a woman said at his side. She had a point.

"Hunnert thousand people gonna bug out in half an hour?" one of The Boys asked.

"Going up highway 30 and the interstate...maybe," someone offered.

"If Nat says it's missing town," Schmidt said, slapping Nat's back, "That's good enough for me."

"But out here...we're right in the sights of it?"

Stu nodded at Nat.

Nat nodded back.

"We can get a dozen trucks in the cavern," one of The Boys suggested.

"Y'all get back home," Stu said. "Hold your loved ones and hunker down."

He watched the lightning creeping toward them in the darkening sky. He weighed the options and consequences. He was a twenty-year Civil Defense volunteer. Sometimes he led workshops these days with Sam Nichols, who was a firefighter by trade. "Nichols," he called, "Fire up the tornado sirens, will ya?"

"On it," a uniformed man said, then spoke into a two-way radio. Seconds later they could hear the long wail of the siren build and echo across the rangeland.

Pickups and trucks were pulling away, all light racks and diesel rumble. Three remained behind, threading their way into the canyon that led into the caverns of the Springs.

"Are we taking your rig down there?" Nat asked, looking down into the canyon. It was rough going.

"Truck doesn't matter," Stu said. "Let's hoof it."

Together the two scrambled down the slope and into the cavern where they joined six others. They were assembling there when the rumble of thunder was drowned out by the sound of the low-flying airship.

Stu could feel it through his core.

One truck's spots aimed deep into the cavern. Some dust and gravel sprinkled down from the cavern's roof. No point trying to be heard, Stu knew, so he waved and gestured and goaded everyone into their truck cabs. He and Nat were welcomed with some others into a large antique four door pickup. Inside, the shudder of the airship was no less intense. Small rocks pinged off the hood and windshield, but Stu could scarcely hear them hitting the truck.

He looked back to the cave entrance and in the strobing lightning, he could see a curtain of rain. "Damn," he called out, "that came in fast."

"See that?" The man in the driver's seat pointed ahead. He turned to them all and shouted over the rumbling, "You boys think this was the best place to be?"

The cavern wall was slick with rain. A rivulet of muddy water shot out from the wall like a fountain. The Springs were already overflowing and backing up on the cave's floor.

"I'd 'a never made it home," the man in the passenger's front seat hollered. "My place is due west."

"I wouldn't want to drive in this!" Nat said. They wiped at the door glass with a sleeve.

Stu was amazed at the lightning. The cavern mouth was constantly ablaze with white flashing light. It did not look like night at all.

• • • •

An hour later, they were rolling again, heading up to Stu's truck. Headlights did not reveal anything special about the range around them. Some scorch marks, some mud. When they neared the pickup, however, they were all agog. The vehicle had been white, but it was now charred and pitted. Most of the glass was shattered. One tire was aflame.

"Never did like that truck," Stu said with a sigh.

"Hey, look at this," one of The Boys approached Stu with a soggy paper no bigger than his palm.

"They're everywhere," Nat marveled. They peeled one off the pickup, picked another off the ground.

They brought them into the headlight beams and studied them, turning them this way and that.

"I'll be damned," one of them said.

They were printed leaflets from ChompCorp. The cornucopia logo was unmistakable, as was the font.

"What's it say?" someone over Stu's shoulder asked.

"Mine's a little wrinkled," Stu said, but he read it aloud:

"In six days, our airship will return to finish the cleansing in your town. Consider this notice. Everything in the path of our airships will be commandeered for the greater good.—ChompCorp."

"Don't know about you," one of The Boys said, "But I got a big appetite for some thick corporate fat about now."

"Eat the Rich!" Nat shouted, shaking a fist in the air.

They all joined in the chant, "Eat the Rich! Eat the Rich! Eat the Rich!"

Stu Wiebe had removed himself from them. He was watching the departing lightning storm, his jaw tight, his fists clenched. The Eaters might have it right, he thought...but he wasn't so sure it was all so black and white. By some measures, even the Wiebes were rich. He remembered some very wealthy ranchers who he would count among the rich, and he had no grudge against them.

Corporate people had been trying to broker deals for the last year, pleading for locals to sell out. Their motive was bad. Their approach was dead wrong and going nowhere, but they weren't outright evil.

Even the ChompCorp execs were giving locals a week to retreat before they took over.

None of The Boys were going to back down. That was as sure as the sun coming up in the morning. Nobody that owned so much as a trailer park lot would let ChompCorp take their land without a fight.

He studied the remains of his pickup and knew this was going to be a fight they would not win.

• • • •

S ome people left town with just the shirts on their backs, not trusting that the ships would be six days away. Non-essential businesses were encouraged to board up and move on. By the second day, Laramie residents were clogging the highway with their RVs and pickups loaded, ready for escape. Trains out of town were packed to standing room only.

Rumors were rampant throughout the city that something big was going down, that the Eaters were going to send their own message back to ChompCorp. At night the bars rang out with old TurnCoat songs and brave speeches from the Eaters. Loudmouths like them had come and gone. This strain called themselves the Rebels of the Plains.

On the fourth day, under police protection, the fancy MagLev first class cars were loaded with the families and executives of ChompCorp. Again, Stu thought, looking on, these weren't the filthy rich people the Eaters demonized. Some of them went to Stu's church. He'd played golf with one of the fellows sometimes. Nat was standing with him at the train crossing, watching the spectacle of it all. "There's the Gibsons," Nat remarked, waving at them subtly.

At 2 pm, an announcement was made for final boarding.

Dozens of news drones from CommCorp were buzzing overhead. They were here to capture the story for the world to see. If the Eaters were going to get even, like they had been bragging they would, it would be on all the channels, simulcast in every HeadGear on the Interface.

Mooring brackets released the train cars with a pneumatic hiss, and the train rose a foot off the tracks. It floated there only an instant, then was propelled ahead silently by the magnetic forces that moved it.

It shot east on the tracks, a silver bullet glistening in the afternoon sun. Stu had to hold his hat on as the train streaked past.

Voices were shouting up ahead then. The drones all left the depot together, speeding east.

The train charged ahead and disappeared, car by car, flashing into the void.

• • • •

He hadn't seen a Hot Wire in so long it was hard to believe. That one could consume and transport an entire train—he couldn't fathom it. Altogether, it left him with a strange sense of déjà vu. Awash in shock, confused by the almost memories, Stu stood there, mouth agape, for the longest time.

People around Stu were revealing their hidden mobile devices, armatures and apparatus, HeadGear and implant modulators, tuning into the news. Others were running east to see for themselves.

Reporters were shouting out the story in a Tower of Babel blitz of shock and awe. The Eaters had rigged a homemade Hot Wire big enough to erase a thirty car MagLev train! Cheers and hoots and hollers were deafening. Some people shot their pistols in the air in celebration.

This was their counterstatement to the Lightning's Hand, the ChompCorp airship threat: two hundred men, women, and children had been ported into oblivion.

Stu pulled Nat to his side, and they shared a side hug. This just wasn't right. There had to be a better way. He wagged his head in sorrow.

"Effective!" a stranger said. He was an old man with long hair and a long white wispy beard. He dressed like Moses from the VBS play. He had a distinctive face that Stu might have recognized in other circumstances. The old man was not rejoicing with those around them. Neither was he too upset by it all. He was not a reporter, just a commentator.

"Next time, however, *if I might suggest...*" he smiled at Stu, then pointed at the drones, then up, then back to the west, "They'll aim higher."

Chapter 09 Kept Man

K rystal Price was coming to the Installation.

Normally, Lark would have been excited. He would have hired a cleaning service. He would have gotten a haircut. He would have bought her a gift and decorated the place. It was tradition. Krys came out only once a year, at Christmastime, on Christmas Eve. Once a year. Every year.

Popping in on him now wasn't just unusual, it was a bother.

Yesterday, it was her security company. He was napping at his desk when he heard the commotion out in the foyer. Two men and two women, all in aquamarine uniforms. They looked more like a pool service than a security force. He watched them on the closed circuit, poking around. The logo on their backs looked familiar, but he didn't recognize any of the faces. Of course, he wouldn't know them. She used different people every time, claiming a fresh set of eyes made her feel safer.

Lark tossed them his keyring and trudged back to his office, where he resumed cleaning. He would stop now and then to watch them looking behind filing cabinets and under desks. They spent an inordinate amount of time in the old labs. When they were rummaging around in the basement, he turned up the volume on their banter. They were annoyingly thorough, but stupid.

He hadn't saved the money to hire a cleaning service, so he was left to do it himself. He had been at it since her message service had forewarned him of the visit. "Ms. Price will be on the premises in twenty-four hours," the AI voice had stated. "She requests you go to no special effort in preparation for her arrival."

Cleaning was a strategic effort. Over the years, he knew she preferred a quick tour and a perfunctory exit. He cleared a path down the residence hall wing, shoving aside boxes that had collapsed and tumbled since his last trip. She liked the residence hallway, sometimes reminiscing on the days they had spent there as kids. As he mopped, he worked up a sweat and a thirst, and soon was again in his office, feet on the desk, tipping back a beer.

Lark mocked the voice aloud again, "no special effort in preparation for her arrival," meant exactly the opposite, of course. He was sure the AI was ignorant of the effect it had on those it informed. The scrambling and the arrangements, the anxiety and the expense—all were amplified for most she would come to call on. Lark, however, had tired of working to make an impression.

· · · ·

The pool service left late, forcing him up early the next day for a quick trip to the barber. He was surprised how packed it was when he got there at 10. The only empty seat was under the wall-mounted television, but he wasn't interested in the news CommCorp was broadcasting, anyway. He slumped in his seat and pretended to read the paper.

"Lefty, you're up," Baxter called to him, eventually. They went through the ritual of asking about family and confirming the length and manner of cut. They argued about sports and cussed the government, as it was. Baxter was good at lulling customers into routine.

His customers were not.

"Lefty," a fat man said in the adjacent chair, "I heard Lemmert's was out at the Installation."

"Lemmings?" the fat man's barber asked. Lark never let that guy cut his hair. Conversations with a deaf old man were tedious.

"Lemmert's, that security firm outta Oak City."

"Tourists," Lark said, not even opening his eyes. Baxter had him laid back with a hot towel on his face.

"Between them an' exterminators, you prolly clockin' to set a record this year, then," someone smirked. "You're prolly going to have to hire more help."

"Now Higgins," Baxter said nearby, "Installation's still a big deal. Guys from NASA took interest once, you know."

"NASA's gone TransCorp," another voice offered. "They're not digging around for space junk these days."

It was quiet again, save the droning of the televised babble from CommCorp. As usual, it was something about some rich bastard getting his just rewards. Lark tuned it out and thought of Krystal Price. He wondered if she'd like Baxter's aftershave.

"Hey, Lefty, you still living out there?" someone asked.

"Installation? Yeah, why?"

"Some guy was asking about you."

Lark raised his eyebrows against the towel. His prosthetic flexed involuntarily.

"I told him you was there," the voice said. "He said he'd already tried there and your mom's, too."

Lark lifted the towel to look in the direction of the voice. It was Hughy from the tire shop. "He tried *my mom's*?"

"Didn't know any better, I guess," Hughy shrugged. "Said he'd try again."

"When?" Lark sat up in the chair, handing his towel to Baxter.

"I dunno," the tire guy said.

Some stranger and now Krystal Price...more people were taking interest in him than he was used to or comfortable with. It didn't sit well with him.

· · · ·

After the government had abandoned the Installation, Krystal's mother, Sybil, had snatched it up. Altogether over a square mile of land west of Guthrie, it was a long-term investment.

Someday the world would completely forget about the Guthrie Fall of 2024, then the Prices could have the property platted out and sold in parcels. Meanwhile, the grounds of the Installation were thoroughly picked over. Enthusiasts had been coming out for years. The land was practically tilled by scientists, explorers, and even *astrophysical archaeologists* from Roswell, New Mexico.

Krystal Price strolled into the Installation like she owned the place because she did own it. She had talked her mother out of it, then talked Lark into it. He owed her so much. It seemed the least he could do. Essentially, all she asked was that he would host tours and maintain it as a museum. Neither had really panned out. The facility was huge, and the Guthrie Fall was all but forgotten.

Lark suspected Krystal had no true interest in preserving the Installation. She didn't care about the memory of that night the meteor shower had bombarded the former golf resort neighborhood. Establishing it as a museum and a national historical landmark kept the place in the flow of grant dollars. Keeping it occupied kept the insurance rates low and served as a deterrent for thieves and vandals. Anyone could have fulfilled those expectations.

Krystal kept Lark on site for additional reasons. She had been married, and before and after that marriage, she had spurned his every advance. He still liked to think she cared for him.

After all, she had provided bail, attorneys, and moral support when he had been charged with felony arson. She had funded his entire case, arranged a retrial, and he was sure she stopped up CommCorp with so much money they had just looked the other way. His prison term had been commuted after only five years. Fines that totaled over $100,000 just disappeared. She did all that for him, kept this roof over his head, provided a ridiculously generous medical and benefits package, and she made sure he had the best prosthetic technology money could buy.

It wasn't a bad life, then, being her kept man. He was sure there was a twinge of guilt there, probably some pity for him, too, but he saw it another way. He served a vital purpose in her life, keeping her grounded, offering a safe place to come back to, should she ever need him. Keeping him here, she knew where he was.

He knew the underlying reason she supported him was not the guilt, nor the pity, nor anything that might approximate true feelings for him. She was obsessed with tiny white tablets, the size of a fat grain of rice, the shape of a Tic Tac candy, the secret to TransCorp's teleportation technology. She kept him there year-around in search of more Tic Tacs.

So, he had played along.

In the basement of the Installation, Lark had fashioned an impressive if not improbable screening station. Every December he would load buckets of dirt into the hopper and sift it out with several sizes of framed screens. He would make a convincing mess of it, adapting the display a little every year for authenticity.

And he would run a handful of Tic Tacs through the station. Sometimes he would sprinkle nearby buckets with more, anticipating those times Krystal had wanted to try it herself. Nothing stole his heart like her smile, and she never smiled bigger than when she had screened her own Tic Tacs.

He had kept her away from the soil sampling and the screening station as best he could on this visit, for he had not had time to set it all up. Instead, he entertained her in the original office of the Installation's commander. This was the central piece of the Installation exhibit, clean and well-preserved. It was also the plushest room of all of them, and Lark had kept it tidy and relatively authentic.

They were sipping at snifters of top shelf cognac she had gifted him with last Christmas. Lark planted a small glass bottle of Tic Tacs on the table between them. This was his gamble. Though it was oddly out of season, she would have no other reason to pay this visit. If that were the reason she was there, maybe she would just take it and go, eventually. Quite possibly, if he just engaged her in small talk long enough, she would be content to take the bottle and go on her way without a full tour, without the screening sham downstairs.

If Larkin Wayne Fortune had a superpower, it would be small talk. In his annual visits with Krystal, he liked to offer up the most tantalizing tales he could, but on this impromptu visit, he had not yet collected himself entirely. His news was old and his tall tales, robbed mostly from the barbershop, made no impression.

He began by complimenting her. "Gotta say, Krys, you've never looked better."

"Thanks," she said with that smile she made when she was just a little uncomfortable. She never thought she was all that pretty. Some of their talks had centered on that very subject.

"I mean, you look young enough to be in college. You still get carded at bars?"

"It's the sun," she said, "Or avoiding it, actually, I guess." She ran a finger over the brim of the hat that rested on her knee. It was a broad brimmed, white straw hat—her trademark was that hat and her big lacy white parasol. Lark knew she had been very faithful to staying out of the sun.

"Well...whatever. You look fantastic."

They talked of sunscreen and moisturizers, and when that died out, a quiet settled down between them, pressing an awkward reaction out of Lark.

"You believe in ghosts, don't you, Krystal?" he blurted out.

"Ghosts? Why?"

"Sometimes—you're going to think I'm crazy—sometimes I swear things get moved around here."

"Like you misplaced your keys or something?"

"More like, well, I'll have all my bookwork laid out on the desk here, see, then I'll go into town for groceries or whatever, and when I come back, they'll be moved around, flipped to another page. Rearranged on the desk."

"Hmmmmm," she said doubtfully. "Maybe you misremembered it."

"Doors left open, drawers ajar, lights off or on that I'd not messed with in days sometimes...."

"Probably just kids looking for something."

"Sometimes, I swear, they're getting sloppy in their surveillance."

"Who's getting sloppy?" she asked, then took a sip. Lark heard it in her voice and saw it in her eyes again. She was falling into that camp that did not believe him. People did not believe he heard voices, either, or that he smelled cigarette smoke once in a while when no one other than himself had been in the building for months.

"Watched the news lately?" he asked abruptly. He was hoping to erase that doubtful, pitiful tone from their conversation. He was struggling to remember the stories he had just heard at the barbershop, the only real news he had heard in months.

"You mean, like on *television*?" Krystal chuckled, looking across the room at the Commander's old TV.

"Yeah, that or on the Interface. I dunno."

"I know food prices are going up," she said.

"That's not news," he said.

She looked at the watch she wore on the outside of her long, lacy glove. "I don't mean to be rude," she said, "but this is going to be a come and go, Lark. I'm sorry."

She was eyeing the bottle of Tic Tacs. His plan was working a little too good. There wouldn't be a tour, but neither would there be the time together he was accustomed to. It was going to leave him yearning for more.

"Yeah. Yeah that's cool," he said, then asked it outright. "When will I see you again?"

"Christmas, of course," she smiled. "Couple-three months."

"Sure." He nodded emphatically. "Sure."

"Thanks for the rush order on these," Krystal said, sweeping up the Tic Tac bottle.

"Any chance I'll see you again, *early like this*?"

She stood, thought a second, as if deciding whether or not to confide in him. "Tell ya what, Lark... Got any Headgear in this joint?"

"Of course not," he said.

She set her hat in place on her head, used the built in HeadGear then: "Wilson?

You get that?"

Before Lark could even generate something small to talk about, Wilson, the security guy, was in the doorway, a Visor in hand. He extended it to her, then she handed it to Lark. State of the art HeadGear.

"*Keep your Head' on Straight*," she said, quoting their slogan. "You'll see me soon—in the news," she smiled. "I'm fixin' to make headlines."

A major victory in the War on the Wealthy.

Rebels of the Plains flex their tech and toast a train. That's right, you're reading it here first.

This week marks the first time our side has made a strike back that had no reply. Why? Because we wiped them out and didn't break a sweat. Over 200 Rich are now ported to the great hereafter. Gone and nobody but the news to tell about it. What can you say to that kind of power? Sorry?

The Rich might think they have all the toys. Better weapons. Lots of bodies and billions of dollars to throw against us. They might think they still rule the world.

The 1% thought they'd crush us. For generations they were the ruling power. They used us. They ran all the governments, and by that, we know they were behind them all the time. Lobbyists were calling the shots. Rich people were calling the lobbyists. Finally, they got outed and the rest is history. Except now we're making the history!

In just five years, we took 22 million millionaires down to 10 million. Whether by choice or by voice, by God or by gunpowder, we prevail. All the money we liberate goes right into our war chest, and we use every dimc for the cause.

They owe us. They come down taking our land and what we raise, and they found out we raise HELL.

Why did they drop a Weekly out of orbit and burn that swath south of town? They killed a lot of livestock (over 200 head in Albany County alone) and grassland. Eleven people were put in the hospital, and a couple of them, Father Lemke and David Hanks, died. All that for what? To scare us? Did that work?

The fight is far from over. The reason for our latest success is the support we get from you. You area farmers, ranchers, and businesspeople want to keep up a quality of life that you can pass on to your kids someday. We're fighting that fight for you. Support the cause and Eat the Rich.

This is a statement to ChompCorp. The Rebels of the Plains won't stand for it. This is just the start. The train job should tell you this much, we bite back.

Chapter 11 Trading up

L ark knew he was in no state to drive, so he walked. He was mobile, and so long as he was moving, he was winning. "So they say," he said aloud, sometimes softly, sometimes loud. "Allowed to be aloud," he read off a sign he thought should exist. It ought to be a T-shirt, maybe.

Whenever he'd see someone out early, he'd wave, and they'd nod or ignore him—didn't much matter. School buses would rumble by, reminding him he loved the diesel, though he despised the dread. Every bus that went by was full of dread. Dreadful kids on dreadful trips to awful places. One went by as he was stopped to light a smoke. "Dread!" he shouted to the little faces pressed against the windows.

His jacket wasn't warm enough for this cold morning hike to town. He rubbed the sleeves of it briskly, puffing his cig as he bit down on it. Clint Eastwood would smoke like this, his eyes squinted, his lips in a snarl around his smoke. Eastwood, however, wouldn't be cold and crying on a dirt road. He'd be wrapped in his poncho. He'd be whipping his horse, left-right, left-right, on his way to seek revenge somewhere.

That guy was too damn ambitious.

Besides, Lark knew, bad guys weren't so easy to defeat these days. Who was he going to fight to win the day? Not some sweaty gaucho with a six-gun. His enemies were bigger, badder, and less tangible. His enemies had no friends to befriend to make them into enemies of, "so they say."

At least he had that now, a catchphrase. If he were young again, he'd spray paint that on a grain elevator or a train car. He loved tucking it into conversation with a knowing Eastwood squint. "No one's what they seem, *so they say.*"

"What's that, Mr. Fortune?"

It was the Spangler kid, rolling alongside him in a new truck. Lark Eastwood gave him a glare. *Where had he come from, anyway?*

"You need a lift or something?" the kid persisted.

"No," Lark shook his head, "I'm fine."

The kid looked up the road toward town. "Where are you heading?"

"If I keep on going crazy, I'll get there, by and by," Lark smirked.

"What?"

"Why don't you get to school before you're late."

"Mr. Fortune, I'm... I run Bigley's now. You know that."

"Why isn't it Spangler's then?" Lark plucked the cigarette from his lips with his plastic hand and twirled it. He expected the kid to say something about advanced robotics or some other wisecrack.

"New lid?"

"What?" Lark followed Spangler's glance. "Yeah."

"Visor, isn't it?"

"Guess so."

"Trade you straight across," he patted the door of his pickup.

The gravel muttered something under the oversized tires as they moved along. Lark shook his head at how upside down the world was. Everyone wanted HeadGear, even strapping young men.

"Are you a strapping young man?" Lark asked.

"Sir?"

"What do strapping young men actually strap?"

Spangler shrugged. "I... I don't know."

"Bad trade anyway. I couldn't take advantage. I only had it for four days, and it's already broken."

The Visor had winked out on him sometime overnight. Sometime near the bottom of his bottle, the projection quit, leaving him in the dark. He was wearing it so he wouldn't lose it, but a cap would have been warmer, and now, he thought, attracted less attention.

"Broken?" Spangler said. "Let's go to the shop. I'll take a look at it for you."

"It's not a tractor, kid."

Spangler looked hurt. His beard twitched. "Still," he kept on, "I can hook you up with a coffee, and we could look it over."

"No offense," Lark wriggled his mechanical fingers and said, "Kenny Hinman does all my work."

"Henny?" the Spangler kid snorted. "That guy's a hack."

"He is at that," Lark agreed. Then he gave Spangler his most menacing glare, "But I trust him."

The kid brushed up his flannel sleeve and gave his own wrist an exaggerated look. He was sporting a high dollar arm appliance. With that gadget, he could probably hook up to diagnostics in his shop or order lingerie for his girlfriend with little more than a thought. Lark thought it made him look like a hillbilly Power Ranger.

Spangler glanced ahead on the road, then back at Lark. "*Shart's* don't open for hours. If you change your mind, come by. I'm right on your way."

"Thanks. I might," Lark said, taking a long drag on his cigarette. "Now run along, Spangler, you're interrupting my traversal of town."

"Sir?"

"Piss off," Lark said, flicking his cigarette butt at the boy.

· · · ·

S pangler was right...and wrong.
        Henny's was closed to the public until the lunch crowd would congregate. Meanwhile, the Hinmans would make ready, thawing out chicken fritters and generally getting set for the day.

Lark trudged in the back door behind the guy bringing in beer on a dolly. He gave the dishwasher kid a nod and kissed Darla on the cheek as he passed through. Henny was hunched over his bookwork at the counter.

He looked up, glanced at the clock, then back at Lark. "You're in early!"

"Yep." Lark ran a finger over the brim of his Visor, saying, "Do you keep up on the news in this dive, Henny?"

"Not on HeadGear," Henny said, turning back to his ledger.

It wasn't the reaction Lark had expected.

"It's new."

"Yes," he said. "I can see that. Why's it off?"

"I...it...you know where I got it?" Lark set it on the ledger. "Krys brought it out."

"Yeah," he said, gently pushing the Visor off the page he was attending to. "I heard she was around."

Lark was surprised. He looked around. Was there a camera crew, some set up? Was he being spoofed? He thought he might just get a rise out of them, beat them to the punch. "You heard she was around, but did you hear she just left this morning?"

"Did she now?" Darla said from down the bar.

"Just spent the last few days cuddling," Lark said.

"Dressed like that?" she said. "Smelling like you do?"

"Why didn't she give you a ride into town?" Henny asked.

"I... I needed my daily walk and meditative self-loathing," Lark said. They weren't buying it, but something else was going on. He began to wonder if the camera crew was actually some sting operation, co-opting the Hinmans, ready to spring on him at last. He watched his words as he continued. "This device is defective, Henny. Wanna look it over?"

Henny glanced at it like it just showed up. "Visor," he said, "a '55. Didn't know they were out yet."

"It's broken."

"Doubt it." Henny said, picking it up and turning it this way and that. It looked like a blackjack dealer's visor or like something a golfer or tennis player might wear. When Henny put it on his big head, it looked like it might break. It cast a green shadow over his eyes. "Go. Launch. Fire up." Henny said.

"It's dead," Lark said. "And that's not the start command."

"Krystaline," Henny tried. Still nothing.

"Honey, I need a—" but before Henny could even complete the request, Darla handed him a Brick. It was a wireless charger like any of a dozen laying around the bar.

Henny waved it around his head in a broad, slow loop.

"Looks like you're doing an exorcism," Lark said.

A little green status light winked on the rim of the Visor.

"Command?" Henny asked, the glint in his eyes directed at Lark now.

"Gimme that," Lark said, reaching over the counter.

"You want me to fix it, give me the command word."

"Mandolin bandana," Lark sighed.

The Hinmans snickered. The Visor glowed warmly and executed a welcoming tune.

"It was a band I liked."

"It was the band you took Krys to. Bunches of times."

"Dozens," Darla tossed in. On her way back to her chores she said, "Shoulda played your wedding."

The Wedding that Never Was. He had sat around and talked that out with Darla, daydreaming in the neon sun, more times than he could remember now. It was a rabbit hole, and this morning, he had no time for what might have been. "So, it's fixed?"

Henny leaned against the back bar and issued a line-of-sight command. Lark could see it in the optics reflecting in Henny's eyes. "I'm running diagnostics," he said, but he was such a bad liar.

"You're running history," Lark said, reaching for the Visor. "Give it back."

"Krys left four days ago, Lark. You've been Jacked In ever since?"

"Have not."

Henny's eyes were darting over some projection he was studying. "Yeah, you've been on the Interface a lot, pal."

"Research," Lark said.

"Four days of 'researching' Krystal Price!" Henny smiled.

"Give me that. You ever think waving a Brick around your head might have caused you brain damage?"

"This thing's a toy," Henny sneered, setting the Visor on the back bar. "Come with me."

Lark looked at the Visor, glowing green, piled on the counter with liquor bottles and a couple of Bricks.

"I'll keep an eye on it," Darla said. "Go with him."

Lark followed Henny to the back room, then upstairs. The Hinmans were both acting strange. He couldn't remember the last time he'd been up to their place. The sting operation again came to mind.

Henny tinkered with something on the far counter.

"I'd take a coffee, if you're making any," Lark said, dropping into a chair at the kitchen table.

Henny turned abruptly, holding a silver-plated Stetson. It was glowing blue in its undercarriage, making it look like it was floating in Henny's palms. The finest appliance. One did not even classify it with HeadGear. *It's not HeadGear, it's a Stetson*, one of the less creative campaigns touted.

Lark had never seen one before in person.

"It's yours," Henny said in reverence, holding his hands out to Lark.

"Mine?" Lark leaned to look at it from different angles. "It's not mine. If I sold the Installation and everything in it, I couldn't buy that thing."

Henny nodded. "I'm not comfortable even holding it."

"Thing could raise attention."

"That's why you're taking it home. Put it in the lead room. Bury it under some crates of space junk."

"Yeah," Lark said, distantly thinking of the power and potential of that Stetson. "Don't they have Measures?"

"Take it," Henny commanded, and Lark did. "If they have Measures, maybe it's safe enough to use—sparingly."

"Did you try it on?"

"Nope. The guy said it was single-purpose. Underwired."

"*Underwired*?" Lark looked past the Stetson to Henny.

"Yeah," Henny hadn't looked so concerned in a long time. "It's a dedicated channel, he said. Untraceable."

"I know what underwired is, but to single-stream a Stetson? That seems—"

"Criminal," Henny said. "That's why it's going home with you."

Lark set it on the kitchen table. Sleek, silver, contraband on a tablecloth of pumpkins and ghosts. They both watched it glow.

Finally, Henny sat down and offered, "Since it's on, anyway, want to test the theory that it's an exclusive? Want me to tweak it?"

Lark had just spent four days mentally intubated in the Visor. It had been trippy, all-consuming. He had never felt closer to Krystal than over those hours reviewing every recording of her on the Interface. Constantly, however, he had to tolerate streamers and footers and other commercial interference, all of it damning the rich. A Stetson was, he knew, commercial free... and *that* made it all the more tempting.

"Wait. Wait. Wait," Lark said, suddenly free of the Stetson's spell. "*Who* brought this? What guy?"

Henny did his full body shrug. It was his trademark. It should have been on a sign out front of the bar. "Same guy that's been poking around town for a few days now. Said his name's Alex Gault."

Lark shook his head. He'd never heard of Alex Gault.

Henny leaned in closer. He smelled of pickles. "He was looking for you," he said, whispering in his own kitchen. "Looking for *candy*."

"Tic-Tacs?" Larked mouthed it.

Henny nodded.

Lark's eyes ached from his look of surprise. Only three people in the world knew about them, and two of them were at the kitchen table. The third was Krys, and she would never tell anyone about them because she was cashing in on them.

Except now there weren't only three people.

Lark's eyes moved to the Stetson.

Chapter 12 Incongruities

"What's my job again?" Kelli Chase asked. Though she sounded like she was speaking in the bottom of a swimming pool, Ashley did not miss her cross tone.

The two were facing one another, helmet faceplates touching, hands on each other's shoulders. They stood atop the *Necromancer*, a Nebulosus class airship that Ashley favored above the rest. It had been her home for years. This little alcove was hidden among the whirling, churning, shape-shifting surfaces of the ship. It was like the space between the wings of a bird, if that bird had a dozen formless wings. This one spot on the surface of her ship was as close as one could get to privacy in the sky. She called it the 'bald spot.'

"You're my second," Ashley said.

Kelli dipped down a little, getting Ashley's full attention. "I'm your right hand."

Ashley nodded just a bit, and their helmets clacked together. That was a bad idea. Too hard and a crack in the glass could mean death.

"What happens, Ash, when the right hand doesn't know what the left hand's doing?"

Ashley sighed, and her helmet glass fogged for an instant, then the climate controls inside erased it. "I'm sorry already," she said. "I thought I saw him."

"Ashley," Kelli said firmly, "Rory's dead."

"Not him," she said. Her space suit felt too large then, and she was nothing but a puddle inside.

Kelli shook her by the shoulders. "Not him? Then who?"

Ashley looked at her friend. They had become the best of friends through these years. Kelli's green eyes twinkled with the stars.

"Who?" Kelli asked again, concern working at her features.

"Blackbeard," Ashley said.

"The man, the myth, the killing machine of the Barbary coast? You did a pivot and took her down on a myth? A hunch? What?"

Ashley didn't want to talk about it, but she knew she had to answer for this. It had been a stupid, stupid move to pull out of the Rainmaker formation and double back, out in the wide and clear, out where they could have spotted her airship. Even a Nebulosus could be seen with the naked eye—and floating contrary to the wind and weather?

"It was stupid. I know it... but I thought I saw him. Myself, with my own two eyes."

"So, drop a pin in it. Chart it. Let the next week's wave take him down."

"No one's ever taken him down." Ashley said.

"But if you know his shore, we could drop a lot of squirrels. We could drift in *all* the girls if you wanted. If you *commanded* it."

Here it was. Ashley pulled back from the helmet-touch contact for a second. This was the speech she knew was coming. Again. *A leader's got to lead.*

Kelli pulled her back in. The helmets tapped together. The vibrations coursed through Kelli's air, her helmet glass, then Ashley's and it was as if she was talking inside her suit to her. "Ash, I know you feel you are going too far. I know you realize it. I don't know if you realize the girls think you went too far. They get tired of you going too far. They are tired of you leaving them out and just doing things on your own. We're all tired of you taking Point all the time when some of us are just as capable. What they need, Ashley, is for you to take charge. What they need is for you to quit being a foot soldier and to start being their Commander again."

"Is that what they want or is that what you want? Are you speaking for them, or are you speaking for yourself?"

Kelli smiled. "Little bit of both, maybe?"

"I need *you* to lead them."

"I train them. I bandage them up. I chew their asses," Kelli reviewed. "You inspire them. You are, and always will be, their Princess."

Kelli had learned a lot about leadership in the last few years. She had become quite the diplomat. Kelli had come to realize it wasn't all barking orders and bravado. Sometimes motivation was cloaked in posturing, in finesse. Regardless, she was right. She had called this moonwalk meeting for a reason, just as she had the last one a month ago when Alex had left their sky.

That visit had been even harder.

· · · ·

They had been out there in the bald spot arguing over the helmet headsets. They had tried to keep their talk loosely fitting around the problem at hand. They spoke in code, and they added charades, as much as their bulky suits allowed.

"My subordinate is not coming around," Kelli said. "He's directly disobeying orders."

"He's civilian. He's not obliged to obey."

"I'd like to think otherwise," she gestured to her ring finger, "you know, to love, honor and *obey*?"

They shared a chuckle, then Ashley remembered Rory, and Kelli realized it. She moved the conversation to intercept: "He's on a mission taking him down and inland."

Ashley shook her head and twisted her shoulders left and right to better pantomime that gesture.

They both knew his odds weren't great inland. The man had no filter and no fear. He could handle himself well when put upon, usually, but he would be put upon constantly down there. He would be mistaken for the Rich, simply in the way he carried himself.

"I just don't understand," Kelli pleaded then, so worked up she forgot all about radio seep and security. *"Why's he leaving me?"*

Ashley pulled her to her, and in their hug, their helmets touched as Ashley was saying, "He's not LEAVING YOU FOR LONG." The helmet contact doubled the radio headset voice and volume.

They both cocked their heads. Kelli shut off her comms on her wrist. Ashley did the same. They touched helmets again. "This is better," Kelli said, understanding the analog secrecy they had discovered. "Can tell it like it is now."

Ashley noticed the tears streaming down Kelli's face, trickling on the inside of her helmet. Ashley looked away but said again, "Alex won't be gone long."

"Did he tell you the same thing he told me?"

Ashley did not answer. She remembered what he had said, however, and it did have the sound of a one-way ticket. *"I'm going to set this right,"* he had said, *"no matter what."*

"I mean, what if he goes back—you know—and can't get back to us?" Kelli said, "To our time?"

"He promised you, remember?"

"He might break a promise," she said, fighting back tears. "He blames himself for all this. All the loss."

Ashley knew it was true. Alex had told her as much, explaining that had he just seen the way things were going to go, he could have stopped Spexarth and the subsequent years of brainwashing. All the Eat the Rich unrest. He should have seen it, he argued. He should have known. When she argued with him, Alex started berating even himself for not giving himself up when the authorities came for him. Had he done that, Rory would still be with them.

"He'll come back," Ashley said, consoling her friend, "or we'll go get him."

. . . .

"The girls need a fresh fight," Kelli persisted. "All of them, from all the ships."

"I don't want to lose any more of them to raids, if that's what you're driving at."

"That would be good, too," Kelli said, "but I'm saying, if you're after this Blackbeard guy, let's do it right. Not some rogue heiress on a whim. Let's swoop in with all the Neb's and all the girls. The guy wouldn't stand a chance."

The prospect was entertaining. She liked the idea of saturating the sky with her squirrels. She liked the thought of them all working together to find that bloodthirsty monster. He was unhinged, taking the Eat the Rich campaign to the extreme. Blackbeard was the soulless killer, rumors said. He was probably a cannibal.

Ashley could not resist the infectious grin on Kelli's face.

"We'd be out of formation," Ashley said.

"We'll draw our boats in tight," Kelli countered. "With all twelve, we'd look like a Rainmaker front."

Ashley searched her friend's features for any trace of doubt. There was none. It would be dangerous to even deploy so many squirrels so densely in the sky. It would be a challenge for the boats to ever round them all up. There would have to be strategy, scheduling, precision leadership. That was Kelli's strong suit.

"Okay," Ashley said at last. "I'll call it up, you make it work."

Kelli squeezed her shoulders. "You gotta do more than call it up. You gotta bark it out. Scream it out. Rally the troops."

"Yeah, yeah."

"You have to make this a mission. Amp up the rumors on the guy. If this is going to be a manhunt, and he's as deadly as you say he is, then when you talk to the girls, you'd better say he's ten feet tall and dripping blood. You'd better paint him as evil incarnate."

Ashley remembered the Mennonite's encampment and realized nothing she was hearing was that far from the truth. It would be easy to embellish something that was already that horrible.

"Don't let anyone question your leadership again," Kelli said before they broke contact.

"You're right. I know you're right, but doing things to plan takes forever. Sometimes I just want to do it myself."

Kelli growled. "What's the sound of one hand clapping? Cuz that's the sound you're going to hear, clapping upside your head if you go solo again. Remember, right hand, left hand, working together, okay?"

Ashley nodded. She was so grateful for the tough talking Captain Kelli Chase, formerly of the Franklin, Texas militia. Kelli Chase, who was also almost as brokenhearted as she, herself. She smiled to herself at the incongruities as they walked across the top of the airship, weaving between the wispy wings, holding hands like schoolgirls through their space suit gloves.

Chapter 13 Droning

Stu Wiebe stood out in the rain, wearing a knee-length oilcloth duster, a slicker. It was his riding coat, the one he wore when they worked cattle in the weather. The Boys all wore them. They stood out, outside. Their collars were turned up, their coat tails hung low, their broad-brimmed cowboy hats tilted down against the rain. They stood apart. They were there for a reason: to keep track of the Rebels of the Plains, this newly organized, consistently stupid, batch of Eaters.

The Boys had other reasons to be on watch as well. A second-tier corporate type was coming into town, someone with TransCorp. The corporation had the nerve to pitch a Portal in the Civic Center, downtown. They'd tried to draw attention and muster a crowd, red carpet and all, but most folks were more curious about what the Rebels were up to. With both groups in town and that storm moving in, there would be trouble. If the law would not do anything, the Boys would. Peacekeeping wasn't their thing, but they did like to be where a brawl might break loose.

The Rebels of the Plains had taken over the Albany fairgrounds just south of Laramie—everything at the fairgrounds—every outbuilding, every pen, every shelter. They had made a mess of the place. The county crews couldn't keep up, and the Rebs didn't care to.

Since it was raining, all those indomitable Eaters went indoors, leaving The Boys outside on watch. Stu didn't mind. It was like the rain he was accustomed to. Just the good country rains that kept his pastures rich and green. This was the rainy season in natural times. Once in a while, even the paths of the Rainmakers some 500 miles south might have nudged a storm like this up north. Stu knew a good rain when he felt one.

Rainmaker storms didn't pass over Laramie or Billings or anywhere in cattle country... or they hadn't until last week's Lightning's Hand. Stu knew the side effects of a Winston Weekly, like everyone up his way. He had driven through the storms. He knew the land the programmed rains had painted all vibrant, verdant, and misleadingly green. He had been on such ground with the extension agents and learned how the soil had changed. Thousands of miles of dirt, amended by ChompCorp scientists, was left with no water retention left in it. The whole swath of it depended on Rainmakers. Weekly rain had made that land too valuable to live or ranch on. Over time, and with the influence of the corporations, almost everyone had evacuated the fertile farmland.

Then five years ago, it all changed.

Eat the Rich took credit for rerouting the airships, but Stu knew better. Someone with some real power had made some really terrible decisions. The new flight paths made no sense, inconsistently crisscrossing properties that had been high producing corn fields, neglecting entire regions of countryside. It left a strange cross hatching of dead soil and virile crop patches, but the patches had gone to weeds. The Boys had a theory they kept close to the vest: those airships were aimed at high populations now, no longer at crops. New leadership had new objectives, and it resulted in new side effects.

Stu had seen the psychological effects that stirred up trouble like the Eaters. He knew that the effects of those storms wore off after about a week, just in time for the passage of the next Rainmaker. It had been six days now since the Rainmaker swooped down low over Laramie. Stu half-expected that the rebels might back off a little. But they didn't seem so inclined. They seemed to be all the more charismatic and excited and involved in their venture.

They had fired up the people of Laramie. Together, they rounded up a drone armada. The Rebels of the Plains commandeered the best drones, ones used for crops and surveillance, to get momentum around the idea. CommCorp donated crates of drones, some just like those that swarmed *whenever news happened*. A few ChompCorp models were shot down and repurposed. More were rounded up from some gaming enterprises.

Stu became more concerned when he saw how many drones were donated to the cause by the people of Laramie. Easily two hundred were personal and antique drones that kids might use. These all had been rounded up and traded out in various ensembles over the last few days. The techie rebs had tuned up the drones so that the controls from one device to another might not interfere. So many drones and pilots, so much teen angst and bravado. Victory seemed unlikely. They were David; the Lightning's Hand would be their Goliath. Stu thought of his pickup again and the pounding it had taken. Survival seemed improbable at the very best.

His concern grew every time an outsider came to town with ideas. First, it had been a trickle of Rebs, now hundreds of them camped at the fairgrounds. They were bubbling over with ideas. Fire up the National Guard hardware, out of service now for a decade. Make cannons from air compressors. Engineer a way to divert lightning back at the airships...

That old man who had shown up at the train porting incident continued to linger. He offered advice, always with his "if I might suggest." Some called him "the Wizard," others called him Dumbledore. Stu worked with the Sheriff's office on him and could find nothing, not even a name. He was benign but always underfoot, always marveling over the simplest things like squeeze chutes and milking stations. Today, it was mud. "Yesterday, it was just dirt, innocent and fluffy. Puffed up when you kicked at it. Just add water and voila, it's mud. Sucking at your boots. Stopping up traffic. You know, man-made mud in his own image, himself being made of mud..."

While Stu looked on at the droneworks, The Wizard continued his nasally small talk, lapsing into thoughts about county fairs. He was waxing on about the biological engineering of crops and genetic crosses in chickens. Some of it sounded suspiciously well-informed, as if the old man had defected from the ranks of ChompCorp.

"Are you ChompCorp?" Stu asked abruptly, interrupting a diatribe on the prospect of boneless chickens.

The Wizard stopped mid-sentence, his hand mid-gesture. "No," he frowned. "No, Wiebe, I'm just an admirer of progress."

"Best to keep your admiration to yourself," he advised. "They're not favored in these parts."

"That *is* good advice," the old man said, pausing to look at his chunky old watch. "Might I suggest some in return?"

Stu turned to look him over. The man was tall, over six foot three, by Stu's estimation. He was not hunched nor frail, but the years had not been kind to him. He was standing in the rain under an umbrella he had offered to share several times. His long white hair and beard were sopping wet with rain. He had talked about the rain since it had started. He never flinched at the thunder.

"What would you suggest this time?" Stu said.

"When the big ship gets here, tell your fellas to stay dry and plug their noses," he said, pulling a wad of cotton from one nostril. "Trust me on this one."

• • • •

S tu believed the world was largely populated with crazies. He knew that even The Boys would be considered such, and by extension, so would he. A man just had to choose his crazy.

That had come to him suddenly when he was in high school, and his entire world burned down around him. Crazies had detonated a nuclear bomb over his grandfather's ranch in Oklahoma, disrupting generations of Wiebes. Torching his future.

Crazies were nothing, if not elusive. He had spent years with The Boys, seeking out trouble, fighting to get revenge. When that went nowhere, The Boys headed out to nowhere for a fresh start. They settled in a state with low population density, where the crazies were few and far between, and the Wiebes flourished.

Crazy was coming to town again, however. There had been increasing reports of goons like those who had once haunted around Guthrie. Add that to the Rebels and this strange old man. Add that to the crazy that was coming on the storm in the morning. It was building to be a very volatile situation.

He had just been handed a note from the Sheriff's office. The spark that might set it all off again was due in town soon, a rep from TransCorp Stu had never expected to see again: Krystal Price.

His days of armchair quarterbacking were coming to an abrupt end, like it or not.

He left the old man babbling about the ChompCorp land grab and strode across the riding arena. His boots were coated with muddy slurry, but he did not have time to take the long way. He didn't have time to wipe his feet when entering the Exhibition Hall. He pushed through the foyer and out into the main hall. The place was teeming with people Stu did not know, but he raced toward a knot he knew by their slickers alone.

"Where's Rae?" Stu asked on approaching them. The group spread some to let him in and reveal his wife. She was down on one knee working on a drone with Nat. "Honey, I need to visit with you," he said, putting a hand on her shoulder.

She stiffened and turned to stand and face him. "Is it about *her* coming to town?"

"Let's go—somewhere. I need to think out loud."

"Nat, you got this?" Rae asked, then led the way.

She was from a big ranch near Cheyenne, and she was used to being in charge. By the way the Rebels of the Plains bowed and scraped to her, she was in charge of the whole damn drone project.

They cut through the tangles of strangers and their drones, cut toward the kitchen and concessions, then once inside, Rae took him to a room labeled "Nursing." Inside was one chair, and she pushed him into it, then shut the door behind her. "Why here? Why now?" she asked.

"Rae, I—"

"You know how I feel about her!"

Stu took off his hat. "I do," he said. "And I know she's trouble."

"Don't tell me she don't know you're here."

"Of course, she knows we're here," he said. "We've been here—"

"That bitch is going to do it again! She's going to get you all twisted up and out of here like nothing else matters."

"Rae, I'm not going anywhere. I got more than I can handle right here."

"She's going to play off the good old days, Stewart Wiebe, mark my words."

"That was a long, long—"

"She's a homewrecker," Rae said, red in the face. "She has men all over the world."

"Now, I don't think that's—"

"I heard her say it on a vid, 'a port in every storm, a man in every port.' Something like that."

"I think you're watching too much Interface."

"I think you're a damn fool!" Rae waved her arms overhead in frustration. "All over on the HeadGear they're calling this the Standoff. They got *your Boys* on vids talking shit on the Corps, Stu. The Comms are looping Rebs spouting off how this will set things right." Rae leaned in, "Krystal Price smells trouble and comes running at it. Headlines. You know I'm right! Here we are, on a whole powder keg of trouble. And Hot Wires—just like you two used to toy with!"

Stu stood. "Don't you think I know we got trouble? Don't you think I know she's mixed up in it? I ain't stupid, Rae."

"Do you know why she's coming?"

"She's bringing the Tic Tacs," he said, confident in his answer.

"Do you know why it's her coming in with them?" Rae took a step closer and jutted her chin at him. "You don't, do you?"

"I..." Stu shook his head. "I... don't. No. Do you?"

"Damn right I do. This isn't about the pissant Rebs pushing back at ChompCorp. It's not even about the train massacre. This is TransCorp coming in to square off against Chomp."

"Listen, I don't care if it's—"

"So, they send in their figurehead, their White Witch, with the Tic Tacs," Rae said. "Then when the fight begins, she pulls you through a port to God knows where, and I'm left here in the lightning."

"Rachel!" Stu said. "I am not going anywhere."

"Have you seen the coverage? CommCorp is practically a *sponsor*!"

"That's what's bothering you, isn't it? The attention. You think I can't stay out of the limelight."

"You can't."

"I'll go back to the ranch right now!" Stu said.

"No," she said, taking in a deep breath. "You can't. You're here front and center."

"The Boys can handle it."

"They can't put their boots on the right feet without you," she scoffed. "Besides, we got a stake in this now. Nat's in deep. They put in a drone. They're going to pilot, too."

"Let's take Nat home and lock 'em up," Stu said, though he wasn't even convincing himself. He couldn't let Nat down. He'd never seen such conviction in Nat's eyes, ever. He couldn't leave Rae here to fight without him... and she was right. The Boys needed him, too.

Out in the exhibition hall it sounded like a million mosquitoes. Stu and Rae darted out to see what had changed. All of the drones were airborne, hundreds of them, holding a pattern in the confines of the hall. The buzzing changed pitch, and every drone turned 90 degrees in synchrony. Another change, and they moved again into another pattern.

Nat looked over a shoulder at them, beaming. The test flight was working. Stu smiled back. Rae took his hand. She leaned in and shouted in his ear, "You better not be lying to me, Wiebe, or I'll personally kick your ass."

He chuckled a bit.

The improbable was joining in on the crazy.

Now all they needed was the Tic Tacs.

The Warrior liked the days when the fog lifted from his mind. He could remember more than his mission. He remembered the horrors of the ocean, and he rediscovered the name of the ship he had found himself missing. He knew he had once known the captain. He speculated why the airship had crashed where it had, but none of that was returning to him. It seldom did.

While everyone on earth struggled to survive, the Rich drifted in the sky, looking down on lowly peasants. He had heard as much on broadcasts. After Rainmakers passed, he would study those people stranded on the islands ranting, shaking their fists at the rich, and at the airships in particular.

When he stalked the Rich for slaughter, the Warrior spent hours in the dark just outside the encampments, listening. Hadn't many of them commented on the grandness of the flying circus that was Winston Water Works? Hadn't they all sounded envious of such wealth, themselves?

It tormented him.

He would often ask them, threatening with a knife to the neck, if they could tell him more about Ashley Winston. The details were as distant as paparazzi, as vague as a news vid. Seldom did someone know more about Ashley Winston than he, himself, and even those few were not spared his wrath.

The information he had gathered had come and gone with the weather. He was wise enough to write down what he could, and he carried that inside his vest pocket to review with fresh astonishment from time to time. The facts galvanized him in his mission.

Yes, he had known her, perhaps to capture her and torture her for information. He had known even her tenderness, and though hard to come to terms with, that suggested he had once been very

good at infiltrating enemy lines. He was both repulsed and
strangely proud of himself.

On the seventh day of a Rainmaker's cycle, the Warrior would
sometimes stand with his feet in the sand and his head in the clouds
and miss her. At those rare moments, he knew truths about her he
could not write down.

He knew, for instance, that he loved her.

• • • •

The Warrior kept record in his mind and on his flesh. He had
an intricate scarification system up and down his arms that
noted his days on these islands. He had trolled these shores—he
calculated—almost five years. The Winston Weeklies had passed
overhead 241 times. He had drilled a dot into his arm at each
passing. His kill count, something a merc would never be sloppy
about, was lost to him. This was a never-ending source of
aggravation. The rain would still be dripping from the trees, the
blood from his weapons, but he would not be able to recall the kills.
Dwelling on them too long caused him to become physically ill.
Bodies could be counted, piled and burned, but he could not be
certain they had all been his workmanship. It seemed unlikely from
the quantity of them. How could he be so manic, so violently
abandoned, that he would not keep an accurate record of such
things?

He could, however, recall the waves of nausea and guilt, the
irrepressible sorrow and self-hate that the dead would bring him.
It was a stunning mix, this illness and the accompanying ecstasy.
No one was so efficient, so disciplined, as he was at fulfilling his
mission. Still—in the nights that followed the storms and
bloodshed—he had doubts.

He brushed his fingers absently in his woolly black beard and
long, knotted hair. Over the years he had made note of especially

significant kills. Each time he killed one of the flying women, he would rip a bit of her wingsuit into a little ribbon and tie it in his hair. He was adorned with twenty-three of these colorful snippets. Some were faded. Some were forever stained in blood. Some of the older ones had to be tied and re-tied in the curls of his mane.

He could vaguely recall faces and fighting styles of a few of these girls. He could appreciate the training they had been through. His most vivid memories retained the techniques they used, for such memories had spared his life, time after time. He thought he recognized the fighting stances sometimes. He was sure he had known a few of these women by name. They all died the same, however, named or not. They all were trophies in his beard now, nothing more.

Thunder rumbled from storm 242 as it neared. He appreciated the number. It was an even number. It had balance. Twenty-four hours, 2 twelve hour turns of the dial. This was a significant day; he just knew it. He would add a twenty-fourth woman's ribbon to his beard on this 242nd day, and that symmetry pleased him and pained him, though he could not say why.

When the rains came, he felt the familiar surge of energy and surety that helped him dismiss his doubts. He was able to swallow his gorge and choke back his tears. The Warrior was about to fulfill the commands that had blared from the underbelly of the Rainmaker. The ranting would come from a battery of loudspeakers high above. He thought he could still hear it loud and clear: "Eat the Rich. Eat the Rich."

The Warrior screamed it into the face of the rain and lightning and wind and storm. He cried it out so fiercely it caused him to cough up blood and bite his tongue. It did not matter. Nothing did. He would slay them all. No one of Wealth would survive his—

Then he noticed something with his predator's eye: there were many, many more clouds than normal, and there was no broadcast coming from them. He was yelling it by himself, and his compunction to do so was...gone. This storm was different. The rain even felt different.

Wiping it from his eyes, he saw more. The flying women were not waiting as long as usual. They were descending even now... and even more of them were in flight than usual. In fact, as the storm clouds moved through, the Warrior's surprise grew to absolute astonishment.

He lost count at 102 of the wing suited women cutting through the sky. He thought there might be 144, another number he liked for its balance. A dozen dozen. A gross.

The Warrior pulled his two scimitars from their scabbards and enjoyed the weight of them in his hands. He did not remember where they had come from, probably some cruise ship museum. He did not know how long he had had them. He could only remember the delight he felt in lopping limbs and severing spines with them.

This day the women from the Winston Weeklies were here to war with him, and he welcomed it with a deep, guttural roar.

Chapter 15 Formalities

Krystal Price despised rain, even regular rain like that falling outside the Laramie Civic Center. Rain was pernicious. It wriggled into every nook and cranny. It leaked and dripped and eroded through everything. Rain ruined the party. It played havoc with her hair.

Generally tamed and predictable these days, this *au naturel* rainstorm was ruining her entrance. The rain lapped at the foyer glass. It coursed in a chorus of rivulets and wrinkles, obscuring her view of the street. It gurgled down the gutters with gay abandon. It was laughing at her.

She stood in the foyer, waiting as patiently as she could.

It was 12:21, local time. Her arrival had been flawlessly executed and applauded politely by a small crowd. She had crossed a continent in a stride, arriving confidently at this destination and ready to move on to the next, albeit by car. The display inside her Kentucky Derby hat was merciless and precise in its timekeeping. The airship was predicted to be at the outskirts of town at 1pm.

She sniffed at her sachet. Just the act of it helped her fight back anxiety. "If you're on time, you're late already," she always said. Though the Civic Center was only blocks from the fairgrounds, she did not want to appear rushed.

Krystal examined herself in the window's reflection. She was a shimmering white blur. Cameras and HeadGear, bright lights and fast talk, all of it swarmed around her. Though she was not at her best, she had to look her best. Though she could not see her reflection, she switched vids with an eye gesture, and there, projected in her hat, was her radiant image. She smiled and twirled her parasol. The projection she was watching did the same.

The locals had recommended the limousine roll around back, that she be loaded into it in a sheltered docking station, like a bag of flour. It simply would not do. Their approach might have kept her from the rain, but it would have kept her from her public, which was not an option. They had approached with a plan to flank her down the sidewalk, holding umbrellas tightly overhead as she walked the ninety feet to her waiting ride. That had been an equally repugnant thought. She was not being escorted by six men surrounding her like clingy children. They would have been a clumsy lot, out of uniform and with mismatched umbrellas. They would have huddled around her and again separated her from the cameras.

"A saber arch," the mayor proposed, "with white umbrellas."

As the citizens busied themselves with the idea, Krystal had appraised the mayor. She was a local, obvious by her shoes alone, but she had panache and leadership Krystal could admire. She stood in the foyer with Krystal, close enough to be in her camera frame, absorbing the attention in her sleek golden blouse. She was standing there like a model, being seen with Krystal Price. Seen, but not heard. She was smart enough not to attempt conversation. She had listened to her mother, no doubt, "Do not speak unless spoken to."

Krystal sniffed at her sachet and tapped her toe.

"They're back from the department store with matching white umbrellas," the mayor narrated, quick and soft, not to be broadcast. "I had my assistant choose volunteers from the best dressed he could find at your reception. They're out there now, Miss Price, at the ready."

Krystal nodded her huge white hat once. The media frenzy scrambled for the best angle. The mayor swung open the door to the storm with an exaggerated gesture sure to be caught on screens worldwide. *Glory seeker,* Krystal thought, then smiled. "What was your name again?" she said over the hissing of the rainfall.

"Barb," the mayor said, "Barb Randall."

Krystal said, "Your honorable Ms. Barb Randall, I need you to do me a favor. Would you lead me to my car?"

"Why, yes! Yes ma'am!" the mayor said with a broad smile.

"Good!" Krystal said. "And do this, would you? Put your fingertips on your head, point your elbows out wide, like my hat brim, you see? Now blaze a trail, would you?"

The woman looked stupid, like a child pretending to be a charging deer. It kept the umbrellas at the proper height and angle to avoid complications with Krystal's hat, which was the intent. As an added value, the mayor's silly pose revealed sweat stains in her armpits. It was glorious.

• • • •

She touched up her makeup and re-tied the ribbon that held her hat in place. Time had not allowed for her to check in with anyone on her HeadGear. When the limousine was slowing at the turn for the fairgrounds, the driver spoke over the car's audio, "We are arriving. As scheduled, between the storms. Which building will we be stopping at?"

Krystal ducked down in her seat to look out the side windows better. She flopped the brim of her hat up some to see out better yet. The fairgrounds were more substantial than she had expected. There had to be a dozen outbuildings.

"Miss Price?" the driver continued.

She was looking for CommCorp drones, hoping an array of them were in position for her dramatic entrance. Instead, she saw the sky was simply full of drones, all of them in a pattern, deploying in a huge line that disappeared in either direction out of sight in the mist and sun. These were the rag tag drones that would carry out her plans. It was going to be sensational.

First, however, she had to find the right building.

It was frustrating that she did not have people for this... or a memo... or even a better-informed driver. Krystal cleared her throat and asked, "Which building might you recommend?"

"I've been told they came from that large one, the Exhibition Hall. I guess it was quite a sight. Pity we missed that."

"Take me there, then, driver, and don't waste any more time," she said, and switched off his comms.

The car wheeled around to the largest building on the property, a tan structure with blue trim and a tasteless sign painted with grass and cattle and other assorted livestock. The driver came to her door and opened it. The sound of drones buzzing unnerved her.

Krystal almost stepped in the mud, then noticed and saved her stunning white heels from ruination. She frowned at the hundred yards of mud from the car to the door. "Can't you park anywhere else?"

The driver looked around. He fought a smile, "Perhaps at the back door, at the cattle chutes?"

"Get some help. Have them lay something down—or drive me to the door."

"Yes, ma'am," the driver said. "I will return presently."

She shut herself back inside the car. The world outdoors was buzzing and dripping and muddy. The fairgrounds smelled of animals and feed, like they seemed always to do. Krystal tried to ignore the time flashing inside her hat brim. She would have only moments to spare once they rolled out a suitable carpet for her approach.

Someone knocked a knuckle at her window. She waited for the door to be opened. The rapping again. She sighed, and opened the door only to face a tall, lean cattleman in a dripping black slicker. His hat obscured his features at first, but then she recognized him. "Why, Stu Wiebe, what a surprise!"

Without ceremony, he reached inside and grabbed her wrist, then pulled her from the car and tossed her over his shoulder. He carried her without a word. She swatted at the oilskin cape on his back and wriggled. It was indecorous. Her derriere was in the air.

Arriving at the building, he sat her down on her feet inside the threshold. "No time for formalities," he said. "They're waiting for you inside."

She was adjusting her dress and hat. Out of the corner of her eye, she saw cameras training on her. She stood a little taller, took a sniff of her sachet, and said, half to Stu, half to the cameras, "There's always time for formalities," and she kissed him on the cheek.

The strobing and clicking was as familiar as her heartbeat. She smiled at all the paparazzi, then followed the lead of her entourage into the large Exhibition Hall itself. The place was monstrous. One could park a space shuttle inside. They approached a dais featuring a number of pilots and dignitaries. She waved to the cameras as she scaled the steps, greeted a few of the dignitaries, and found her place among them.

It was entirely too loud inside for a speech. She would have CommCorp overlay something later. She nodded to a man who looked to be in charge. Two drones were summoned closer. These were each holding the ends of a hair-thin thread that was miles and miles in length. At the tips of the thread, each drone held a tiny nodule, a receiving piece just the size to hold a Tic Tac.

Krystal made a production of peeling off her long white gloves. She smiled again to the cameras when she opened the locket dangling from a necklace she had never been seen without. With great care and delicacy, she extracted the Tic Tac within, and mounted it first into one nodule, then popped the other nodule onto the other end of the Tic Tac. The drones raced away with it, as if it might explode in her face.

She knew the time it would take for the tiny tablet to take effect over the distance of this massive portal Hot Wire. It gave her just enough time to turn to the cameras, smile, and curtsy.

Behind her she heard the unmistakable hiss and pop of the portal coming online. The crowd was temporarily blinded by it. The drones, in unison, swept it out the giant hangar doors to join the rest in forming the largest portal mankind would ever witness. Krystal held out her hand for her parasol, and when no one placed it in her grip, she sighed and took the hand of the nearest bystander to escort her to the hangar door.

If the Lightning's Hand came in as predicted, this door would make a fantastic vantage point. The cameras in her wake could frame her up with the action commencing behind her. She was going to be part of history.

She looked, then, at the person whose hand she was holding. This person would be immortalized with her in vids and programs of historical significance for a millennium. He was not a wedding cake topper, not a handsome stand-in stud rented from the locals.

It was not a stud at all. She held hands with a slim, dour ranch woman who smiled at her coldly. "I'm Mrs. Wiebe," she said, "Mrs. *Stewart* Wiebe."

Chapter 16 Reverse Engines

The *Necromancer*, Ashley's ship, was equipped with dozens of cameras trained on the sight unfolding below. She watched as her squadrons of squirrels jumped ship and sped down in formation after formation, all of them intent on finding and dispatching that vile man known as Blackbeard.

Her monitor also kept up a feed of current events, the CommCorp version of news. She ignored that frame in the top left corner, glancing only if she saw something about 3dub in the stock price ticker. Otherwise, she was soaring with pride, self-assured they would win this day. One hundred and forty-four trained fighters to one madman—she liked the odds.

So had the girls. They had flocked to the *Necromancer* from other vessels for this excursion. Though Blackbeard was a constant threat, with these numbers, they were much less afraid.

Dozens of women waited in full flight gear in the main hall of the fuselage. On cue, lines of them would rush to the helm, then deploy from the ship's rear deck. As each team cleared the ship, Ashley felt a pang of longing. She so wanted to be out with them, to lead their charge... but Kelli had been right. These girls wanted her to lead from here, not fight. They were much braver when she strutted among them in her dress uniform. The high fives and fist bumps from her meant more now, since she wasn't a traditional soldier in the ranks.

Some of the girls even flipped to their backs after jumping, so they could ham it up for the camera, flash Ashley big grins and thumbs up. Morale was at an all-time high.

And then it wasn't.

The screen in the top left corner was flashing, and she kicked the sound on in the cockpit. "—the likes of which this reporter has never seen. The largest Hot Wire in creation was fired up at

1:02pm, Mountain. Estimations are that this Hot Wire's nearly ten miles in diameter."

Ashley flipped a toggle, so the tiny screen became her primary view. The flying girls were in frames skirting all the edges of her screen. It was a very, very large Hot Wire, but it glowed differently than those she had seen. It seemed bluer. It could have been the monitor, she thought.

Beyond the Hot Wire, she saw what the broadcasters were also carrying on about: an airship was cruising low to the ground, scorching everything beneath it with constant lightning. Camera angles were switching rapidly, and finally CommCorp got one view they must have liked best.

The frame featured a rainbow from a front-line natural storm, then beyond it, the blue glowing portal, and beyond that, coming directly for the portal, was the Lightning's Hand.

She forgot all about the girls for a moment. She forgot everything, even that she was in an airship herself. "You can clearly see in this image... the airship is being targeted now by the Hot Wire. It's a *mobile* portal, a renegade port that's being trained on the airship by the hundreds of synchronized drone craft that support it." The reporter's urgency held her attention. "If this works, the reign of ChompCorp will be over. If it fails, I pity the townsfolk of Laramie, Wyoming, which will be called hereafter 'Blackhole, Wyoming.'"

It was too far away to see the exact vessel, but the airship in question was clearly a sizable Cumulus. ChompCorp had weaponized a Cumulus, ruining its humanitarian purpose by running it aground. The ship was valued greater than the GNP of several nations. It would be a terrible, terrible loss. It was floating into a trap it could not escape. The entirety of the ship and crew would be ported into oblivion.

She did not know which she hated most at that moment, the Corporation that had stolen the Cumulus, *her father's ship*, or the Eat the Rich rebels about to destroy it.

Ashley could do nothing about it but watch. She hated herself for watching the ship and portal drawing closer and closer together. "It's the *Cumulustrata*," she gasped with woeful recognition.

She abandoned the monitors and called into the brass voice tube, commanding they abort the mission against Blackbeard. She ordered her crew to drop smoke canisters, aborting the mission for all those already airborne. They flashed morse code signals to the fleet of Nebulosus vessels, ordering the change of plans. She sent out charges to the reconnaissance boats, commanding them to retrieve the squirrels immediately and meet at the rendezvous points for pick up.

Ashley took another peek at the monitor as she passed through the helm. It stopped her in her tracks. The camera angle had changed to one that had the airship in profile as it was crossing into the blue glow of the portal. The massive airship was being consumed and transported away entirely. The Hot Wire in the sky created a rogue port sucking up all the energy of the violent storm. Nothing was coming out the other side. No rain, no lightning. Nothing.

"Set a course for—where the hell is that? Wyoming? Someone, get a bearing and speed. Set a course for Wyoming, full stop. We leave as soon as the girls are aboard, got that?"

"All of us, miss?" a crewman at the flash pot asked. "Every ship we have?"

"*Every last one*. All of 'em, underway now! We'll retool on the way."

"Yes ma'am," Lucifer Pruitt said, taking his station. "What should I say, should they ask why?"

"Revenge of the *Cumulustrata*," she said through teary eyes. The lump in her throat was painful, yet she spoke around it, "Revenge."

• • • •

They were now well-versed in ship-to-ship transfers. Fuel, food, and personnel routinely moved from one vessel to another in mid-flight umbilicals. Four years ago, such maneuvers were unthinkable, and of all the Winston fleet, Nebulosus class airships would have been the least likely to succeed in such stunts. Those ships were just too wispy, too unpredictable.

Ashley had dismissed all non-essential personnel from the *Necromancer*, and for a few hundred miles, she flew only with her crew of four. She had agreed to an umbilical with a sister ship over Florida, but only because Captain Kelli Chase was part of the transfer.

Ashley greeted her in the aether tankroom, one of the more remote sections of the ship. Though not completely private, these chambers often allowed them room to spar and speak privately. The tankroom always roared with enough noise from the ship's Transpiration that the two of them could speak freely.

Before the Necromancer had even decoupled, Kelli was asking questions. The vessel surged and drew a strong draft of troposphere. No time to delay. Kelli's ship would spool the umbilical while underway.

"So, we're just hard charging into what? Some Eater's prank? Some CommCorp propaganda event?"

"I smell TransCorp all over this. *I think it's real.*"

Kelli scoffed. "They ported a whole ship. You really buy that?"

"No one's been able to raise the *Cumulustrata* for hours."

"So?" she shrugged. "Maybe Comms are down. Maybe they're out on the raggedy edge, just chilling."

"Did you see the vid? That ship's gone. Vaporized just like the train."

"What train?"

"Get your Head on. See for yourself."

"Oh, I heard about it. I'm just not buying it. Where would they port to? How would that even work? A train—at speed—ports off the rails into some remote partner port half a world away?"

"If they're lucky. They could port right into a mountainside... or a busy city."

"That would be a weapon no one could reckon with, a train hurtling into... well, anywhere you set up the port." Kelli shook her head.

"I don't think there is a partner port, programmed or otherwise. I think they're just ported into atoms. Messing with Hot Wires is just stupid. Unregistered porting is suicidal... or in this case, outright murder."

"But you don't know that. Maybe it's all publicity. TransCorp's flexing their muscles. CommCorp's going for attention and hits. And the ETR? They're just pompous—"

"Have you kept up at all? Chomp's out there terrorizing ranchers with a Lightning's Hand. *Weaponized one of my ships!*" Ashley shouted, "Again! And the ETR's claiming this is all their counterstrike... and Trans is backing it!"

"You're sounding a little *tin hatty* there, Ash. You know better than to believe anything you see on the Interface."

"That's why we're on the fly. We're gonna see for ourselves."

"And then what?"

"Then we'll do what has to be done

Chapter 17 Coda I

A million viewers from Canada, Montana, and Wyoming were cheering. They were no longer threatened by ChompCorp's Lightning's Hand. Even should that corporation (or anyone, for that matter) steal another airship and bring it low, the message had been issued. The Rebels of the Plains would not tolerate it. They would vaporize any airship that posed a threat.

A MagLev train and now a Winston Weekly—such wins left the Rebels of the Plains heady with power. They would celebrate in the streets of Laramie all night long.

• • • •

It was a testament to TransCorp's industrial might, that they had spun a Tic Tac and synthesized its essential, extraterrestrial elements into something so fine and pure it could hold a charge. At 40 microns, it was thinner than human hair, yet it conducted the power of that single Tic Tac through the course of 11 kilometers. It was not large enough to encompass a *Nimbus*, but it had taken in almost all of the *Cumulus* ship it had been designed to teleport.

Another day they could concern themselves with the leavings of the ship, the four miles of wing that did not fit into the Hot Wire and was thus severed to float down to earth, blinking lighting as it crashed on the mountain ranges of Wyoming somewhere. They would think harder about where the bulk of the vessel had gone, try to find it still aloft somewhere, even shorn of a few miles of wing.

The accomplishment was something TransCorp's R&D would celebrate for quite some time. They knew now that synthetic ports were incredibly potent. It was a game changer.

• • • •

The Boys were not celebrating. They were not even holding vigil over the rabble tearing up the town. They were out at the Springs, reckoning with what power they had just witnessed. While the destructive power of the Hot Wire brought others to giddiness, it left The Boys feeling very old.

Chapter 18 Ruined

Alex had been patient, and he had done his due diligence. When the Stetson *finally* informed him that he had a call, he felt prepared. He slipped into it, and the familiar relaxing-back-into-the-bathtub sensation greeted him with a smooth jazz jingle. He opened his eyes, then smiled at the familiar face. He had been studying up on him. Larkin Wayne Fortune was squinting skeptically into his screen, his Stetson setting a little cockeyed on his head. As soon as Alex's image rezzed into clarity (.04 of a second if one believed the hype), Lark's expression changed from curious to furious.

"IT *IS* YOU!" Lark growled and severed the connection.

The Stetson tried to compensate by projecting a pastoral scene of rolling hills and heather. Alex sighed and removed the device, setting it down in his lap. He looked out the window of his bed and breakfast thoughtfully. What had Lark seen that ignited him so? How should he have handled introductions differently? He had tried meeting him at the bar. He had knocked at the Installation several times. The Stetson had seemed like a safe and pleasant way for Lark Fortune to have reached out, on his own terms.

Lark had instantly arrived at some conclusion about Alex. On that alone, Alex felt the man had simply mistaken him for someone else, someone he knew (and obviously did not like). If it were later in the day, Alex might have thought Lark long into his cups, that his judgment might not be too keen.

As it was, Alex decided to take another chance at it. He set his Stetson down atop his head and enjoyed how it bathed him in warmth and light. He did not need to verbalize it, but he spoke Lark's name, anyway. Even as advanced as Alex was technologically, it was nice to imagine oneself at least partially still in charge.

The "requesting access" light blinked gently with the rhythms of the smooth jazz playing in the HeadGear waiting room. Eventually, the hue of the room paled, and the message "denied" was presented in an understanding script.

"Kenneth Hinman," Alex said then.

Henny's big face was tinted green from the Visor he wore. "Hey man!" Henny said over the din of the bar.

"What's going on there? Is business always so brisk, mid-afternoon?"

"Celebration," he explained. He was working the bar in his foreground, watching Alex's reaction in his peripheral view. "Rebs stuck it to ChompCorp. Surely, you've seen it."

He had not. He had kept his options open. Kept his mind open. Stayed off the JackChat altogether in his vigil, waiting to speak to Lark Fortune.

"Stuck it to...? ChompCorp?"

"Oh yeah!" Someone rushed past Henny; the man was hoisting a keg overhead. "Hey! Where're you going with that?" Henny called after him.

The man's off-screen comment was drowned out in the revelry at the bar.

Henny's attention returned to Alex. "Come down and join us. Drinks are on CommCorp."

"CommCorp?" Alex leaned his head forward, ever so slightly, and the Stetson took his cue and zoomed in a little closer on Henny. "Why?"

"I dunno, but it's the good stuff. Bound to attract Lefty," he raised his eyebrows and grunted, "if you know what I mean."

Alex checked the time in his display. It was 4:45 in Guthrie, close to sunset out in the Caribbean. "Be there in a bit. I have to make a call."

"The appetizers are going fast. Fancy stuff shipped in. Better hurry."

Then Henny's image was out. The Stetson compensated for Henny's uncouth exit with an image of airships and tropical islands.

"Nah," Alex said, talking to the HeadGear as he removed it. "Intuitive, but no."

• • • •

Though he always moved about frequently and fluidly, Alex referred to south Texas as his home. If pressed, he would claim San Antonio as his hometown. Few people knew of his personal life in Springfield, Texas, and fewer yet of his actual job. Only one man had known anything of his life prior to 2034, and now even that man was dead. No one, not even Kelli, truly knew his past—and that was the way he liked it.

Guthrie was more than 600 miles from Springfield, and Alex had never gone there directly. He had, however, been to the town dozens of times. He owed his very existence to Guthrie, Oklahoma, in ways no one else could claim.

In all the times he had rehearsed it, Alex had yet to get it right. This time, he told himself, was the time. In the last twenty years, he had been angling toward a conversation with Lark Fortune, and at last they had seen each other face to face, even if it had been through a Stetson. He would make this visit happen. It was imperative. Find him in Henny's and work things out together.

But first, he scaled the narrow back stairs of the B&B, unlocked a door to the attic, and entered his local lair. Alex privately owned the Stalwart Arms Bed and Breakfast, and on several visits, he had stayed there. Other times, he took the fire escape up to the top floor, then made his way to the attic. When left with no other option, before his promise to Kelli, he had sometimes arrived by Hot Wire.

As this was his inner sanctum, and the most secretive of all his various perches and places to stay, he had taken care not to draw any attention to it. The windows were covered with blackout curtains. The room did not even have electricity. Alex had fabbed a foot pedal-powered generator years ago to operate his radio unit and a lamp. He sat at his desk, pumping at the pedals and blowing dust from the ham radio.

He wiped down the leather-padded headset, smiling at the contrast between this antique and the comforts of the Stetson. He slipped it over his ears and began tuning in signals, listening for anything Astar and Zana might be circulating for him to hear.

It was only half an hour before he picked up on it: ghost ships were coming to haunt Laramie, Wyoming.

· · · ·

Waiting in *Sharts N' Grins* brought its own amusements. No one particularly trusted him there. He was alone in a corner booth, facing the mayhem of the place. Between broadcasts and the related hooting and hollering, curiosity would grow, and the locals would steal glances at him over their drinks. Alex would tip his beer at them and smile broadly. They would generally look away with a curt head bob or mutter to their companions, then the lot of them would stare at him skeptically until the next distraction presented itself.

Televisions, antiquated as they were, provided patrons with CommCorp loops that had caused all the stir. Alex could see two of them from his booth, and he watched them off and on. A Winston Weekly had been run low, turned into a fierce electromagnetic monster. Somehow, a band of Eat the Rich activists, the Rebels of the Plains, had fashioned a Hot Wire consuming the airship. No matter how many times he saw it, the vid took his breath away.

It should not have been possible. It had never happened in any timeline Alex had known. Teleportation was not done on that scale—it never had been. Here and now, however, it had been done. It was so diabolically simple that Alex both admired and despised the act, all at once.

Someone had engineered a synthetic material from a Tic Tac. That was the only answer, the only way a Hot Wire thread could be conductive over miles and miles. Someone knew of Tic Tac pairings, and somehow, that same someone had spun up a synthetic thread from one Tic Tac, then used the other to close the loop.

An image was on the screens that stirred up the whole bar. Listening over the chaotic cheers, beyond the endless yawling of the jukebox, Alex could just pick up snippets of the newscast. The story was clearer from neighboring booths, and he eavesdropped on all he could catch.

A woman was smiling at the camera, kissing a rancher on the cheek. Cut to her fingering a locket. Close-up on the locket. She was inserting something from the locket into two couplings of a Hot Wire. This was it. She was the engineer behind the event.

"Girl made good!" someone said.

"She was in my class... well in school when I was. Year ahead of me."

"She's still hot as balls!" a man in another booth was saying.

"Krystal Price—who knew?" Another said.

Alex stood and put an elbow on the top rail of the neighboring booth. He was looking on at images of the woman, acting disinterested in anything else. He mused aloud, "She's from here, isn't she?"

Without looking up or over a shoulder, men in the booth acknowledged his comment, adding local color to the comment. "Much as anybody of her stripe would claim us."

"Always a little too good for the ol' hometown."

"I dunno," a man said, sipping at a can of beer, "I've seen her pass through now and again."

"Recently?" Alex asked, still careful not to make eye contact, staring instead into his beer.

"Was she in that big stretch that rolled in a couple days back?"

"Why would she come through here?" A man standing nearby overheard. He pointed at the television, then gestured broadly at the bar. "She's rich."

"Eat the Rich!" someone in the bar spouted off.

Amid the grumblings, Alex heard several comments suggesting no harm would come to *this little rich girl*. She was one of them. She would put Guthrie on the map again. She was the hometown hero.

The broadcasts seemed to side with her, too. Though he could not hear it over the din, Alex could generally follow the story. Corn Belt map, sideswipe to Oklahoma, zoom in on Guthrie. Footage of the Guthrie meteor fall. Still of the Installation. More current footage, possibly a live satellite feed, an aerial view of Guthrie today. Then a cut to somewhere else altogether, a cityscape he did not recognize. The woman was on screen again, wearing her trademark white ensemble and comically large sunhat. She was being interviewed, but Alex could not hear it. The scrolling text at the bottom of the screen was obscured by patrons of the bar, all crooning and gawking to see the screens themselves.

Someone new was leaning against the bar, and the sight of him took Alex's attention away entirely. He recognized the lanky frame, the clothes that hung loosely from his drooping shoulders. Alex caught him in profile and was positive then. The sarcastic smile. The bent of his nose. It was Larkin Fortune.

Henny had pointed at Alex just then, and Lark panned back and forth. Spotting Alex, he cursed something at Henny. He snatched up his beer mug, sloshing half of it on the bar as he whipped in Alex's direction.

Alex stood his ground. In his peripheral vision, he could see patrons piecing it together, looking from him to Lark and back. He had his guns, should he need them, even for a diversion, but he hoped it would not come to that. He hoped it would be a civil conversation.

"IMPOSSIBLE!" Lark coughed as he drew up to Alex.

"Hi, I'm—"

"SACKERSON!" Lark yelled at him.

Alex stepped back as much as the booth allowed. "I... I most assuredly am not—"

"You!" he yelled. Only the music and television noise remained. Everyone was watching the altercation. "Her!" He pointed at a television. "And all that... *and now you*!"

Alex held up his hands to calm Lark. "Easy now."

"EASY!" Lark threw his beer on the cement floor between them. The mug shattered and the beer splashed at Alex's pant legs, but he did not move. "EASY?" Lark was shaking with rage.

"Yeah. Yeah. Let's just chill," he gestured to his booth. "I'll buy you another, and we can talk."

"Whaddya want? *A milk, maybe?* Like old times?"

Alex cocked his head. Lark seemed more out of sorts than he had been reported to be. "Milk? No. No, just have a seat, I'll go get us a couple cold ones."

"Only if I can keep this!" He held up the black hatbox. Alex hadn't even noticed it. The guy was striking a bargain with him. A Stetson for some conversation?

"I'll even unlock it," Alex said. "You just sit tight. Okay?"

"And don't crack out the guns again. And no Hot Wires, either!"

"Right. Right." Alex nodded. He turned back toward the bar but was intercepted by Gail with the beer mugs.

"On the house," she smiled.

"Keep giving it all away, you'll go belly up," Alex smiled but took the beers gratefully.

The crowd had already lost interest, turning their focus back to the televisions. Henny was sweeping up the broken mug.

Alex sat across from Lark and studied him. The man looked even older in person. Haggard. Haunted. Lark's attention was fixed on the television.

"So... you know her?" Alex asked.

"Know her? Know her! Yeah. It's Krys. Remember Krys?"

"Uh... can't say that I do."

"Lissen," Lark said, pointing a finger at Alex. "You can act like you don't know anything, go asking all around town about every damn thing, but the fact is, you do. You know too much."

"I... I think you—"

"And you have single-handedly ruined my life!" Lark guzzled his beer. He finished the whole mug and wiped his mouth with his sleeve. "Ruined."

Chapter 19 Staring Down Death

The hangar was solemn as a church service. Stu knew this silence. It was like the time they came across a beached whale when he was on vacation—something bigger than life, epic in its presence, was now void. As with the MagLev, Stu thought of the lives aboard that airship. He doubted they were all evil minions of ChompCorp. He doubted they all even knew what they were doing.

Nat bought into the hype, however, and was sure that a Lightning's Hand—an airship electrified—was on autopilot. Nat would sleep at night, believing that no lives had been lost at all.

As with the train job, most people had watched the spectacle on their various HeadGear. The pilots were particularly jacked in for they had precision work to do and depended on the instrumentation displayed inside. All of those immediately around him in the shelter of the hangar bay were jacked—pilots, press, most of the Rebel rabble. Only his twenty men stood out in the rain, looking at the place the Lightning's Hand had been. They were staring down death, then in a blink, they were gawking at a glow in the sky.

The cloud cover made afternoon look like evening, and the shock and awe seemed to stop time altogether. Stu thought he was the first to break the spell of the spectacle. He nodded to one of his men outside. He smiled at Rae. He tipped his hat at Krystal. They all acknowledged him, sort of, but their eyes were saying, 'Yeah, but did you see that?'

Stu turned to Nat. Nat was awash in the blue of a HeadGear display. Eyes darting as they read some projection, sized up something to do with the spectacle they'd just witnessed. Stu had never adjusted to seeing Nat all jacked in. *Not as bad as some kids,* he had told himself. "What's it telling you?" Stu asked, tapping on Nat's HeadGear. He knew it was a breach of etiquette, like pounding on a bathroom stall, but he didn't really care. "What do you see?"

"We did it," they said in a hushed tone.

Then, as if Nathan Wiebe was the voice of the people, they all seemed to sigh collectively and snap out of it. Stu registered the communal shift in body language, the suspended judgment passed—replaced by relief. Then ecstasy burst in.

"It's gone!" someone yelled. Cheers were bursting out all over the hangar. Someone slapped Stu on the shoulder in the giddy moment, instantly apologizing and moving on. The hangar, even the grounds outside, were filled with happy people. They were a massive mosh pit of joy, swaying and teeming. The whole lot of them shared high fives and chest bumps. The whole of the fairgrounds was surging with uproarious hooting and hollering.

Stu stood solid, a bump on a log, and as he surveyed the crowd, he realized there were others like him, not so giddy. His men, to a soul, were uncharacteristically reverent. On another occasion, they might have been shooting their guns in the sky, popping open beers and pouring them over each other's heads.

The annihilation of the airship was an overpowering statement.

Thirty years ago, the Wiebes had been dealt a similar blow. Someone had detonated a nuclear bomb over Horse Thief Canyon Ranch, the Wiebe ranch and others surrounding it. They had torched a region to send a message to The Boys. They had killed 32 of the locals and spread radiation poisoning to countless others simply to say, "Back off, Boys."

The Wiebe family and The Boys had no recourse. It was a bitter pill. If whomever was going to chuck nukes at them, they had to tuck tail. It was humiliating pulling up stakes and moving away. It was a few bad years of getting their footing in Wyoming. The worst of it was that the enemy, the 'whomever,' had never been pointed out. Stu knew Lefty Fortune and his strange friend, Sackerson, had something to do with it. He knew it was all tangled in those Hot Wires, somehow.

And Kenny Hinman had betrayed them all, siding with the Spooks.

Now a Hot Wire as big as a nuclear mushroom cloud glowed overhead, and a ship once as big as a ranch was nothing but vapor.

• • • •

S he had had her moment of glory, but even Krystal Price had to admit it was getting dangerous to linger. Stu had escorted her by the elbow out the back door of the Exhibition Hall, where Leon was waiting with the limo. He carted her to her car and deposited her inside, all poofy in her white wedding dress and all puffed up from the big event.

"Get in," she commanded, patting the seat beside her. "I won't bite."

Stu grimaced. "Why are you here, Krystal? And when are you leaving town?"

He glanced at some Eaters firing off guns in glee. A couple of the Boys met his glance and sized up his situation, then looked away discreetly. One of them shook his head, but Stu noted his grin. They would talk later.

"Oh, come on, Stewie. I'll leave *now* if you'll ride back with me. You said it yourself. Laramie's no place for a girl like me." She gave him that smile he had never quite got over, threatening, "*Otherwise...*"

Stu could not think of all the stupidity she could get herself into, unattended. The crazy was at full tilt, and eventually the Eat the Rich mob would realize their new ally was one of the richest women serving one of the biggest corporations in the world. What then? Krystal Price traded in the currency of souls. Even wild outlaws should know that. Sure, she'd powered down a Lightning's Hand, but she would have something back in trade. He suspected it would be more than good publicity.

He removed his hat and folded into the limo but knew better than to sit beside her. He settled into the seat across from her. Even being *seen* with her was a mistake. Riding back to the Civic Center was against his better judgment, and like Rae, his judgment was always right.

No sooner had the driver started the limo than a couple of pickups surged around the building. Stu leaned forward, gripping the door handle for a quick exit. The Boys, however, were in the gap between pickups and limousine, weapons drawn. The Eaters downshifted and spun a couple loops, spraying both the Boys and the car with mud.

Stu tapped the window between front and back, and the chauffeur lowered it a bit. "Yes, Mr. Wiebe?"

"Take third, Leon, and if you see more of them, go the long way around fifth."

The divider whirred up. Stu could not spot a threat, if there came to be one, out the side windows through the coat of mud. It was not an ideal situation.

"What are you pouting for? You got your sky back. Chomp won't dare bully farmers around here for a while."

"Ranchers," he corrected.

"Farmers, ranchers, grocers, and brewers, all of 'em's ChompCorp's makers and doers," she sang.

"Is that their latest jingle?" he grumbled.

"No, silly. It's a nursery school song."

He wanted to ask her how the rest of it went, but then, he did not want to listen to her sing more. Even the way she sang that little tune was too much. It reminded him of high school musicals they had been in together. He did not need more reminders.

Once Rachel had been gifted with a new perfume, the same as *Krystal's perfume*, and Stu acted as if he were going into anaphylactic shock. His attempt to cover up his recollection just made things worse. He'd had to buy her a new pair of boots to make up for that one.

"How about the show?" Krystal asked, beaming. The mud on the windows was washing away in the lingering showers, and it cast her in golden ripples. It softened the radiant White Witch. "The world's never seen nothin' quite like it. R&D call it imploding fireworks or something like that."

"It's gonna bring a shitstorm of trouble."

"Might swing some tourism your way, though. Especially if I leave my portal behind for you."

"Not for me," Stu said. "Besides... New York. Paris. *Laramie*. I don't see your clientele popping by anytime soon."

"Stewie, baby, get some perspective. Laramie could be the Portal of the Plains."

"Too many crazies coming around here lately as it is."

They both flinched when some vehicle with no mufflers roared around their car.

"What's the point of it, anyway, your *show*?"

"Really, you need some perspective," she sniffed at her little perfume pouch. "TransCorp is about to make it really big. Teaming up with the Eat the Rich gang a little's going to win us a whole new market, and that—"

"Eaters can't afford to port around. Hell, nobody can."

"But they will. Everybody will. You should climb aboard, Stu. I'll make you rich."

The way she said it, the way she sat, suggested climbing aboard more than a money train. Stu fiddled with his hat. He wondered how damn far it was yet to the Civic Center. He wondered if she was really leaving town tonight.

"Wait a minute," he said. "How's everybody going to afford porting all the sudden?"

"We're going to Henry Ford it: a port in every garage," Krystal smiled. "Like that twist? Won't need a car anymore, see?"

"Ports won't haul my cattle. I'll still need my truck to—"

"Ubiquitous. Instantaneous. Free." Krystal painted the campaign with her hands between them in a sweeping move.

"First of all, folks out here won't even know what that means, at least not but the free part. Besides, y'all tried that with the One World thing. Fool me once, shame on—"

"That was different. We're keeping it at travel and transport this time, not all that foo-foo about borders and boundaries. We're keeping it real."

"Yeah, well, you can keep it."

She frowned. Shrugged. "That's your prerogative. I'm just telling you, as a friend, there's no better time to hook up."

Climb aboard. Hook up. The way she was sitting. Her smile and her perfume.

The car slowed to park. At last.

"Well, while you're out hawking teleportation, I'll just stay here herding cattle. I chose my lot."

"You're a fool, Stewart Wiebe." The White Witch glowered. "You need to think it through. We put Chomp down, and we might as well own CommCorp. Water Works is a mess and..." Leon opened her door. "*And* who do you think just acquired PetroCorp?"

Leon Williams, a discreet professional chauffeur, could not ignore this news. He was slack jawed, himself.

"You're kidding," Stu scoffed, looking out the window through the mud and tinted glass toward the Civic Center... except it wasn't the Civic Center. It was the Grand Marquis hotel.

"You don't get ahead of it, and you'll be walking... on my shale."

"So," he said in a measured tone, "if I wanted in?"

"I'm staying in your little burg a couple nights. If you want to get in deep, I've rented the whole hotel. Come see me?"

Just then his four-door dually truck rolled up. Double parked. Rae hopped out and was making her way toward the limo.

"*Miss Price*," Leon urged.

"Oh, hello, *Mrs. Stewart Wiebe*," Krystal cooed. "Come to fetch your hubby?"

Stu could not get out of the car fast enough to block the haymaker.

Rae clocked Krystal out cold.

Leon caught the withering White Witch and dragged her toward the hotel.

"Get in the truck," Rae said and clomped back toward the pickup without giving Stu a second glance.

The limousine was still idling.

One of Krystal's white shoes was abandoned on the sidewalk.

Rae revved up the diesel truck, and it blew billowing black smoke.

People on the sidewalk were gawking.

A hotel porter was approaching. "Anything I can do to help, sir?"

"No," Stu said, pushing his hat down tight enough to weather a tornado. There wasn't much anyone could do to help him now.

Chapter 20 The Shark

The Warrior snapped his neck, a quick left and right. His soaked hair flapped over his shoulders and face. He smeared it back with the rain, trying to get a better look above. This was not right. It wasn't only that the sky was filled with the winged women—now they were turning away, breaking formation. *They never did that.*

He roared and shook his swords at the sky.

Those most near him had veered from their usual coastal sweep off toward the sea. They did a sharp break in formation, then made a pivot and, like a murmuring of birds, reformed and regrouped on a different course.

"Come back!" he screamed, but when they did not, he had a flash of memory, first just a glimpse, then several more memories roiled through. The women would splash down and board rafts. He had a vivid memory then of one woman in particular who had seen him across a cove. When was it? Who was she?

Maybe she was one of those now drifting away. Maybe he could intercept them shore-side. He roared again and sheathed his swords as he ran for the beach. He had seen them fold and plunge into the water. He knew where they would be. If they were not coming to him, he would surprise some of them at sea. With each footfall, he calculated his arrival and theirs, planning the most efficient intercept.

If he knew anything, it was the water. He had spent months marooned at sea, so very long that water was his first comfort. Whenever the killing was scarce, the Warrior returned to the water to float for hours. The sea was his solace. He meditated in its lulling waves.

He also caught most of his fish by hand, swimming in for the kill like the predator he was.

He crouched in the last stand of trees at the edge of the beach, intending to watch for them to splash down nearby. What he saw instead was a flotilla of inflatable speed boats. Crewmembers were signaling the flyers.

The Warrior was confident he would yet have his kills. Only the filthy rich would have such elaborate means to hunt him. The girls he had slain had no qualms about attacking him. Somewhere in his core, he knew this was all about him, and he knew he had been hunted and outnumbered many times before. There was no fear in him. He sat down and waited for his spoils. A broad smile crinkled his sunburnt face.

He watched carefully as the crew untethered their ships and made way. Two boats remained floating here as if baiting him. He waited. He looked skyward, following the gaze of the crewmembers, and caught his breath. He wiped his eyes and squinted. Something was drifting *counter to the storm*, some feathery cloud swooping more up and down than anything else.

He cocked his head. Had he actually seen the Weeklies before? Nothing like this faint ribbon of gossamer. It flew so low, if he had a bow, he thought, he could run an arrow into it. He allowed himself to entertain the idea, how the arrow would deflate the faux cloud, and then he would slaughter everyone on that airship. In this fantasy, he was victorious, slashing and fighting so many of the Rich while their craft sank into the sea.

His attention snapped back when he heard yelling and struggling at the boats. The crew were kicking and swatting at sea creatures surfacing all around them. The boats were being boarded by men camouflaged with seaweed and grass.

The Warrior stood and frowned. He swiped away the rain again to get a better view, to really grasp what was happening. Those boats were *his* trophy. The winged women were to be his kills, along with the entire crew. Who could be ruining his plans?

"Eat the Rich!" raiders cried out as they jumped up and down in the inflatables. They waved weapons overhead, and they cheered. The crew had been thrown overboard, likely dead.

He groaned as he unbuckled his belts and pulled off his holsters, scabbards, and vest. He tucked it all under an outcropping and charged. The Warrior knew that victory, however small, might blind the hijackers, even for a moment. He dived the moment he could and slipped along the seabed. His strokes were strong, and he closed on them fast. He was in the shadow of the boats, corpses drifting down around him in clouds of blood.

Had he brought a knife, he could have quickly slashed the bottom of each boat and then dealt with each of the revelers as they entered the water. They had crossed a line, however, trying to ruin his kills, and they would pay for that with the most physical and manual of murders.

The Warrior surfaced behind a boat, just his head to get a breath and his bearings, then one arm to snake up and grab the boat's mooring rope. He tangled the props with rope. He swam toward the other boat. They would not be going anywhere.

He swam underneath and came up midship, this time grabbing the mooring ropes that hung on the side. He brought himself up, standing on the sidewall of the boat and jumped up and down, leaning back with all his weight and strength. As he expected, this sudden movement caught the Eat the Rich revelers off guard, and they fell toward him. All the weight, his included, caused the raft to flip over on him, spilling five men into the water with him.

A few random shots detonated in the water, stray gunfire that shot streaks of bubbles off and away. One that came close to the Warrior's head continued on up to puncture the other boat's inflatable hull. He turned back from seeing that to a slow-motion punch in his face from one of the ragged men.

Fighting underwater was uncommon. Few knew how to do it. Anything that would normally be a powerful blow could be so slowed by the water to be nothing but a love tap. One had to be considerate of the water's resistance. One had to strike in a streamlined slice, not a conventional punch. These men, clustering around him, had no idea. He dodged most of their blows, chuckling bubbles gleefully.

He considered himself a creature of the sea, and he moved like one of them. He had found he was already disciplined at measured breathing, but during those months on the sinking *Undulatus*, he learned to hold his breath for minutes on end. He had taught himself to hold his breath, even under strenuous activity, far longer than those struggling around him.

One of the five had made it back to the surface, apparently, for now shots were being fired down at him. Like fists, bullets slowed and lost trajectory, but the Warrior did not trifle with them. He redirected the others into the line of fire with something like underwater judo, letting their own weight and thrust propel them into the rain of gunfire. One survivor not shredded by bullets was quickly dispatched when the Warrior choked the life from him. His arms and legs curled around the last man and crushed his bones; his ribs and vertebrae snapped satisfactorily.

He waited under the boat, floating with his back against the underside of it. He could feel the frantic darting around through the rubber floor. He could see a dip in the boat where most of the men were scampering, at the aft, likely struggling with the engine. He shook his head, smiling at the snake-like tendrils of hair that moved around his face. Idiots. He could have reared up again then and capsized this boat, too, but it was more fun to wait them out. Soon, he thought, they would swim for shore, but they would never make it. He would see to that.

The Warrior felt, more than heard, something drop distantly into the water in a downspout of motion. As he turned his head toward it, he felt another, closer, to his right. Another behind somewhere. It was the winged women, and they were coming right for the boat. When one spied him, she pulled a knife from a sheath on her thigh. One from the other side of him had a rapier out, waving it slowly, menacingly. These two knew the resistance of the water and sliced with it, one with the currents. They swam like mermaids. They were closing in on him.

A third one had no weapon drawn, but she was the most bothersome, for she seemed not to see him at all. She was more intent on boarding the boat. When the Eat the Rich imbeciles saw her, they would kill her. *His kill.* His trophy. They followed no code.

He had to make a quick decision.

She drew up to reach for the mooring ropes.

A shot was fired above.

The Warrior ripped the sword from one of the women. She recoiled and kicked at him, but he did not bother with her. Instead, he sliced the boat from end to end. Six men dropped through the slice as it opened. Then it was a flurry of curses and blood, startled cries—and the Warrior's laughter, which came out in barks and bubbles, nearly blinding him from his work.

• • • •

As he was tearing his trophy strips from the deceased, he heard the approach of more boats. He saw more downspouts and bubbles where more winged women were plunging into the water.

Over a dozen were dead in the water, drifting downward, leaving smears of blood. The boat he had rendered in two was sinking slowly. A corpse was tangled in the slice, like a lure caught in the mouth of a fish. Winged women continued to splashdown, and now three fresh boats were circling around the site.

He measured his options.

He could lurk. He could float among the dead and strike out when the women came to inspect.

He might just thrash his way through all these additional people and boats and make a bloody mess of it all. That had appeal.

He considered taking refuge in the upturned boat, buying time for a stealthier attack.

Ultimately, however, the Warrior swam deep and low along the belly of the bay. Before long, he was far enough away he could creep back on shore. He watched the crews retrieve the women as they landed. He watched them all, aghast at the bloodshed and brutality surrounding them. They were at high alert. Afraid, and rightfully so. They were looking all about, scanning the waters, perhaps for a shark. He smiled a wide and toothy grin. *He was the shark*, and he snickered at his kill. As he watched, he tied three more strips of flight suit into his beard.

It had been a very prosperous morning.

Chapter 21 Sackerson

Kenny Hinman had seen it all, all types of patrons at all hours in all ways, always bucking for a beer. He'd sent some packing, he'd thrown some out, and once in a while, when the situation called for it, he had sat down with someone and just listened. Lately, he'd let the girls handle all the consoling and cajoling.

He had shooed away everyone at closing time, for the day-long celebration over the Laramie vids left a lot to clean up. Henny and the girls had been at it for a couple hours before he had called it a night and told the others to come back to it early tomorrow.

Not an hour later, however, Gail (still on the job, still mopping floors) came up to report that a strange old man was asking for him... and a glass of milk. That brought him down the stairs two at a time.

"You let your hair grow out," Henny observed, setting a frothy, brimming glass of the white stuff in front of the man hunched over the bar.

"Felicitations!" the old man cackled. "You've done well for yourself, old friend."

"Sackerson," Henny said. "I can't believe you're here."

The old man cupped the frosty glass of milk, studied it in earnest. He nodded and smiled across the bar between them.

"I thought I saw you on the Vids—out in Wyoming."

Sackerson tossed his head, his mane of white hair taking on the colors of the neon light. "Can't believe everything you see."

Gail was hovering, acting busy wiping down glasses. Henny tried to wave her away.

"What brings you around, after all this time?"

"What's it been for you, more than a little while, I guess?" He eyed Gail, panned the empty bar. "That your wife?"

"Daughter," Henny said under his breath. "You should know that."

"Haven't kept up on my history," Sack winked.

"It's been a long while, Sack. It's been thirty years."

"Thirty years," Sackerson nodded, then took a long gulp of the milk. He fussed at his bushy mustache, wiping it clean.

"Are you here because of what's happening out in Laramie?"

"Mmmmh. Bumped into a mutual friend out there," Sackerson confided.

"You got a loose way of using that word, 'friend,' my friend. Wiebe still blames me for everything. He's not been back to Guthrie since then."

"Stu Wiebe's all tied in knots."

"And Lefty, he still blames you."

"That's fairer than you know."

Sackerson ate peanuts and stared at the flat screens for a while. He brushed at his braided beard.

Henny turned to watch the screens with him, monitoring Sackerson in the mirror behind the bar. Finally, he said: "Whatever's in the air, it's like a magnet, bringing strangers into town."

"Is this the guy?" Gail asked, her curiosity getting the better of her.

"So, which am I, Henny? A friend? 'The guy?' 'A stranger?'"

He shrugged and turned to Gail. "This is my old friend, Sackerson."

"Oh?" Gail said, stepping forward and extending a hand.

The old man stood and shook her hand. "And you are?"

"I'm Abigail," she bobbed. "Sackerson, eh? I haven't heard *a thing* about Dad's old friend Sackerson."

It was her mother's look. Henny didn't even need to turn his head to see it: head cocked, just the pinch of a frown, hands on her hips. He would be telling her Sackerson stories now for a week to make up for it. No hiding this one in the closet. The skeleton was out and about.

Sackerson acted a little hurt. His acting was exaggerated. He was a model of exaggeration and always had been. Since he was on his feet anyway, Sackerson took a spin around the place. Henny knew this one, too: Sack was appreciating *Sharts N' Grins* like a museum of antiquities. If Sack had ever been in a museum, he had doubtless ignored the "Do Not Touch" signs—he had to run a hand over everything.

"Abigail, if I might suggest, ask your daddy sometime. Ask him all about how he saved the lives of so many people when he was your age."

Henny had a tickle in his throat. "Sometime," he allowed, "but not tonight. What're you here for, again?"

He knew the answer would be slow in coming. Sackerson was poking a finger at a static lamp, fascinated with the way the light pooled at his fingertip on the shade. "Can't believe I'm seeing one in person," he marveled, smiling at Henny and Gail. "One of these burnt down—"

"You don't get out much, do ya?" Gail asked. She joined him for the tour, clearly enjoying his appreciation for the little things he was so drawn to. He was fascinated with the neon signs, then went on a riff about Neon and Argon, Mercury and other things. She listened with enthusiasm and continued the tour. The bar itself and back bar were over 100 years old. Hardwood. The wood flooring was original, and though they re-stained it, patrons could still imagine a bloodstain or two from old west shootouts. She explained the taps, offered him a beer which he politely refused. They talked over the jukebox, and Gail hummed a few tunes for him when he recited the titles.

It gave Henny a minute to regroup. This little visit in the middle of a Wednesday night just confirmed it all. Something big was going down, and now with Sack here, Henny knew that something big was going to suck him in again, too.

He'd thought he'd seen the old man on the flatscreen. In one frame, he did a double take when it looked like he was getting chummy with Wiebe. Time had not been good to either one of them. Sack looked twice his age, and Stu Wiebe was now a weathered ranch hand, no longer a homecoming king.

First, it was Krystal passing through town. Then Lefty had gotten to him with his usual freak on. Then that wild-haired guy, Gault, came around with all his high-tech stuff, friendlying up to—of all people—*Lefty Fortune*. To top it off, an airship swept the two of them away! The whole thing—from the CommCorp hype to seeing Sack on the vids—led Henny to pack his bug out bag.

He'd gone out of his way to spend a few extra hours with Peg and the baby. He took some Krugerrands out of his stash and doled them out to the girls, pocketing a few for himself. Henny didn't know where this was going, but it couldn't be good.

"How'd you do that?" Gail was marveling over the dart board. "Three in the bullseye!"

"Beginner's luck," Sackerson said. "Did I do good?"

"You're grifting me, pal." Gail left the darts in the board and escorted him to the kitchen. Something had been said about coffee.

Henny touched the red feather flight of the darts. They were grouped in a perfect triangle. They had been thrown deep, all the way to the hilt. The red cork bullseye was cracked in two.

Maybe Lefty was getting to him, or maybe it really was a message. Either way, he'd be buying a new dartboard. He sighed and followed after them. Sackerson, once the most lethal man he'd ever met, was learning how to brew coffee with his little-girl-grown-up.

"Guthrie wasn't always this peaceful," Sack was saying. "Once it'd been a wild—"

"Oh, I know this one. I'm a barkeep. I gotta tell the tourists all the stories about the Wild West, the Land Rush and the oil boom and—-"

"Apparently," Sackerson nodded at Henny, "you don't know the half of it."

"So, what's the other half?"

"Nowhere near as interesting," Henny jumped in. Damage control. If stories were to be told, they'd be on his terms. "I was in high school. It was right after that meteor shower that started the whole hubbub and the Installation. There were some terrorist types flitting around town. Spooks, we called them."

"They were after Larkin Fortune's dad," Sackerson added, "and, for that matter, Lark himself."

"Wait, wait, wait. Lefty? *Terrorists* were after Lefty?"

They both nodded.

Henny continued, "That coffeehouse on the corner? Used to be Mack's, a greasy spoon cafe. That's the place ol' Sackerson here shot a couple terrorists dead on a Sunday afternoon."

Sack was taken aback by this, returning with his flavor of things. "Your father infiltrated the terrorists, got on the inside with them, and when they set off a nuclear bomb, he ratted them out and saved a lot of lives."

"Oh, come on!" Gail tittered. "Dad? A nuclear bomb?"

Sackerson nodded adamantly. "That patch out east? The ranch land all staked off? I bet it's still toxic."

"*From a nuclear bomb*?" Gail scoffed. "Two headed cattle and ten-foot corn out there, eh?"

"Well," Henny shrugged, "we'll never know unless they let us back in there."

"Lefty's talked about that, now that I think about it. Yeah... he's always going on about how we're sandwiched between two government black ops or some such thing. Installation on the west, the Quarantine on the east."

The coffee pot burbled its last surge, and Gail poured three cups.

"Oh, I can't drink the stuff," Sackerson said. "Too much caffeine."

"Why didn't you say so? I can make you some decaf upstairs if you—"

"That's okay, honey," Henny said. "He won't be staying long."

· · · ·

"You can pout all you want, Henny, but you ought to own it, man."

"Different times."

"You should be the hometown hero."

"Not for me. I pour beer."

"You don't even tell your family?"

"Oh, I'm going to have to answer for this for a long time, thanks to you."

Sackerson brushed at his beard again and asked if he had anything in it. He acted like it was new to him, to be eating when he was so wooly. This was a different side of Sackerson than he had known, a self-conscious side. Back in the day, he had been more devil-may-care. More... flamboyant.

"You ain't here just to eat peanuts and stir up my family. Why're you really here, Sack?"

"Well, I *was* coming by to visit our mutual friend, Lark," Sackerson said. He stood and faced the mirror to inspect himself, like he wanted to look his best. He then sat back down. "Gail tells me he's not around."

"That's right. Lefty flew the coop. Literally. Damnedest thing. I've *never* seen a Winston Weekly fly over town, ever. Today one dropped low and slow to pick up Lefty."

"Is that so…" Sackerson muttered, lost in thought.

"Isn't that something?"

"It is. It is."

"What do you know about it?" Henny asked. Strange things and Sackerson went together.

"Not a thing. Tell me more."

Henny wanted to keep it to himself. He really did. He did not want to be drawn back into the Sackerson madness. Then again, who else did he have to confide in? Who could he trust? Who better to talk to than Sackerson, a man who knew the score. "Well," he shrugged, "anyone in town could tell you the same thing. They flew low, dropped down this tube thing with, like, ribbing inside, then Lefty and this new guy around town climbed right up and the ship floated off. That's all there is to tell."

"New guy, huh?" Sackerson's eyes were penetrating.

Henny was on a roll.

"Yeah, yeah. He came into town just like you did, back in the day. Asking around all over town for Larkin Fortune. Hung around here a lot. Racked up a hell of a tab. Must've bankrolled 'drinks on me' three, maybe four times."

"Lubrication," Sackerson observed.

"Yep. Limbered folks up a lot, I'd say. And he did his share of talking, too, like all the damn time."

"Really? About what?"

"Asking questions mostly, but sometimes he'd get folks riled up from the Eat the Rich camp. Get 'em all going down that path, then just, you know, screw with them."

Sackerson nodded sagely. "Tripped them up on their own rhetoric, right?"

Henny fought off a shrug. "I... I dunno. He'd confuse them anyways, ask them if they didn't all want to strike it rich someday, then question that like a double standard. 'You want to get rich, but you want to wipe out rich folk'? Stuff like that."

"And you say he and Lark left together, by airship?"

"Yeah, that's right."

"So, they got to be friends of a sort?"

"Not at first," Henny chuckled. "At first Lefty thought the new guy was you!"

"Really?

"He drinks a lot these days."

"So I've heard... but he and this new guy—what's his name?"

"Alex. Alex Gault."

"Lark and this Alex fellow, how'd that play out?" Sackerson seemed more curious than even he should be.

Henny wanted to feather back on his answers, but he wanted his own answers, too. Give and take, the code of the barkeep. "Why are you so interested? Why do you want to catch up with Lark so bad?"

"Ah, that is the question, isn't it? Why Larkin Fortune? Why did they hunt him and his daddy? Why did this Alex Gault come visiting?"

"Yeah, and why are you here?" Henny asserted again. He thought he knew the answer, but he wanted to hear it from Sackerson. He wanted him to say, "Tic-Tacs."

"You saw the Vids, Henny. You know that's some big mojo. Big corporations squaring off. Big Hot Wires in the sky."

"But why Lefty? And why now?"

"It's confusing as hell out there in Wyoming. I'd bet my beard that's where Alex Gault and that airship are heading, am I right?"

Henny nodded.

Sackerson was getting his edge on. The old Sackerson, under all the hair and wrinkles, was still in there. It made Henny catch his breath. It made him feel a bit like he did back when. Clever. Spry.

"I need you again, Kenny Hinman. Only this time, I have a feeling there're bigger stakes. Bigger even than the last time."

"Me? What can I do? I just slosh beer—"

"Folks say you're the only one ol' Lefty trusts. Gail says he depends on you, even so far as keeping his claw machine working." Sackerson's gesture was a reasonable exaggeration of Lefty's prosthetic.

"He is my best customer."

"Ah, he's more than that to you."

Henny squirmed.

"*I need him to trust you* out there in the wild."

"Yeah, but..." Henny added meekly, "me*?*"

"And just like before, even if it puts you in the shit house, *I need you to trust me.*"

Chapter 22 Alignment

Ashley was waiting at the Umbilical hatch. She started asking questions before the airlock had even finished venting. "Who's this?" she asked Alex of the man panting at his side.

"Ashley Winston, meet Lark Fortune," Alex made a sweeping gesture of introduction. "And Lark, I present you with her majesty of the airship, Ashley Winston."

"Where's the head?" Fortune asked. He was tall, but his shoulders slumped with the weight of the world. Ashley gave him a once over: late fifties, graying red hair, crooked nose, not one to make eye contact. "I feel sick," he announced, and the look on his ashen face confirmed it.

"We might have just polished off some oysters from the bar about the time you pinged us," Alex explained. "And Lark here's not a fan of air travel."

"Not when I'm swinging in a tube slide a hundred miles in the air!" Lark said.

"Bah," Alex said. "We're not even at altitude yet."

"Toilet?"

"Third door on the left, but knock first," Ashley said. "We're at capacity, and that's the only lav on this end."

Fortune pushed past her into the hall. He went the wrong direction, but Alex ducked out and set him straight. On his return, Alex was shaking his head in dismay.

"What is it? Who is this guy?"

"He's my wild card." Alex slumped down on the pile of Umbilical tubing. "He's the *only* card I have, tell you the truth."

Ashley studied Alex. Without Fortune in the room, Alex let his guard down. He was a wilted court jester whose jokes had gone flat.

"Are you getting any sleep?"

"Sleep is for the weak," he said. "Besides, there's hijinks happening and no time to spare."

"This guy, Fortune, what's he to you? Why's he on my ship?"

Alex encouraged her to join him on the Umbilical pile. She sat beside him, noting he smelled of beer and stale cigarettes. "Larkin Fortune found the first Tic Tac. His dad figured out how they work. He's the rightful founder of TransCorp's Teleportation."

"That guy? The washout?"

Alex nodded vigorously.

"And you found him in the middle of Oklahoma?"

"All a matter of historical record." Alex attempted a smile.

She wasn't buying it.

"If he's the 'rightful founder,' why's that White Witch strutting around Wyoming bragging about torching my airship?"

"Ah, so you're up on your news at least, if not the history."

"Catch me up on everything, Alex. Can't trust the news. Can't trust anything these days, it feels like."

"Here's a newsflash you *can* trust: Lark Fortune's the key to it all."

"Him? The guy in the toilet?"

"Him."

"How?"

"His dad worked for TransCorp. Your White Witch? She's Fortune's old flame. If we play him right, he can spring the whole thing."

Ashley sprang to her feet. "*What whole thing, Alex?*"

"How long till we reach Laramie?"

"Alex!"

"How long? Eight hours?"

"Why?"

"Cause that's how long I have to get him in alignment. I'd like to capitalize on your gifts. I need you to Affect him."

Ashley took a deep breath and blew it out her nose. "You have to give it to me straight, Alex. Swinging south like this put me half a day out of whack. The rest of the fleet's going to be waiting on us, but the longer they wait, the more anxious they'll get."

"Okay, okay. The only way I got him up here was to promise we'd speed him to her side. Once he's there, he's got to—"

"Well, I'll be damned!" Kelli Chase said, pushing Ashley aside. "If it's not my darling hubby back from his sojourn."

Alex lumbered to his feet and spread his arms wide. He was all smiles. "Come in for it, Scrumptious."

Ashley stepped back, farther out of the way. After weeks at large, he had the gall to expect a warm welcome? She was sure Kelli would punch him in the gut.

"My spidey man," Kelli cooed, closing in for a loving embrace.

They hugged and kissed passionately.

Ashley waited.

She poked her head out the door, looking for Fortune up and down the hall.

She turned her attention back to the airlock and rattled at the workings loudly.

She cleared her throat.

"You're an asshole, Alex!" Kelli said, pushing him away at last.

"But I'm a loveable one."

"You couldn't spare a minute to ping me on the Interface?"

"You were running silent. I was on a caper."

"Ops said you brought on a passenger," Kelli stated. "Just who have you been hanging with?"

"Me," Fortune said, stumbling over the threshold. "I'm Lark Fortune," he said. He nodded at Kelli, then extended his hand—his *left* hand—for a shake.

Ashley cocked her eyebrow and glanced at Alex.

Kelli crossed her arms and looked Fortune up and down. She, too, turned to Alex for answers.

"We're just giving him a lift," Alex smiled, "so he can reunite with his girl."

"I'm looking for Krys," Fortune said. "Krystal Price."

Ashley knew Kelli well. She knew her down to that hitching movement in her shoulders. She was fighting off a laugh, as subtle as keeping back a burp. "Well," Kelli said, recovering, "I sure hope you find her."

. . . .

"That's the last of that," Sam Barlow said, tipping the contents of a pan into Fortune's bowl. "I'm sure glad to find a man so fond of my stew."

"Best I ever had," Fortune said, wiping his mouth. "Thank you."

"Anything else, missy?"

"No, thank you, Sam. Thanks for putting that on for us."

"My pleasure," he said, fussing over the empty bowls. "Let me know if you need anything else."

Ashley smiled at him, then returned to the conversation.

"So," she whipped around directly to Lark Fortune, "riddle me this: why's she getting involved?"

"Salt of the earth, that girl. She's doing the right thing by the poor folk. The ranchers."

Ashley smirked and looked to Alex and Kelli. They were holding hands and not too focused. "Those *poor ranchers*," she said, "could probably stand up to ChompCorp just fine."

"They were fishing around for help. That's what they say on the Interface."

"And?"

"And TransCorp rolled in to help 'em out."

"Strange bedfellows, farmers and corporations," Alex said.

"Helped them... by porting away *my* ship?"

"That was a Chomp ship, so they say," Fortune tossed back.

"I hate ChompCorp," Kelli offered absently.

"They're all bickering these days, all the corps... all their board members... chest thumping and posturing. Bad moon's a rising, if you ask me."

"I'll give you that," Kelli said. "Chomp's been nothing but trouble for Franklin, lately."

"They *stole* my ship," Ashley said, gritting her teeth, trying to be civil. She poked a finger at Fortune. "Then your friend Krystal toasted it."

"Acting as a bona fide agent of Trans—"

"You got the nickel tour, Fortune. My ships... my *Poppy's* ships... they're not something to steal or shoot out of the sky. They're living, breathing works of art."

"I'm not saying it was right or wrong," he pushed back from the table. "I'm just saying I think it's a bigger deal than some ranchers fighting a land grab."

Alex perked up some, lifting his head from Kelli's shoulder. "What's your theory?"

"I don't have a theory. Honestly, I don't know what the hell's going on. I just want to catch up to Krystal before she gets in trouble."

"Tell them what you told me about the Spooks," Alex prodded.

Ashley noticed a hardening in Fortune's features. She looked at Alex and caught his subtle nod. She released an Affectation, a slow, gentle one, to release serotonin. It wouldn't hurt Alex or Kelli, either. They probably all needed it. That and a good night's sleep.

"I could use a drink," Fortune bargained.

"We run a dry boat," Ashley said. "Maybe you don't need a drink, anyway."

"Maybe I don't." Fortune jutted out his chin. "But I want one."

Kelli wrapped her arms around Alex's arm and squeezed. He leaned against her.

"Alex?" Ashley prodded. "Spooks?"

"C'mon Lark. Tell us about the ones that cop friend of yours was after."

"Don't see how it matters. I thought we were talking about Laramie."

Ashley sighed and turned up the juice. The Affectation was palpable for her, surely overpowering them.

Kelli giggled and kissed Alex on the forehead. She reached out to Ashley and squeezed her hand. "Hoo doo," she said softly.

"What's that?" Fortune asked.

"Whooo dooo you think was after you?" Kelli recovered.

"Spooks." Fortune adjusted in his chair. He leaned in and whispered aloud, "People from the *future*."

"And on that, friends, I believe my missus and I shall retire," Alex said, wobbling as he stood. "May the rest of youse muse on our good Fortune, pardon the pun."

Ashley watched them drift away.

She watched Fortune watching them leave.

An awkward moment passed while Fortune studied the table between them, as if he were searching for the topic they had just been going over. Another moment passed, as an idea came to him. "It's a prosthetic," he said, holding up his right hand. "Little bit twitchy right now, but it's mine."

Ashley chastised herself that she had not noticed. The hand was passably good, no *very* good, but it was acting up some. Fingers were trembling. He seemed to be fond of his alcohol. She could have written off his shakiness to withdrawal.

She had never been introduced to a prosthetic before, and she had little to say about it. Should she ask what happened to his hand? Should she compliment the craftsmanship?

"That's how I found the first one, you know, the first Tic-Tac. The first Hot Wire." He chuckled. "Somewhere out there, my right hand's still wriggling."

Ashley wondered if she had pushed too far with her Affectation. She thought about a stimulant, maybe to counter with dopamine, but she did not want to befuddle him too much. Fortune did not seem solid enough for what Kelli had called a "double whammy."

"And so's that train on the news. And so's your ship, miss Winston. I think some Hot Wires just port stuff... I dunno... *elsewhere*."

She narrowed her eyes though she did not want to discourage him. "Part of my ship's been sheared off and dropped in a field. And the crew—what of them?"

"That's reason enough to go look around there. That's what's bringing you to Wyoming, isn't that right?"

Ashley shrugged. Yes, she was angry. She was vengeful. But she was also concerned about how many souls had been aboard the *Cumulustrata*. At least four were her crewmen, she knew that for a fact. Very few knew how to keep her airships afloat and under sail. Even fewer could pilot one as a Lightning's Hand. She wanted to know who they were and why they had betrayed her.

"Right," she said at last. "I'm after my crew."

Chapter 23 Let them Eat Steak

Krystal winced when her makeup artist dabbed more foundation on the bruise. "Imbecile!" she said, glaring at the girl.

"Sorry, Miss Price, I'm sure it's a little tender." The girl stepped back and assessed her handiwork in the mirror.

Krystal tore away the bib protecting her newest white dress. She glanced at her reflection in the vanity mirror, then at the girl behind her, and graced her with a biting smile. "That's fine, now. Yes. Good work, Priscilla."

"Stella." The makeup girl mumbled as she packed her kit.

"What?" Krystal brushed everything from the vanity in front of her off to the side. She was acutely aware of the time, and she had no time for chit chat.

"My name is Stella, Miss Price."

"Right. Right. Well, go to your room or whatever. I'll need you again tomorrow at 7pm. I'm hosting a soiree at 8."

"Yes, of course. Anything else?"

Krystal sighed, scooping up a handful of cosmetics and dropping them in the girl's bag. "I have people, Stella. People for everything. Y'all—*you all*—go dream up something fabulous for me now."

"Yes, ma'am." The girl melded into the others waiting in Krystal's suite. Four of them were bowing and scraping on their way out.

Krys sighed again when the door shut behind them. She spun in her chair to admire the suite, the honeymoon suite of the Grand Marquis. It was much nicer than she had expected, but then, her people had obviously been busy that afternoon, bringing it up to her standards.

She stood and approached a floor-length mirror. It was *her* mirror, one her entourage had brought along and set up while she was at the fairgrounds. It was a CommCorp creation, one she absolutely adored. She studied the image of herself in her searing white gown, and she tipped her head side to side to review again the makeup Stella had been working on. No visible bruise. The split in her lip had been glued and painted over. It was passable.

She looked beyond and at what was in the frame of the mirror's reflection. It would never do: her bed, complete with the dirty dress and a bloody towel. Luggage askew. She almost called in more help, then in a flash of inspiration, turned the mirror with both hands so that it took in a more refined view: the balcony and two high-backed white chairs. She nodded once, then raced to shut the curtains and position herself in one of the chairs. She repositioned. She tried to look casually preoccupied.

The mirror chimed. It was time for the show.

The reflection flashed away then, only to be replaced by the TransCorp board room. As usual, the four board members were in silhouette, as they preferred, with the steel gray of the boardroom walls shimmering behind them. A black table reached into the foreground, the image so crisp it looked as if she could set a drink on that table, even from her room in Wyoming.

"Oh," she feigned surprise, smiling at them. She had chosen the correct chair; her best side was facing the mirror cam. "Is it meeting time already?"

"Let's be brief, Krystal. You've much to do and I'm sure much yet to accomplish in your time out there." She knew who was speaking by the slight gesture of his hand on the boardroom table.

"Wouldn't have it any other way," she smiled, then began filling them in. "I arrived early, before the crew, and set myself up simply. Hailed the limousine we had arranged. Found my way to the fair—the facility serving as the launch—"

"The cowboy, the one who seems you're familiar with... is he this Stewart Wiebe you have spoken of?"

Krystal struggled a little with her expression. She was annoyed. She was surprised, but the image on her mirror projection would surely appear as placid as she was settling on. How had they noticed this? What was CommCorp broadcasting? She blanched at the thought of the street fight.

Clearing her throat in a tiny cough, she replied, "Why, yes. He is an acquaintance."

"Is he ETR?" asked another board member, a woman with a drawl that Krystal abhorred.

She thought of several possible answers. Yes, he seemed to be, for he was everywhere the ETR had done anything of note lately. No, but he was surely a sympathizer, as he was himself a beleaguered citizen of Laramie. Hadn't he even groused around some about ChompCorp?

"Miss Price?" a third board member prodded. "Is he with the allies?"

She chose the answer that would put her in the best bargaining position: "No, I don't believe he is, quite yet. However, since we do go way back, I may have influence with him, should TransCorp find it useful." They would get a full profile on him now that she had admitted acquaintance. They probably had it already, glowing off screen somewhere in their office.

"Leverage?" the drawling woman asked.

Krystal weighed and measured again. This was her most difficult audience, one that set her teeth wrong no matter how many times she had dealt with them.

"It could be argued," she said carefully, still thinking of Mrs. Stewart Wiebe and her right hook and how very badly she hoped that Vid would never surface.

"If he's not ETR and not one you can cashier, don't waste time with him."

"Of course," she nodded once. "Should I continue my briefing?"

"I believe we've seen it," one of them said. "The drones made good footage."

"The locals are thrilled," Krystal offered. "One for the win column, I'd say, both here and on the Interface... so that's two wins, right?"

There was no applause, not even a nod of affirmation on the screen. It was so quiet she could hear the partying down on the street.

"Wouldn't you agree?" she asked at last.

"Our research has yet to find a head of the Eat the Rich rabble. What do you hope to accomplish by continuing on there?"

Another of the silhouettes held up both hands in a question. "Just why are you staying around? You could just as easily port back for any engagement there, anytime."

Everywhere, any time.

It was a TransCorp advertisement. And while it was true, the marketing department had not spent as much time porting as had Krystal Price. They had no idea of the toll it could take on one's tummy.

"I want to be seen as... approachable. The same reason as my early arrival, and the same as why I did not arrange our port for the launch site itself." Krystal stood and approached the mirror. "I am, for the weekend, a familiar." *Not some corporate big shot half the globe away.*

"Does that mean you'll be wearing flannel and jeans?" one of them asked, and they all chuckled. It sounded a bit like the signal was breaking up with their "hee hee hee."

"Approachable, not local," Krystal clarified. "I will be eating with them, tomorrow night, and I'll find your leaders then. I will not be going native, if that's a concern."

"No concern," a board member said, "just an amusing portraiture."

"It would get a lot of hits on the Interface," the silhouette closest to the camera offered, his voice smiling.

"Imagine her," one tittered, "at a Ro-day-o." Again, the mechanical laughter, a laugh track that was old and crackling.

"Or noshing at a calf fry!" another said, and the mirror trembled with their full-on laughter.

"Back to her roots."

• • • •

She stripped the dress, scrubbed the makeup, and called again upon Priscilla—who was about her size—for some workout gear. Krystal had not packed any gym clothes. It was as if no one in her away team seemed to think she exercised at all! She tied her hair in a knot and stormed to the hotel fitness center—without an escort.

Laugh. At. Me. She said to herself again and again as she ran. *Shocked. I'm. Fit.* She panted as her bare feet pounded the treadmill. (None of her entourage had shoes her size, not even Priscilla, and she forbade them to go buy any. Surely that would have gotten back to the board before she had them laced up!)

Hers was a public presence, and her job did not allow for anything less. She would be seen in court and at dinners, sign autographs and smile at the camera. It was what she signed on for, to be their figurehead, but how did they think their figurehead kept such a figure?

Krystal Price had never been seen in a sheen of sweat. She was nonplussed and was to remain aloof, beyond the effects of heat and cold. As a TransCorp power player, she was different by design. Distant. She was not to dabble with something so lowly as exercise. Surely, her public must think, she had people for that.

. . . .

"You don't want to exercise, Krissy," her mother forewarned. "You'll perspire."

She said it in a way that sounded like 'expire.'

Distasteful. Un-lady-like.

"But momma, I want to go out for track."

"Track?" she sneered. "To run around in circles in your underthings! That would be so unbecoming."

She had heard of Jim Thorpe, also from Oklahoma, who ran barefoot in practices. He won races in the Olympics with mis-matched shoes.

She knew of others in history who had to keep their athletic interests in secret.

For years, after school, Krystal found her way outside of town. She would change into shorts and t-shirts in her mom's Volvo, then run barefoot on the red dirt roads. When she grew up, she would slink off to the gym. Her role in TransCorp demanded that she continue to keep her fitness rituals under wraps—decades after her mother had died.

. . . .

Krystal ran and ran. She ran past her internal ranting that had set her pace. She forgot all about the laughing board members. Her footfalls were graceful as a gazelle. Krystal Price had run miles from her problems, if only on a treadmill.

She was pouring sweat and breathing heavily when a woman from her entourage interrupted her. "The delegation has confirmed," she announced meekly. "We will have them in the restaurant. We expect standing room only."

Krystal hopped off the machine and took the towel extended to her.

"Well," she said, renewed. "Let's learn just what else these Eat the Rich clods like to eat. Crow? Shit?"

"Pardon?

"Have a buffet arranged. A potluck maybe. Something local. I don't care. Let them eat steak."

"And for the dinner, what should we lay out for you?"

Krystal entertained the idea of attending their dinner in her sweaty T-shirt. *Fit right in.* It brought a smile to her lips, cut short by the pain of that Wiebe woman's punch. Her lip was bleeding again.

She dabbed at it, then tossed the towel to the floor and stood a little taller. "I'll pick something myself. There's stores downstairs, are there not?"

"I doubt they have your color, ma'am. We can have something ported—"

"Whatever. Take care of it. I have a lot on my mind." She thought about the board again, about how they had chided her. As much as she wanted to see Stu and poke at the locals, distancing herself seemed most prudent. "You know, I need more time to myself. Clear my slate tomorrow. And tomorrow night? Just let the people downstairs eat without me. I will be down when I am good and ready."

"Yes, Miss Price. Should I have something brought to your rooms then?"

"Steak," she said. "Steak tartare."

Chapter 24 At the Helm

Alex agreed to this meeting, just him and Ash, first thing in the morning, but it wasn't going well.

"That's your big plan?" Ashley rolled her eyes. "Flip Krystal Price?"

He closed the flap on the voice tube horn. The ambient noise of the creaking, breathing ship was unnerving, but it made the helm a safe chamber on the ship. "You're not listening," he said.

"I'm going to need that horn whenever Pettijohn has a course change."

"I'm going to need the privacy even more," Alex said.

"Fine," she said, turning her high stool in his direction.

"Don't you—don't you need to turn knobs or something?"

"She'll drift along. We're in the stratosphere. It's a long way down."

"Right."

"If it makes you feel better, I can glimpse a gauge now and then."

"No, no," he said, "it's not that."

"Need a hit?" she asked. He declined. No affectations, not this early. At least she was asking and not Affecting him on the sly, at least he hoped she wasn't.

"Ashley, we've been through some trouble. Seen some things."

She nodded, and her brow tightened.

"What if I told you—"

"I don't know if I like this warm up. Just make the pitch."

"We're flying blind." Alex wiped a hand over his face, rubbing at last night's grogginess, and continued, "That incident, the Showdown or whatever they're calling it? Didn't happen in my history."

Ashley glanced over his shoulder at a gauge or something, then sighed. "Never?"

"It's like there's a new player, turning things around."

"What do you mean, a new player?"

"It's like TransCorp is too sure of themselves. It didn't go down like this in any version of anything I can recall."

He paused and let her work it out.

She was quick. She perked up on her stool and blurted, "*Another* time traveler?"

"Maybe?" Alex said. In his scope of the world, everything was a variable. The changes a static person might cope with could present as any of a hundred variations or more.

"So maybe Fortune's not so crazy after all?" she asked.

"Maybe not."

"'The Spooks from the future?"

"I never claimed to have a monopoly on it."

"Sheee-it," she marveled.

The *Necromancer* moaned as the Transpiration cycle reversed. The ship yawed, and Alex clutched at an instrument cluster. Ashley turned her attention to the dials and levers and gauges and foot pedals, talking while she worked. "So you're saying everything he told me last night is true?"

"I don't know what all he told you last night, honestly, but he's told me some whoppers."

"He said time cops were trying to get the Tic-Tacs. Said his dad was so worn from running from them that he ported himself to oblivion."

Alex nodded. "Along with his twin. That seems true by all records I've scared up. Christian and Tristan Fortune were never seen nor heard from again."

"*Time cops*, though?"

He swallowed hard.

It would have been easy to say, *Remember those guys, the ones with the laser rifles? The ones hunting me?* Instead, he bit his lips together.

Her features had changed again by the time she turned back to him. She had put it together. "Like the ones who were after you."

He nodded.

"Like the ones... on the *Undulatus*?"

"Just like them, yeah."

"You think they're back? Maybe in Laramie?"

"I think somebody's changed something. Maybe back in Guthrie, back at the time Lark was a kid."

"But that's not what you really think, is it?" She wiped grease from her hands onto her jeans. "You think this other player guy's done something."

Alex ran through his thoughts. He tried to sense her messing with his mind. He smiled wanly remembering the ridiculous group Rory had talked him into joining, the *Don't Mess With My Head* gang or something like that. How did she know he was withholding his deeper thoughts, if she was not wielding some kind of telepathy?

"Why do you think Fortune's your wild card? Because he got away from his *time cops* unscathed?"

"Maybe that."

No one got away from them unscathed.

"That's not it either," she surmised. "Do you think Fortune did something way back when that changed the here and now? Is that why you've pulled him in?"

"It's like I told you: We need him to get an audience with TransCorp. He needs to get in good with Krystal Price so we—"

"If he can get me within shooting distance, I can change her timeline," Ashley spat. "Forever."

"If we can understand her—not shoot her—maybe we can straighten things up."

"That's never bringing back my boat!"

A tiny bell tinkled by the voice tube. They both looked at it.

Ashley hopped off the stool and stepped closer to him. "Time cops," she scoffed. "The past you love or the future you knew. Turning Krystal Price around or getting inside TransCorp—none of that means a thing to me."

"I know." Alex glanced at the bell. "Do you need to get that?"

"I want to teach the White Witch a lesson."

"I know, I know."

"If time cops, or whoever they are, show up again... those bastards Rory saved us from..." Ashley's features were distorted, her teeth clenched. Her fists were balled up. "I'll kill every last one of them."

"I know," Alex said softly.

The *Necromancer* tilted abruptly, and Ashley was thrown at him. Alex pulled her into his arms and held her. She was weeping and pounding at his chest. "Why won't you go back and change things, Alex? Why? Go back and get my Rory?"

He shuddered with her pain. It was his pain, too, to know and harbor forever.

"You know it doesn't work like that," he said into her hair. "Can't bring back your ship. Can't bring back our Rory."

She pulled back to look him in the eye. "Can't or won't? It's all your stupid promise to Kelli, isn't it?"

Alex held her by her elbows. "It's infinite outcomes, time travel. We went over this. It's not like TransCorp and their silly ports of call. It's not mechanical teleportation. It's messy, Ash. If I could, you *know* I'd save him. I'd die a thousand deaths for that guy..."

The ship was groaning and listing hard to starboard.

The little bell was jingling frantically.

Ashley sniffled and bobbed her head toward the voice tube. Alex let her go.

She grabbed the little bell to quell it, then popped the brass cap on the voice tube, which released a tirade from the bridge.

"I'm on it," she shouted back and snapped it shut.

Ashley was back at her controls in an instant, whipping left and right to change the ship's rate of Transpiration and to correct its descent. In minutes, it was back to gliding gracefully again.

"I'm sorry," she said, turning back to him. "I know you—"

"I think we're in the same boggle," Alex said, composing himself. "We're frogs in hot water, but we're wide aware of it."

"*What*?"

"The heat's been coming up, and we knew it wasn't just a sauna. It's about to boil and we can't jump the pot, no matter how aware we are."

"Alex, did you bump your head?"

He sighed. "We can't do a damn thing about anything, and we both know it. It's not a history I know. It's not a situation we'd like. I had the gift of time, swore off it. You had an armada of airships, lost 'em. We both feel the heat, am I right? Time cops or no, Laramie's a big deal and we know it is... but what are we going to do? Something radical, like TransCorp or something smarter, like your daddy would have done?"

"Poppy lost," Ashley said, spinning a couple of wheels absently. "Rory lost."

"That's not true. We wouldn't be here—"

"And who won? Spexarth. He's dead five years, and Eat the Rich still rages."

"Listen to me, Ashley, if we can bring down TransCorp—hell—if we can even *tamp down* TransCorp, we may still win." He knew the doubt on her face. It was the same every time he looked in the mirror, but he continued, "ETR's lost their mojo and without TransCorp's support, they'll eat themselves up before this is over."

"Plug your man into TransCorp, and we save the day?"

"Maybe," Alex said. "It's all we got. Diplomacy."

"Our diplomat's a drunk."

He shrugged and nodded the concession. "He's all we got, Ash."

"I have a dozen Nebulosus class ghost ships circling. Don't even make a shadow from our altitude."

"And what will you do with them? Light up Laramie? What good would that do when Krystal Price can port away before you're even in range?"

"Stealing my ships, that's one thing. We can fight and get 'em back. *Porting one*? That's not something I can let go."

"Could you let it go long enough to try my way?"

"She's just such an arrogant bitch about it!"

"Could you help me with Fortune, then wait it out a week?"

She nodded her head reluctantly.

"Just a week," Alex assured her. The world was askew. He didn't even know if it would hold together that long. A Hot Wire portal like TransCorp had ignited would bring the Spooks. Alex had no doubt about it. If he could lie low for a week, they'd lose interest...he hoped.

It was the other player he was even more worried over. Some resourceful soul had Tic-Tacs on crack. History was changed, and the future was unknown. Alex was living life like everyone else, careening toward the next sunrise at a thousand miles an hour, without a clue.

"Promise me you won't torch the town?"

"We'll work with you... with finesse," she pledged, but he wondered what that meant.

Chapter 25 Clean Your Scene

He woke on the beach in the remains of a boat. The searing pain of sunburn had woken him up. He had no idea why this boat was mangled and deflated. He had no recollection of it at all.

The man noticed the markings on his forearms, and then the counting came back to him. He had to account for yet another sunrise. He had to account for himself. Somewhere in the maze of his mind, he knew that keeping count mattered. He measured his breathing and numbered his thoughts.

He was lost at sea.

He was lost in his thoughts.

He had lost something or someone significant.

He was marooned—no—he had marooned others.

He was hungry and alone.

Had anyone seen him, they might have mistaken him for dead. That crossed his mind, but he was too tired to sit up or roll over or even to avert his face from the sun's intensity. Instead, he squinted at seagulls squawking overhead, knowing from their voices that something of interest—maybe food, maybe another shipwreck—could be nearby. They were stirred, and from the look of the vessel he was in, they had been with him in it, for it was spattered with their scat.

The man found a few feathers, too, in the raft. Maybe in rolling over he had frightened them off. Maybe they had been picking at his matted beard and were the reason he was waking now.

Some seagull's offal was on his shoulder, and he struggled to the water so that he might wash it off. His limbs were aching and reluctant to take his direction, but he was able to wade into the water and cleanse himself.

The water felt so comforting and natural that he waded out into it and swam a while. An odd idea passed over him that he was a shark, so he moved like he thought a shark might swim.

Returning to shore, he noted that it was littered with other detritus, including two dead bodies. It surprised him that the bodies did not surprise him, and all at once he knew what had befallen them: *he had.*

He was The Warrior.

A mantra cycled through his mind and touched his parched lips again, *Eat the Rich.*

These bodies and this boat were part of his latest conquest, and he had no remorse for it. This was his calling. He had no other mission in life but to rid the world of this scourge, the rich.

But then a question came to him, a deep question that was not the thoughts of a beached Warrior at all. It was a cutting question: How would one ever accomplish the goal? Rich was relative. He would never run out of the rich, by this new insight, for so long as there were two people, one would very likely have something more than the other, and that would create the inequity.

Rich. Poor.

Haves and have nots.

It made him growl. If his mission was without end, how would this end? What was he doing here, sunburnt on a beach? Why was he slaughtering people on intuition?

It struck him that perhaps he was more logical than that, and that was what troubled him. Why didn't he know more about himself? What *did* he recall about himself? He sat cross-legged at the water's edge, enjoying the way it lapped at him, prodding him to think.

Think.

Think.

He was not a man of epiphanies, he somehow knew, but he thought he might be having one. He was the Warrior, but hadn't he always been a soldier of some sort? Yes, he had taken unpopular sides, and both won and lost before. He had lost so much, but he was unable to divine just what it had been.

As he searched for some foothold on reality, he noted again the scars on his arms. Two dots were fairly raw and fresh. Two days—he knew it now. The dots on his arms were a calendar of sorts. Two days had passed he had no accounting of but the holes he'd drilled in his arm. Two days ago, he nodded to himself, it had rained.

The Warrior looked to his left at one of the corpses, as if it might provide him some answers. It was lying on its chest, crumpled and sodden. The face was turned toward him, but the eyes were empty sockets plucked clean by gulls.

· · · ·

He had walked along the oceanfront the entire day. When it got hot, he waded in the water. When he grew hungry, he foraged for food. The Warrior continued to surprise himself. He knew what plants were edible and where to find them. He knew how to catch fish without proper equipment. As he passed through the rubble of villages wrecked by storm, he rummaged for tools, food, weapons.

When he came to an inhabited beachfront, he hid in the foliage and waited for an opportunity for a raid. Boats like the one in which he had started his day were pulled up in the sand. He would have one.

Two men and four women were talking among themselves and also engaging in communication devices on their heads. HeadGear.

He knew HeadGear belonged to the rich.

He thought he hated HeadGear for other reasons, but he could not place them.

Though it seemed wrong, he would take their HeadGear from their corpses, and he would tune into the Interface.

The Warrior pulled two massive swords from the scabbards on his legs. He examined the blades, exposed all day to saltwater and grime. That could not be good for them.

Six of the Rich, by his measure, would be a good test of his metal.

"Test my mettle," he said, finding himself wittier than he knew.

• • • •

Four of the six dropped dead with his first slashes. One of the remaining, a man in a strange uniform, got off a shot that knocked the Warrior off his feet. The man did not inspect his work; instead, he ran for the raft and pushed off to sea with it. He had left a woman behind, and he had left his kill dishonorably.

The Warrior respected that man for getting off a fair shot, but otherwise, he felt him to be a coward. Leaving a woman behind?

It was a breach of code that would not be tolerated. The Warrior nodded at the woman, threw down his swords, and raced into the water. He swam swift and strong, intent on catching the coward and teaching him the code.

The outboard motor was just turning over when The Warrior caught up to the boat. The man at the rudder popped off another shot, then another, but he was afraid, and the boat was bobbing. The Warrior scaled the side and brought his weight down on the other man as he tumbled in on top of him.

A third shot went astray.

The Warrior swatted the weapon out of the man's hands and off into the water.

He crouched low over the man.

"Blackbeard," the man gasped. "You... you're invincible."

The Warrior cocked his head. Blackbeard?

"I... I shot you, yet you're—"

"Always inspect," the Warrior said. "Even in the fray, be sure your enemy is dead."

He had a grip on the man's throat. He was pressing him down into the rubber floor of the raft. The Warrior thought he could press him completely through the flooring and hold his head underwater. He thought about it.

The other, greater infraction crossed his mind when he looked back at the woman on shore. She was picking up weapons and HeadGear.

"And never leave someone behind. Not a witness. Not a dying victim. Not an innocent colleague. The rule is: clean your scene." The Warrior slapped at the man beneath him hard. Left. Right. Left.

"Now say it with me, 'Clean your scene.'"

Though his eyes were bulging and his lip bleeding he said it on the third pass. "Clean your scene." This one was not a rich man but a fellow soldier, if maybe a little green. This one had pulled off a shot that would have killed the Warrior, if his vest were not packed inside with a sodden journal he had not found time to read.

For the first time in recent memory—for that was all the memory he had—the Warrior entertained the idea of saving this man. He could be educated. He could be useful.

Shots were fired from the beach, and the Warrior dived down beside the soldier, still clutching him by the throat. The soldier, however, had found a knife and plunged it into the Warrior's meaty shoulder.

He stabbed again and again, erratic, untrained, but adversely effective. He had meant to kill the Warrior, but his mistake was in making him angrier. "Shouldn't have done that," the Warrior growled. "I was wrong. You're not worthy."

In a sharp twist of the wrist, he tore at the soldier's windpipe. Then with both hands, the Warrior wrenched the soldier's head fully around. He shoved the soldier's face into the pool of blood and water in the boat's bottom.

Another shot cracked from the shore.

"Clean your scene," the Warrior reminded himself. Staying low in the boat, he piloted it directly at the woman. He jumped off the back and used the boat and motor as a shield as he closed in on her.

She cursed when the gun clicked empty. A second weapon was jammed or mucked up from the sand. She cursed again, but she did not run away.

She was one of the winged women. Unlike all the others who had shrieked and fled, this one stood her ground. The boat slid up beside her in the sand. She glanced at the dead man inside, then glared at the Warrior. She spat out a rant in some foreign tongue and waved him toward her.

She taunted him.

The Warrior grunted. He admired her grit.

He sloshed on out of the water, stopping a few yards from her.

She unclasped her collar and the wingsuit parted. She shook it off her shoulders and stepped out of the harness. The wings sloughed off into the sand. She flexed her fingers. "You've gone too far," she said. "You must stop here and now."

The Warrior knew her voice, her accent. His mind was ajar with the thought of it, the incongruity of killing someone he once knew. Why would he have ever associated with the rich? Or was she?

She was airborne in a kick no one should have been able to execute in the sand. Her feet hit his midsection, left then right in a pummeling he felt at his core. The Warrior grasped at her. He would crush her if he could get his arms around her. He would pull her head off if he could get his hands around her neck.

She was up, behind him now, cracking at his ears and temples with rapid blows that made his vision flare. Her hands were digging at his hair and yanking it out by the fistful while she squeezed his neck with her thighs, a powerful sleeper hold.

The Warrior did a forward roll, knocking the wind out of her.

They both struggled to their feet.

She had a rifle for a crutch. She was panting, but fearless.

"I want HeadGear," he rumbled. "I'd let you live if you'd show me how to use it."

"I won't let *you* live," she snarled, then whipped the rifle at his head. It narrowly missed. She was so fast swinging it that the Warrior could not catch it to pry away from her.

In his clumsy grab for it, she found another weakness, whirling again with her kicks, this time connecting with his groin.

The Warrior was a man of honor. Even in fighting, he would not resort to hair pulling and low blows. It angered him, and he roared as he clutched at his groin and dropped to his knees. He saw it coming but was too late to protect himself from the rifle butt that cracked hard against his face. He was leaning over to his left, as if the hit had him on full tilt. He was going down.

It was a fake.

When his hands hit the beach, he swung up his hips and spun his legs lightning fast to trip her with an improvised crab swing. He had her ankle in his grasp then, and he was about to snap it. He would break her, from her ankle to her hips, bone by bone, and leave her on this beach to crawl until the seagulls ate her!

She kicked sand in his eyes and struggled to get the other foot free. She kicked him in the face, and he felt his nose crunch from the impact. He knew the pain of a broken nose, and he expected the gush of blood and tearful eyes that followed.

What he did not expect was the wash of emotion that swept over him. On impulse, he released her ankle and his mooring on the fight.

He flopped onto his back in the sand. He could hear his own pulse and the waves and his grunting and her panting. He could feel the heat of the sand and the dampness of the clothes he wore. He could see the horizon of the beach in his foreground, the ocean far behind, and in between, the woman with flaring dark hair was rising to her feet. She was still glaring at him in disdain. "Is that familiar?" she sneered. "Ever felt that before?"

The Warrior was paralyzed with sensory overload. His senses were an erratic kaleidoscope. He was so overwhelmed with all he experienced that he could not even find his voice.

"The gift of clarity," she spat the words at him. "Know thyself."

She kicked him in the throat, and he choked and gagged for air.

Clarity, he thought, and the words came to him. Programmed words from another person in another time: *A moment of clarity without any action is just a thought that passes in the wind.*

"For my sisters!" She screamed and brought the rifle down in a hard drive at his head.

It was his moment to act.

He snatched the rifle from her hand and sat upright. He tossed the gun away and smiled broadly. "HeadGear," he said, "and we both live."

The Warrior was spent. The knife wounds throbbed. Pain coursed through every point of contact this woman had delivered.

The fierce fighting woman, too, was ragged and worn down. She was sizing him up, considering his deal.

"Stay down," she commanded and slung a bag over her shoulder. "I take the boat, then I toss you the HeadGear." She nodded toward the bag.

She was taking steps backward toward the raft, her eyes never leaving his.

The Warrior might have bolted up and dived the span between them, knocking her back with a mighty tackle. He could then have pounded her into the sand or drowned her in the shallow water. He could have dismembered her or fed her piecemeal to the sharks.

However, she was a worthy fighter, herself a warrior. She was the most formidable opponent he had any recollection of... and she had done something to him. Her gift had somehow opened his mind and frayed his senses.

Another moment of clarity stung him. As she was gliding out to sea, he knew the word for what she had done. He mumbled it, first to himself, then aloud. "Affectation."

She threw the bag at him. He dug around in it as her boat's engine roared to life. He found what he was looking for, the HeadGear the woman had been wearing when he first spotted her.

The Warrior sat down hard and wedged the HeadGear down over his brow. The heads-up display was superimposed over the retreating boat, the blue of the ocean. This was no military grade utilitarian model. This HeadGear was a personal piece, customized to its owner.

Though he had not worn any kind of HeadGear in so long, it was quickly coming back to him. He snapped his head and the screens advanced to an account profile and the name of the fighter, his worthy foe: *Katrina Covarrubias*.

The Warrior glanced beyond the name, through the profile to the sight of her speeding away in the raft. He tried to match the name with the woman's back and billowing hair. He measured her height and replayed every word she had said, and yet, he could not quite grasp how it was he knew her.

He hoped the charge in the HeadGear would last long enough that he might find out.

Chapter 26 Potatoes and Gravy

S tewart Wiebe brought his Boys, almost all of them, to dinner.
Twenty-two ranch hands and men he knew as family, if not by
blood, then by the blood they had spilled together.

The Eat the Rich leadership numbered less than a dozen. They
looked a bit on edge when they drifted into the school
cafeteria—the restaurant had proven too small for even The Boys,
alone. Since Stu's people sat closely knotted together in the middle,
it forced the rabble to sit at tables along the fringes of the room.
The thought was that this might diffuse them. The chaplain
presiding over the dinner had required everyone to remove their
hats, hardware, and HeadGear, and this too, might unravel the
Eaters—at least that was the plan the chaplain had shared with Stu
in their advance meeting.

The high school cafeteria was a shrine of hometown heroes.
Banners with state records hung proudly from the ceiling.
Life-sized posters and projections of some of the greatest athletes
of Laramie smiled down at them. Stu found it inspiring. He knew
some of The Boys' own kids were up there. Some of the records had
been made by some of the Boys, themselves. This was their arena.

"I was in a band once," the chaplain, Brother Chris Thompson,
shared. "Sides Touching."

"What?"

"The band. We called it *Sides Touching*. Know where we got
that?"

Stu just shook his head.

"*Place biscuits in pan, sides touching.*"

"Let me guess, some acoustic folk band?"

Brother Thompson chuckled. "Ravers."

Stu turned from studying the room to size up the chaplain.
"*Ravers*? Huh. Who knew?"

"No one around here. That was Phoenix. A while back."

"Why're you telling me now?"

Thompson nodded out to the room. All of them, ranchers and rebels, sat at tables too small for them, packed in tightly. Sides nearly touching.

"In my opinion, one of two things will come of this. Either they'll find commonality by proximity, or being packed so closely will set them off."

"Would you like to place a bet?" Stu smiled.

"Gambling?" Thompson smiled with a tut-tut. "That's not the way of the Lord, Mr. Wiebe." He fished a twenty from his wallet and pressed it into Stu's palm as they shook hands. "My money's on community."

"Thanks for the cash, Chris. I'll put it in the plate on Sunday."

"We win either way," the chaplain said, and headed for the podium.

Stu and an equally imposing member of the Eaters, Stokes, were appointed as guards of the hardware. Only these two men wore weapons on their hips. All other weapons were locked in a ball cage, along with all the hats and HeadGear. Stu tended the lock and latch. The Eater leaned against bleachers a few paces away, looking on with disinterest. The chaplain had appointed Stokes, for he had proven to be hard of hearing. He would be slow on the draw. He would not catch much. Stu would have every advantage if it came to it.

"Gentlemen," Thompson said from the podium, "Please bow your heads and join me in a moment of prayer."

Stu did not bow his head but chose the moment to study the room. When his scan reached the front again, the chaplain winked at him. "Prayer," Thompson had told him an hour before, "is pacifying."

• • • •

S tu's first confirmation that it would end in a brawl was the food fight that started in the buffet line. Someone, he was later informed, complained about the locally sourced beef looking tough. The Boys took offense, and one of them tipped a platter of potatoes on an ETR member.

It was messy, but at least they were throwing food and not fists, or worse, exchanging bullets. Brother Thompson brought it to an end when he fired a gun and yelled over the PA: "That's your supper, whether you eat it on plates or off the floor. Now settle down!"

Men were frozen in place for an instant. One had a handful of baked beans. Another was lifting up a serving tray of potato salad. One of Stu's guys had his arm cocked back, about to launch a vat of salad dressing.

Stokes looked at the ball basket, still locked, then at Stu.

"Don't worry, just a starter pistol. Brother Thompson's also a track official."

"Huh?"

"Preacher can pack if he wants to," Stu said more loudly. "Blanks."

"Whatever," Stokes nodded. "I'm getting in line. You keep watch."

"Suit yourself," Stu said, resuming his post.

A couple of The Boys checked in as they walked past, asking if he wanted anything to eat or drink. Stu declined, choosing instead to keep his eyes on the Eaters.

He was looking for their leader.

A crew was only as good as their leader. Usually, he would stand out. ETR leadership liked staying tucked away, subbing in proxies and fall guys. Somebody in this bunch of Eaters was herding scapegoats and propping up scarecrows. Chances were, none of those present were very high up in the food chain.

Altogether, they looked ridiculous: forty-five men in a cafeteria gym, most of them splattered with food, noodles and salad hanging in their hair. Still, this was an important meeting. TransCorp was coming. Stu hoped he was wrong, hoped that the Eaters did have their leaders hidden in the mix. If he could get a bead on the leadership, he could neutralize all this on his own terms. He could talk them down. No more porting innocent train passengers or passersby. The Boys wouldn't get locked up again. The Eaters would disperse. Then Chomp and Trans could duke it out for themselves without middlemen as fodder.

• • • •

It had been over an hour of petty bickering. Membership of the Eaters bewailed the evils of ChompCorp. They could not understand why anyone would tolerate such pressure. They were here, they claimed, to bring justice. Put Chomp in its place. Take the bite out of the bully.

"You *invited* us here," one of the Eaters shouted, and his whole crew joined in.

"Did not," locals retorted.

"Did so! You was all over the Interface whining and bitching, begging for help."

"I don't think our Boys would be so inclined," one of Stu's men grumbled.

"Mighta been townies, but it weren't us," another said.

"ChompCorp won't slow their roll for a couple-dozen cowhands," an ETR rep scoffed.

The Boys puffed up, swearing they did not need any help. ETR was just making it worse. If it could get any worse, they had the media in tow. CommCorp was bringing them too much attention. Even tonight, their drones were pressed against the skylights and transom windows, capturing the show. It had been a media circus from the first shout out on the Interface.

"We're here to tell ya... Chomp won't stop without us stoppin' them," a whiny Eater said, rising to his feet. He brushed crumbs from his hoodie absently. "They'll keep buying up your land, clogging up your markets. Hell, by the time they're done, you'll all be begging to work for them."

Eaters pounded at their tables in support.

"Seen it before," another Eater shouted out. "Turned farmers into sharecroppers. They got all the clout now."

"Damn right!" another affirmed.

"As much as I hated regulations," a lean man began, unfolding his limbs to stand as tall as Abe Lincoln, "regulations did slow down mega-madness. Nothing's stopping Chomp now from starving the world into compliance." The Eaters paused a beat, as if mouthing his words to themselves to better understand them. Finally, they cheered the comment.

Mega-madness. Compliance. Stu studied the man. He wanted to hear more from him, but he didn't want to be called out himself. He fingered the kerchief around his neck, a ready mask if CommCorp cameras came around.

One of the Boys, Paddington they called him, had noted the speaker, too, and he engaged: "Eat the Rich is a *slogan*, a vigilante rant." Paddington was a school district administrator. "How're you and your rabble going to stop anything?"

"Our rabble assimilates sympathizers," the tall, well-spoken Eater said.

"Join the gang!" someone else shouted, a ready translator, and they repeated the chant as they banged on tables for a bit.

"Frisk me? I don't think so!" a woman's voice cut through the chanting. Everyone turned to look.

Krystal Price was waving away the guard detail near Stu's station. The two men were looking his way for answers.

Stu sighed and nodded. "Let her in."

"Stewbert!" she acknowledged him in passing. She stood out in stark contrast to the messy, grizzly men. She was radiant and graceful—and clean. Her white heels clacked on the gym floor as she made her way toward the front. She made an exaggerated step over a broad swath of gravy and stepped around a dinner roll.

She plucked the mic from Brother Thompson and said, "Y'all are messy eaters!"

It brought a big guffaw from the crowd.

She set to it immediately, working the room. She told jokes and read the athletic records and banners out to the Boys, stoking their pride. Always careful to sidestep so much as a smudge of food, she circulated among them, mesmerizing them. As she wove through the men at the tables, both Eaters and ranchers, she moved in a way that accentuated her curves.

Stu looked away, finding Paddington at his side with Brother Thompson.

"Now that girl's fluid," one said.

"She's like an exotic dancer," the other said, "fully clothed."

"Yup," Stu said.

He was listening to her commentary, her careful articulation of the problem. Gone was the testosterone and bravado of the previous speakers. Hers was calculated malice chipping and slicing at ChompCorp. "What gives a corporation the right to starve you out?" she said, then picked up an apple and took a bite from it. Food, as she explained it, was a God given privilege earned from the sweat of one's brow. Putting food on the table was what made the Midwest strong. Not toiling for another's profit but raising up your own.

Chomp wasn't improving anyone's lot in life, now were they? They were throttling the free enterprise of farmers and ranchers, free trade as old as the barter system. What else was so old and integrated? Transportation. Moving food to market. TransCorp was making life better, letting goods and produce flow more freely than ever before. A potato from Idaho could be ported to anywhere in the world and sold at a premium.

"For a tariff," one of the Boys shouted from the middle of the mix.

Krystal cleared her throat. She rolled her eyes. "The price of progress," she said.

Stu could concentrate on what she said when he kept his eyes averted. However, whenever an Eater would speak up, he would look up and take note. An older Eater in the crowd argued that no man could serve two masters. Another voiced a common concern: "How do we gain advantage, picking Trans over Chomp?"

As it all wore on, the tall, articulate man clarified that they were "affiliates of the ETR but an independent franchise, providing regional support. We are the Rebels of the Plains."

"We don't answer to nobody," another man elaborated, drawing cheers again.

When she would circulate past Stu, he could smell her perfume, feel her smile radiate in his direction. One time she slowed before them and said, "Oh, here's the making of a good joke: a pastor, a principal, and a cow poke walk into a bar..." then she flitted away.

On another pass, she covered the mic and said close to Stu's ear, "It's that tall drink of water, in case you haven't sussed him out yet."

"Abe Lincoln?" Stu asked.

"Don't put the pinch on him too bad, Boys. I'm sure he's just being strung along..." she looked directly in his eyes, one of her rare, sincere looks, "like the rest of us."

Chapter 27 Mandolin bandanna

L ark was seasick. How could anyone get used to riding in an airship? What had Gault told him? "Smooth sailing, like a pleasure cruise."

It was more like riding a whale, bareback.

If he wasn't sitting, he suffered vertigo.

He thought he could sleep it off, but like his worst benders, laying down just gave him bed spins. Unlike a good bender, he did not pass out. The rocking just kept on rolling.

He was sure he had purged everything left in his system, but for good measure, he took up residence in the bathroom, curled in a fetal ball, for hours. No matter who pounded on the door, no matter how hard, he just cursed at them to go away.

Gault had been by more than once. It all blurred together. He'd reassured Lark that his precious Stetson was safe. He was sure the HeadGear had countermeasures programmed in that would fight seasickness, but he wasn't about to ask Gault to get it for him. Lark Fortune didn't need his help. He didn't need anybody.

All he needed was to get to Krystal ASAP and protect her from herself.

Despite the weightless and then oppressive surges of gravity, Lark knew this was the quickest way to reach her. He also knew airships were not passenger vessels. They were not cargo vessels. They were wispy animals that provoked storms. It was a weather machine crewed by four sailors. That was the whole of it, yet they said over forty women were aboard, and he had a hunch they were busying for battle.

With his ear to the floor, he could almost make out the arguments in compartments nearby. Something about sitting ducks. Something about squirrels. *Ghosts*? Lark sat up to examine his reflection. Was he losing his mind?

Sitting up normally meant throwing up, but his head was clearer and his stomach was no longer over-reacting. Lark got to his feet, clutching the sink, staring at himself. He gave himself a pep talk. He would charge in—well, *surge* in—and save the day. Krys would have a newfound respect for her old buddy Lark.

"My pristine Krystaline. I know why you wear white," he winked at the mirror. He recalled the JackChat: *Two annulments and she still won't speak to it. Is Krystal Price a virgin? Is the White Witch that frigid? Is this why she wears white dresses to this day?*

On that terrible day she had walked away, leaving him at the altar, she had said there was no one else for her. Lark was holding onto that. He believed her. Even if she'd married and divorced twice since then.

The Interface was brimming with speculation as to her every eccentricity. *What was with that hat? Did she have a problem with sunshine? Was she a vampire or something?* Lark knew. He'd known since grade school.

Her wealth was presumed boundless, yet she did not own anything on record, not even a vehicle. *Price flies, alright, by the seat of her pants and her faith in portals. She has put all her stock and value in TransCorp's teleportation infrastructure. But the questions run rife. Why? When she could own entire nations, why not own her own car? All the rich collected antique cars, but not Krystal Price.*

Lark had ported with her when they first discovered the magic of it. He would never forget how entirely absorbed she became with it. She was a marveling child, utterly astounded at the potential. Through teleportation, Krystal was able to harness the heavens, make magic bend to her will. Porting was heady... and dangerous.

He was reminiscing over his father and friends and their early porting adventures when someone pounded at the door.

"The girls have gotta make water before we make Laramie, Fortune!" It was Gault. Pesky. Frisky. Annoying at every turn—and not to be trusted. He was too much like the damnable Sackerson.

"How far yet?" Lark asked through the door.

"Under an hour," Gault replied.

"You need to come out, Mr. Fortune, 'cuz we're coming in." He knew that voice, too. It was the pretty TurnCoat captain. Gault's girl. They probably wanted a turn at the mile high club, Lark smirked.

He ran his hair in the water, styled it to his liking. He splashed water on his face and toweled off. He stood tall and in profile, he thought, he looked pretty good. Maybe a bit of a beer—

A spurt of light and heat burbled through the door just below the handle. The glow and molten metal snaked up through the latch. Lark was backed as far away from it as he could get, clutching the towel at his chest. A blob of glowing slag poured to the floor and smoldered.

Kelli Chase kicked the door in and holstered her plasma pistol.

"Clear out, or I'm going to piss right here in front of ya," she said, unbuckling her belt.

• • • •

"You think I got that kind of influence?"

"Maybe at least you can gain her ear..."

The Winston girl came up in back of him and rested her hands on his shoulders, asking, "Who else does she listen to?"

Lark hunkered down over his plate of food and did his best to ignore her. He couldn't remember the last time *anyone* had touched him, let alone a woman.

Gault persisted from across the table. "She listens to you. I think you said as much back in Guthrie."

"I was probably drunk," Lark said.

"You said she comes to your place every Christmas for advice."

"Yeah, I... well..."

"Trust," Ashley Winston said, her whisper right in his ear. "Trust is precious. It means even more to a woman in her role."

"Ahhhhh but why would I ever break her trust then? Just for a trip on your ship?"

"You've built the trust," Gault said, nodding his head. He glanced at Winston, continuing. "She wouldn't believe this coming from anyone else."

Ashley continued: "If you want to protect her from harm, like you said, she needs to listen to you."

"I... I... I do want to keep her safe."

"We know. We do, too." Ashley squeezed his shoulder in support.

Lark had a question flit by, but he couldn't catch it. He found another. "You're sure there's trouble ahead for her?"

"Sure as I'm sitting here," Gault said. "Can't you feel it now, too?"

Lark nodded. He *could* feel it. She was in danger, and she needed his sage advice. If he could help her, keep her safe, then she'd come around. He couldn't put it into words for them—it would sound dumb, anyway.

He patted the hand that rested on his shoulder. He felt another bolt of confidence surge through his left arm. It coursed its way to his heart.

"Well, why wait then?" he found himself saying. "Where's my new Stetson?"

"That's what I hoped you'd say," Gault smiled. He fished around under the table and pulled up the silver-plated Stetson. "I polished her up while you rested."

"That *is* a damn fine Stetson," Ashley said, taking a seat by Gault. "Why don't you slip it on. I want to see it on you."

He set it on his head and thought of his password, not eager to voice it.

"Go ahead, give her a ping," Ashley smiled. "Remember, you're not asking for much."

Lark adjusted it on his head. He sat up a little straighter and smiled into the HeadGear. "All I do's think of her?"

"Password first," Gault said.

"Mandolin bandanna," Lark sighed. He heard their aborted chuckles. When was he going to change that password?

He saw his own reflection fade in the HeadGear's screen. The room beyond the visor faded, transitioning to a mountain scene. He heard birds and a tranquil ripple of tones.

He could feel the ebb and flow of the airship again, but it wasn't making him nauseous anymore. He felt Ashley Winston hold his hands in her own, cupping them supportively. She was sitting across from him now, both her and Gault looking eager.

"For her own good," Gault said softly, like he didn't want Krystal to hear him. "Just get Ashley an audience with her. We'll make it all better."

"I'll have to be there," Lark said, his vision briefly penetrating the projection.

"Be where?" Krystal Price washed into view. Lark hadn't been this close to her since they were engaged, all those years before. She was vivid, and real, and he wanted to reach up and stroke her cheek.

"Oh, erh... Hi Krys," Lark chuckled. "Did I say that out loud?"

"Yes, you did. You want to be here? In Wyoming?"

"Yeah, yeah that's it," Lark recovered. "I'm on my way, to tell you the truth."

The image before him glowed even more warmly, soft tones cycled up with her broad smile. "Why, Larkin Wayne Fortune, what a surprise. Leaving the bunker, huh?"

He nodded. In his peripheral vision, he saw Ashley's hands holding his own. He saw Gault nodding with encouragement.

Lark did not know how to ask her for anything. She had done the asking. He had done her bidding.

Ashley was smiling at him beyond Krystal's superimposed projection. She was confident in him. What had she said? He *wasn't asking for much*, after all.

"Yeah, I want to be there, and I want to see you. In person," he said firmly, adding, "tonight."

He could see a 'no' starting to form on her transparent visage. He saw it with a clarity he might normally not have had. Maybe it was because he was sobered up?

"Now don't say no, Krys." He thought fast. "I might have a little *candy* for you."

She gasped and beamed brightly again. "For me? So soon? That's great news, Lark."

"Guests," Ashley whispered a prompt.

"What's that?" Krys was coy now, her head turned a bit, giving him her best side.

"I said... I said, I guess." He swallowed hard. "I guess that's a yes, then?"

"Nine o'clock," Krystal said, then reconsidered. "Make it ten."

"Krys, I... I'm bringing the Tic-Tacs... but I'm also bringing some friends."

"Friends?"

Lark could feel her souring.

Text materialized in the space between them. BRING IT HOME, PAL. CLOSE THE DEAL BEFORE SHE GETS TOO DOUBTFUL. Lark squinted and saw Gault typing on a keypad.

"Right," Lark said, clearing his throat. "Good friends. Good intentions. They're coming with me to help out."

Krys couldn't stop the frown of curiosity, but she corrected to a mild smile. He could see she was trying to think of what to say.

Lark knew the Tic-Tacs were irresistible for her. He knew he was in.

"Ten, then!" He said with a wink, then pulled out of the Stetson as quickly as he could.

The device closed out with a happy melody.

"Ah-mah-god!" Lark said. "I'm *sweating* here."

"You did great!" Ashley said, patting his hands. It was as if he could feel her touch even in his prosthetic.

Chapter 28 Settlers

Despite the way Sackerson had left town back then, gone in a flash without so much as a goodbye, Henny still liked the guy. He'd made a lasting impression. Now they picked up about where they left off, thirty-some years later: Sack, on some wild spree, tagging Henny in to help.

He was aching to throw in, but times had changed. He had family to think about. He had the bar. Besides, he wasn't the linebacker he once was. He'd put on some weight. The girls called it 'settlement.'

Sometimes that brought a chuckle. Settle down and settle out. Beer went flat. Dough went wide. Henny had, too. It was the way of things.

Staring up at the ceiling, unable to sleep, Henny remembered their high school reunion. Some folks had done great things. Krystal Price, of course, was the crown jewel of success, but others had gone on to college, too. Some folks were war heroes. Some had invented stuff. Some were climbers. Some were movers and shakers.

A handful of Guthrie grads, however, were referred to as 'settlers,' at that class reunion. It was glossed over and gussied up, but everyone knew what it meant. Settlers were the people who'd just settled for life in town. No ambition.

Henny knew better. Ross Waterman had inherited his dad's lumberyard. Petie Johnson had a great yard service. Jill Brooks and her husband were working up a franchise all over Oklahoma with their fried pies. None of them had left Guthrie, but all of them had ambition.

Some Settlers had family ties and responsibilities. Sometimes, for kids like Henny, the scholarships just weren't there. Not everybody in town ate from a silver spoon.

Larkin Fortune was the Settler who'd never settled. He had been in Guthrie his whole life, except his turn in prison and his time in college. (Lefty once told him that he considered these to be equally low points in his life.) He lived with his mom, then in some trailer house, then in Henny's own RV for a while... all before Krystal set him up at the Installation. Through all these years, he had never settled into a normal life. People around town thought he had been star struck at that meteor shower.

• • • •

*T*he night of the reunion, Jackson Crosby, class salutatorian and now a pipefitter in Tulsa, joked that Lefty Fortune was "one settler who hasn't died from dysentery, but he's been through a whole lot of shit."

They were huddled around the makeshift bar. Henny set a drink down in front of Penny (Leffler) Carlson, a mocktail with an umbrella.

Penny Carlson's husband, some guy who only ordered the fancy cocktails, said he had never heard of Lefty.

"Don't call him that, Lyle," Penny said. "It's mean."

"Why? Southpaw, right? He any good?"

Jackson laughed, "Never pitched a ball in his life. Ol' Lefty lost his hand. Nothing but a stump."

"He's doing okay now," Henny said, wiping the counter. "Got a fake hand."

Lyle Carlson smiled curtly at Henny. "You know him, then?"

"Yeah, I know him."

"Henny here used to play some mean football," Crosby offered.

"And now you tend bar?" Carlson asked. "At your own class reunion?"

Henny shrugged. The money was good, and he was going to be there anyway.

"Where is ol' Lefty, anyway?" Crosby asked.
"Out with the typhoid?" somebody asked.
"Cholera?" Carlson chuckled.
"Broken leg, maybe?"
"Yeah, what's plaguing him, Henny? Why isn't he here tonight?"
"He's allergic to people," Henny said. "Agoraphobia."
"Fear of spiders?"

• • • •

Henny was shaking his head on his pillow. People could be so stupid. It was people that made Lefty hole up out at the Installation, staying clear of town. Then again, it was people who peopled his bar and drank his beer and laughed at Gail's jokes. People were a necessary evil.

Even the evil people seemed necessary.

He came back around to Sack's offer. "Won't be a week away," he had said. "Promise."

All the excuses welled up, and every last one of them made him feel like a Settler all over again. Hell, when was the last time he had even gone shopping in OKC? Been on a vacation?

"And nobody's getting hurt?" Henny had asked for clarification. "Cuz last time—"

Sackerson had looked shocked. "No. No way. We're going out to help people, Henny. I'm going to put you right where Larkin Fortune needs you. He's going to need a friend."

Before he laid back down, Henny spent some time in the walk-in closet, illuminated with his new Visor. He was careful not to even let a hanger scratch too loudly on the rod. He was looking for his look. Leather jacket? A long coat? He had a great black wool coat he wore to funerals and sometimes on Sundays. What would a man wear on a job like this? What still fit him?

He smiled at his letter jacket, holding it out to admire it through the dry-cleaning plastic.

His wife swung open the door. "What *are* you doing?"

Henny hung the jacket up and smiled broadly. "Just reminiscing, honey."

"You can do that in bed, Ken. Now settle down and come to bed."

"Sure," he sighed. "I'll just settle down."

"It's that guy bugging you, isn't it? Got you thinking."

"Who?"

"Alex what's-his-name."

"No," Henny said, winking out his Visor. "Sackerson."

"Sackerson?" Darla said. "Haven't heard that name in a long while. I thought he was dead."

"Figured he was... but he was here tonight."

"Well," she said, pounding her pillow back in shape, "whatever he's got you thinking, forget about it."

"Yeah. Some epic save the world stuff."

"Oh, I'm sure."

"It'll wait."

"It will." She wrapped a meaty arm and leg over him and nuzzled close. "Leave the world for someone else to save."

"Yeah," he said, but as she dozed back off, all he could think of was romping around in that black coat on some big adventure with Sackerson.

Chapter 29 Aeronautical

Alex turned to study his woman from behind. She was sexy as ever, bending over in her skivvies to slip on her leather uniform. Ashley had shared her quarters with them, and she'd left them alone while making ready for the jump. Alex stepped up behind her and pulled Kelli close. She had one leg in her pants, but she dropped them and turned to kiss him.

"When do we get some privacy, some *real* R&R?" Kelli asked. "We never even got our honeymoon."

"Darlin' I hear Laramie is the honeymoon capital of—"

"*I'm serious.* When this gets settled, let's plan on Rio or Cabo or somewhere else that's warm."

"I'm all about it, babe."

"This is a bigger deal than you're letting on, isn't it? We're not just going to chew someone out and move on, are we?"

"Fortune's introducing Ashley to the TransCorp woman, Krystal Price."

"The one on the Vids?"

"Yep."

"He *really knows her* then?"

"His fiancée once, according to record."

"You've got to be kidding."

Alex assured her he was not.

"We'll be overhead in half an hour, in her parlor by ten."

She shook her head. "Don't tell me this was your idea. Bringing Ashley into it?"

"Well... it *is* her ship," Alex squirmed. "And so was the one they zapped."

"But you're worried, I can see it."

"Like I said, they zapped her ship. I've never seen her so angry."

"I think it's the only thing in the world that could have turned her from the hunt—somebody messing with another airship. She's vowed to get them all back."

"Oh, I know, I know." Alex shook his head in disbelief. "She told me all about it. Said she saw the Vid right when she had Blackbeard in her sights."

"*Blackbeard*," Kelli said, flatly. "She thinks ol' Blackbeard's—"

"Rory?" Alex offered. "Do you think she thinks he's Rory?"

"What do you think?"

"I think it's unhealthy. I can't tell her though. I can't tell her anything."

"Why?"

"She's already mad I'm not looking for Rory, and she knows I don't want her on the ground, but we need each other."

"You cut a deal with her, didn't ya? For passage?"

"It was the only way."

"Whatever happened to Fortune being your ringer?"

"He still is."

"You're just adding Ashley, too."

"Right," he tossed his reply. "She can do some head games, if it comes to it."

"And you're okay with that?"

He had no response.

"So... you're going down, too?"

"Of course," he said. "Can't leave out the *architect*."

"More like ringmaster," Kelli scoffed. "Or referee."

"She promised me she'd behave."

Kelli looked at him skeptically. "Really?"

Alex shrugged and gave her his best pouty kitten. "Maybe?"

"That's funny, because she told some of us girls to be ready to jump."

"Really?"

"Speaking of which, just how *are* you getting down there? Taking the tube?"

"Won't get Fortune in another one of those any time soon," he said, "We're going for an airdrop. Skydiving."

"A night jump? Where's your drop zone?"

"Ash called ahead, made plans with the locals. Something about pickups with light racks. I'm following her lead. Fortune's tandem with me."

He said it lightly, but he was more than a little worried. Skydiving wasn't for the feeble. Night jumps were even worse. He had his questions about Lark Fortune and his fortitude, but he kept them to herself.

Kelli had other questions she was worried they just weren't considering. "And the weather? Who's looking into that?"

"Look. Porting would be smoother, I know. Our host, however—"

"—would rather die than port," Kelli completed. They had both heard it from Ashley a number of times.

"It is too bad there's nowhere to land this thing," Alex said, "not even a good-sized lake."

"I've seen them fly so low you could practically step off."

"What about the ground effects, the lightning?"

"Only in the right conditions and the right vessel. But a Nebulosus is mostly floof."

"*Floof*," he smiled. "Nautical term?"

"*Aero*nautical," she corrected.

Alex busied himself with his gear, checking and rechecking the harness.

She put a hand on his. "You want me to talk to her?"

He shrugged. "What good could it do?"

"You want her to stay behind? Maybe I can talk her into it."

"Pull that off," Alex smirked, "and I promise you an exotic honeymoon, soon."

Chapter 30 Fall Guy

They met back in the bald spot, and they'd been talking again, helmet to helmet, when Ashley was pinged. They were over the drop zone.

"Can't tell Alex, though. Promise?"

"I promise," Ashley said. She was positively aglow. "I promise I'll keep quiet for... a day, maybe?"

"Give me some time. These things are to be breached delicately with men like him."

Ashley sighed. "Fine." She stepped into the airlock, then whirled and gave Kelli a big, sisterly hug. She tapped her helmet to Kelli's again and added, "I'm just so happy for you!"

In the depressurizing blast, they stood firmly in their EV suits. Entire conversations went unsaid between them. They waited for the all-clear lights, and in that span, resumed comms conversation about the matter at hand, the Laramie visit.

"So, I'm not making any daring night drops. Understand?

"I wouldn't ask it of you."

Once they'd popped off their helmets, Kelli continued, "I want you to know that I sure will, though. I'll jump without a chute. If I hear one word of trouble down there, I'm coming. You want that?"

"No. Of course not."

"So why not stay with me? Let the men handle it. They can tame your White Witch."

"I can't stay, Kelli. This is my moment. I got a few words for Krystal Price."

"Promise you'll not lay a hand on her?" Kelli affirmed. "You won't go beating on her?"

"I'll not beat her within an inch of her life. I promise you that."

"Really? That's all you—"

"I'll leave her an inch... and a half."

"Seriously. Think of the backlash. The bad press."

Lark Fortune interrupted their talk as he crossed the hallway. A question was forming on his brow, but he was thinking about it a little too long. Finally, he asked, "About ready, ladies?"

"Ready when you are," Ashley said. "We're in a pattern over Laramie, descending."

"I need to walk off some energy. Maybe hit the can one more time. Where can I find Alex, tell him I'm about ready?"

"He's in the Tank Room."

Ashley steered Fortune in the right direction. She turned back to Kelli and smiled disarmingly. "He's like a puppy," she said.

"A mongrel," Kelli replied. "The guy gives me the creeps."

"Puppy love," Ashley said. "Pining away for that nasty TransCorp woman. What a waste."

"You must see something more in him than I do," Kelli shuddered.

"I've been in his head," Ashley smiled again. "He's not all bad."

"Yeah, but... yeah, I guess you're right." Kelli sighed, "Just once I wish I knew someone who wasn't bad at all."

• • • •

"I wish you'd reconsider," Kelli pleaded. She was checking Ashley's gear. Alex was idly leaning against the doorframe. Cocky. Confident. Ashley didn't even know how many times he had jumped. Only a handful from her ships, yet still he had that devil-may-care attitude.

"I don't even want to be here, Kelli." Ashley continued. "I don't want to go down there... but they're ruining my fleet, and my reputation. This has gotta stop!"

"You gotta be careful," Alex said. "Diplomacy, remember?"

"You're not hearing me. TransCorp's been getting the Eaters on their side, crazy as that sounds. Eaters! Why would they wanna side with the most money-grubbing—"

"People see your ships as the trouble," Kelli said.

"And that means you're trouble, by default," Alex added.

"Pollutants spreading mind control. Airships turned into Lightning's Hands. And everybody adores Krystal Price. You go punching her around, and it'll be bad news for you. Bad news."

"Kelli... guys... I have to tie this up quick and get back to the coast," she said. "I gotta just pound it out and move on. If that means breaking a few eggs or noses or jaws or—I'm all about it. But I need your support. Both of you."

"I'm in," Alex said, offering a makeshift salute.

"Oh, I'm in, Ash. I'm in to the end. If you gotta go, I get it, but don't make me come down there. Don't do anything stupid."

Just then bells were set off ringing at every voice tube. Lights were flashing up and down the cabins. Ashley flipped open the brass flap of the nearest one. *"All hands. All Hands. Passenger has jumped ship! Repeat, a passenger has jumped ship."*

Alex, Kelli, and Ashley looked at one another in astonishment. There was only one person aboard who qualified as a passenger: Lark Fortune.

· · · ·

Ashley was falling at seventy miles per hour, but unlike her target, Lark Fortune, she was in a controlled descent. Fortune was spiraling akimbo. If she did not have him by the outline of his heat signature, she could have tracked him by his hoarse screaming as he fell.

She had no time for bearings, but she did glance at her altimeter again. His chute was going to open in seconds, unless he'd screwed that up, too. Her warning signal was already chirping in her headset.

She would not deploy until she had to. Her gear had no automatic activation device, but his should.

Ashley closed in on him by making her body an aerodynamic knife cutting through the sky. She fanned out the wingsuit some as she leveled off near him, astonished with what she found. He wasn't even wearing the parachute right. Much of the harness wasn't even buckled. His main chute would never open, even had the pull been done right. When the reserve chute opened, he would be jerked from the harness entirely and fall on to his death.

He wore no HeadGear, no comms at all.

"Spread your arms and legs," she yelled, drawing as close as she dared. "Spread 'em."

Fortune did more cartwheels, then leveled out. He looked at her, astonished that she was floating there with him.

"Hang on tight," she yelled. "Hang onto those belts. Hold those to your—" but before she could finish the idea, the AAD snapped, and the wedge of his chute shot out.

Ashley folded flat and shot into him hard. As soon as they collided, she grasped his cords and clutched them tightly. His chute unfurled. His harness was a confusing mess, barely holding him. She had an arm and both legs around him. Her other arm holding the cords had been pulled nearly from its socket when the chute snapped full.

"You're under 2000," a voice in her headset warned.

"Alex?"

"I'm coming in behind and to your right. Are you fouled?"

"No, I haven't pulled yet. Fortune's falling out of his harness. I can't clip him on."

She saw Alex taking shape in the dark nearby as he descended.

"I can intercept if he falls, maybe?"

"Won't matter, he's not strapped in."

"I won't let go," Fortune hollered into the wind.

"You gonna pull your chute or wing it?" Alex asked.

Her wings would give her some resistance, and she could glide on her own, but with Fortune in tow, and with the cords of his chute wrapped around her wrist, she was unsure of her options.

"I'm gonna deploy," she said to both Alex in her HeadGear and Fortune in her clutches. She put her mouth to his ear and said, "Hang on."

In the same instant she pulled the rip cord, she Affected him. Fortune was in a terrible fright. In a night jump, even an experienced skydiver was disoriented by the dark. He was anything but experienced at this. She filled his head with peace.

Her full canopy opened, and as it did, she released Fortune's cords. His chute drifted away without tangling with her own. She could control her chute, even while holding Fortune, but it was sluggish from the poor weight distribution.

She leaned back to get a better look at his face, to confront him, but he was unconscious. Whether she had let loose a bit too much Affection or the fall itself had taken its toll, she couldn't be sure.

"He's passed out," she reported to Alex.

"Why'd he jump without me?"

"He heard us talking. Me and Kelli. We followed him to the tank room."

"He was off. Suspicious."

Ashley adjusted the lens of her aviator's helmet, pulling the bearings into view in her HeadGear display. They were miles from the drop zone. She would have to ping her contact and make a new plan.

"But... why?"

"He was in a big hurry. Said he was going to save Krystal."

"From what?"

"From me," Ashley admitted.

• • • •

Four pickups escorted them from the improvised drop zone to a hotel in Laramie. Fortune was riding in a truck up ahead. Ashley and Alex were riding with a teenager, at the rear of the convoy. The kid was talking the entire trip. Ashley thought he might be trying to make a good impression on them.

By the time they rolled up to the hotel, the other three pickups had parked. Fortune and the rest had gone on inside. As Ashley scaled the steps to the lobby, her eyes were slow to adjust to the bright lights. They entered the hotel, and Ashley was aware that everyone was armed, and some of the weapons were unholstered, casually pointed at... her.

"*No, no, no*, you gotta keep her under guard," Lark Fortune was screeching. "She's a threat to Krys."

Fortune was pleading with a couple of tall men wearing black raincoats and cowboy hats. He was very animated. They were not.

"This little tweaker?" one of them asked.

"Meet Miss Ashley Winston!" Alex announced proudly.

"Now, *she'd* have a grudge against TransCorp, then, for sure," the other one said.

"You bet your ass I do!" Ashley said.

"There. *See*? So... So, keep her away from Krys, you hear me?" Fortune was waving madly.

"Stow 'em."

The men holstered their weapons immediately and stood a bit more solidly. An even larger and more menacing cowboy strode into the room. He looked Alex and Ashley over, then turned his attention to the gesticulating man. "Lark Fortune! What's dragged you up this way?"

"Stu," Lark acknowledged. Nothing more from him.

"Lark's here to save the White Witch from the Princess," Alex explained.

"What?"

"Ashley Winston—we call her the Princess back home—is here to avenge her airships," Alex completed introductions.

"Fortune thinks I'm gonna put the hurt on Krystal Price."

"And? Are you?" the cowboy-in-charge, asked.

"Just who are you, anyway?" Ashley asked.

"That's my dad," the teenager interjected. "Told you about him on the ride over."

"I'm Stu Wiebe."

"So..." Alex nodded at the kid, then asked the father, "You're not an Eater, then?"

Nat scoffed.

Others chuckled.

"You're not even in their leadership?" Ashley asked.

"No, miss. I'm a rancher. Plain and simple."

"Not so plain or simple, truth be told, right Stewie?" A woman dressed all in white entered the room behind him. Ashley recognized her immediately: Krystal Price, the White Witch. Ashley fought back an Affectation.

"Ah, Krys, I was so worried. You okay?" Fortune rushed to her, almost hugged her. He seemed to think twice. He didn't know what to do with his arms.

"Why wouldn't I be?"

Lark looked at Ashley, then around the room. His gaze settled on Stu Wiebe's son. "I hear there's plans against you. Threats on your life."

"There's always threats on my life," the White Witch said. "Surely you can relate."

She was addressing Ashley!

Blinking did not make her go away. She was being... *chummy.* Ashley did a double take, tipped her head at Alex, questioning, then at Krystal. "What?"

"Since Sarah Dawn got knifed, I've been following your story. I hear all about the death threats. Seems we have something in common."

"We have *nothing* in common," Ashley growled.

"We both deal with the other corporations pecking at us."

"The only corp 'pecking' at me is TransCorp. *You* took down my ship."

"We took out a threat. A Lightning's Hand. We neutralized it before ChompCorp could use it to terrorize this town." She spread her hands, then her arms, widely. "*We* sent a message to Chomp to back off."

"Eat the Rich!" someone blurted from the gathering crowd.

Both Ashley and Krystal rolled their eyes.

"You destroyed a billion-dollar 3dub property."

"And you should be *thanking me,*" Krystal hissed, leaning in. "You want your ships causing more damage? Wreaking more havoc?"

Ashley felt her fists clenching up. She felt a flutter in her chest. An Affectation was welling up and out, and she did not know if she could control it at all.

"Any-way," Alex said, stepping in between them. "We're here for a casual visit, remember?" He chuckled. He looked for assurance from the others in the foyer. He zeroed in on Lark Fortune. "Isn't that right?"

Ashley and Alex had drilled and practiced on Fortune for hours on the Nebulosus. He hadn't been playing his role at all. He had a perplexed look on his face, and he struggled to follow through.

"Krys," he said at last. "Let's go somewhere quieter. Just a few of us. We got a lot to talk about... and I brought you a present, too, remember?"

Like Pavlov's dog, Krystal Price heeled at the mention of the Tic-Tacs. "Right. Okay, Lark, you and your friends here, let's go to my suite."

Someone cleared his throat.

"You coming too, Stu?"

"Wouldn't miss it," he said, sardonically. "But I'm bringing along a couple of the Boys."

It was an awkward wait for the elevator. Ashley noted how Alex kept positioning himself between her and the witch. That woman disgusted her. *The very idea of her suggesting they had anything in common!*

When the doors opened, people piled in. Ashley didn't.

"C'mon Ash. This is what we—"

"I'll take another. Too crowded."

"Oh, c'mon." Alex turned from the questioning, motley crew in the elevator to whisper in her ear. "Grow up, Winston. You've been in tougher jams.

"I'll take the stairs," she said, leveling her glare right at Krystal Price.

"This is important," he gave her arm a tug, pulling her even closer, and added, "*Historically*. Important."

The elevator was packed. It smelled of rain and ranches and more than a little fear. Ashley was biding her time enjoying the thought of Affecting them. As the elevator lights ticked off floor after floor, she imagined it opening at the top. She would step out, stepping over bodies. The rest of them, Alex included for his flippancy, would all be flopping around boneless and numb, begging her to undo the Affectation.

When the doors did open, however, they all faced something worse.

Chapter 31 Reeds

I t was the sixth day since the last wave of the Rainmakers. The mystery ships and their random attack had been only four days ago. His encounter with the fighting woman he let go was just two days past. By dawn, the Rainmakers would pass over again, and he felt unprepared.

Regardless, the Warrior continued his trek northward up the coast. The direction was as good as any, and he liked the sound of it, repeating it in his litany. "Eat the Rich. Find your true north. Don't run from the future. Own it and do better." As he hiked, he wove these words into his cadence. It comforted him to put words into this rhythm. Soon he had built his breathing around his march. His breathing and words were all of his being. They kept his pace determined and driven.

Except when he would Jack-in. He knew this word now, to be *Jacked in* was to be using the HeadGear. He was accessing the Interface. He was tuning into media he had been deprived of for so long. Jackchat seemed like a foreign language, so quick, so snipped and pithy. It did not mesh with his mindful phrases and the deeply embedded quotations that guided his steps.

The Jackchat was static. Busyness distracting him from his business.

However, he found himself gravitating to it more and more frequently, especially as the sun would set and the display would glow more brightly before his eyes. He found he was growing concerned about the HeadGear's battery life and about its reception. He did not want to be away from it.

Something told him this was contrary to his nature. A warrior would not waste his mind on Jackchat. A soldier would not set his march to the beat of commercial blips of nonsense.

But he was drawn to it. He needed it. The reason was becoming more and more clear when he reviewed his viewing history. He had become obsessed with Winston Water Works.

The fighting winged woman, Katrina Covarrubias was associated with Winston Water Works. Just how or why she was tied to the corporation was not clear to him, not straightforward on the Interface, either. Everything in the bag she tossed him, however, was the property of Winston Water Works (WWW, or sometimes in the Jackchat, simply 3dub). The viewing history on most of the devices was scant, providing a chronicle of only their last mission.

He was surprised to learn they had only one directive, all the winged women and those manning the retrieval boats alike: to find him, detain him, and if it came to it, kill him. Orders were issued by another unfamiliar woman, Captain Chase, according to HeadGear captions. Chase's demeanor was resolute, all business. The Warrior could appreciate her as a leader, as another worthy adversary.

Replaying their transmissions, the Warrior could hear the echo of leaders and the rhythms of their command. He stopped marching when he realized that he had led people in battle, that his voice ordered, cajoled, demanded—just like Captain Chase.

He had once been a leader of men.

He flipped up the HeadGear's visor. It was after sunset, but he could still appraise himself in the evening light. His clothes were ragged, but possibly once the remnants of a military uniform. His weapons were a hodgepodge of ones he had collected in his campaign against the Rich. And his beard... woven into his beard, he noted again, the trophies of so many of these winged women he had killed. Women of Winston Water Works. Women who were themselves warriors. They were mercenaries of the Rich but not themselves of the Rich. He had been killing the drones, not the Queen Bee.

The Warrior remembered again what he had known just a week before.

He had been going at it all wrong.

He wasn't some berserker on the beach bathing in blood. He was—or had once been—a taciturn planner. Methodical. The Warrior was eager to revisit this side of his old self, to resurrect the someone inside who was an even better—perhaps less bitter—killing machine.

He dropped to his knees, then slumped back to sit on his haunches. He ran his hands over his wild hair, his bushy beard, and his chest. No, this was not regulation. It was not him.

The Warrior pulled a favorite knife from an ankle sheath and eyed it lovingly. Then he set to cutting his hair, sawing it away, talking to himself. He chopped off the ratty beard and all the bloodied ribbons of wingsuit material knotted into it. Before he was finished with his work, he was inspired to use the knife to carefully shave strips from his temples back over his ears. He did not quite remember why this mattered, but it was significant. It said something about him that he could not yet hear.

· · · ·

In the cover of darkness, in the gathering wind of the coming storm, the Warrior set about crafting a makeshift shelter. He was tired of suffering the weather, standing in the cold rain, snarling at the clouds. He was going to sit this one out.

He chopped long sticks to serve as support posts. He sliced the HeadGear bag into long strips. He harvested piles and piles of seagrass and reeds. He then set about building his shelter, a grass hut backed up to an inset washout on the bank. He worked by the flaring light of a lantern he had scavenged. He set the lamp inside his sandy alcove and built up the woven grass wall quickly so that it would be difficult to see the light from the sea. Then he sat in the shelter and continued weaving together reeds to comprise the roof.

The Warrior worked quickly. His hands wove the grasses and reeds together with an automatic ease that left him time to think. He might never find Katrina Covarrubias, she moving by boat, he on foot... but then again, perhaps the raft ran out of fuel, or she capsized in the coming storm. He had many questions he wanted to ask her, given the chance. He wanted to know more about the mission the winged women were on. Why him? Why now?

As the night wore on, he remembered more, and he listed his questions in his sodden notebook. Sometimes these many days after a Rainmaker passed, the Warrior remembered more. He knew what the Queen Bee looked like. He knew her smile, and that made him smile. He even knew her voice. Occasionally, just before the rains fell again, he could hear the words she had said when he had known her before.

"*There's nobody I'd rather be numb with*," her voice repeated in his head. It would disturb him from his plans. It would interrupt his mantra, "Eat the Rich. Eat the Rich."

Then, in a voice not his or hers, he could hear this: "*We can revel in us now*," and that was even more disturbing. It left him with a buzzing in his head... like bees... no, not the Queen Bee... not the Queen... the Princess... someone called the Princess haunted him.

These things, and surprising memories of the smell of her hair, the sound of her laughter... altogether confirmed that he had known her. Each week, pieces of the puzzle came to him, confused him, and left on the next storm, leaving nothing but some cryptic note in his book.

Why would he have had a relationship with this woman he so loathed? Why would he long to hold the one person he found more abhorrent than any other alive? Winston Water Works, her company and her airships... she was at the helm of the most showy, most aggravating display of riches.

He stopped weaving.

He held the reeds in his hands and looked at them as if they had spoken aloud to him. There was something about them. It was outside his scope, out of reach of his lacerated hands, bloodied from weaving the sharp-edged grasses. Weaving reeds mattered. Reeds.

He shook his head and shook off the not-quite memory. Whatever it was, he hoped it would come to him again.

The Warrior held up his latest work, a door, and laced makeshift hinges on the side of it, tying it to the sidewall branches. His shelter would be snug from the coming storm.

He sat back in the sand and admired his hut from the inside. This was evidence of yet another survival skill he could not quite own.

He shrugged and blew out the lamp, intent on settling down for the night.

The Warrior fought with his most worthy opponent all night long: dreams. He could not know if they were his own, if they were memories or fantasies. He would wake and process them one by one, then drift off again to revisit and revise them to his liking.

Chapter 32 Wet Work

Krystal rolled her eyes at the silly leather skullcap on Ashley Winston's head. The shorter woman was in front of her in the elevator, facing the doors, her arms crossed. Krystal studied the back of Winston's bomber jacket, wondering what the trim black metal bracket contraption was that went up the spine and across the shoulders.

Ridiculous, she thought. Clunky hardware on a fashion jacket.

The elevator dinged, announcing they had arrived at the top.

The elevator bobbed, the doors whisked open—and everyone panicked.

"Spooks!" shouted both Stu and Lark.

"HALT!" men yelled from her penthouse floor. They hefted huge guns to their shoulders and aimed green lasers at them.

The Boys crushed around Krystal as they whipped shotguns from their long coats. Winston's wild-haired friend cocked twin pistols.

She peeked over Winston's shoulder, then hunkered down in the clutch of wet ranchers. Lark was holding her. Stu encircled them both with his bear-like arms.

It would do no good.

Krystal knew this was her last moment, that the corporations had sent an ambush.

"We're all gonna die," Lark whimpered.

Then it was all weapons rattling and men yelling.

We're here for the—

Drop 'em.

Stop.

Everyone was shouting and frantic.

Everyone, that is, except Ashley Winston.

"Alex," she snapped, "Brace."

The men outside the elevator crumpled like rag dolls. Their weapons clattered to the floor. There was no other sound. No suggestion of violence. Nothing.

Alex was the first to move, as if a spell were broken. He uncocked his guns in a flourish and holstered them.

"What the—?" Others around her verbalized the shock Krystal couldn't put into words.

What had she just witnessed?

The elevator doors started to close, stirring them all back to reality. Someone poked at buttons. The knot of men around her came loose as Stu barked orders. "Check them." There was a tremble in his voice. "Check everything. Stay sharp."

"You okay?" Lark asked. He was the last to release her.

"Yeah," she said.

The ranch hands jostled the four bodies on their way past them, but they kept their rifles and attention pointed ahead, wary of more trouble. Alex and Stu took over in the threshold, crouching over the downed men. Alex was rummaging through the men's pockets. Stu was searching one of them for a pulse.

Winston leaned against the persistent elevator door. She didn't seem to notice it bumping her. She looked withered and woefully unhappy, but she did not take her eyes off Alex and Stu.

Lark caught Krystal's attention. "Spooks," he offered the explanation again for the men at their feet. "Like Guthrie."

Krystal shook her head. She remembered nothing like this, not anyone like these men. That had been a lifetime ago.

"Are they..." she blurted, "Are they...dead?"

Stu was checking another man's carotid artery. He exchanged glances with Alex, then with Winston, and then looked up at her and nodded. "All four."

The Boys reported sporadically down the hall at each door they checked.

"Clear."

"Nothin' here."

Some were shouting the all clear from within her rooms.

Lark crouched with the other two men. "You won't find nothin' on 'em. Not a label. Not a lint ball. Just look," he said, and lifted a hand of one of the dead for them to inspect. "They don't even have prints."

"Mob?" Stu asked. "CorpseCorp?"

"Spooks," Lark said again. "After us again."

"Not you," Alex said, rising. He shook his head, then made eye contact with Winston. "They've found me."

"You?" Krystal found her voice again. "They're in *my* penthouse."

"You lit up the sky, dumbass. Lucky it took 'em so long," Winston growled. "Might as well send up a flare for them next time."

"What are you—" Krystal turned on Lark, "What is she *talking* about?"

"She's talking about the hot wire, I'm guessing." Lark guided Krystal out of the elevator, through the pile of bodies. "Am I right?"

"Yeah." Winston studied them as they passed through. "That'd get their attention."

"Whose attention? Who are they?"

Lark pointed at the corpses, gestured wildly, "They're guys from the—"

"Investigators," Winston interrupted. "Corporate spies, more or less."

"And you *killed* them?"

"She saved our lives," Lark said, guiding them both into Krystal's bedroom. "Thanks, by the way."

Winston cleared her throat. "I didn't..."

Krystal glanced at the magic mirror. "Stop. Not here."

The three of them turned into another room, the suite's lounge. Her people had previously swept it of surveillance. "You didn't what?"

"I... I didn't mean to," Winston said sitting down.

"And what's Alex mean—they're here for him? What's he got to do with *anything*?"

Just then Alex ducked into the room. He gave Krystal an exaggerated smile, then looked to Winston with concern. "Tapped out?"

"I'm fine," she said. She drew a hanky from her pocket and dabbed her eyes. "I just..."

"Don't think about it. We don't have the time. Locals are hauling out the garbage, but we need to split, too, just in case."

"In case a' what?" Lark took an interest in this. "Think this'll tip off more of them?"

Alex cocked his head at Lark. "You know something, or are you just paranoid?"

"Both," Lark replied.

"Then come with me. They're safe in here."

Krystal did not like the way he was assessing the windows, studying the doors that opened onto the room. She could see doubt through his smokescreen of confidence.

"Krys?" Lark asked. His mechanical hand was flexing, giving away his anxiety.

"We're good," she said.

"Right outside," Lark said.

"Okay, Ash. You got your meeting with her." Alex nodded Krystal's way. "Say your piece. Then we gotta go."

"But..." Winston started, then slumped into a chair.

They left but left the door ajar.

Krystal sniffed at her sachet. She took an instant to ensure her HeadGear was off.

"I should call this in," Stu was saying in the hall.

"You can't," Alex replied. "Don't call anyone. This is my mess."

Krystal huffed. "Why's he keep saying that?"

"Huh? What?"

The voices faded back down the hallway. She was left alone with this *brilliant* conversationalist.

She dropped into the chair across from Winston and studied her.

For being once the most powerful woman alive, Heiress of the Air, Ashley Winston seemed like something of a space case. Krystal shook her head, dismissing the idea that this woman, in her silly Red Baron costume, had done anything to the men outside the elevator. Why, she could scarcely keep her head up!

"Why's he keep saying this is all about him?"

Winston did not respond. She was wrinkling and straightening out a rag in her lap.

"And what's with you? You wanted a meeting. What do you want?"

A flame flickered in Winston's eye as she looked at Krystal, suddenly intent. "What do you know about Rory Reed?"

"Never heard of him."

"Blackbeard?"

Krys couldn't stifle a chuckle. "Who?"

Winston looked more agitated. She was clutching the rag in her hands so tightly her knuckles were white and trembling.

"Why'd you have to do it? Why my ship?" she snarled the words, clipping them sharply. Then, in a shift to something Krystal could not mistake as anything else but sorrow, Winston asked another question, "Why now, dammit? Why now?"

Krystal did not reply. She would not respond to badgering. She only tolerated such questions from her board. Besides, she had stated her views. *Watch a Vid and get in the know*, she thought.

"You don't know why I'm here, then?"

"Like, *other* than the airship? No."

"Do you know where my ship went? Where your ports dump?"

Krystal blanched. The question was coming up too often of late. Her best answers were never good enough. She had tried answering questions with more questions, humor, diversion: *Do we know what happens to a log when it burns? Where's that go? Or how about that missing sock from the dryer? Now there's a mystery...* but she knew better than to try these on the woman growing ever-more incensed with her own questions.

Before she could compose something scientific-sounding, Winston continued.

"Do you *really* not know about the time cops?" Winston asked, her questions climbing in pitch and desperation.

"The time—"

"Do you work for the same people Spexarth did?"

"Who?"

"Do you know the Family?" Winston squeaked.

When Krystal moved to shake her head, even in the slightest, it set Winston off in a private tirade of profanity growled under her breath. She was pounding her thighs and the rag spread out on them. Something was written on it, but Krystal couldn't make it out in the flurry of fists and foul words.

"Can't you help me?" Winston seethed, standing now.

They glared at each other for a long instant.

Krystal blinked. She found she was biting her lip, and that brought back the pain of Mrs. Stewart Wiebe's right hook. She was ready this time, making a fist around her sachet.

"I don't know what you want," she said through gritted teeth.

Winston grabbed her lace lapels and pulled her to her feet.

Krystal was taller than Winston, yet she feared the ire burning in Winston's eyes. Her expression was wild. Possessed. "What?"

Krystal leaned back a bit, fearful Winston might bite at her.

A noise in the hall wafted into the space between them. It was a cart, something on wheels. They both looked to the doorway, and Krystal caught a glimpse of a large laundry cart, like hotel maids used for morning bedding. The sides of it were especially lumpy. A leg and foot, clad in black, stuck up out of it.

"Now that's takin' out the trash," a gravelly voice stated from the hall.

Some chuckles and groans followed.

"It's a good quick fix," someone else said. "Saw it in a movie once."

"15 atmosphere's pressure," another offered. "Squeeze'll make 'em unrecognizable."

"Ugh," Krystal recognized this voice. It was Winston's friend, Alex. He was nearing their door. "I'm not one for the wet work. Just get them as far away as you can, as soon as you can."

"Truck's out back," Stu was saying. "You tend to your problems. We'll tend to ours."

Krystal was shaken to attention by the wiry Ashley Winston.

"What can you tell me? What can I do? What's our next move?" She was ranting now as Alex pulled her away.

"Ash? Ash-ley? We handled the problem. You can relax. Really."

"I said I'd kill them, didn't I, Alex? Didn't I?" She shook her fist with the rag clutched in it. "I said it, and I did it, and then... and then... this!"

Alex took her lead and gently took the rag from her hand. He read it aloud, "Just ask."

"What the hell am I supposed to do with that?" She collapsed in his arms, a growling nightmare of anger.

"We better go for now," Alex said, excusing himself and Winston. Passing by Krystal, he said to her in confidence, "You'd better be glad she had orders, Miss Price. Things could've gotten ugly."

Could have?

Alex ignored the elevator. They took the stairs.

The moment the stairway door shut behind them, Lark Fortune said, "See there? Did you hear that? *Things getting ugly.* That's why I'm here, Krys."

"Right. Right," she said, urging him to relax.

"He isn't wrong," Stu said, low and slow. "Getting ugly."

"What?"

"Last time I saw them, my whole life was over."

Krystal turned her full attention to him. He was holding his hat, looking out a window.

"Stu?"

"In Guthrie. Guys just like that. Just like Lefty said." His deepest voice trailed off in a mutter.

"I TOLD YOU!" Lark crowed. "Krystal, I told you so. Now, do you believe me?"

She was going to dial him back. She was going to put a hand on Stu's shoulder and pry more of his story out of him. That was her intention, but as she moved to him, she stopped cold.

Alex hadn't taken the elevator. The light bar above it reported the elevator was idle on the ground floor. He hadn't even bothered with it. Why? Had they made a hasty retreat down the back stairs? She heard an unsettling slam out back, something huge and metal, much larger than a back door.

Krystal walked through her suite to the walk out window and fire escape. She stepped out onto it, gingerly touching the railing just enough to lean over it. No sign of Winston and Alex in the alley.

However, a trash truck was completing its compression cycle and returning to stasis with a loud slam. Two garbage men were talking with Stu's men. It looked as if the older one, a lanky man with a long white beard and ponytail, was refusing something offered to him. The other trashman, some good ol' boy on the stout side, shrugged and tossed his head, 'maybe so, maybe not?' Ultimately, he took the thick envelope from Stu's man, and they made their way back into the garbage truck.

Something bothered Krystal more than the fact four men had died in her penthouse. Something was itching at her more than Ashley Winston being their killer. It felt like déjà vu. She lingered on the fire escape, even after Stu joined her. She watched the truck maneuver through Laramie.

As it rumbled off, so did the feeling. Almost.

Chapter 33 Half-life

Stu would never own the truck he sat in. He shook his head in frustration and swiped the dash screen, then did the gesture before the interior camera again, just like the salesman had shown him. He couldn't tell if the damn thing was off or on. He couldn't hear it idle, but then, it was some new hybrid-drive out fresh from TransCorp. The dash screen was illuminated. The interior lights were on.

He pushed another button, this one to open the door. All day this had surprised him, and it did again; the door swooped *under* the cab. It was a dumb design that wouldn't last a week of Wyoming weather. Snowpack or mud, it seemed there would always be something mucking up the undercarriage. TransCorp's engineering had to be a bunch of city kids. Shaking his head again at the stupidity of it, Stu listened for the hybrid-drive—for a humming, an idle, for something suggesting it was still on.

Nothing.

"Whatever," he grumbled.

He was halfway across the farmyard when he remembered the carrot cake he'd brought home for Rae. The truck door was just rolling back into place, and the lights powering down when he approached. "Open," he said. "I'm back," he said, then thought of how odd it would have seemed to his daddy, watching him now, talking to a shiny plastic truck. He tried another gesture his salesman had taught him, thinking this one might open the door on a visual rather than verbal command. Nothing happened.

"Just wanna get my damn cake," he said. His breath clouded in the cold night air.

He rattled the door handle. He rapped a knuckle on the side window. He tried several more verbal and gesture commands. He was reaching for his pistol when Nat called from behind him: "Palm it."

Stu wondered how much of his antics had been observed. He felt his shoulders sag as he turned around to face the inevitable heckling. Nat waved from his loft window, and catching Stu's attention, he repeated, "Palm it." He gestured with his own hand, pressing a palm to his windowsill. "We put in your biometrics, remember? Anywhere on any window."

Stu rolled his eyes, sure the kid didn't see that in the shadow of his hat. He did as recommended, and the interior lights snapped back on.

"Now do the hand thing again," Nat directed.

Stu ran through a few moves before the door retracted again underneath the cab. He fetched Rae's dessert, then turned to look up toward Nat's window only to find it empty.

It was just him and the plastic pickup now. At least he would be alone in his humiliation. "Shut," he commanded. "Close. Door up."

He decided to wait it out, to see if the SmartTruck from TransCorp was really all that smart. After a time, the interior lights gradually faded to black. Stu was getting cold. He wished there was a manual override, so he could just wrench the door up and shove it into position. He thought about the barn cats that would make a home of it inside the dealership's loaner truck if the door never shut, and he decided that was about what they deserved for making such a chucklesome truck.

He turned toward the house, and just as he did, he heard the servos and hydraulics pulling the door up and into place.

That was his opening story, and the carrot cake was his peace offering, but Rae was already in her night clothes and all out of interest. She did still have an appetite, however, and she did not turn away his dessert. She sat at the kitchen bar and ate the cake, but she had little to say.

Nat came through, raiding the fridge and making small talk with him about the new truck. Like many of his conversations, it was more of an information dump. "Tracy says it's a limited edition. She says the all-wheel drive is lots more fuel efficient than the four wheel, and she says it'll still smoke the tires if you step on it. It'll take some getting used to for you, I know, but it's really cool. Mom's gonna love it, too, and Tracy says they can even order it in white to match the other...."

Stu wasn't able to focus on the mundane. He didn't give two shakes if the truck just up and drove itself away. Some could these days. It was midnight, and he wondered what these two were still doing up. The whole house was lit up like they hadn't even thought about bed. It wasn't like them to stay awake on his account. He knew they were wanting a report, and he knew they'd be hearing all kinds of stories tomorrow that would just get him into worse trouble.

The problem, as he saw it, was one of degrees of honesty. Stuart Wiebe was an all-out honest man. The dead men crushed in the garbage truck, however, were a truth he just couldn't tell. The men and their iron were probably two counties away already, probably the whole load dumped in a distant landfill. If Rae asked him, what else could he say? If Nat wondered why he was so late, how much could he honestly hedge?

And if he was being honest, what was he to say—what was he even to *think*—about Lark Fortune's claim? Men from the Future. It was too stupid to put into words. He hadn't seen Lefty in decades, but the ol' boy seemed pretty sure of himself. Stu had heard about his conspiracy theories, of his crazy antics at the Installation, so he wasn't expecting the conviction Fortune carried with him.

"You damn well know I'm right, Stu," Lark had said. "You said it yourself. Spooks."

"I was just spooked, that's all," Stu replied. "Hell, I mighta said anything."

"They're the same outfit as what came through when we were kids. I have footage of them at my dad's place. I have one of their laser pistols out at the Installation."

"You got a regular Roswell going on there, don't you?"

"I don't get it. I don't know why you won't admit what you know is true. They're the same black ops types responsible for your place getting torched."

Stu had gritted his teeth, and he was gritting them again remembering the conversation. There were some things from the past that had to stay back where they were. Adults in his family at the time had signed non-disclosure agreements. Even the kids had to swear to never bring it up again. In exchange, the government, or at least some government-type agent, had promised them relocation and a fresh start.

No one knew that. Everyone believed there was a hush-hush cash settlement with a bomb manufacturer that gave the Wiebes and all those around their ranch money to compensate for their losses.

It was actually money to stop their tongues.

"—isn't that about it, Stu?" Rae was saying, frowning at him.

He had learned years ago not to admit he wasn't listening. He knew, too, not to agree to anything he had not heard, himself. These were always tricky situations.

He nodded but did not speak.

She took it and ran with it. "And that's why we're calling Barb in the morning and insisting that White Witch gets issued notice to leave town."

Stu blinked and looked around for Nat. No one was around to help him out with this one. Stu sighed and spread both his palms on the counter. "It's not her doing."

Rae said nothing. That was always a bad sign.

"What?" he asked defensively.

Rae crumpled the paper bag and clamshell with half her cake still uneaten. She stuffed it into the trash vigorously.

"You think I'm taking her side?" he ventured. He shouldn't have said it aloud.

"You've been at her place two nights in a row... and tonight, on into morning," she looked past him at the clock.

"Now, it ain't like that, Rae. Last night it was dinner with the Boys and the riffraff. Tonight, Lark Fortune came to town, dropped in off an airship with Ashley Winston herself."

"Ashley Winston?" Rae asked. "Just dropped out of the sky here in Laramie?"

"I swear to God."

"A regular congregation of rich bitches, is it?"

"Rae, c'mon. I couldn't make this stuff up."

"Wasn't on the Interface."

"We tried to keep it that way."

"Nat didn't say anything about it, either."

He wanted to say they were in on it. Nat always confided in her. Maybe this time the gravity of the situation had been clearly conveyed. No gossip. No Jackchat. No Interface.

"It can't get out, what happened up there," he said, instead. He was getting dangerously close to too much information. "It got ugly."

"And you were there *because*?"

Stu sighed. "Like I told you last night. I thought I should be there since Krystal didn't bring any security with her."

"Laramie PD was there. The Boys stood around the hotel all day. Cort Bradley said he ran off some ETR himself."

The same Cort Bradley who pissed himself in the elevator? There was so much Stu wanted to tell her. He looked her over. She was at once the wisest and most incendiary woman he had ever known. She reminded him too much of his mother sometimes. It seemed unwholesome, like marrying his own momma. Rae was her height, her weight, and she had her same mouth. "'Don't have much to say about that? How's it matter if you were standing around with the rest of them, pissing testosterone?"

It had been a long week, and it was only an hour into Wednesday morning.

"I'm the only one Krys knows around here. I just wanted to be around just in case something came up." *Like an ambush from time-traveling spooks.*

"So?" She had the same keen insight as his momma. There was no lying to her for long. The best he could do was buy himself time; if he knew her at all, he knew that much.

"So... nothing."

"You'll tell me over breakfast," she stated.

* * * *

He was left alone in the great room, watching the fire from his oversized recliner. His stocking feet were toasty warm, and the leather chair formed to his body like it did most every night. With his hands behind his head, he stretched and sighed, taking stock of his current situation.

His ranch, his hands, and all the good people he knew were in the middle of a corporate grab for land and power. His son was not his son, and far worse, Nat was getting suckered in by the Eaters and their spin. His wife didn't trust him, and he couldn't tell her even enough to restore her trust. That left him feeling guilty all over again, telling half lies and living his half-life like he had been ever since they'd left Oklahoma.

Now Lark "Lefty" Fortune, up from Guthrie, thought he was showing up to what—save the day? Some hero he proved to be! He was probably already deep in his drink. No, he was probably fast asleep at the foot of Krystal's bed, like a faithful dog.

Rae's theory was that Stu never got over it when Krystal chose Lefty. That was ludicrous. It was a high school thing. He'd moved on. Hell, he'd moved a thousand miles away. He'd done fine for himself.

Lefty hadn't fared so well. Talk about not letting go. He'd hardly left town, and he'd never gotten over being jilted. Sometimes folks couldn't get over or around a tough time, they had to work through it. That's what his shrink said.

There was a time when Stu Wiebe went to anger management, an hour's drive to Cheyenne just to keep it all on the quiet. It was years ago, just after they'd gotten married, but Stu remembered every word that therapist coaxed out of him and every idea he'd put into him, too. Lark Fortune and Kenny Hinman were not the root of his problems. Losing the ranch was not their fault. It was not his fault, either. It was something cosmic, beyond anyone's immediate control. Relinquishing control, that was the way through it, he was told.

Stu rolled over there every Wednesday for two winters, spending petty cash to keep it off the insurance and off Pharma's books. He told Rae that Cheynne had a better sale barn, and he had gone to the effort of checking in at the auction every single week. Nobody questioned him about it, not even The Boys, which meant he had been crafty or they all thought it was good for him.

In the end, Stu didn't think it was so good for him. Therapy sessions were like burn treatments he had known. They stripped off the crusty outer layer, leaving him raw and vulnerable. They brought up memories he'd buried, dug them up like the dead, and the dead walked beside him, his constant, pestilent companions.

No amount of reasoning with them could talk them out of their vigil. Stu's memories plagued him like an invisible leprosy. The smell of them, burning hair and flesh, hung on him like charcoal sweat. When he'd close his eyes to sleep, the blinding flash would sear him awake.

When his meds would kick in and his eyes rolled up in his head, the nightmares rolled out. Screams of family burnt beyond recognition. His own horse, scorched to the hide all down one side. Stu had been, too, singed by radiation down his whole left side. He woke beside his dying horse in red dirt and snow.

The final jolt that horse had made when he shot it in the head would shake him awake again, and he would struggle with his memories the whole night through.

Chapter 34 Paddington's Pie

A lex was a firm believer in chaos.

It was an undeniable force in his life. Others lived oblivious to chaos as a force, simply recognizing its effect.

Alex could feel it surge around him like a wind gust. He could predict it like a natural storm. He could feel it in his bones. Chaos had come again... and he had seldom known it to well up like it was in Laramie.

Others might be buffeted around by it, their best laid plans snapped off like a brittle branch, but Alex always felt better when he was in motion. He was a willow tree, or better yet, he thought, a jellyfish.

He made a face that was more puffer fish than jellyfish, and the question of a jellyfish's face passed through his mind in the process. He was puffing against the cold Wyoming wind that pressed in around the visor of his motorcycle helmet.

Inside the helmet visor was a carnival of news and information he was consuming from the Interface. It was important for a man to be in the know, and he was learning all he could about the TransCorp woman, Krystal Price. He found no reason she would have been part of a time-travelling ambush. She was a shareholder in TransCorp, but she didn't have enough money to control anything. She had bought in early, and she had ridden every wave of TransCorp teleportation ventures. Krystal Price was a big splash of white on the Interface whenever porting snared a headline in the clutter that was CommCorp excuse for news. She was a figurehead.

He knew her to be one of the Kids of Guthrie. Probably no one but Alex thought of them as that. Capitalized. Like they were a piece of history themselves. That was what he knew of them, that they had been tangled up in the Guthrie Fall and the Air Force's coverup. They were little more than names in history from his vantage point, but meeting them now, he was learning that each of them could trigger interest from all the wrong people.

Krystal Price was, as Alex had told Kelli, "Just a puppet, poppet." She was nothing to worry about, but she *did* have access to those undiluted elements of teleportation, what the Kids of Guthrie had first dubbed Tic-Tacs.

Lark Fortune might seem like little more than a little man, but Alex was gathering he was more in the know than any of the rest of them, even in their teen years. According to him, he'd mixed it up with Spooks. He'd escaped from their clutches. He'd alluded to someone, too, who was now Alex's person of greatest interest. He'd finally admitted that other guy, The Other Guy in Alex's accounting, was who he had first mistaken Alex for. Someone named Sackerson, *from the future*. Lark's far-flung sci-fi stories and erratic behavior had earned him scorn in Guthrie and left him there with no options.

Alex reviewed his initial notes on Stuart Wiebe, comparing them to the man he'd just met in Laramie. In high school, he'd been the star quarterback. He was from the equivalent of (literal) landed aristocracy—his family had ranch land east of Guthrie for generations. His life was looking good, and then it wasn't, all in the span of a few weeks. First the Guthrie Fall stirred up the whole community, then... then what?

Records were vague. No one around town strayed from the published stories, and that had Alex curious. Whatever had happened to their land first seemed to have no bearing on the current situation. From Wiebe's reaction to the time cops, however, Alex was sure now there was more to the story. The story needed to be told.

The fourth of the Kids of Guthrie had served as his best informant to date, Kenneth (Henny) Hinman. Maybe he was reading too much into it, but Henny's role in Guthrie was the least pronounced and, maybe then, the most crucial. Alex had buddied up to Henny, but now that he had spent more time with Fortune, he wondered just where the truth about him might lie. Was Henny covering for him? Was Henny hiding something else?

The dynamic between them would be interesting, should he ever get the four of them in the same place and time. He had been hoping to observe at least the three, Stu, Krystal, and Lark, when the time cops had pre-empted their reunion.

He was running information on a group of local militia who called themselves "The Boys." He listened to Roy Orbison and Daft Punk mixes, and that was peppered with sound bites Kelli had recorded for him to replay when he missed her (all the time).

He was also processing all he could about the trash company that had hauled away his time cops. All he had to work with initially was a vague description from one of The Boys: "You know, a trash truck. I dunno. Grimy. Blue maybe. Had a picture of a bird on it. A stork I think." That did not hold true with what he learned of Laramie's trash service. Theirs was a fleet of HydroDrives, shiny, new... and white. This blue truck, he guessed, was an independent.

Drilling down into TransCorp records was no help at all. There was simply no stork-related trash service. The nearest trash service with anything related was a pelican logo, and that was coastal, hundreds of miles west.

Before Alex left town on his wild pelican chase, however, he caught another break. He learned which of The Boys had paid for the truck to haul off the trash, a fellow named Paddington. "Yeah, like the bear," the man said over coffee.

Donnie Paddington reported that Stu Wiebe had asked him to find a garbage truck and to get it in the alley immediately. Paddington had scarcely tapped his HeadGear when a trash service washed by on his Interface feed. The very man he spoke with in his visor was the same who rolled up in the alley not five minutes later. It had truly been, as Paddington said, "fortuitous."

"Bet you a slice of pie you can't find that service in your 'Gear again," Alex challenged. "And if you do, I want everything you can pipe me on it."

Paddington flipped down his visor with a confident smile. "Thanks for the pie, mister," he chortled. Two minutes passed. Five. His smile was gone when he flipped up the visor and shook his head. "I... I dunno. It was there not two hours ago, all over the feed. Now I can't find it at all."

Alex sighed and asked him for all he could recall about it. Brilliant blue background, like the city buses TransCorp was running everywhere. Blue like that, but "enamelly." The logo was a gold pelican with an expression on its face like it was in charge. Winking. Hands on its hips, somehow. The words and contact information, however, were not Paddington's forte.

"I'll buy you a *whole pie* if you let me tinker with your HeadGear a bit."

"Oh, I dunno. I put off two years' vacation for this baby." He stroked it lovingly. His attention did drift to the pie cabinet more than once, however, and after some techno babble and the promise of some upgrades, Paddington surrendered his Head.

"Play with this one a while, if you want," Alex smiled, and extracted a thin filament model from his sleeve. "It's called a LiceWire, surprisingly powerful for its size."

While the man tried it on and marveled aloud at its resolution and speed, Alex combed through the metadata within Paddington's head piece. In a few seconds, he had the entire viewing history for the last four hours scrolling on screen. The pelican trash service proved to be a bogus overlay listing. Someone had been toying with the locals. Someone was tapping their feeds and knew just what they were looking for and how discreetly and immediately they needed it.

"The Other Guy," Alex said aloud.

"Hmmmm?" Paddington asked absently, still spellbound by the Lice.

"How can I find this pelican truck, anyway? Do you have any idea what route it took from here? Where's the landfill, maybe?"

"Umm-hmm."

Alex pried the Lice off Paddington's face, "You can keep this if you tell me what I wanna know."

Paddington blinked. He appraised Alex carefully. "You're not with the Eaters."

"Hardly," he smiled. "I'm an independent contractor."

"You're one of them? An assassin?"

"Aw, no, nothing like that. Think of me as a free agent, but I'm anything but free." Alex winked at him. "I'm hoping to unplug this whole ChompCorp/TransCorp thing before it gets too big."

Honesty, Alex had found over time, was usually the best policy. It was working on Paddington. "That's good to hear," he said. "That's my take on it, exactly. Let the Titans fight. Don't get crushed in the wake."

"Yeah, Godzilla and Mothra—"

"And Kong."

"Right. And Kong... so... what can you tell me?"

"Landfill's out north of town—"

"Great," Alex said. He waved for the server and asked Paddington, "What kind of pie do you want?"

"But you won't find them there. Stu told me to send them at least to Washakie County, further if they'd go for it."

"And did they?"

"*Said* they would," Paddington said, his eyes on the Lice.

"So, that's farther north, right?"

"Landfills don't open for another two hours. I told them to drive 'til they found one open."

"And they were good with that?"

"The round guy acted like he'd drive to Canada for the cash in that envelope."

Alex smiled. A trash truck might run 60 miles an hour, maybe a bit more. On the motorcycle he'd bartered for, he could likely go closer to 90. He was sure he could catch up with them.

"Oh, you know, I just remembered this," Paddington said. He took his HeadGear back and swiped manually a few times. "There. See? We put a wire in the envelope. You can track it from this display."

Alex palmed his face. "You had a tracker all along and never thought of it?"

"I'm a superintendent, not a super spy," he said. "And I'll take the pecan. Warmed up."

Chapter 35 Jump Around

Henny was walking along a pier off the coastline. It was not a dream. He felt the shock of it on every level, from the time change to the temperature change. It took him a bit to get acclimated. One step through Sack's portal had taken them from Oklahoma to California.

They had ported into a sleepy seaside town. The air was humid and had the tang of the ocean to it. Henny took in a deep breath and held it in. His chest was puffed up and out, and he was proud of his decision. Kenny Hinman wasn't settling for anything. He was taking up the offer. He was on Sackerson's big adventure. Sack left him to himself for a bit, claiming he needed to "round up some resources." That could mean anything, Henny knew, from recruiting more help to gathering up armament. It might not mean anything more than raiding an ATM or a bank. Hell, when Sackerson said resources, it could mean a couple of convenience store sandwiches.

He slipped off his knit cap and held it to his chest. He marveled at the waves lapping at the shoreline, so peaceful, the Pacific... but it was not to last.

A cobalt blue truck lumbered up, brakes squelching as it came to a stop beside him. Sack waved from the cab. As Henny rounded it, he discovered it was a garbage truck. He frowned, shrugged it off, and opened the passenger-side door.

"Where to now?" he asked, as if he were in a "choose your own adventure" game that was none of his own choosing. He was going to play along. It was a big adventure.

"We're going on a little trek in my truck, my friend... a cross-country truck trek."

"Where we going?" Henny asked. "I like it here."

"We're goin' to Wyomin' and we're gonna get there fast," Sackerson sang.

"Never heard that one."

"I just made it up," Sack cackled.

He wasn't a very good truck driver. He popped the clutch when shifting and killed the engine at most of the stoplights. But he managed to get the rig up to speed and out of the little village. Henny settled in, hoping they might stop for a snack soon.

Then, not a mile past the last traces of town, Sack ground down the gears and pulled into a highway maintenance lot. It looked to Henny as if TransCorp had abandoned it, and the state of the road they were traveling would confirm that. Sack aimed the truck at a round top that gaped open, a Quonset hut made of corrugated tin. The doorway was darker than the surrounding night. When the headlights flashed over it, there was nothing remarkable in it.

Sackerson glanced at Henny's chest and hip. "Good, you're buckled in."

"What?" he asked, but Sackerson had already popped the clutch and floored it. The truck grunted loudly and snapped forward. "What are you—"

Before Henny could complete the question, they were in the doorway of the shed and then the headlights flared to a blinding flash of blue.

Then they were slowing to a stop in a city alley. A spark and tendril of flame caught Henny's attention in the passenger's rear-view mirror.

He smelled bleach again.

They'd just ported again.

Guthrie to the ocean to this alley... presumably in Wyoming... now in a truck.

He felt queasy. Lefty had told him of the side effects. Henny himself had never ported over and over, back to back, but Lefty had. One night over drinks he told him everything he knew of serial teleportation, from stories in his father's journals to his own far-flung experiments.

He didn't recall any of the stories to include teleporting a trash truck.

"Did we... did this thing just...?"

"Good gas mileage, eh? Sackerson laughed again.

"Why are we here, and why are we in this? And... and *where* are we at?"

"Hold on," Sackerson said. He produced a battered HeadGear unit and slid into it.

"What are you—"

Sackerson held up a finger to shush him.

Henny shook his head. He thought for a moment about asking to be returned, right now, to his sleepy little bar and grill in his comfy little town.

"Yessir, we're on it. Quick as a cat. We'll be there before you can bring it out, sir." The glowing light on the helmet went from red to blue, and Sack flipped up the visor. "*Pack it up, pack it in, now let me begin,*" Sackerson was singing again, this time something of a rap song. He was egging Henny on to join in. "You know... *won't ever slack up.*"

Sackerson was jostling around like a geriatric hip-hop artist. He threw the truck into reverse and gunned it, grinning at Henny and continuing, "*Guess I'd better back up.*"

Henny looked in the mirror and braced himself.

The truck careened backward down the alley, then at the intersection, barreled across a street, and continued down the alley beyond. Somehow, even with his rapping and dancing, Sackerson managed to not sideswipe a building or hit a pole or crush any back-alley debris.

He slammed on the brakes, singing repeatedly, "*Jump around! Jump. Jump. Around!*" Sackerson was singing along, as if on cue, as if with a silent karaoke machine.

The HeadGear was off. The radio was off. Of course, Henny knew the song, something they'd played at football practice, something in one of the oldies sets on his jukebox. But it was something in Sack's repertoire?

"Time to take out the trash, Henny."

"But..."

"Get out. Let me do the talking. You help me load up. Easy-peasy."

"Easy... peasy?"

Sackerson was already out of his door and talking to someone behind the truck when Henny had collected himself enough to join them. It was so cold here he could see his breath. He was all in a huff.

"That hamper and all that's in it," a man said, but he stopped short when he saw Henny. His glare, even masked by the brim of his black cowboy hat, was fierce. "Who're you?"

"I'm Ken—"

"Spush!" Sackerson interrupted. "He's with me. He's my muscle." He turned to Henny and winked, saying, "You heard the man, load 'er up."

Henny shrugged and looked beyond the cowboy to a large laundry cart. It wasn't a trash trolley. He approached it and tried to push it toward their truck. It was really heavy. The wheels were made for inside use, not the rough concrete of the alley. Henny stopped and flipped up the tarp to see what was so heavy. He retreated with a yelp.

Sackerson tossed him an envelope. "Pocket that, will ya. We gotta get this loaded and get gone. There's still trouble coming."

"Trouble?" Henny stuffed the envelope inside his greatcoat. He still clutched the tarp with one hand, waved it over the corpses to get Sackerson's eye. He glanced toward the cowboy, finding he was already on his way back inside.

"Oh, c'mon." Sackerson tugged at the cart, dragging the wheels over the rough surface as best he could. Henny lifted and pushed, easing the job.

When they had it near the truck's back end, Henny stopped again. "You can't be serious."

"It's a job, Henny. A little clean up. It's what I do."

"*What's* what you do?" Henny screeched.

"I rectify and tidy up. Sweet as a peach. Now come on." Sackerson busied himself with controls near the taillight assembly and after some fussing, he found one that opened the back of the garbage truck wide open. Another lever lowered the bottom jaw of it to the ground. "There. See? Help me get this on here."

Together they hefted the cart's wheels and then forced it fully onto the landing. Henny draped the tarp back over the body he had seen and tucked it in. He had been in town less than five minutes. He was still catching up with the weather here. He was just getting used to the stink of the trash truck. Everything seemed to be moving three steps ahead of him, and Henny couldn't quite register the here and now. *Another side effect of porting so much?*

Sackerson flipped levers again, and the truck went through several gyrations before he found the right one. The bottom jaw lifted from the ground and the entire apparatus tilted to consume the cart and dead men inside it.

As the truck continued its operation, Henny realized suddenly what was happening. "Oh my God, Sack, you can't do this!"

He dashed at Sackerson, but the wiry old man did a quick twist like a matador and deflected him. He stopped the machine, however, and he turned on Henny.

"You are absolutely right. How stupid of me!" Then, before Henny could even gawk at him, Sackerson snapped open a knife, bound up into the back of the truck, and sliced open the side of the laundry cart. Well-dressed corpses tumbled out into the maw of the trash truck. As they fell, Sackerson fished around them and pulled out weapons, tossing them at Henny's feet.

He just watched as the mad man wrenched and wriggled the last of the guns and hopped down. "You are so right!" he continued. "Imagine what would have happened if we crushed these!"

Sackerson laughed at his own stupidity, shaking his head.

Henny looked at the weapons, like none he had ever seen before. Like oversized Nerf guns someone had chrome plated. They looked like they belonged in a cartoon, not at his feet in this alley.

"Load 'em up, Ken. We have miles to go before we sleep."

Sackerson threw some levers, and the truck's compactor roared into action, slamming and grunting. Pneumatics hissed, and the back gate of the truck thunked down into traveling position.

Henny held the bundle of guns like an armload of firewood. Dumbfounded. When Sackerson waved him into motion, he followed him back around the truck to the passenger door and poured the weapons on the floorboards at Sackerson's orders. "Just don't kick 'em," Sack said. "Could punch a hole in the space-time continuum."

"The... space..."

"I kid. I kid. Just hop up there and let's roll."

• • • •

Henny had the hardest time finding his words. The one condition he had was that no one would get hurt. It curdled his stomach to think what might have become of the men in the back. "You said..."

"Hmmmm?" Sackerson said, not taking his eyes off the highway.

Henny cleared his throat. All his teenage fears of the wacky Sackerson were throbbing in his head. How could he have forgotten just how unhinged the guy could be? Maybe it was his new grandfatherly look. Maybe it was that Sack's edginess was just what Henny had been missing.

"You said we wouldn't hurt anyone," Henny managed.

"Oh. That." Sack cocked his head back. "We didn't hurt them, silly. They were already dead."

"But... but..."

"I know it seems a little grizzly, but we have to be *thorough* on this one, see? We're too close to the action. Gotta help neutralize things as best we can."

Henny was whispering back Sack's words to himself, trying to take them fully in. As the miles rolled by, Sackerson shot him a grin now and then.

Finally, they slowed to pull into an abandoned rest stop. The building, once a full-on bathroom and break station, had crumbled and been vandalized with graffiti. To the side of the station was a dilapidated awning and frame. A faded sign dangled from the framework, offering a wash. Sackerson pointed at it. "Gonna give our trash truck a little scrubbing."

Henny followed Sack's lead and climbed out into the cold night air. Out here, far from the shelter of any town, the wind was stronger, and the wind chill was more cutting. He pulled his knit cap down.

Sackerson was inspecting the awning's frame. "Still looks good," he hollered over the wind, giving Henny a thumbs up.

He approached Henny and grinned again, as if he was in on a private joke at Henny's expense. "You got anything in the cab?"

"Nah, just brought what's on my back."

"Got the cash?"

"The what?"

"The envelope?"

"Oh. Yeah." He pulled it from his pocket and handed it toward Sackerson. The weight of it gave him pause. Cash? Just how much money was in there?

"Take all you want," Sack said.

"Really?"

"Just gimme the envelope," Sack asked for it again.

Henny pulled out two banded bricks of 100-dollar bills. He held the envelope out to Sack absently. He inspected the cash as best he could in the dark. He sniffed it. The real deal. Thousands of dollars. It was more paper cash than he thought he had ever seen. His mind reeled with what he could do with all that. He could help the girls with college. He could buy Darla anything she wanted. All off the books.

The truck revved up and stuttered forward. Henny looked in his open door across to the driver's side. Sackerson had wedged one of the chrome rifles into the drive mechanism. He jumped from the truck with a cackle.

The truck rolled toward the awning, crushing weeds and rubble under its wheels as it approached. Sackerson wadded up the envelope and tossed it in the back end of the truck and dusted off his hands.

The truck groaned as it moved on under the awning, and then in a flash, it was gone.

The envelope hadn't made the jump. It just flittered away.

The grumble and rumble of the truck was replaced by the sound of the wind.

Henny looked all around. It didn't appear they had another source of transportation. He didn't look forward to teleporting somewhere again. The thought of it upset his stomach.

"That went well," Sackerson said, his attention on the drifting envelope. He seemed to be debating the merits of chasing it down.

Henny stepped closer. "Why?"

"Why what? I told you, it's the job. What—you don't like the pay?" He patted Henny's breast pocket.

"Why way the hell out here? Why didn't we just do that in the alley?"

"I told you. It was getting too hot back there. We had to hurry. Fortunately, I had this rig set up for just such a situation."

"You had a Hot Wire out here?" Henny asked. "Set up in advance?"

"That's right." He turned, hands on hips, to admire the awning and the remnant of a hot wire that sparked from the framework. "Any port in a storm, so they say."

"Why *here* though?" Henny continued questioning, "And whadda we do now? Teleport somewhere else?"

"We're here because that's here," Sackerson thumbed back over his shoulder. Henny turned his attention behind them. Not far away were the lights of an industrial plant.

He turned back to Sackerson. "Yeah. So?"

Sackerson put an arm around his shoulders and guided him toward the road and, generally, toward the plant. "That is a nuclear power station. It's close-enough it masked our truck's departure. If anyone was tracking our friends, they wouldn't find a thing."

"Wouldn't the... compactor have done..."

"Oh, that made soup of them. Yeah, that was good. This is better," he cackled. "We even ported their weapons. There's not a cufflink left of 'em now. Plus, we're not porting out of here. No way. That'd leave another signature we don't need."

Henny's head was spinning. Soup? Signatures? Sackerson was carrying on now, as he was so prone to do, about how frustrating it would be for anyone pursuing them. It was funny, he said, from this vantage point. He could just see the looks on their faces. His narrative continued, complete with pantomiming a mad search, darting around the lot.

Henny was curious just who might come looking. He wasn't too certain he wanted to be around when they arrived.

"So... we're going... *there*?" Henny looked ahead at the well-lit plant. It looked vaguely like the Emerald City in the Wizard of Oz.

"Yep. Dole out some of that cash, buy some wheels from some Homer Simpson type, and we're on our very merry way."

• • • •

Despite the roaring, cold wind, he had a random thought of a water park ride. It was a tube slide that went in ever-tighter circles, then poured guests out into a huge funnel. They called it the Toilet Bowl. He remembered times he had whirled around and around in the Toilet Bowl, how he had fought for a way to just slow it down, maybe to swim upstream and out of there completely. The worst of it, though, was dropping out at the bottom of the funnel, hitting the pool below in an awkward flop. It was always a little painful. The pain was inevitable.

He could feel the bundled bricks of cash press against his chest. This time, he decided, he would enjoy the spin. Go with the flow. The pain would come. Later.

Chapter 36 Lost and Found

The Warrior prided himself on his vigilance. He did not miss a thing. Even in sleep, he was wary and alert. It was the way of a warrior, to keep watch.

However, he found the sun was already high in the sky when he woke in his shelter. It seemed odd to him. Had he *ever* missed a sunrise? Deep in his core, he felt he was a morning person. "Early to bed, early to rise..." he mumbled. That bothered him, too. He seemed to remember more words from others sometimes than his own words.

From the doorway of his hut, he surveyed the damage from last night's storm. Had he slept through it, entirely?

His beard was close cut, as was his hair. He had no memory of this, either.

Something else was different, too, but he couldn't quite determine just what it was.

He enjoyed a long, languid stretch.

He felt a nagging itch to be about his mission, to set off again on his journey, but another part of him argued otherwise. The quote came to him, *"The only journey is the journey within."*

The Warrior did not think he had ever done this before, but he sat in the sand and read his notebook, every smudge on every page. He did more stretches, and then he went through a series of controlled, calculated motions. He knew these were part of his training, for they came naturally to him.

By mid-day, the Warrior felt more attuned with himself, and he felt much less like denying himself. Oh, the Rich were bastards who he would destroy, but at least for now, he wasn't going to destroy himself in the process. The hunt was his calling, but he was listening, also, to his body.

. . . .

Through careful calculation of the marks on his arms and the rhythms in his notebook, he was certain that this day was a peculiarity. As far back as the tallying went, the seventh day was his most lucid, then a few days would be scattershot, then he would gradually come to clarity, only to experience the cycle over and over again. The pattern corresponded with the storm cycle exactly, so from this, he inferred that something about the storms had a horrible effect on him.

Yet last night's storm had no effect on him.

He had taken shelter.

Maybe it was the first, maybe the *only*, time he had done so.

He eyed his rain catcher with suspicion. Though the canteen under it was brimming over, the Warrior had yet to take a sip. It was getting hot, and he was getting thirsty, but hours had passed, and he had yet to drink the water.

His notebook told him not to. The warning was scrawled in a manic script. "Rainwater rots your brain." He had written that over 40 weeks ago. It had been revised to read, "Rainwater *washes* your brain," just 4 weeks ago. It made no sense to him. His entire situation made so little sense.

His notebook told him other things, equally baffling. "EAT THE RICH," it commanded in all capital letters on page after page, so violently written many pages were torn. More than once it was written in blood. His blood? Someone else's? In contrast, in the neat lettering of an engineer, he read, "You owe it to her." When this same lettering showed up again in subsequent weeks, it stated again and again that he owed something to a woman named Calissa.

The Warrior only knew two women by name, and both of them wanted to kill him. One was the white-haired Ashley Winston, a rich woman who led the hunt for him. The other was the dark and sultry fighter whose life he had traded for HeadGear, Katrina Covarrubias.

This Calissa was not someone he knew. He had no face to match her name. Every time he read of her, he racked his brain, trying so hard to figure out who she was and what it was that he could possibly owe her.

Another time his torment had left him, his hand was steady, and he had written, "You did good. You fought hard. You died fat and happy." Whenever he read that passage, it made his head and heart swell, but he did not know why. It read like a motto, like someone's credo, but it was not his own. *Was it?*

Recently, on the lucid days, he had recorded what he was sure were not his own words. Some rhymed and felt like song lyrics. Others were pithy and astute quotations that he knew as soon as he read them. He had taken to reciting and recommitting these to mind. On the good days, he could recall several without looking at his notes.

He was so curious about his past, but all the notebook would suggest was that he was a collector. He had collected words and phrases, lyrics, and quotes. He found names repeated over and over throughout the notebook, names he collected. Saying them aloud did not bring back memories, only feelings.

"Zana and Astar," or more commonly, "Astar and Zana, A to Z" made him smile warmly. Those names were always together, and they were the first names he had written down, back when his handwriting was crude and violent. The feelings those names gave him made the Warrior think this might be his parents.

"Alex and Kelli" he had written frequently, sometimes with an asterisk or a star. There was something special about these names, but he could not guess what it was. Again, they felt close, like family.

He had written "The Family," on a page about a year ago, and he had revisited that page to underline the words, to draw arrows at them, to warn himself about them. Sadly, that was all he knew: be wary of The Family. What if it was his family he was to avoid? What if they were after him like the winged women of Winston Water Works?

"Ashley Elizabeth Winston" was more than the sum of her parts on the Interface. The repetition of her name, scrawled in his early, ape-like hand, then as recently as yesterday in a thoughtful script, told him what he suspected. She was always paramount on his mind.

It made sense that her name was so prominent in the notebook. She posed the greatest threat to him. She had orchestrated the winged women. She owned the ships they came down from. She wanted him dead.

When the Warrior lived by his code, by his mantra, he wanted her dead as well. It was his mission to eradicate the Earth of all of them. The Rich must die... and she was the richest person he had ever heard of.

When he sat in the shade of his shelter, when he sat in his own presence, he could see past his rage and hatred and programming. It had been the wickedness of the water that had driven him to kill so many Rich so violently. He inhaled the salty air through his nose and puffed it out of his mouth slowly. No need to be so angry about it. No call for such wrath.

He would find her and carry out his mission, but he would stay away from the rainwater so he would keep his wits about him. He would kill her like the professional he knew himself to be.

He thought it might close the gap to close his contract at last.

Then he might find peace.

Then he could find the others on his list and once again find himself.

Chapter 37 The Other Guy

A lex thought it should have gone smoothly. His bike was fully charged and an absolute dream on the open road. He coaxed it up over 100mph and felt safe at even higher speeds. Traffic was sparse, even by Wyoming standards, for it was only 5:30 in the morning. Road conditions were tolerable. He felt good.

He was popping along, a happy jellyfish.

Then the screen changed dramatically.

Everything he had on the trash truck tracker stopped. All the trajectory estimations, all the telemetry readings, all of it froze up.

Even more surprising, the readings he *did* have told him the truck was dead in the water just a mile ahead.

He slowed, appreciating the silent-running electric cycle even more for its stealth. He crept up on the rest stop where the trash truck's tracking had last reported in.

There was nothing in sight. Even the rest area had been long abandoned. No vehicles were pulled in there, let alone a blue trash truck.

Alex dismounted and walked the grounds, talking to himself, reasoning through it. He was annoyed that maybe his work was about to get a lot harder. He was getting mad at himself for his complacency.

Then he chased down an envelope blowing across the lot.

It fit Paddington's description, but it was void of cash. There was, however, the remains of a tracking wire crumpled inside. It had been burned by some high energy surge. "All signs point to yes," he murmured. It might not be the only cause, but the most likely cause of such a surge was a Hot Wire teleportation. It all seemed to fit, that the truck and occupants ported away from this ever-more-volatile area. The question was, were those who took the truck hiding it from him or from an even greater source of concern:

the future. Who would have had the knowledge of the elevator ambush, other than those who had arranged it? Someone—not from around here—had been at the right place and time to intercept the dead... but who? And why?

If they were hiding the time cops—what a stupid moniker he had hung on them since his teen years—that was in Alex's favor. Such people might even be considered on Team Alex. If, however, they were hiding the bodies *from Alex*, there could only be one reason: regrouping.

Alex flipped the envelope over in his hands and held it up to read it in the glow of his HeadGear: "*We got this.*"

"Sackerson, my eye!" Alex recognized the handwriting from the directions he'd been given to the Installation. Back in Guthrie. From Kenny Hinman. *Henny was the Other Guy!*

• • • •

Like it always tended to, the return trip seemed to take forever. When urgency mattered most, like on this drive at this moment, Alex felt conventional travel was painfully inadequate. He could have ported back to town in a stride... but he had made a promise.

The sun was coming up, barely able to overcome the inertia of the horizon and the blankets of clouds keeping it down. The wind was tormenting him at every opportunity. The motorcycle was now fighting both the headwind and more traffic, but Alex pressed it.

Henny, a sleeper agent in a pivotal but sleepy little town? He so did not fit the type that he fit it perfectly. A great spy didn't remotely resemble James Bond; instead, he fit in with the locals. No one seemed more local than Hinman.

Alex tried it on. He reflected on their every interaction. He wondered if he'd revealed too much over drinks. A spy would ply his interests with alcohol. A spy from the future might even slip in something now and then, like scopolamine.

"Nahhhh," Alex said into the wind.

The Interface history on Kenneth Hinman was either an incredibly good forgery or a record of a very mundane life. Surface level information only offered that he was 58 years old, married twenty years ago to his wife, Darla. He'd owned the bar, *Sharts N' Grins*, for over a decade.

Alex peeled back the onion. Young Kenny Hinman was an average student. He had played high school and junior college football. He hadn't set a record, broken a record, not even recorded so much as a song. His "criminal" record only listed a few vehicle citations. His history was so scant he was a ghost, or, as the Kids of Guthrie had dubbed them, a Spook.

He nearly sped right off the highway when Alex saw an addendum on Henny's record. He slowed into the stream of traffic, then even more to the edge of the highway. A government record, though almost impenetrable, taunted him. Alex ultimately had to park the cycle and employ both hand and verbal gesturing, and some of it he was uncomfortable stating aloud. Cars and passersby ignored him. Alex was counting on it.

In 2028, the year of the Guthrie Meteor Fall, Kenny Hinman had been detained by Air Force operatives. He had not returned to the other Kids of Guthrie after that. Instead, he had been, as best as Alex could gather, ostracized. Some of this he had read before. It was what had led him (and others like him) to Guthrie, Oklahoma. The search had fallen out of vogue years and years ago, but not everyone had Alex's perspective. Quite likely no one had his latest suspicions.

Allusions in the records suggested Kenny Hinman had been seen with "agents." Eyewitnesses had reported that he was otherwise not a major player in what went on at the Installation or at the Horse Thief Canyon Ranch. That struck Alex oddly. Henny was one of the gang, then suddenly he wasn't?

Alex wondered how much of the historical record had been factual. Maybe Henny was much smoother than he seemed when he was futzing around the bar. Maybe he had altered everything in order to lie low. Alex asked himself, if he were a sleeper, how better to serve his purpose than to befriend Lark Fortune and wait it out. But to wait it out twenty years in Guthrie?

He peered through his visor at Laramie.

Something caught his attention a few blocks ahead. Cars were clogging the street. People had parked in all directions. A crowd was building.

Alex guided the bike quietly closer. This was not Eaters and ranchers, but townspeople, wives, and children. The threat of gathering like that in times this volatile gave him cause for alarm. Anything could happen. That they were shaking fists and carrying on at 7:45 in the morning was what concerned him more. Only serious protesting happened at that hour for truly egregious things.

A brick arced over the crowd and bounced off a plate glass storefront. The window vibrated and sounded like a gong. People closest to it in the crowd jumped back, then pressed in again. Some were beating on doors and windows. A chant caught on, "Can't starve us. Eat the Rich."

Alex got off his bike and worked into the crowd. He picked up the story quickly from customers streaming out of the grocery store. Shelves were empty, they claimed. People outside were pushing their way in. People inside were fighting to get out, then fighting those outside to let them pass with the odd grocery items they would be clutching with both arms. One woman clutched four long loaves of French Bread, swinging a fifth like a weapon to clear her path. A man who was faring worse was unable to clear the crowd with the cases of beer he was trying to make off with.

By the look of things inside, customers had already started panic shopping. Some had carts full of bottled water, toilet paper, and canned goods. Official-looking ChompCorp security stood, arms crossed, at the checkout lanes and exits. One man in a store smock was yelling over the crowd. *No supply trucks. Wasn't his fault.* Just as a battery of flashing lights and sirens were closing in, he tried to announce that medical attention would be provided for ChompCorp customers injured in the...

Alex's attention went from curiosity to white hot concern. There, on the floor with other battered customers, sat his ragamuffin! She was sprawled awkwardly, leaning against a broken produce display. *Had someone knocked her down and gotten away with it?*

"Dream lover!" he said, sliding up to her on his knees. "Are you okay?"

Kelli Chase, the most badass woman he had ever known, was weeping.

"Are you hurt?" he asked again, giving her his best medical once-over.

She was laughing and crying then. She folded into him, a tearful and snotty mess.

He didn't care, she was *his* mess, and he squeezed her as tightly as he thought it might be safe to do. She squeezed back harder.

"How'd you know?" she cried into his chest.

"I didn't know—"

"You're cold."

"You're... you're crying."

"Am not," she said, pushing him back and smearing away her tears. "I'm fine."

"What happened?" Alex glanced around them, trying to put it together.

Kelli pushed away stray fruit and debris. She was getting frantic in her search for something in the mess around her. She snatched up something and clutched it to her chest.

ChompCorp security staff were leading in medical personnel from Pharma. Together they were running triage. Alex waved them away.

"You're sure you're not hurt?" he asked, trying to give her another look.

"I'm fine," she said, swiping a sleeve under her nose. Then she reframed and said, "I'm cursed. I mean, really!"

"Really!" Alex repeated, not knowing what it was all about.

"We gotta get out of here," Kelli said, pointing at the entrance. People were pouring in.

The riot was going shopping.

One of the first of the looters snatched up an armload of the pears behind them.

Kelli refused his help and got to her feet. They found they could not fight the incoming stream and followed store employees out the back. A few others trickled out with them. They were in a back parking lot, all of them milling around in shock.

"I should pay for this," Kelli said. She had a crumpled box clutched in her hand. She approached the nearest clerk. "I want to pay for this," she said.

The boy was dazed, but he came into focus when she offered him money. "Thanks, but just take it. We're insured."

Two others refused her money.

"Let's get some coffee," Alex suggested as they threaded their way through an alley and back onto Main Street. They steered clear of the mob. CommCorp was descending with camera drones and reporters, and he did not want the attention.

Alex was able to retrieve his cycle, and in minutes, they were blocks from the grocer. They sat facing each other in a gas station booth, drinking terrible coffee.

Kelli tossed the box on the table between them.

"Might as well tell ya," she said. "Just picking up a pee stick when a riot breaks out."

Alex frowned at the mangled box. *Pee stick?*

He flipped the box over and tried to smooth it out some. He was reading the words, but they had no meaning.

"I'm preggers," she said. "This is just to make sure."

"Preggers," he repeated. It sounded like a word from another language.

"Great time to raise a kid, eh?" she asked, as more emergency vehicles flashed by outside.

"Preggers!" Alex said it with a smile and increasing clarity.

They were going to release their own breed of chaos on the world.

Chapter 38 Grounded

S tu had quit eating at the Golden Hen years ago when he'd found a cellophane strip from a pack of cigarettes in his biscuits and gravy. A thing like that could ruin a place for a man for good. He tried not to judge, but he didn't even trust the coffee he was huddled over. Who knew what lurked in the black of it?

Krystal had called a meeting there. She'd just asked him a question he had no answer to. He sized up his game face reflected in the coffee. "Who's to say?" was the best he could do.

"*You're* to say. You. That's why I asked you."

It was five after seven, though the Kit Kat Klock argued it was straight up seven. Stu fixed his attention on it, willing it to fall silent if not fall off the wall. Its tail wagged on after the meow chime, narrowly missing plants that vined all around it. The clock had apparently come first. The philodendron, growing like a weed, kept its distance from the tail.

"You know the people here. You're a born leader."

"Even if I had an answer, why would I tell you?"

She clicked her tongue and sat back abruptly. The booth hissed around her as she sank into its red Naugahyde. There was the girl he knew. Spoiled. Demanding.

Then she leaned in again, whispering fast: "You'd tell me to save your ass."

Stu adjusted in his seat, raised his eyebrows. He was about to make a comment about his ass when she continued.

"They're overreacting." She said it like he'd know what the hell she was talking about. "I think they were just looking for an excuse. I think that's why they let me stay over."

"Who let you do what?"

"You know, the board." She was talking like they were picking up right where they'd left off, but he had no clue.

Krystal was more frantic than usual. He realized, a bit slow on the draw, that she wasn't made up. Her hair was tied back. She was wearing a blue sweatshirt from the gift shop. It featured a bucking bronco circled with a lasso advertising the Cheyenne rodeo. If she only were to have two hair ties, blue ones with the yellow pom-poms, she'd have been a cheerleader all over again. Coyle Yellowjackets. No, that wasn't it. She was from the city, not Coyle. She was from Guthrie... the Bluejays.

Stu returned to examining his coffee. He had forgotten how to argue with her properly. Shades of Rae crept in around the corners of his mind. He had skirted the morning argument with her by leaving early—when Krystal called. When Rae caught wind of that, there would be hell to pay.

"But to answer your question... well... I don't know, honestly," Stu sighed. It was the truth. "And I don't know why you're interested. *Outside of work?*"

She traced her hand above her brow absently, like she was brushing away hair that was already tied back. Women did that when they were self-conscious. Krystal didn't act self-conscious. Usually.

"Yes, outside of work." She studied his hairline. "Are you Jacked?"

He laughed aloud. The diners across the way looked to see what was so funny. "Never have been, never will be."

He realized then that she was doing something to her Internals with that gesture, maybe shutting something off in her head. He leaned in just a little and asked, "Are you Jacked?"

She rolled her eyes. Of course, she was. "I'm offline," she said, and she seemed to be assuring herself as much as she was telling him.

They looked at their coffee cups and not each other. Stu wondered why she had chosen the Hen over the swanky hotel restaurant. He still wasn't clear why they were meeting at all.

He tried to see the place through her eyes. A dozen diners, all locals, all talk, and no HeadGear. It had to seem pretty lame to her. The walls were covered with local grip and gear, and covering all that, all over the room, were the plants. Gretchen, the mother hen of the Golden Hen, had a green thumb. It wasn't a place he would think to find Krystal Price.

"You know, Stu," she said, getting his attention, "I'm actually very self-aware."

"Are you now?"

"You remember..." She let it hang when the waitress stopped by.

He ordered wheat toast. She ordered eggs, over medium, but with the yolk still soft, and could they cut off the whites. She really just wanted the yolks. Three of them. Two slices of bacon, crispy. Toast. White, not wheat.

Ordering gave her something she needed. She'd bucked up some. "I'm onto myself. I know who I am. Do you get me?"

"I dunno," he said, wondering where this was going. Wondering what it had to do with her big question.

"Stu, I am what I want people to see me be. It's a job. It's a damn *good* job, being the face of TransCorp's Teleportation. I know they call me the White Witch, and I know the corporation plays that up. I don't care. I get more stock the more bitchy I become."

"That's not gonna get you very far out here. You should know—"

"Oh, I know. I told them so. They don't listen." She sipped her water, *served in a glass. No ice. Not tap water, but not chilled either. From a glass bottle, not some plastic bottle. The glass bottle, from the gift shop no doubt, sat on the table proudly. Spring water from France or somewhere.*

"So, you're out here being bitchy, but...?"

She smiled and swallowed his jab. "They amped it up. Way over what they said. I should have known when they wanted me in and out fast. But I asked to stay on. I asked for it, and now here I am. Then nothing happened but a food fight with the Eaters. Then when I was almost murdered last night—"

"That Alex guy says they were gunning for—"

"Doesn't matter. See? That's not the way it works. It's perception."

"Uh-huh."

"They wanted us winning big over ChompCorp, and they got it. They wanted me here for the big standoff with that airship, and I brought it to 'em. But when those guys threatened me with the big guns, professionals, it lit them up. Then it was a whole new story."

"Believe it or not, I get all that. What I don't get is why you're telling me, and why you're asking me about..." he mimicked her now, "*the climate*."

"Because—" she lowered her voice and continued, "because I think it's a rhetorical question. I don't expect you to answer me, really. I want you to think about it. Will your fellas work with the Eaters or not? And more importantly, do you really think you'd stand a snowball's chance in hell, even working together?"

Stu rubbed his chin. He'd not had time to shave.

"Because the answer to that one is a big 'no,' Stu."

"It depends on what you're talking about. Is Trans gonna close the roads, same as Chomp's trying to starve us out? Is Trans gonna send in their militia—" he smiled at that prospect, "—cuz that'd be... colorful."

"In an hour, the Interface will be lit up with lies."

"What's new?"

She shook that off and continued in earnest. "Lies I did not tell. Lies that will bring a lot of heat on Laramie."

Krystal bit her lip and jumped to attention, like she had a new idea. "That's what I'm here to tell you, Stewie. It's not my fault. I know I've been played. I'm always being played. This time, *I think maybe they hired those guys*—for all I know, they might have been actors—but they arranged the whole thing. Staged it. Somehow, they have good footage, *great* vids of the whole thing. It's like they took it off the elevator cams or off one of us in the elevator. It'll be hyped all out of shape."

"And you think it's a setup to justify... what exactly?"

"To justify something I did not sign on for, Stu. I'm great with product roll out and 'more ports for the people.'" She shot him one of her radioactive smiles, quick and insincere. "*This* though... *this* time, I think they let me stay over here to *take me out*. If they'd have successfully bumped me off, even made it look like it... well, it would have set the world afire. I think they were counting on that."

"I think you've been hanging out with Lefty too much. You're getting all conspiratorial."

She pressed on, ignoring him. "But when that failed—because of whatever the hell Winston did in the penthouse—they've grounded me."

"Grounded you?"

"They told me not to leave town. They told me not to leave my room! I dunno if they're playing it off like I'm dead or injured or held hostage or what. I know they're in deep with Comm, so they're going to spin it however they want. I can tell you this, too. It won't make you look too good. They're some real spin doctors, Stu."

"They bein' your board?"

"Yes."

"You're not grounded, Krystal. Nobody's grounded. Rent a car. Take a limo. Just roll out." Stu shrugged. "Besides, there's worse places to be."

"You don't get it. There's *nowhere* worse to be than here."

"Ah c'mon. What could they do?"

She looked away.

It was like she called for the delivery of their food to buy herself some time, for it was brought to the table just then. The waitress went through the questions, "This look good? Need anything else?" Krystal went through her usual complications, asking for a special hot sauce. Touching her egg yolks for consistency and heat. Requesting sand plum jelly, or if they didn't have it, just strawberry.

"Krystal? What could they do?"

"You never hear about it on the Jackchat because we pretty much own CommCorp now. There's things. Bad things. I can't go into it." She looked around like she was worried about eavesdropping. Any other day, she'd no doubt be sneering at the mismatched furniture, judging the place for its "quaint decor." He hated it when folks came into town calling everything "quaint."

"You're as nervous as a cat in a room full of rocking chairs," Stu observed. "You want to go somewhere we can talk?"

She fluttered her eyes, and he felt himself blush.

He went on, "I'm talking about the ranch, not your room."

"There's not much time."

"Right. One hour." The cat on the wall gave them an extra five minutes. "What about a Lead Room. Think we could talk there?"

"There's a Lead Room in Laramie?" she narrowed her eyes.

"Old TurnCoat place," he said. "Just around the corner."

· · · ·

From anywhere in town, tourists could still spot the rebel stronghold. It had been a dumb idea, holing up in a grain elevator, for there wasn't that much practical space to bunk or drill or much of anything else. Like many cities on the plains, grain elevators were the skyscrapers. They formed the skyline.

Laramie had several prominent buildings still standing that contributed to the skyline. ChompCorp had erected one of their ugly prefabs not a block from the elevators, and they, of course, made certain it measured up a little taller.

Stu had sat out the rebellion, but he'd always admired their grit. He'd toured the remains of their fort like any other tourist, and he'd taken visiting friends through it a dozen times.

His buddies on the Force had taken him on behind-the-scenes tours. They'd scaled ladders to the very top and had a few beers up there. They explained—in honest terms—how this stronghold had been brought down. Grain dust. While the tourists heard another story altogether, the truth was a recirculating air handler went down when the power did. Grain dust swirling in an enclosed space like that was volatile. A simple match would have blown the whole joint. Stu's buddies thought maybe a flaming arrow had done the trick. Half the elevator had exploded, and they were never going to get it all picked up. Hell, they invited tourists to take souvenirs of it, and there were still a thousand chunks of concrete littering the lot.

They'd also shown him what they said had been a torture room, explaining the walls were a foot thick, made of lead. The center of the room had a drain and grate just like the one at the Laramie meat locker. Big iron studs were still poking up from the floor where they'd once had a table bolted down. A Lead Room was soundproof, but more, it was CommCorp proof. Lead was the one known substance that thwarted every signal on every device, even HeadGear... even Implants.

Extractors worked in Lead Rooms, prying out Internals, never using anesthetics.

Stu tried to shake it off. The Boys had shared some details too graphic for a morning recall, especially when Krystal was acting edgy. He'd skip the details if she asked.

Leading Krystal through the rubble seemed surreal. Taking her behind the curated displays and on into the depths of the elevator seemed... daring. Had anyone, even a drone camera, been privy to their passage, Stu would have felt dishonest.

Given the circumstances and her sense of urgency, however, Stu felt a little heroic. He was providing a safe place for her to get whatever it was off her chest. He tried not to think about it, but he couldn't help but wonder if she had something very personal to tell him, something about the two of them.

"So here we are," he said, shouldering open a stretch of wall that had seemed like any other wall. The Boys kept a lamp handy for their backstage tours, and Stu felt for it fast, struck a match, and lit it up. The flickering fought back the blackness inside. It fluttered as he pulled the thick door closed behind them.

They were alone in a place no one on Earth could hear them. The privacy of the Lead Room was sacred.

Krystal bobbed on her feet, seemed eager to be in this space with him. She was again the teenage cheerleader. All perky posture and sparkling eyes.

"I thought we were co-opting the Rebels of the Plains, the Eaters out here. I thought that we were really sticking it to one of our rivals, ChompCorp. That was the story they fed me."

He had read her wrong. She wasn't eager to be alone. She was in a hurry to talk. She felt instantly safe in this space and wasted no time filling him in.

"Truth is, they're going to drop the hammer on rebellions before they happen again," Krystal said, "and they're starting with Laramie. They're coming in heavy. I've already seen Port Authority uniforms. *Port. Authority.* 'You heard of that? It's the new TransCorp, bigger, all about the ports now. Coming in hard against the rebels. Oh, there's Eaters everywhere, of course, all over the world, but there's not another place known with such a history of militia groups, paramilitary survivalists, anarchists—"

"I get it."

"And they all pose a threat the corps can't stand for."

"The corps... plural... in spite of the show yesterday."

"That *did* swing us a lot of social capital," Krystal said, "but according to CommCorp ratings, *overnight* the ambush scored even higher, and had even more a direct hit on metrics that mattered."

"The audience loves an ambush."

"Exactly. Are you up on the whole fall of the house of Winston?"

"Uhhhh..."

"Stu, c'mon. Her dad's assumed dead. She's accused of murder. Dad comes back after decades to order her death. Brainwashes the civilized world. That story?"

"I've heard some of it."

"The girl she murdered—allegedly—was a Parker."

"Uh-huh."

"The TransCorp Parkers? Really! Stu, how can you live out here—"

"I know this one," he said. "Just like Ashley Winston, same song, second verse. And now they're framing you up for something?"

"Like my murder at your orders."

The fumes of the lamp made the room squiggle. It was all too heady for him.

"Krys, how stupid do they think folks are? These corporate types need a new playbook. People will figure them out. Murder. Abduction. Absenteeism... People would get savvy to it."

"You're a lot more savvy than you used to be," she said, appraising him.

"I got a kid now. Conspiracy nut. Keeps me sharp."

Krystal walked the perimeter of the room, running her hand along the wall. He'd seen a woman from the charismatic church do that, but with holy water or oil or something. Anointing the room. Surely, she wasn't walking it off in prayer, but she was muttering something.

Eventually she returned to the light between them. She seemed more resolved than even before. "Your kid could probably tell you. A corp fires up CommCorp and anything they say goes without question. They turn towns upside down. They can turn families against themselves."

"The Swipe against the wilds. Civilization against rebellion." Stu shuffled a boot against some debris on the floor.

"Yeah. If the story now goes that I was brutally gunned down by anti-corporate types, Eaters, rebels, whoever they want to throw shade on, well... then you're exactly right. Those *living with* corporations are going to despise those they see as *threatening* corporations. Murdering me would be seen as unforgivable, and it'll bring corps sympathizers together."

"*So, don't die.* Don't roll over and play dead. Wave at a camera. What's it take but that?" Stu shook his head. "You really do sound like Lefty."

She resumed pacing, setting off puffs of dust as she crunched in the debris. "It's not that easy."

"Maybe it is."

"If I play along, I get Severance. More money than you've ever heard of. I could buy your ranch and all of Wyoming, lock, stock, and barrel. If I don't, if I rear up my head for even a sound bite, they'll follow through, and then my murder won't be a sham."

"They already offered you this Severance?"

"They did," she nodded. "And they told me I was more important to them dead than alive... and that told me the rest."

"If I believed a word of it, I'd say you're as good as dead either way. If you fake it and play along, you might be rich, but you'd watch the world burn down because you brought it all on. If they kill you off and keep their Severance, that's cleaner for them. It corroborates their story, *and* you're kept quiet."

She hugged herself and nodded.

"But I don't believe it."

"What?" She took a step closer. "Why?"

"Because I talked to that guy with Winston, Alex, and his story makes yours seem like a joke."

"What could he—"

"His story makes everything Lefty's ever said make sense, actually."

"Oh, come on."

"And if he's right, all this between corporations and rebels is... petty. Those guys in your suite weren't after you, and they weren't from TransCorp. They were after Alex Gault."

"Why?"

"All he'd tell me is he's run out of time."

Chapter 39 Armageddon, Wyoming

L ark rolled over and about fell off the couch. Something was under his hip. A remote control, maybe? No, it was the vial of Tic-Tacs. He held it in both hands as he sat on the edge of the couch, puzzling over it. Krystal hadn't even wanted Tic-Tacs?

The night had folded in on itself after the Spooks. He was sure now someone had spiked their drinks, for he could scarcely remember how he came to be on the couch. Krystal's couch in Krystal's suite. He stood, smoothing out his clothes. He caught a glimpse of himself in a mirror, approached it, and tried what he could with his hair.

He cleared his throat theatrically.

Nothing.

He tried again, then called her name through the double doors that were open to her room.

Nothing.

He peeked in at her bed, ready to avert his eyes or look preoccupied—but she wasn't there. At all.

His suspicions set off alarms in his already aching head. She was gone. Stu's cowboys were gone. Everyone was gone, even Krystal's staff. The whole penthouse was empty.

Lark was pulled from his search by an explosion on the street below. He stumbled to a window closest to the sound and looked out between the drapes. A tornado siren wound up to full from a nearby rooftop. He peered at the clouds. These were not the churning storm clouds of a tornado. The blanket of an overcast sky reflected the colors in the scene below. All across the town, in every direction as far as he could see, red and blue lights were flashing. Thick plumes of rolling smoke rose into the cloud bank. People looked like ants scurrying before a rain.

Another explosion rattled the window he was at, and Lark backed away from it. He sat on the arm of the couch, dumbfounded. *What the hell was happening?*

Concern pushed confusion aside. Krystal. She was out there in all that, stumbling around in her white dress and heels. He just knew it. She would be such an easy target for anyone, for she was not wise to the ways of the world. She would probably take shelter with anyone who offered it, and then—he couldn't think of it.

Or had she been whisked away by Stu Wiebe and his cowboy buddies? None of them were around now. Where had they gone off to? If Stu was one of the Eat the Rich type, then Krystal would be in even bigger trouble. They might have taken her hostage.

He held his greatest fear back as long as he could, but it surfaced all the same.

He hadn't seen a mess like that since Guthrie. Back then, the emergency services from all the surrounding counties, some even from Oklahoma City, had poured in to help. The western edge of Guthrie, the entire golf resort development, was a smoldering mess. It was still smoldering even when they let him out of detention 48 hours after impact. The Guthrie Fall, as it came to be known, was one of the biggest meteor falls in the northern hemisphere. The greatest concentration of damage reached five miles west of town. They'd fenced in the whole thing in a day, and a tent city grew up around it.

Then, a week later, a nuclear warhead exploded east of town, leaving square miles of land untouchable for decades. Part of that stretch had been the Wiebe ranch. That was the last time he had seen Stu Wiebe, in the wake of all that.

History was haunting him. Stu. Spooks. Krystal... it was all pulling into an ugly focus. This time it was further complicated with Eaters and rebels and all these damn corporations bickering.

He looked out the window again. Something he hadn't noticed mixed in with the red and blue emergency strobes: white-blue blinks now and then, bright as lightning. He knew those flashes anywhere, but he couldn't believe he was seeing so many here, now, in Laramie.

Hell's a poppin' so they say.

Armageddon, Wyoming.

Dozens of port flashes, like those from his Hot Wires! Hundreds, maybe.

Lark just didn't know what to make of it. Spooks coming in hot? All of them, all at once, and after what? Who? Alex Gault claimed they were after him. Ashley Winston had said Krystal's giant portal might have brought them around. Lark wondered if they might be after *him* again.

Lark looked around the room. He had nothing. Not a weapon. Not even a change of clothes. He thought he'd lost the HeadGear Gault gave him, but it was tangled in his blankets on the couch.

He put it on his head like it was made of glass. Before he could say a thing, the Stetson hummed a gentle chord, then he was awash in color and soothing sensations. How could it know he was ruffled? How did it know to play Mandolin Bandanna softly in the background? The color wash faded. It was just a glow around the edges of his visor. He could see the room again beyond.

"I'm sorry," a woman's voice said, "Krystalline Price is offline. Whereabouts unknown."

He hadn't even asked, but it was all he wanted to know.

"What do you mean, offline? Can't you do a search or something? When was she last... online?"

"Last known intake, 7am, local, at 104 South Conde. Would you like to see it?"

"What's an intake?" he asked. "Whatever it is, yes, show it."

Colors from the perimeter washed over his vision and painted a disorienting view. Stu Wiebe was in the foreground, plants and plates and colorful decor behind him. He was sitting across a table, frowning at his coffee. The vid ended abruptly with a flesh-toned swath, very close, across his screen.

"What was that?" Lark asked. "Where'd they go?"

"Intake terminated by user."

"She shut it off?"

"Correct."

Why would she shut it off? Krystal wanted a legacy. She was recording her own biopic. The only time in the last decade he had ever seen her without her hat camera, or some HeadGear, was inside the Installation. She said she only shut it off for their conversations.

"Users may opt for reduced telepresence, even numbing nodes by choice or by inebriation," the Stetson explained.

Lark's thoughts flitted over inebriation for a second, and he smirked. *No telepresence could keep up with his lifestyle.* His eyes darted over the scene the machine graciously replayed in a loop. Stu shaking his big head, not making eye contact. He had bad hat hair, and he looked like he hadn't slept a wink.

"Wait. Wait. You said *reduced* telepresence. What's that mean?"

"Only under certain circumstances would a client of this stature be entirely unavailable. It is the policy of CommCorp to retain audio and transcribed records around the clock." The Stetson chimed a little tune, continuing with a jingle: "CommCorp Cares, Everywhere."

"Am I on your Everywhere list?" Lark asked, feeling the weight of his Stetson.

"You are not. Larkin Wayne Fortune, your voice record is registering, but your whereabouts are not entirely known. Your device is not company standard. You are not Jacked."

"Of course, I'm not Jacked," he scoffed. "Now, where is Krystal?"

"Whereabouts unknown."

"You said she was a special customer, that you had her locked in all the time."

"Environmental circumstances have been known to interfere with CommCorp Cares."

Lark was pacing like a caged cat. It was disorienting. "So, the last you have of her is there with Stu?"

"The last capture is the last visual record. Auditory trace continues for eleven minutes, then a corrupted signal has since interfered."

He slumped down on the couch. He didn't think he wanted to hear it, but he didn't think he had a choice. If he was going to find her and help her, he had to hear it all. Even if Stu Wiebe was wooing her away.

Lark didn't need to ask the Stetson to play the audio. It read his biometrics, considered the situation, and began the broadcast before he let out so much as a sigh.

Chapter 40 Sunrise

These islands were getting him nowhere. The Warrior knew that much. He could circle around their shores, patrolling for the shipwrecked Rich the rest of his days. He could paddle from one to another, row from one to the next, do it all over and over again—as he had done for years now—and for what?

Visions in HeadGear offered a more prosperous life. He might somehow migrate to the mainland and find himself, maybe even those he cataloged in his writing. The mainland, if there were one, was out of sight over the horizon, but like so much else, it seemed tangibly close at hand.

The shoreline he was tracing this morning was not familiar. He wondered if he had some time recently drifted to a new hunting ground. This island seemed surprisingly developed. Drain lines snaked to the sea from somewhere farther inland. Solar cells still provided power to lights on a ragged pier at night. A few dwellings on the coast here seemed intact, but as always, they were abandoned and looted.

Other signs suggested recent occupation. One morning he found campfire coals still smoldering. That day he walked especially quietly, his hand always on a pistol butt or sword hilt. That night, he slept very lightly.

The next day he discovered an inflatable power boat, and when he studied over it, he was more and more certain it was the one Katrina Covarrubias had piloted away. By midday, he was following tracks in the sand, confident he was closing in on her.

That night, he did not sleep, but he rested, knowing he might need his energy.

• • • •

"Wake up, mister!"

"Get up!" a second voice commanded.

Several people surrounded the Warrior. He had dozed off. He was cursing himself as he counted them out. Altogether five, and of them, two were old or frail, one or two of them women—he could not quite tell in the darkness. One of them, a larger man, was holding the Warrior's swords, but they seemed too heavy for him. He was resting the tips on the ground.

"What's your name?" one with a rifle pointed at him asked.

"Rory Reed," he said, astonishing himself.

His shock registered as something else with those before him. They cocked weapons and shook them with menace.

"I'm... I'm Rory Reed," he said again, and memories were flooding over him like a torrent on an Interface feed.

"Well, if you wanna live to see the sunrise, you better get explaining yourself," a woman said. She was behind him, pistols in her hands.

He turned to look at her, but the clacking and rustling of weapons again threatened, so he laid back in the sand, his hands where they could see them.

"I'm looking for my friends," he said. "I'm looking for my daughter, Calissa."

"We're all looking for someone," one of his captors said, lowering his weapon.

"How did you come to end up here?" a more skeptical one asked.

"You Rich?"

"You got a boat?"

Rory could hear the edginess in their questions. They were fighting the Just Cause, just as he had been all this time. They were hunting for wealthy swine to sacrifice. He could relate to them, even though he was coming now to know better.

"I'm a hunter," he said, sitting up. "I've killed more Rich than you'll ever encounter."

Two more of them lowered their weapons.

"He don't look like much," another said. "He can't have a pot to piss in."

"Still," the woman behind him said, "Why trust him?"

Rory was processing. He was considering the order in which he could neutralize them. She would be first, maybe second to the one still pointing a rifle at his head. Then again, he could deflect the rifle, grab it by the barrel, use it as a bat to swing at her. With a good power stroke, he might crack her wrists, maybe break one, before she could even get off a shot.

"I'm trained in combat," he warned them and confessed, though he did not know he was trained, and he did not know why he was telling them this. "I was in the rebellion."

"A 'coat?"

"Yeah, Springfield, Texas."

"We're from Houston," the old, frail man said, stepping closer. "That was a while ago."

This was his reason for the confession, he realized. Rapport. "I was at Winter Games. I survived a Smoker."

One of the others took a knee, bared his forearm, and showed Rory a tattoo: 10:1.

Had he already scoped out the tattoo? Was he playing off that kinship? Had he heard something in their language that told him he was of their ilk? He was catching up with himself.

"You're a ways from home," the woman said, holstering her pistols, cross draw style on her hips. "How did you end up here?"

"Where's here, exactly?" he asked.

"Arpeggios off the Canary Islands."

"How did you end up here?" He felt safe in asking the counter question. He needed time to learn his own answer. He did not know if he even knew how he had come to this. Rory's mind was spinning, calculating, mapping the Canaries and the continents, feeling for his own place back in Texas, not Springfield... but Franklin.

They looked at one another but did not respond to his question. Instead, another of them stepped forward, this one the frailest among them, and helped Rory to his feet. The man with his swords returned them to him, relieved of their burden.

"So, how did you end up here?" she asked again, somehow again behind him. He turned in a circle, but her voice led on around. He turned in the sand until he saw her, farther away than he remembered her.

Rory walked toward her, and the others were surrounding him. "I ran aground in a hurricane."

"A hurricane?" one of them asked. "Lucky you survived that."

"Where'd you strike land?" They set out walking down the shore, a knot of dark figures around him in the pre-dawn dark.

"It wasn't land, exactly." He cocked his head, trying to understand the place in his memory. It was like a rubber island, some man-made thing. Vast. Waving with the ocean. Rolling with the tide. Undulating. "It was the *Undulatus*."

A man at his side registered surprise. It was still too dark to tell, but Rory thought this might be the brother in arms with the 10:1 tattoo. "That's a submarine or something?"

"It was an airship," Rory said. "One from Winston Water Works. One they brought down in the Bermuda Triangle."

"A hurricane swamped you on an airship in the Bermuda Triangle?" the old one cackled. "You really *are* lucky."

"That's a ridiculous story," the woman with pistols said from behind him. She poked him in the kidneys. "You have to do better."

"I was there a long time," Rory remembered. "Not quite the Triangle. That was CommCorp hype."

"How long a time? Overnight?" a younger one asked. "Was it like a trampoline? Was it fun?"

"I wouldn't call it fun," he said. When he turned his head to address the young man, he recognized her, a young *woman*, but she was looking straight ahead, as if she hadn't asked a thing. Rory just shrugged and continued, "I was marooned. Alone."

"Nobody there, just you?"

That wasn't quite true, he realized.

"At first..." but he couldn't get to the first of it. He had woken with the dead. Dozens of the dead. Some were his people. He had sorted them out and taken their weapons and waited for something to improve. "It was just me, in the end. For a long, long time, I was alone. Then I swam. I think I died at sea."

They all seemed to find that agreeable, shaking their heads knowingly.

"I was a teacher," one offered. "Before the Eaters, before the storms."

"Bricklayer," another said.

"I was in the service," the kid said.

"I was an Extractor," Rory said.

They stumbled as they kept pace with him, all at once as if they all had felt a tremor he had not noticed. He felt, however, like he had been gut punched.

"That's a rough life," the tattooed man said sympathetically.

"Had to hide it from my girl," Rory said, and a knot formed in his throat.

"Truth comes out," the old man said.

They walked on in silence for a while. The sun was never going to come over the horizon, as if it just waited under the sea. Rory looked out at the gray glow where it should be turning pink—then one of them, the pistol woman, was in his line of sight.

"Ever wonder what we're doing?" she asked, the edge gone from her tone. "I mean, really. Eat the Rich?"

"How many have you killed?" the kid asked.

Rory felt for the ribbons and felt for his beard. All of it was gone. He felt for the wad of papers in his vest but thought better of revealing his notes. "I don't really know. Too many."

It made him nauseous. Any feelings of hunger he had were replaced by this queasiness that would not leave him.

The woman was behind him again, so over his shoulder he said, "I'm done with the mission. We're all Rich in our own right. There's no way to win that fight."

"Let the dead bury the dead," the old man said. He seemed full of wisdom, like an old man should be.

His fellow TurnCoat slapped him on the shoulder. "You're all right, Reed. This battle's done. Let's get in the fray."

"I suppose we ought to get on with it, Sargent Penley," Rory said, and with the name, recognized the man as one who had gone down fighting on the flaming helicopter, the *Feldergarb*.

Rory turned to the kid, the girl, Rose. He'd seen her die in Franklin during the siege. "I killed far too many, kid. I'm sorry for it."

"We're a forgiving bunch," a woman said. "We're all a bit worse for the wear."

"Die another day, Reed," the withered old man said, but in the voice of Rory's old comrade-in-arms, Nick Grimes.

"You've got to forgive yourself now, Rory," she said from behind, a strange accent tinging her words. "You must find it in yourself, as you once found some forgivable thing in me."

The others disappeared as he whipped around to face her. She held her hands up in surrender. It was Katrina Covarrubias.

The nausea faded away.

The sun resumed its rising.

She smiled, "Welcome back."

Chapter 41 Port Authority

Henny pawed another handful of candied popcorn and poured it into his mouth. He was on his second bag. He hadn't had the good stuff like this, sticky caramel and candied nuts, in years. It had to come from some Swipe city, certainly not from the Skirts or the Wild. The whole can of it, a big Christmas tin with elves and kittens all over it, was thrown in on the car deal. The guy at the plant, Peterson, didn't care. "There's sunglasses, probably some junk in the trunk you'll just wanna throw away." He cleared his throat and with a wary look, continued, "How you feel about hot iron?"

Sackerson looked at Peterson, then at Henny.

"Oh. Yeah," Henny said with a bolt of realization. "You left a gu—"

"Yeah. There's a piece under the driver's seat. Extra shells in the trunk."

"And... and you don't want it?"

"Like I said, it's *hot* iron. It's seen some action. I want it as far from me as possible."

"That we can arrange, my good man," Sackerson said.

"Car's a hybrid, but damn thing only runs on gas now," he smiled widely. It wasn't uncommon for locals and rebels to rig their cars for internal combustion only. People called them Poppers. Peterson shrugged, and feigning ignorance said, "I can't figure it out."

"Don't you worry you'll run dry?"

"I don't worry," Peterson said. "I don't worry about *anything*. Why, just today I was wondering how I was going to make rent, and here you fellas show up giving me a ton of cash for that shitbox."

Henny had mulled that over for a good twenty miles. It wasn't a bad way to live, a life without worry. The fella stopped just short of "The Lord will provide," when he was explaining himself. Then again, it reminded him of a song, an oldie from some animated movie he could barely recall. "Hakuna Matata," he sang to Sack.

Sackerson raised an eyebrow. They belted out the chorus together.

"So, Sack. What do you think of Peterson's philosophy of life?"

"Peterson?" Sack asked. Something was consuming more of his attention than Henny was used to. That couldn't be good. Henny wanted him in the here and now.

"The name on the title? Richard Peterson? Didn't you hear what he was saying about fate or whatever? He doesn't worry about anything."

"Hmmmm. Mmm-hmm." Sack was looking out the window.

That was all he had to say. Sackerson could talk for a solid hour about landfills or waste management. He could go on and on about ways to dispose of trash, from launching it toward the sun to porting it into the unknown. When something really mattered though, like whether a guy should live by a plan or live on a whim, he had nothing.

Henny drove on, continuing to process Peterson's whole lifestyle, what he knew of it. He was on what his wife, Darla, called "trickle charge," like a battery. He was juicing up a great conversation to have with Sackerson about living on a prayer versus by the book.

"Ha!" Henny said, suddenly. He thought he might have woken Sackerson from a nap.

"What? What is it?"

"That guy. Helluva name to grow up with, eh? Richard Peterson. Dick. Peterson?"

Sackerson looked at him, annoyed. "I don't get it."

"Wonder what his *middle* name is." Henny gestured toward the glove box. "Think it says on the title?"

· · · ·

"**S**till," Henny said around a mouthful of popcorn, "guys like me don't matter, not in the big picture. Guys like me lie low."

"How can you say that? You went to state all four years in high school football."

"Sack, I can forgive your ignorance. You're not from around here." He swallowed, then fished his bottled water from the console. "Let me explain it to you."

They were driving back toward Laramie. The sun was up, but it was overcast, just the kind of day a guy could get lost. Henny had a hell of a time with his sense of direction. Fortunately, it was a straight shot south for them, open highway all the way.

"Being unremarkable has its merits," he reminded Sackerson. "Like you said, 'gives a guy some anonymousness.'"

"Anonymity." Sack nodded. "Has its privileges."

"You said I was easy to find, but that's because you knew where to look. Otherwise, I'm like the Invisible Man, man."

"Balderdash. A guy like you—*big boned*—you stand out. Had I needed to, I could have found you all over the historical record. I'm sure you broke records in discus. In powerlifting. In wrestling, too."

"No, no, and no. And that's the plight of the plump."

"Plight of the plump," Sack snickered.

"See, we get lumped together in this weight class at the end of the line, like, it just doesn't matter anymore after you're a certain weight."

"How so?"

"Lessee. In my senior year, I weighed 285. Put me on the heavyweights. Problem is, powerlifting pitted me against these guys that were just massive. Same age, same height, but I remember this one fella, Tony Jonas. He must've been over 500 in high school.

Strongest guy I ever seen, to this day. And we were in the same weight class."

"So, it was unrestricted in your weight class, leaving you tough competition."

"Yeah. With impossible odds. Crazy competitors. I'd have to compete with, say, Bart Rodgers from down the road, a big ol' cornfed boy. He weighed 360 or so. He crushed me in wrestling. Guy was like a Sumo."

"Leaving you at a disadvantage."

"Leaving me a loser," Henny said, loading more popcorn. "Way I grew up, second is first last. Nobody's ever heard of Kenneth Hinman, and that's fine."

"What about your bar? That place is a *bounty*. I'm sure you've set some records there, no? I heard you basically brought it up from a dingy dive to what it is today."

"Literally brought it up from the ashes," Henny admitted. "Place burned down a few years after I bought it. Had to start all over."

"There. See?"

"I'm not making it to no CommCorp screens. Too far into the wild for Swipe folk. Nobody's coming around to interview me... and I like it that way."

"Guys like we cleaned up, what you kids called 'Spooks,' they could have found you all along. There is no place low enough to lie that they could not find you," Sackerson said, then switched it up, "So! Might as well live loud and live large. You should have some pride, Kenny Hinman." Sack looked at him knowingly. "Remember? People owe you."

"Only thing I'm proud of in life's waiting for me at home. My girls."

Sackerson turned his attention to the windshield. Henny glanced at him once in a while, wondering how he'd turned off the conversation tap. Maybe Sack didn't have anybody, and he was mulling that over. Maybe he was a lonely old man.

"I could make you famous," Sack said eventually. He was coming at it from another angle. The smile returned to the corners of his eyes, even if his voice did not reflect it.

• • • •

The first phase of the mission, disposing of the Spooks, had been grizzly and strange. Already, Henny felt he was in over his head. Phase two, by his reckoning, was something Sack was making up on the fly.

They sat in the car outside a hotel, a front-row seat to what Sackerson called the Real Showdown, the start of something profound. Henny felt the weight of it. They'd be talking about this one with the grandkids. It reminded him of vids of New York City's streets the day of the twin towers bombing. They'd watched that in American History. This street in Laramie was starting to look like some war-torn blocks of Israel. Except there was no war, no bombing, no tornado... just people acting like it.

"Flames are being fanned, my man," Sackerson said.

"What?"

"See the sheeple out there? They're believing what they see here." Sack pointed to his head. "They're believing their visors and not what's right in front of them. And that is *manifesting* the scene they see projected. Confirmation bias. Wish fulfillment. Call it what you will... It's like time travel a bit. What you see beyond the visor is on a bit of a delay, see? But it *becomes* the scene you're told to expect from the broadcasts over the Interface. Those vids on screen are becoming reality for these people."

Henny shrugged. It was all he had.

"Check it out." Sackerson tapped a button and the windshield inside the car—even this old beater—flashed to a similar street scene, only this one featured looting, stores aflame, and angry men and women rushing in every direction.

Henny looked out his side window. Sack was right. The windshield broadcast was a hyped version of the true scene, an escalation of the scurrying and anxiety he was witnessing.

"You, sir, are going to disrupt this programming."

"Me? What do you want me to do about it?"

"You're here to be heard, Hinman."

"You're a better speaker. You have all the big—"

"I have big words, yes. But you have the *right* words for the right people. I have every confidence in you. I know Lark listens to you."

"Lark... right..." Henny's eyes were tracing up the hotel's exterior. "What's he doing in the penthouse? Lefty Fortune in the top of that joint?"

"He's meddling," Sackerson said. "Someone—wish I knew who—is putting him up to it. I'd bet my beard. He's being set up."

"Set up?"

"Exactly," Sackerson said. "You need to listen to him, really hear him out. Then you gotta talk him down, Henny, talk him down. If you can't talk some sense into him, he's going to make the biggest mistake of his life."

"How do you know?" Henny turned on him. "How do I know you're not setting *me* up?"

"Henny, ask yourself who was there thirty years ago? Who helped you help them back then? Me. Who knows Lark Fortune better than you and me? No one. And why is that?"

"Yeah. Why is that?"

Sack closed his eyes and made a production of shaking his head. "Don't you remember?"

"Bah!" Henny said. "I didn't believe that then, and I sure as hell don't believe it now."

"Suit yourself. The point is, you can trust me. I wouldn't do anything to hurt you guys. It's self-preservation."

"Riiiight," Henny said with doubt. "Besides, talking to Lefty's not gonna stop whatever all this—"

Trucks rumbled through, too loud to speak over. They obscured his view of the hotel. They looked like military transports, big, beefy, all-terrain things in TransCorp gray. It was as close as paint could get to the official titanium of the fancy teleportation terminals Henny had seen on the HeadGear vids. The truck doors featured a logo he had not seen before: an upright rectangle in radiant blue, framing a bold red exclamation point.

Henny looked from the logo to Sackerson, and he did not like what he saw. The old man was riveted, focusing solely on those trucks as they rolled away. His face was ashen, and his wrinkles multiplied.

"Sack?"

"Port Authority," he whispered. "Already."

Chapter 42 The Perch

A shley snugged her aviator cap over her ears to shut out the wail of the tornado siren as it made another pass. Built in HeadGear functionality in the leatherwork activated noise suppression. "End sequence," she commanded verbally, before it could initiate a pastoral view. She cued it to Interface Now, a mosaic broadcast of news, and quickly honed in on the situation.

She hadn't thought it out too well, she realized again. Somewhere a few thousand feet above, hidden in the overcast sky, lurked her airships. She, on the other hand, was stuck below. Given the circumstances, no Nebulosus could sweep down to fetch her with an umbilical. It was far too risky.

She stood on the rooftop of the Grand Marquis. It was a well-developed roof, hosting an open-air restaurant, The Perch, but today, of course, it was largely abandoned. She was surveying the developing mess. She had a version of it streaming in on her HeadGear, and she tried to give both views equal attention.

The CommCorp version showed shiny TransCorp heroes coming in to break up the riotous Rebels of the Plains. The local version of the global scourge, Eat the Rich, were sacking Laramie to hunt down and persecute the beloved Krystal Price.

With her own eyes, Ashley saw a different view. TransCorp soldiers were rushing into Laramie through portals, then fanning out to establish more ports of entry. The portal growth was viral and varied. The first were little more than Hot Wires, but as more and more troops arrived, more elaborate ports were erected. Equipment was being ferried through. Massive weaponry was rolling into Laramie through portals larger than garage doors. Even larger machinery arrived when portals larger than hangars were hastily propped up. Soon, the city was overrun with militarized TransCorp personnel.

The HeadGear version had a running narrative that was not filled with screaming and gunfire. It was scrubbed of sirens and explosions. According to their story, TransCorp was acting swiftly and justly on good information. Miss Price, and therefore the civilized world, was endangered by rebellion. TransCorp was moving in as a peacekeeping force.

Local law enforcement, as well as the Eaters and the Boys, had receded into the background. Ashley wondered where they were hiding, but she understood why. They were going to have to unite to have a prayer in this battle.

CommCorp continuously emphasized that this was a peaceful takeover, for the good of the citizens. It was foremost an effort to find Krystal Price and bring her captors to justice.

One commentator proposed this was, "a protective measure keeping predatory corporations from taking advantage of the poor community ravaged by rebels. TransCorp is bringing sanity and consistency to a wild west town."

• • • •

At the helm of Winston Water Works, Ashley had become a competent armchair meteorologist. She knew the storms her ships caused, and she knew what everyone referred to as "Naturals," which continued to roil around the planet. The heavy overcast was all natural that day. Had the weather been clear, she wondered if TransCorp would have been so bold. Would CommCorp have such a confident grip on HeadGear broadcasts if there was not such heavy cover over the region? Others could send in their own drones and get a completely different perspective.

Ashley considered rallying her armada to push the darkness away with their own front. She even consulted a few captains circling high above. Yes, it could be accomplished over the course of days. Nebulosus vessels were not full-on Rainmakers, however, and it would not be as dramatic as Ashley was imagining. She wanted her airships to pull back the Naturals and reveal a brighter tomorrow. She wanted a prominent presence from Winston Water Works that could remind TransCorp and CommCorp that they were not the superpowers they might think themselves to be.

Her captains went so far as to suggest pulling a Cumulonimbus off-route from the Rockies. Though it would take a while to arrive, it could sweep the sky in its wake. They also suggested it could be weaponized if it were to fly low and slow.

She was not trying to make a statement like that.

A clock tower chimed that it was ten o'clock. Ashley confirmed it in her HeadGear display. She was astonished she had been pacing so long, sizing up the situation from every angle.

Some hotel staff, though alarmed, remained professional and frequently came up from the hotel with food and drink. Ashley recognized it for what it was. They needed an excuse to survey the city.

Hotel guests would come and go from tables at The Perch, sipping coffee from paper cups. These patrons expected waitstaff to meet their needs, and the few who were around did their best. Tablecloths flapped in the wind. Guests pulled coats up tighter, yet otherwise ignored their environment. They acted like the world was not crumbling around them. It reminded Ashley of stories she had heard about people on the Titanic. Denial.

"What happened to the sirens?" a server asked, as casually as he could. He was a guy in his twenties, maybe. His Marquis jacket was haphazardly buttoned. His nametag—pinned on upside down, no doubt in a rush this morning—read William, but she could call him Willy. He was her most frequent attendant. He had recognized her even last night, obviously a big fanboy, but he was too professional to ask for an autograph.

"This closest one was shot up hours ago," Ashley said. "The last one wound down just a bit ago."

"That's a blessing," he said. "So loud early-on I thought it'd blow me off the roof."

They stood looking west. Though he had brought her another coffee, he had forgotten himself and was drinking it. She didn't care. He needed it more than she did. His eyes were red rimmed. He had a shy smile they had almost trained out of him, and Ashley liked it. Poor kid was probably worried sick.

"You have family in town?" she asked.

"No, just me. I'm laying out a semester. Got a job here in Laramie to save up." It seemed to help him to talk about the mundane. Earlier they had talked about the weather. Another visit had been about how symmetrical the town looked from up above.

"Where did you tell me you go to school?"

"Garden Seminary, down in Denver."

"Seminary," she repeated. "Are you going to be a preacher?"

"I like the mission work, mostly. Garden gives us lots of field time."

She wondered what the field time was like. Soup kitchens? Ministering to the homeless? She wondered what he would have thought of Franklin and the hard cases she'd encountered there.

And she wondered what a nice boy like that was doing sidling up to her.

"Where do you stand on Eat the Rich?" she asked before she could stop herself. Talk of the movement cleaved the well-intentioned from the nutjobs in a quick slice, by her reckoning.

Willy raised an eyebrow and took a sip. "I wish the gap wasn't so wide, the rich and poor."

A TransCorp truck moved by below, rumbling loudly. They both looked over the brick parapet as it passed.

"Did you know they could do that? Transport whole armies like this?"

Ashley shook her head. "No, I had no idea."

But she did know. She had known for five years. Sarah Dawn Parker had warned her of such things. War was coming, Sarah had said. Get ahead of it, she had said. She had proposed an alliance between her family company, TransCorp, and Ashley's 3dub. She had promised they would make millions and show the patriarchs where they could stick it.

Ashley tried to think of anything but the last image she had of Sarah Dawn Parker—a gutted, bloody mess sprawled out on a mess hall table. A sacrifice for the machinations that seemed now to be coming true.

"You got a car, Willy?" Ashley asked.

"I have a bike," he offered. "Electric."

"I'm sick of the view. You think we could go for a spin?"

It was another sorting question. Was he one to be contained by TransCorp patrols, or was he a guy that wanted to race through Laramie with her at his back?

He tossed aside his coffee cup and smiled like a kid at Christmas. "Let's ride!"

Chapter 43 Thawing Out

K rystal laughed. "Really, Stu. That's ridiculous."
He had rattled on for a frenetic half-hour, but she'd heard him out. It was a sci-fi fairytale, but she couldn't remember a time Stu Wiebe had believed anything with such wholehearted zeal.

His plan, his happy ending to the story, however, was nothing short of stupid.

"It's genius. We gank the goons, go back to Guthrie 2028, stop the problem before it starts."

"That's what Ashley's friend suggested?"

"No, no, it's my plan. I ran it by Gault. I thought about it all night."

"That guy's crazier than Lark. I don't know why you even—"

"If I could be there, that night of the God damn meteors, maybe I could blow up the one with all the Tic-Tacs. If there never was a Tic-Tac, there'd never be all this."

She knew what he really believed, that just maybe he could go back then and stop the clock their senior year. Stop the bomb. Restore his life and ranch and his teenage dreams. The guy needed a reality check.

"Even if you could travel through time, haven't you seen the movies? You can't be in the same place as your younger self. There'd be some kind of time warp or something, a black hole, the world would melt like a Dali clock."

"I don't think so."

"And... hell-o... TransCorp manufactures ports from *synthetic* Tic-Tac tech now, Stu. The meteor doesn't matter anymore."

"I don't think you understand time travel."

"Like you do?"

"Nah," he said, kicking at some bolts in the floor. "I don't. But I do think even half a chance of stopping things would be worth a try."

The lamplight softened his craggy features, painted him in gold. He looked like a quarterback who had just lost his last game. If she remembered right, he never got to play his last game, not even his last season, due to all that happened that year in Guthrie.

She put a hand on his shoulder. He pulled her close. They held each other, first in an awkward embrace, but then, it melted into a long-lost comfort. She pressed her cheek against his chest. He laid his head against the top of hers.

Then he ruined it all by patting her back.

If only he had stroked her shoulder or held her tighter. Instead, a back pat, a "you'll be okay," patting of her back he could have given anyone, even a man. Even in his culture.

She started to pull away, but he didn't really quite let her, did he? His other arm wound around her lower back, snugged her up against him like he had in those high school slow dances. His back patting turned to a full-on hug.

"What're we going to do?" he asked.

What was he asking her? Her mind was racing. The hug, burrowed deep in his wool and leather coat, felt so good, so right. She frowned, chewed her lip in thought—then the pain reminded her once again of the punch Mrs. Wiebe could pack.

Krystal broke the hug and stepped back clear of him. "We're going to the last place anyone would expect me to hide out. How's that?"

"I... uh... me and the Boys got a place out on the property. Call it the Springs. We could stash you there a while."

"Let's do one better. Put me up at your house."

"Whoa, whoa, whoa. I don't know if—"

"Exactly. Nobody'd believe it."

"Krystal, I believe you met my wife. She's not exactly your biggest fan."

"Yeah... well..." She didn't even know why she liked this plan herself, but it seemed like the right thing to do. "She'll warm up to me."

Stu was shaking his head. "I dunno..."

"And I've never met your kids."

That set strangely on his features. He looked away. "I only have the one kid. A teenager."

She felt something come over her that felt a little like guilt. "Stu, we've gotten too far apart. I've never talked with Rachel, never even met your kid... your teenage kid."

In light of all the chaos brewing, she felt propelled to keep talking. "Can't travel time, but we can make up time. I want to make it right. I want to make up the last twenty years. I want to get to know you again. You and your family."

"Krystal, I..."

"I know Lark lots better than you anymore."

"You do visit him every year."

"And I don't want to sound like a drama queen, but things are going to shit here. We don't know what's next. I want to make amends while we can."

Stu was shaking his head again, but she also saw a hint of a smile. Maybe he was thinking of the meet up. She was. Maybe he'd grab his wife from behind and hold her until she wasn't ready to swing.

"You'll like Nat," he said at last. "My kid."

"Bit of a rebel like ol' dad?"

"Nothing like his dad," Stu said, then faltered. "But, you know... I guess maybe he is a bit."

"I look forward to meeting him, then."

"Except, there's this thing. He's not comfortable being a he." Stu squirmed, but continued, "His birth name is Nathan, see, but he's—"

"It's okay. If Nathan's more comfortable being Nat, that's fine. I'm from the city now, remember? I can navigate that, no problem."

Stu sighed. "Some of the Boys won't know what to do with you around. Like at dinner. They'll be embarrassing themselves."

"Any of them from the old days?"

"A handful. You'll know them when you see them. I'm sure they'll introduce themselves. Thoroughly."

"Great. Let's do it."

Krystal wasn't sure how to bring the conversation to a close. It wasn't a business meeting, after all.

"Great," he said, and he extended a hand.

They shook, but then held hands a little longer.

"Stu, I..."

"You're too skinny."

"I'm what?"

"To make it out here." He smiled. "You'd have to beef up some to suit any man in his right mind."

"That's the first time I've ever—"

"And you need some fat on you for the winters, too. If you want to hide out in Wyoming long, you better start eating."

She smiled back but didn't know what to say.

"Yep, another twenty pounds and you might turn some heads."

She chuckled. "I might, huh?"

"Maybe, once you thaw out some."

· · · ·

As he pushed the wall open to the Lead Room, they could hear sirens, a mix of them. One was the long, mournful wail of a tornado siren. She immediately swiped at her forehead and tapped her temple. Nothing. They'd shut her off completely.

Stu was looking over an appliance he wore on his wrist. It was battered and scratched, but the screen display was scrolling text quickly. "Reports coming in all over. People being pulled right outta their pickups. Everyone's told to stay home. Look at this."

She read a warning screen in red and black, ordering everyone to stay indoors. "*Quarantine?*"

"That's only so much bullshit," he said, fanning the screen for more news. "There's nothing on the national feeds. What I can catch, anyway. Nat sent me something, looks like just a minute ago. Says CommCorp is shutting down."

"I'm blacked out. Unplugged."

"They can do that to your Internals, even?"

She really didn't know. This was the first time it had ever happened. She nodded her head, "I guess so. Can I try yours?"

He was removing his wrist appliance when a ringing in his coat pocket stopped him. Stu pulled out an antiquated phone and smiled at her sheepishly. "Still works," he said, holding it up to his ear.

She endured his one-sided conversation. Someone was updating him. Asking him for directions. "Get the Boys to the Sp—to the rendezvous. See if you can run by some of their places in case they're offline."

He looked at Krystal, though he was now listening to his phone.

The alarm in his features was tempered with a maturity and sense of command she admired. People were counting on him. She was coming to count on him, too.

"And Schmidt?" he said. "Don't leave anybody behind."

Chapter 44 Tropes

A lex had arrived at his own brand of chivalry over the years, and it was what he called, in his mind anyway, *graduated chivalry*. If a woman wanted to be treated like a man, peer-to-peer and toe to toe, he could do that. If she wanted a concession now and then, even tolerating a courteous opening of a door, that was easy to adapt to. If he met a woman like Krystal Price, he knew at once she was in full-on Southern Belle mode, and he'd pour on the syrup.

Kelli Chase, however, was a new animal now. When they first met, she was as much a man as he was. She was Cap'n Chase, and "my eyes are up here." She had no tolerance for his humor, no matter how gender neutral, and she had even less patience for his quirkiness.

It had taken years for him to reach a comfort level with her. In that time, the years of warming up, he had accidentally fallen in love with her. Eventually, after more years of coercion, she accepted him, and finally agreed to marry him.

And now, she was carrying his child. Something only a woman could do. She deserved to be treated differently. *Special-issue* graduated chivalry.

"Easier in Franklin," she was saying. "City square, depot. Now that was a natural rally point. This place, from what I can tell, is lacking. Depot here is just a freight station. There's not a square. There's not a stockyard or anything much."

They were walking in the open down the middle of a street, side by side. The road was closed now, and few people were out. Those who remained outside looked at them like they were aliens. Some well-intentioned locals warned them they were to get off the streets.

Orders.

Quarantine.

At first, Alex had been good natured about it, thanking them for their concern. As they came to interrupt the conversation more often, Kelli would simply draw her pistol or snarl a curt "Piss off" to steer them away.

They endured the passes of the tornado siren, talking over it otherwise when it was rotating over the rest of the town. Once or twice someone in gray fatigues would give them the eye, but Kelli's commanding presence seemed enough to turn them away. *These two must have good reason to be out here*, they seemed to assume. *They must be with us.*

"Years ago, 'Coats stood up a line down at the elevators," Kelli continued. "We could hole up there. See if we can get some local support from those cowboys you were going on about."

Alex entertained the idea of the Boys following her lead. It didn't seem likely. They seemed the type to follow any man before they would a woman, and from experience, Alex knew that was misguided. Even their local leader, Wiebe, had no background to compare to hers.

"Don't you think?" Kelli asked.

"About the cowboys?"

"Yeah, and a call to Franklin."

"The cowboys... around here, they're like a local militia, call themselves The Boys."

"That's *creative*," she said sarcastically.

"From what I've seen, and that was just last night, mind you, they're all about protecting their own, but they have a leadership hierarchy already in place." He was stretching it a little. He knew she was seeing right through it. "Their guy, Wiebe, he's all right. Met him last night."

"What about bringing up reinforcements?" She looked around. "Looks like we might need them."

Not far ahead, gray-clad men and women were rolling out fencing. Others were driving posts. They were enclosing an elementary school.

"That's going to be their base?" Alex asked. It didn't look like much.

"Detention," she surmised. "That's a perimeter fence, I'm betting. It's to keep folk in, not hold them out."

"How can you tell?"

"It's flimsy. It's short. It's a line in the sand for whoever they lock up. Hell, I could practically clear that in a good jump."

"You hadn't better try anything—"

She flashed on him before he even realized his mistake, but he tried to wheel about on it.

"—until we get some help here."

Rule number one: do not suggest her delicate condition would inhibit her badassery. Alex knew better, on any occasion, but now it was obviously going to be a sensitive subject.

"YOU TWO," a woman in uniform shouted, "off the streets. Get to your home or to shelter, immediately."

Kelli stopped and whirled at the voice. "By whose orders?"

"Port Authority," the woman snapped back. She nodded at the others gathering with her. She smiled a challenge. "We're peacekeepers."

"Peacekeepers," Kelli snarled, but she took off for the far sidewalk, dragging Alex by his hand. She was grumbling curses under her breath. She put a few more paces between them and hollered, "We're going. We're going. *Peacefully.*"

Alex didn't look back. The gravity of the situation doubled on him, and an icy realization hit him. They couldn't pop off and throw down like they always had before. There was more at stake now than ever before.

There was Alex, Jr. to think about.

"C'mon," Kelli said, tugging him into a gap between houses.

Once they were in the shelter of the houses and hidden by some shrubs, Kelli pulled him to her and planted a kiss on him that left him seeing stars. She pushed him against the house and said, "I love you, Mr. Gault."

"I love you, too, Mrs. Gault."

"We're not going to die out here in BFE, Wyoming. Got me?" She was in full on combat pep-talk mode. He knew to listen attentively, but he wanted another one of those kisses.

"Got you, lambch—"

"My situation, our new... *status*... cannot get out. Sure, maybe family, maybe Ash, but otherwise, no. Nada."

"Okay," he said.

"And for the record, I've had a day or two to think about this, and I know the tropes. We're going to beat the system."

"The... tropes?"

"The story. The drill. The way it always seems to go. A girl gets knocked up, and all the sudden she's made of glass or something. People treat her like she's fragile, and next thing you know, something bad happens. She gets broken."

"Nothing's going to—"

"You're damn right it isn't. I'm not fragile. Nothing's breaking me."

"That's right," he said firmly, taking her cue.

"And I'm not going to be some object lesson, either. You know, get shot up and die pregnant. Last thing I want at my graveside service is someone saying, 'a woman's place is in the home.'"

Alex thought that anyone who would say such a thing would be haunted by her ghost for an eternity.

"And I'm not going to lose the baby."

"Good."

"I'm barely pregnant. It's not like I'm in my third trimester or something."

"Right."

"I know women who work right up until they deliver. I had a girlfriend who was teaching yoga on the day she birthed twins."

"You'll be the same, I'm sure."

"I'm telling you all this, so you won't fawn all over me, or do something stupid trying to *overprotect* me. I'll still be watching *your* six, right up to my due date, mister. Got it?"

"Got it."

"You'll treat me like you always have?"

"I promise," he said.

"So, job one never changes. We protect Ashley. We protect each other. We get the hell out of this town alive and intact."

"Yes, but..."

She wilted some. "But you have a plan?"

"I have a *mission*," he said, perking up despite her eye roll. "We can't just let the corps roll over this burg. We can't even just set them up and move on."

"I can't say 'this isn't our fight,' can I?"

He shook his head. "It's just the start. It's everybody's fight."

"So, we need a place to bunk," she reasoned. "I'll call in my people, but we have to secure something for them before they get here."

"It took us eight hours by airship," Alex threw in. "Think we have that kind of time to float up Franklin?"

She pointed to a blue flash in the distance. "We could port them."

He chuckled.

She was eyeing him again fiercely.

"I guess it's not impossible," he said. "There's nothing in Franklin for them to catch, but in Springfield... there's got to be a port we could use."

"Ashley's portal," Kelli said with a firm nod. "I'll tell her we need to commandeer it."

The siren washed over them, giving Alex a moment to collect himself. The thought of Franklin's finest trudging through 3dub executive offices was almost too much. In the siren's wake, Alex continued talking, "Comms are spotty. I've tried. I can't raise her."

"*You* can't even raise her? Right here in town?" Kelli's astonishment was fair. He was the most technologically advanced of them, and Ashley was almost always Jacked in.

"I can *follow* her, but I can't get a ping."

"So, where is she?"

"More like, where isn't she?" he said. "She's been ripping around town for hours. If anyone's going to have a good bead on Laramie, it's going to be her... whenever we catch up with her."

"You can't get a line out on the Interface? Can't scare up Kyle or her lab buddy or—"

"Zana and Astar?" Alex completed. "I've been looking for a radio, asking around a little. Even if I can reach them, they're not too keen on ports, or on 3dub. They're not going to be much help on Ashley's portal."

Kelli looked at him, waiting for him to catch up. "*They're family.* Gramma and Grandpa Amin," he said with a smile. "They're going to love this."

They continued their hike through a residential neighborhood, now keeping to the alleys. Peacekeeping had yet to spread that far. Kelli tried again and again to raise her people in Franklin. Comms were spotty, indeed.

As best as he could track Ashley, Alex laid in an intercept course.

They had a lot to catch up on.

Chapter 45 Listening

Henny had to talk sweet to the maid to get let onto the Penthouse floor. Fat guys didn't need a way with women, he knew. It was enough to be affable. He liked the word, "affable," and had told Darla and the girls he wanted that on his headstone someday: Kenneth R. Hinman, an affable guy.

The elevator opened onto a wide hallway with a huge room at the far end that was all glass, looking out over the town. As he passed each alcove to the other rooms, he marveled. One was a sitting room, complete with a chaise lounger affair he always thought Cleopatra would sit on. Another alcove opened onto a nice-sized room that had French doors heading into an enormous bedroom. Henny whistled at that.

"Who's there?"

It was Lefty's voice, slurred like it got after hours. Henny looked at his wrist appliance. It wasn't even noon.

Lefty had crashed on a big couch in the media room. Henny walked in, took a pass through the room, muted the HomeRoom screens, then sat on the coffee table near Lefty.

The guy didn't look too good. He had a Stetson half-cocked on his head, and he was, indeed, drunk. He'd slept in his clothes, and at one point, he'd either tried taking off one shoe or had given up after putting one shoe on. The extra shoe was beside Henny's hip, on the coffee table.

"Rough night?"

"What do you want?"

Henny raised an eyebrow. "Anything seem... odd to you?"

Lefty pried off the Stetson and sat up a little. "Nope."

"Do you even know where you are, Lark?"

"Nope."

"Laramie, Wyoming." He paused, but it did not seem to register. "In Krystal Price's penthouse suite."

"Uhhhhh," Lefty groaned and cursed. He looked over at the bar. Henny followed his gaze. Two decanters had been drained. A third was toppled over.

"What's the special occasion?" Henny asked. "That's some high-end hooch."

"Hooch," Lefty repeated, half-smiled at the term.

"So, you going to tell me what you're doing here?"

"Drowning my sorrows," Lefty said. "Same as always."

"I mean *here*, here, in Krystal's place."

"I'm here to help her out. 'Least I thought I was." He groaned again and covered his face with an arm.

"What is it this time? Aliens? Your dad's ghost again?" Henny pushed a blanket out of the way and joined Lefty on the couch. "Spooks?"

He waited.

Bartenders have a sixth sense when it comes to conversation. Henny could have led a seminar on waiting. Sometimes the wait was measured in shots, other times in jukebox songs.

"She's got her sights on Stu Wiebe," Lefty finally stated.

Henny chuckled. That was an unlikely pair. "Her. And Stu? I don't see that ever happening."

"Already underway," Lefty said, swinging an arm at the Stetson. "Heard it myself."

"You heard what yourself?"

Lefty sighed and let his head loll back on the couch.

"She's *confiding* in him." He made it sound like they were having sex on the street. "She's telling him everything."

Henny wondered what everything could even be. What was there to the White Witch other than showboating for the company? Of the four of them, she had sold out. Completely.

Lefty moaned.

"Dude. Really." Henny tried to get him to quiet down.

"She bought out the whole place. Only people here are her people. If you got the Penthouse, you can make all the noise you wanna."

Henny shrugged. He saw the reasoning in that.

"So, you were... eavesdropping on them with the Stetson?"

"A replay," he said. "Her last conversation before things went haywire."

"Can I... maybe?"

"Sure," Lefty said, nudging the device his way. "You can have it."

Henny Jacked-In and listened attentively. There was a joke about her place or the ranch. There was some playful banter, maybe a little suggestive. It was hard listening to Krystal's voice, for she was really upset. It was harder yet for Henny to listen to Stu, however, for it brought back bitter memories.

"So," Henny said, "they went to the Lead Room at a grain elevator. They had a talk. Who the hell cares?"

It was his tough love routine.

"I care," Lefty said. He was tying his shoe. The laces were in a knot.

"Need me to do that?"

"I'm right here, Henny. Right here," he chuckled, bitterly, continuing, "*in her suite...* and she drums him up to talk to. What the hell is that about?"

"Maybe since she's in his town, she thought he'd have—"

"She sneaked out of the hotel and didn't say a word to me."

"Lefty—Lark, buddy—she doesn't owe you an explanation."

"Now she's out there in that!" he turned to the HomeRoom screens and continued. "CommCorp told the whole thing."

Henny fought back his skepticism. "What whole thing?"

"Just lookit!" Lefty struggled to his feet, then studied the walls of broadcasts. "At one level, it's all what it should be, a lily-white portrayal of this whole thing. There's your world news, served up with regional biases, of course. There's current events—so long as they're the events we're supposed to see. CommCorp is a subsidiary of Trans now, you know that?"

"No, I..." Henny tried to stay engaged. He tried to figure out how his mission was to play out in this conversation, but in the back of his mind, he was thinking less of Sackerson's scheme.

"Below the surface, however, it gets interesting."

"Mmm-hmmm."

"Laramie, Wyoming. See?"

Both walls lit up with protesting and mobs, with fires and violence. Much of it was blurry, fast-paced stuff, obviously from HeadGear feeds. Somewhere in town, apparently, things had gotten much more violent. Locals were being herded into fenced in areas, and even then, they had to be contained by soldiers in gray. Henny wondered how much of this was really happening, how much was fabricated. He opened his mouth to bring up the talk Sackerson had just had with him about it, about the Port Authority, but Lefty continued.

"Watch the editing. I'm convinced, more and more, that some CommCorp editors are with us. They leave breadcrumbs all the time. This one, over here now... see the focus on the signs those picketers are holding. It's crystal clear, where the others are blurred. Riiiight now. What's that say to you?"

Henny squinted at the screens. Lefty had gestured a freeze frame. He gestured again now, and two screens moved in front of the rest. He gestured them together. Half of one picket sign fused exactly with the other. Different ink, different lettering, but a cohesive message: "*Beware the Port Authority,*" Lefty read aloud.

Henny stood and approached the screens, looked at Lefty, the screens again. Sackerson had just shared the most nightmarish stories about the Port Authority. Their logo was rolling around Laramie on everything with wheels.

"What else you got?" Henny asked.

"I knew about the airship before Krystal took it out."

"Oh, how could you—"

"I'll prove it!" Lefty commanded both HomeRooms into action. Some screens featured redacted transcripts. Others were playing vids on short loops. Captioning on those loops repeated phrases, every channel, every format. It was either a complexly woven edit, or it was quite clearly forewarning Chomp to desist or lose both ship and crew.

"So," Henny asked when Lefty finally wound down, "what's next?"

"Proof of concept," he said. "Make an example of Laramie. Subjugate other corporations. All of 'em. Take the whole pie."

It seemed too possible. If TransCorp, now Port Authority, could dominate like it had been projected, it could all be coming true. Henny wriggled. The cold shudder meant someone was walking on his grave, at least that's what his momma had once said. Never mind that he didn't even have a cemetery plot.

"So," Henny carefully asked, as per Sackerson's orders, "What are you going to do about it?"

Lefty stood at the bar, longing for a drink. He righted the decanter and corked it. "I'm going to leave this town while I still can."

Henny was surprised. *Where was the crazy idea to regret?*

"I'm going to kick Wiebe's ass and take Krys with me. If I have to, I'll kidnap her."

Ah. There it was. Henny took off his big coat and draped it over the arm of a chair. He flexed his shoulders, had a good stretch.

Though his bouncer days were far behind him, he knew he could settle down Lark Fortune. He'd done it a dozen times at *Sharts* over the years.

Lefty frowned at him. "What?"

"Oh, nothing."

"You don't think I'll do it."

"I don't think you'll whip Stu Wiebe, that's for damn sure."

"He's not as big as he looks on screen, you know."

"Mmmmm-hmmm." Henny turned his attention to the vids, but he kept an eye on Lefty. He was goading him to keep talking by faking disinterest.

"You don't think I'd take her?"

"I think you're not thinking this through. She's at the heart of a corporate empire," he said. He pointed to a screen montage of gray trucks and soldiers. "*That* empire."

"She's trapped, Henny. Poor girl's already held hostage, and she doesn't even know it. Stock market syndrome."

"Stockholm syndrome?" Gail had been bringing home her psych homework and some of it had stuck. "She's in love with her captors?"

"Stock market syndrome," Lefty continued. "She's so deep in the company, gets so much from it, she's blinded by it. It's not her fault things are turning out like this. It's her board. They own her."

Henny crossed his arms. It was never easy like for a skinny guy. He generally settled for stacking them over his barrel chest. *Don't speak*, he knew. *Let him see how foolhardy it is.*

The whole plan was just insane. They wouldn't even get in a car before Port Authority people would put a stop to it. Though Lark Fortune never wore a wire, never had an implant, Henny figured Krystal's head was stuffed with Implants. They'd be able to track her easily.

All that was assuming she even wanted to get away. He couldn't hold it in any longer. "Lark. You're drunk. You're just not—"

"I am not drunk, Ken," he said sternly. "I'm lit up, sure. I'm... I'm resolved, that's what I am."

"Okay. Okay. You're resolved, but have you thought about this? Really? First, you gotta find her."

"HeadGear."

"Then you gotta talk her into going with you."

"She trusts me."

"Oh, and you gotta have a way to get around."

"She's got money *and* connections."

"Have you been paying attention?" Henny gestured at the screens. "Interface has her as MIA. They're blaming the Rebels of the Plains. Doesn't that seem a little fishy when you know she's with Stu Wiebe?"

"He's probably one of them."

"You know better than that." Henny had his issues with Stu Wiebe, plenty of issues, but he knew him to be a straight shooter.

"So... maybe they have some doublespeak going on, between them and CommCorp." Lark offered. "I bet they concocted all that to slip her out of town. That just means I gotta move faster, get to her before they do."

"You're going to get to her before that whole swarm of soldiers?"

"I got an inside line." Lefty pulled an antique cell phone from his pocket.

"What the hell is that?" Henny laughed. "Get that at the pawn shop?"

"Some suit gave it to me, said it was off grid. A private line Krys keeps."

"For what? Ordering pizza?"

"I dunno, the guy said..."

"The guy's a scam artist. What'd he make you pay for that thing?"

"Gave it to me, last night downstairs at the bar."

"Some random guy has her private line? What could it possibly be for? Think about it, man." Henny continued, "Phone sex? Booty calls?"

Lefty looked at the phone. He clearly did not like that idea.

"I'm just saying, don't embarrass yourself. Wait her out. She'll come back, and you can talk to her then. Maybe sober up some before she gets here. Maybe, I dunno, take a shower?"

"I could use a shower..."

"Dude. She trusts you. She needs you but not you scrappin' with Wiebe and running around town with some half-baked plan."

"But... but you heard her, yourself," he pointed again at the Stetson. "*She's scared.*"

"Stu'll get her back here safe."

"Maybe." Lefty looked at the phone, at Henny, back at the phone. "You're right. Dumb idea."

He pocketed the phone.

Crisis averted.

Lark Fortune's tattered integrity remained intact. *No embarrassing attempted kidnapping today.*

Henny sighed and turned to the bar, and by instinct, began arranging the cut crystal ware. Lefty was quietly looking at the wall screens. Though sirens were wailing, and people were rioting outside, in the Penthouse, for the moment, all was right with the world.

Henny dropped some cubes in a glass. He liked that sharp, bell-like tinkle. He looked at the bottom for a brand. He'd have to get some like this for special occasions.

Then he saw Lefty with the phone to his ear.

"What are you *doing*?"

"Just checking in with her," he winked. "Nothing stupid."

Chapter 46 Interrupting

Stu tried call after call as they walked back toward the Grand Marquis. Gray trucks were thundering past them. Troops were assembling at intersections and stationed at storefronts. The downtown public address system, little used since HeadGear came into fashion, was announcing repeatedly that Laramie was on lockdown. "For your own safety, return to your homes and take shelter immediately."

"This what you expected?" Stu asked Krystal over the din.

She kept her head down, pulled her collar up, and did not make eye contact with anyone. He could see the fear in her eyes, and it surprised him. Krystal Price was as sure-footed as they came.

Three men in gray uniforms stood around the front of the hotel, so Stu led Krystal around the side, then the back. The one woman on duty there was marching off the back of the building, and they timed it just as she was patrolling the opposite direction. They slipped inside.

The place was swarming with Port Authority personnel. As soon as Stu realized this, he turned on his heels and led her back outside. The woman on duty saw them but didn't make anything of it. They were coming *from* the hotel, the *heavily guarded* hotel. No threat.

Stu tipped his hat as they passed her and moved on. His pickup was in a side lot. Maybe they could take back streets and clear town without encountering a roadblock.

They were walking arm in arm, so they might look the part of a couple, but also so they might stay together and move quickly. Stu was impressed with her gait and endurance. They'd walked a mile or more from the elevators.

The lot with his truck was just ahead, around a bend. He slowed some, so they could speak. "Holding up okay?"

"Yeah," she said. "I'm *so sorry* I brought this down on you. On your whole town, Stu. Coming here, the standoff with Chomp, it was all a terrible idea."

"You didn't plan it," he said. "Don't own another man's mistakes."

"Still..." she said. She looked up at him, tearful. "Laramie was my idea," she confessed. "We could have fought Chomp anywhere in the Midwest. I wanted to see you again."

They were rounding the corner. His pickup was in sight.

His phone was ringing again.

Technology—always interrupting.

He released her arm and fished it from his front pocket. An unfamiliar number was on the screen, but he knew the Boys might be using burners.

Just as he brought it to his ear, it exploded. The blast slapped his head, and he tumbled, flopping into the rain gutter. The last thing he saw was blood, so very much blood, blinding him. Drowning the consciousness from him.

Chapter 47 Atonement

"Where'd you get the BobbleHeads?" Ashley asked.

Willy told her a story about a job he had two summers ago, working at a landfill. He had it good, working in the E-waste center. Air conditioned. High tech, clean work. By God's grace, he said, a crate of BobbleHeads showed up one day. They were certified for motorcycle safety gear, just outdated and discontinued. A buddy in the center helped him harvest the best of the lot of them, and he ended up with a pair of vintage BobbleHead helmets.

There was plenty of time for storytelling, for they were touring Laramie at a top speed of 10 miles per hour. "Conserves battery," Willy told her. "Doesn't draw attention," he added when they were waved past a traffic jam by a woman in gray.

She'd never worn a BobbleHead, but it reminded her of her helmet in the high-altitude EV suits. It was heavier, and it didn't have a respirator, but it was otherwise loaded with HeadGear tech.

Willy pulled up a map and simulcast it to both helmets, so they were able to negotiate and navigate to any particular sites she might want to see. Early on, their slow roll let them through checkpoints and snares in traffic. Once in a while, they had to take a sidewalk or alley to avoid trouble.

They had made quick work of the highlight reel of Laramie. She had been all over the world, seen all the wonders of the world, but Willy was a knowledgeable tour guide. He threaded the electric bike through the University of Wyoming campus, navigating both the roadway and the displays on their Bobbleheads. When they rolled by the American Heritage center, with such a unique conical shape, or stopped over to admire the life-sized Apatosaurus recently erected at the Natural History Museum on campus, Ashley was taken in by his steady, charismatic descriptions. They buzzed by St. Matthew's Cathedral, and he made it seem as interesting as the Cologne or St. Paul's. They did not break speed when passing the Wyoming Territorial Prison State Historic Site, for the Port Authority had made it their base camp. Chomp Tower, the tallest building in Laramie, was an ugly thing poured by 3D printer machines, such a monstrous contrast to the cathedral and other structures.

As things got more and more congested, Ashley took more stock in the invading forces. She had been mistaken; they *were* porting in, but they were not TransCorp. They were the Port Authority. Augmented reality overlays relayed the news. The Port Authority was a subsidiary of TransCorp, but it had done so very well that it was assuming control over its former parent company. The Port Authority was confident they would supplant all other transportation within five years.

"That'll be the day," Willy had said. "They'll never replace the freedom of a good ride."

Ashley smiled. The kid talked like he was in a biker gang. His little electric bike hummed along gracefully, but she doubted Willy had ever felt the heat and thunder of a Harley.

"They're going to have to mint a lot of portals," she said.

"There are over four million towns. If you just put a port in every town..."

"They'd be like bus stops, maybe? Public transportation?"

"Everybody'd want one," he said.

She wanted to tell him that she felt differently. She wanted to tell him that she owned one and wished she didn't... but she said nothing.

Willy played a promotional vid on a side screen for them to watch and visit about. He was a great host, a great kid. She was enjoying the respite from the rest of the world, even as they were lacing their way through the troubled town.

"Can I ask you a question, Miss Winston?"

"We've been over this, Mr. Titus."

"Okay. *Ashley* then. Can I ask?"

"Fire away."

He switched the visor images to more prominently display his face and hers. Even though she was riding behind him, even though they both wore black beach ball helmets, it was as if they were face to face. "Why are you here?"

It seemed out of character for him, almost accusatory. Ashley tried to stay poised. "Here? In Laramie?"

"Yeah."

"My ship was toasted." Though only a day ago, it was old news. Surely, he knew all about that. The storm cloud would have been looming over the entire city.

"Maybe I should ask, why are you *still* here?"

Ashley shrugged. "Can't just catch a cloud like you do a plane. Vectors have to be just right."

"And that's why you were on the roof?"

"Yeah, sizing it up... at first."

"Find what you were looking for?"

"I found her, the White Witch, but what a disappointment. I was ready to take her down, but then—well, you work there. You heard about all the commotion, right?"

"I try not to pay it any mind," Willy said, but his expression was inconsistent with his words.

They rounded another turn and were on a residential street. If not for the distant sirens, Ashley would not have known she was in a city under siege. "Kyrstal Price might not be worth my time, but I think I'll stick around a while. This place reminds me more and more of Franklin."

"Franklin, Texas," Willy said, "where you found your strengths."

"You really *are* a fanboy!" she chuckled, but his knowledge of her background felt a little invasive.

"Yes, I am. I know your history. All of it."

She'd never heard anyone talk of her experience in Franklin quite like that, either. *Find her strengths?* It was unsettling.

• • • •

The tornado sirens changed cadence. They were winding down. The final lap of it yawled on for an eternity. Willy brought the bike to a stop. "Let's walk," he suggested.

They pulled off the BobbleHeads and were met with fresh, cool air. They were at a public park, one that paralleled a creek. Tall evergreens had been cut back for a walking trail that meandered along the creek bank. The sky was gunmetal gray. Nothing seemed to be moving. The houses that bordered the park were quiet. Citizens of Laramie were taking the lockdown seriously, it appeared. Otherwise, if not for the distant gunshots, Ashley would have thought the neighborhood was frozen in time. It felt like any sleepy neighborhood on a Sunday afternoon.

"What day is it, Willy?"

He looked at her like she was loopy. "It's Thursday. Why?"

"Just wondering. Lately it's not mattered. My life's a little..."

"Aloof?"

"Aloft is more like it, but yeah."

"It's not like you can settle down when you're wanted."

She nodded. He sympathized with her situation, but he'd never understand it. Hers was a volatile life. "I'm not exactly 'wanted,' like by the law—whatever you consider law enforcement these days. I'm mostly... hunted."

"And blamed for everything spawned by a Weekly over the last five years."

"Right." Ashley wondered if he had somehow been a victim of the Eat the Rich propaganda. She limbered up her arms and legs as they walked, cognizant of the muscles. She could fight or flee. Or Affect him for that matter.

"I don't suppose it matters what day of the week it is when you have a bigger agenda."

She still couldn't figure him out, but she played along. "I'd rather it was Sunday. I've always liked Sunday. It could be Sunday right now, quiet as it is."

"You don't go to church," Willy stated. It was still a question.

"No, my parents weren't... I wasn't raised in a church, I guess."

"Oh," he smiled and turned toward her more directly, "Oh, Miss Win—Ashley—I'm not judging you or anything. Just asking."

"You're in seminary though, so you're probably disappointed or—"

"No, really. I told you, I'm in seminary for the field work. I'm giving back everything I can. My time. My money. My life, I guess."

"That sounds... noble."

He chuckled. "It's not noble. It's payback."

"What?"

"It's my own warped theology. Friends in school say I'm a cafeteria Christian, taking what I want from the buffet, not the whole spread."

Ashley was relaxing, and in catching herself relaxing, she instantly tingled with an Affectation springing up in reaction. It was hard to harness. The guy was posing nothing of a threat. She had to dial it down.

"So, what's your flavor," she asked. "You a meat and potatoes guy, believing in fire and brimstone, or are you a 'hates the sin but loves the sinner' type?"

"Huh. So, you know more theology than you let on."

"I think you're one of those who walks in the world but is not of the world. Am I right?"

Willy beamed. "Really! You surprise me." They walked on, and he continued, "I am one of those types, yes, but I'm no good at it. I lived in a crack house for a year, made that my ministry. Like Jesus, I wanted to live with the people, but I fell into it."

"Drugs?"

"Nah. What I call caterwauling around. I don't want to get into it. I try though. I work the soup kitchens, and I volunteer with the homeless shelters. I keep it non-denominational so I can double and triple time it wherever I want."

"So, the service thing, again. That's what you go for on the buffet?"

"Know your scripture? I get hung up on absolutes, like 'be holy as I am holy.' That's a tall order. I can never be good enough to live up to that. Know another one? James 4:17."

Ashley raised her eyebrows in anticipation. "Which is...?"

"Remember, it is sin to know what you ought to do and then not do it."

"That's a Bible verse?"

"Yeah. Pretty damning, isn't it?"

"I guess, but surely it's out of context or—"

"I know. I know. I think it's just something I hang my theological hat on."

"So, you really believe that if you know something's right then you gotta do it?" Ashley was rushing through a hundred scenarios. "Who'd have the time?"

"Yes. Exactly." Willy looked especially solemn. "So, even though I do know what day of the week it is, I'm otherwise pretty frazzled. I'm always darting off to do what I know I *should* be doing. It's like walking off the job today. Sure, I should be serving coffee, but I knew I shouldn't pass up this opportunity with you."

Ashley frowned. Now this was an opportunity to do good?

"Oh, it's not like that. I'm not saying you're someone to minister to or whatever. Not exactly."

"Then what, exactly?"

The walking path was concrete, well-maintained, and absolutely void of any other pedestrians. On a fall morning, a Thursday morning, even this otherwise chaotic morning, it seemed strange it was all so desolate.

"I thought you maybe need to think about your personal brand of theology."

"I told you. I don't go to church. I couldn't even tell you the difference between a Catholic and—"

"You have a theology, at least it's a system of belief, and it's not far from my own. Wanna hear about it?"

The whole city was under lockdown. A tyrannical force was making itself known. Of all the places she could be and with all the people in the city, she was with a Bible school student flexing his theological muscles.

"Would you be terribly offended if I *didn't* want to hear about it?"

"Atonement."

"What?"

"My mom was a pioneer in marrying neuroscience and advertising. She was the best at what she did. Madison Avenue all the way. The corps all wanted her to spin it up for them. She made a choice, CommCorp. In her thinking, instant communications was a godsend. She used to promote the idea of ending global conflict through honest information. She saw potential for rapid, individualized education via HeadGear. She led the charge on implant tech, too. Her work has led to millions of people—even you, I'd bet—to allow themselves to be wired. Tied to CommCorp."

"And?" Ashley was surprised, but she still had no idea where this was going.

"And the rest is obvious. She was too good at what she did. CommCorp is too invasive. Implants, Internals, Appliances—it's all too much."

"You're Jacked," she argued, looking at the scar on his temple. "We were just on your BobbleHeads."

"Right. She even got us kids chipped." He shook his head sadly. "Anyway, when mom saw what she had done, what the world had done with what she did, she lost it. Ultimately, she committed suicide."

"Willy, I'm sorry." Ashley was reeling from one headline to the next.

"And that's why I do what I do."

"What?" she felt like she'd missed something.

"Atonement," he said. "I'm giving all I have, all I can give, to make up for my family name, my mom's mistakes... and her death."

"Willy, you don't have to—"

"And you're doing the same thing."

"I'm what?"

"You feel guilty about the Weeklies being hijacked and the poison the Eaters spread." He said it without accusation, somehow, and she did not overreact. "You're atoning for your father's invention gone bad. Same as me and my mom."

She stopped him at a bench, and they sat down. She used the time to collect herself. Finally, she spoke. "You got something there, Willy, but you don't have it all. If I were to atone for all I've done wrong, all the people I actually killed—*killed*, Willy—I'd never catch up. Atonement is not enough."

He was stricken.

Had she undermined his theology?

Was it her admission that she had killed people?

He cleared his throat. "Miss Winston, '*There are more things in heaven and Earth than are dreamt of in your philosophy.*' That's Shakespeare, not the Bible, and it's Hamlet talking to Horatio. You know that passage?"

"I have a PhD in Bioengineering, not literature," she said. "But I know the quote. Fun one to share in a theological tussle."

"Theology. Philosophy. The point is the same."

She felt like she was with Rory, parsing out a quote. "The point is, we don't know what we don't know," she said. "That, by the way, is the premise of science."

"*My point is*, there's more than atonement and guilt. There's vengeance, like no one's ever dreamed of—in your philosophy or science or nightmares."

Chapter 48 Ways and Means

R ory Reed. Warrior. TurnCoat. Assassin... and the title he was most curious about: Father.

Katrina answered his questions yet set a demanding pace on the trail.

"Calissa. You say her name's Calissa? How old is she?"

"She is in college, a non-corp private college. Even I do not know where."

None of this was familiar. He flipped through his notebook as they walked. "Her name's in here," he shook the pages, "but not in here." He pointed to his head.

"Yes, it is."

"How can you be so sure?"

She glanced at him but did not answer him.

"Katrina?"

"It is a miracle you are not long dead."

By his count, he'd asked her questions for a mile or more, two dozen questions, and this was the first time she had changed the subject. He logged that. She did not want to talk about his head.

Instead, she spoke of their journey ahead. According to her, they were close to yet another abandoned tourist site, once a robust city, now a refuge for derelicts. It was obvious from the way she carried herself—this was a dangerous place.

Rory had found every place to be dangerous, and when it was not, he brought danger with him. He tried to shake off memories of what he had done.

"And when will we find Calissa and the others?"

Katrina slowed her pace. She looked at him steadily before answering. She was being careful in her reply. "They are many thousands of miles away. They are across an ocean and a continent."

"Not good. Not good. I feel like I need to be there. *Like now.*"

"You *were* a patient man," she offered this as a recommendation.

"Let's grab a boat and set out."

"I suppose you have the means, somewhere in your rags?"

"I have ways *and* means," he said.

"Your ways—the ways of all the rabble—have done little more than punch holes in hulls and scuttle the rest." She huffed at him. "Senseless destruction."

What did she know of his ways? Of a Warrior's mission? He felt a straining in his hands. Something in him wanted to be done with Katrina Covarrubias. Rory shook his head, arguing against himself. She was vital to him. She was, he was guessing, a long-lost friend.

He also found a truth to what she said. Ruining the Rich had led to nothing. There had been no end to it, no contract fulfilled, only more Rich. No one to report to, no one to take orders from but the clouds. What he had done—for as long as he could yet remember—seemed without merit and without end.

"Sometimes we are beyond our own control," she said, as if she knew his thoughts. "We can be guilty and yet not responsible for our actions."

"That sounds like some keen justification," Rory said.

"A wise man once shared this with me. I cling to it when my dreams are dark."

. . . .

"You are a man of many words," she said. "Yet you have forgotten yourself."

"You mean the quotes? All the sayings and proverbs and wise words swimming in my head?"

"You know them, but you do not speak them like you did."

"I used to say them out loud all the time?"

"All of the time," Katrina said, rolling her eyes.

"That had to get old."

The town was rough and tumble, the first gathering of people he did not immediately attack. None of them were what anyone would presume to be the Rich, and his mantra was fading with irrelevance. These people were almost all from mainland Africa, Katrina told him, immigrants who came across the sixty miles to the islands on anything that would float. When tourism failed and travel ground to a halt, the Canary Islands fell into ruin. Cottages and hostels were now occupied by squatters and vagrants. Nearly every structure hosted extended families and friends. The island towns had become encampments of desperate people seeking a better way of life than they had fled in Morocco.

They made it clear to him that he was not welcome here. They went about it in the most passive-aggressive ways. They would just not see him, let doors shut abruptly behind them and in front of him, rather than holding it open. Some would shoulder him in passing. Others would look right through him.

"They will not trust you," Katrina said when they settled at an outside table at a cafe. "If I were not with you, I doubt they would serve you. They may not even serve us."

"What'd I do?"

"You remind them of tourists," she said.

"Me?" he looked at his ragged clothes, his scarred arms. He clapped a palm on a couple of weapons. "I'm a tourist?"

She shrugged. "What would you like to drink? I will order for you."

Rory's perch on the wooden chair was uncertain. He had sat on boulders and logs, once in a while on a ruined gunwale of a boat, but chairs were alien to him, and these rickety little folding chairs gave him no confidence they could defy gravity.

"I will order you mint tea," Katrina decided. "It is what they drink here."

He argued for coffee, and then he had a flash of memory.

"I drank coffee with her every morning," Rory smiled. "All kinds of coffee. It was our thing."

"With?"

"*With Calissa*," he said. He snatched the menu, just a piece of paper with items handwritten on it, from Katrina. He scanned it and beamed, "I'll have a *Kahwa kahla*. It's espresso, you know."

As she had predicted, the server ignored him entirely, exchanging pleasantries with Katrina in some language he did not know. She seemed to light up, animated and cordial, then resumed her more serious nature when they were again left alone.

"You travel a lot."

"I did," Katrina said. "You remember this?"

"No, I can just tell. How many languages do you speak?"

"I don't really know. It would depend on how one counts dialects. Several."

"You've been here before, too, I'd say."

"It was a much different place. I would not know my way here now."

"But you know people, right? You have contacts?"

She shook her head and looked out at the street. "Those I did know are dead or gone. You contracted for lives. I contracted livelihoods."

Rory let that set a beat. He reached for any recollection of the dark woman he sat with. She was beautiful and yet brittle. He could still see the violence inside her, and it made him catalog all the ways she might spring on him—even though he was trying to trust her.

"You worked for a corporation, didn't you? That's what you mean?"

"Yes, TransCorp. Toward the end, I brokered international airways for TransCorp. We commanded tariffs that left many at our mercy. We owned and collected on all major roadways, and assuming control of the air was the venture I was leading."

The server brought their drinks and left with little more than a nod.

Katrina continued, "Places like this could not afford the charges. They came to depend solely on cruise ships and sailboats, and that was only a small fraction of their previous traffic."

Rory could see the regret in her dark eyes.

"Eaters may have popularized sinking the ships, but TransCorp was more efficient at it. We mined the coves and downed many ships at sea. We made it... unpopular to sail. If people wanted to travel to such places as these islands, they had to fly on our aircraft." She sighed. "It ruined entire economies, like this one."

"You commissioned that work?" Rory asked. "And now you regret it?"

"Actually," she said over her coffee, "I *did* the work. It was in doing such deeds that I was noticed and recruited to do *other* things. More regrettable things even than these."

A name came to him, but he could not pronounce it. He knew a woman by name, even the syllables of her name, the rhythm of it. He remembered what she looked like, and how she had died such a gruesome and bloody death. She had been eviscerated. She bled out on a table in a cafeteria. It was a macabre memory.

The woman had been gored and gutted, not by Rory Reed the assassin, but by this woman across from him, sipping coffee from a tiny little cup. Katrina had killed Sarah Dawn Parker.

He said the name aloud, and Katrina's cup rattled as she sat it on the saucer. "She was an unfortunate victim of the Corporation and worse, a test of my willpower. Needless to say, I lost the contest."

"What are you talking about?" he whispered.

"You'll remember, I am sure, but in brief: I was conditioned to respond to threats as assigned. They learned I could be forced to harm individuals, much like you, I believe. My handler, Steven Spexarth, gained control of my implants and forced unspeakable things of me. I could not resist. The pain was unbearable."

She blinked away tears.

"I'm the last one to judge on that," Rory said. He wanted to reach across the table and pat her arm, but he didn't think it would be wise. In reaching, his center of balance would be over-extended toward her, and she could simply pull his wrist, toppling him toward her. She might use the tea service. Break a plate and slice him open. Gouge him in the armpit with the spoon. He did not know what weapons she might have on her.

He shook his head. Here was a woman in pain, not a woman intent on causing pain. He leaned in a little to catch her attention and smiled at her.

That same gesture was one he had used many times with someone else, someone equally pensive and fierce. He couldn't place it.

"There's blood on both our hands," she summed up. "I would like to see us make arrangements for travel without more."

"So then," Rory said. "Guess I'm all out of ways and means. What's your plan?"

Chapter 49 Coming Around

A man in tattered jeans and a Carhartt coat was crouched close up. Another had taken a knee on the blood-soaked sidewalk. They huddled tight in, muttering between themselves. It was impossible to hear just what all they were saying over the clock tower's ring that held onto one unending note.

The kneeling man's pants absorbed dark red blood. It was creeping up his thigh. They didn't notice. Something like a fat tomato worm had come to rest not far from the other man's boot. It, too, was crimson red, wet with blood. It, too, went unnoticed by the otherwise attentive men.

The blood was oozing off the tomato worm, revealing white plate-like spikes on its back, a tiny Stegosaurus slumped on its side. Nathan knew his dinosaurs by name. He'd find this little one interesting. Rain was rinsing it off, and then it was clearly part of a jaw, and the white spikes were jagged teeth.

He grunted a shriek. He joggled on his side, scraping his face on the sidewalk, trying to put distance between himself and this shattered, severed jaw. In his panic, he pushed at the men over him. He tried to bring his hand to his face to feel the damage—pain pulsed from his hand, his wrist and arm. He brought it to his face, noting the hand was coated in blood and slime. He grunted and felt for his jaw.

It was intact.

"Coming around," one of the men overhead warned, and they both—no, all three of them, maybe more—stepped back some.

Stu had not noticed the ones holding a coat overhead to keep the rain at bay.

"You're gonna be okay," the one with bloody knees said, firm and loud.

Then they talked some more between them as Stu scooted around. His head had never hurt so badly. His hand had to be broken, it throbbed so.

"Acoustic trauma... permanent... maybe nothing more."

"Miracle... phone saved his hearing... ask me... eye, too."

"He was on his phone when it happened?"

"Lookit the spatter."

Stu's vision was clearing through blood and rain. He wiped at his face with his left hand. He tried to get a fix on what was happening. The ringing in his ear was constant but fading. Not from the clock's bell.

The men gathered over him looked frightened and stern. One of them offered him a folded-up flannel shirt, which he took to dry his face. "Lay your head down on it and rest," one of them hollered at him.

These weren't The Boys. They were rugged strangers, scraggly and desperate looking men. Another one joined them under the coat canopy. He asked questions rapid fire. Stu couldn't follow it all, but the latest man was familiar, anyway. He was the one they'd called Abe Lincoln. He was the Eater's main man.

Stu scrabbled again to sit up. Just past the men, pooled in rain and blood—a corpse with an exploded head. "Krys," he mumbled, and he crawled through legs and then the arms of men trying to hold him from her.

"Krys?" one of them asked.

"Krystal Price?" another asked, even more surprised.

Their surprise sent a shockwave through him. He had no idea why he said what he said next. "Christ. I said, 'Jesus Christ.'"

Stu reached out for her shoulder and tried to turn her. Part of her scalp was draped over the gaping hole in her skull. Maybe, he'd hoped—ludicrous as it was—that she was just injured. The corpse flopped over like a stillborn calf.

"Who was she?" One of the Eaters asked.

Before they could speculate more, Stu looked up at them, and said, "My wife. It's my wife."

"He's Wiebe," one of them realized aloud. "Who'd a shot his wife?"

They were abuzz with ideas, but Abe was ignoring them. His attention was on Stu. He crouched down by him and put his hand on Stu's shoulder. "Damn shame. Real sorry, Mr. Wiebe. Real sorry."

Stu was fighting against a raging torrent he could scarcely control. He spasmed and gasped for breath, and with every movement, pain shot through him. He brought the flannel, now soaked with rain and blood, to his face. He muffled his cries with it. He raged into it.

Someone had draped the canopy coat over Krystal's body. The rain fell harder. It thumped on the coat as if trying to rouse the dead. It pounded on Stu's bare head, and it spattered the backs of the Eaters. They'd stepped away from him and turned their backs. They were looking out for more trouble, just like his Boys would have done. They were talking among themselves about a sniper and the angle of the shot.

But more, they were giving him a moment to swallow it all, and he was grateful for that.

· · · ·

A black panel van had pulled up. Doors opened and slammed. Lights were flashing. Attendants were zipping a body bag. Someone who looked familiar had led Stu to the passenger's seat. "Figured you'd want to ride with her," he said. "Hop in."

Others in official Pharma gear were working on the scene. Stu didn't want to think about the cleanup, the fragments of her head, the grizzly heap of brain matter they had to be scooping up. It might ride with them in the van. It might be bagged and delivered separately.

It might be scraped off into the rain gutter for all he knew.

Stu sat half in, half out of the van. He didn't care about the rain. He didn't care that his hand was killing him. He was working on what had happened. He was trying not to think too hard on the sequencing of it, for he thought if he just grabbed at it, the memory of it all would get tucked away.

Repressed, his shrink said. That had happened to him before. Memories of the bombing and that night after didn't come back to him for years. This time, he was thinking sidelong about things. Krystal at breakfast. Damn, but she was a picky eater. She sure looked good in the lamplight, even in the most unlikely of places—morning in a Lead Room. She'd called the meeting, called his house when she should have known better than to rile Rachel. How did she even have his number? It was the first time the land line had rang in years. Wheat toast and coffee. That annoying cat clock. Krystal called because she was scared. They'd set her up, she said. He warned her that Severance had a bad ROI, that it would be easier if she were... Hadn't she admitted she'd brought the Showdown here, just so she could see him again? What did that mean, that she was still interested in him?

He looked over the seat at the wet black bag.

Krys wasn't interested in anything anymore. Not him. Not Severance. Not white umbrellas or Tic-Tacs or teleportation. She had already left. That bag of mush was all that was left of her now.

He knew now why he'd lied to the Eaters—to buy time.

CommCorp probably had footage already from a dozen street cameras. They were likely editing the assassination, splicing it with the Eaters who had shown up to help him, making them look guilty.

If they *didn't* have footage, however, and if even the Eaters thought the dead woman was his wife, not Krystal Price, he might have a chance to get to someone and tell her side of things.

He might have a chance, anyway, *to do something.*

The doors were slamming all around the van. Stu pulled himself up inside and shut his door just as the driver was getting in. Stu recognized the coroner now for who he truly was.

"We'll take care of this, Stu," he said, starting the van. "We got you, brother."

"Thanks, Schmitty," Stu said. "Take us to the ranch."

Chapter 50 Introductions

They toured Laramie on his electric bike, homing in on Ashley's signal. It put them in a storybook neighborhood that was too idyllic. "Utopian," Alex said as they dismounted. "Spooky, isn't it?"

He held Kelli's hand as they walked down the quiet neighborhood's backstreets. A man and wife just out for a stroll, ignoring the quarantine.

"What the hell's she doing way out here?"

"My HeadGear never lies," he insisted.

"She's usually in the thick of it. You'd think she'd still be laying into the White Witch."

"Ashley's here, like, *right around here*." Alex stopped and turned in a circle, watching his heads-up display.

"Who's watching over her?"

"She didn't want anyone. She insisted just the three of us jump last night. Remember? Even left you up there. Then... no one around here was really suited for the job. Stu Wiebe's Boys watched the hotel, but... as far as I know... no one was assigned to her."

"And you just trotted away, leaving her alone?"

"Babe, I have worse problems."

"What could be bigger than losing Ashley?"

He did not reply. His mind raced through a hundred scenarios, many of them with more dire consequences than a missing heiress.

What could be worse, indeed?

Losing her for good? Losing this battle? Losing everything?

"Well?"

Was she asking him what to do next?

Was she asking what could be worse?

Alex felt disoriented. *He needed to listen more closely.* According to a vid he had watched recently, listening was one of the most treasured traits of a good spouse. Another, he recalled, was decisiveness.

"We're going down there," he pointed down a footpath. "I say she's down there."

"Based on what?"

"That bike," he spurted, pointing at it. "She was all over town. What else would have let her be so mobile?" He was convincing himself. There were even two helmets strapped to the bike. Though it annoyed people, his leaps of reason and faith seldom disappointed. The more he thought about it, the surer of himself he became.

Alex had guessed himself into a good plan.

"She's just... sightseeing?" Kelli asked, her voice heavy with skepticism.

"The Princess likes her walks, right? She's probably working on her next move."

"Her next move's probably a full-on retreat. Back to the beaches."

It didn't fit with his flair for the dramatic. Ashley Winston tucking tail? What about the thrashing she'd promised Krystal Price? Alex sent a query on his Internal, on an antiquated Clench that only he and his crew even used. Halfway through his message, he quit tapping out the Morse code. Who would respond?

Rory was gone. Calissa had her Clench removed, he was sure, since she was in hiding. A-Z ignored their units, favoring the Ham radio. Ashley had her own Internals, but nothing like the closed-circuit Clench.

What was he asking anyway? He wasn't even sure.

Kelli gasped when they rounded a turn. Beyond an evergreen outcropping, they spotted Ashley and a man on a bench. "I thought he was—"

"—Spexarth," Alex completed. "Me too."

They looked at each other with apprehension, then turned their attention to the bench ahead. He had a six gun at the ready. He noticed Kelli's reflex grip on her plasma pistol.

Ashley turned as if expecting them. She flashed them the welcoming smile of her public persona. Something just the opposite was behind it. "Hey."

"Hi," Kelli returned.

"We were in the neighborhood," Alex said.

"What brought you down? I thought I told you to stay with the girls?"

One did not "tell" Kelli anything, Alex knew, and he knew Ashley would normally never say such a thing. Another tip of the hand.

"Toiletries," Kelli said. "Who's your friend?"

The guy stood up, all smiles. He wore a cardigan and dated loafers. His hair was cropped short, likely a weekly haircut type. If he had been wearing a name tag, Alex would have pegged him for a missionary. Or a salesman.

"I'm Willy Titus," he extended his hand. Alex holstered his gun and gave him a shake. The kid had a winning handshake. Willy gestured toward Kelli, too, and Alex was surprised she also shook his hand. "I'm guessing you must be the Gaults?"

"Alex and Kelli," Ashley said, standing. "Willy works back at the hotel. We were just out for a spin."

"Good morning for it," Alex said, not even trying to pass it off as convincing small talk.

"God is good," Willy said, admiring the sky.

Missionary.

Coming toward them from the other direction were two men.

"Ah!" Willy noticed them, too. "Only He could have brought us together."

Zealous missionary, Alex thought.

Willy stepped back by Ashley, as if to let the men pass.

"Henny?" Alex asked, recognizing the approaching bartender.

"Hello, Gault. What're you doing here?"

"Who's he?" Henny's tall, wizardly companion asked.

"Who are *you*?" Alex returned.

"Ah, introductions are in order," Willy said.

"Willy?" Ashley was incredulous. She also looked a little threatened, and Alex knew what came with that.

"Everything's cool, Ash," Alex said.

"We're all the good guys here," Willy offered, in Alex's same soothing tones.

"If I might suggest, we're all heroes in our own stories. Personal narratives, however, seldom match—"

"Who the hell are you?" Kelli interrupted the taller, older man. Alex was relieved to note that her pistol was still holstered, at least for the moment.

"Allow me," Willy stepped up. "We do this all the time at camps. Okay, tallest to smallest. You, sir, have a full head of height on us, why don't you begin?"

"Call me Sackerson," the old guy said. "I'm not from around here."

"You're not from around *now* either, I'd venture." Alex couldn't help himself. "He's the one. The Other Guy."

"I thought you said Kenny Hinman was the other guy?" Kelli said.

"I'm Kenny Hin—"

"Tut-tut. Not your turn. By my measure, it is your turn, ma'am." Alex swallowed hard. Kelli hated being called ma'am.

"Kelli Chase," she said.

"*Captain* Kelli Chase," Alex bragged.

"I thought she was your wife?" Henny said.

"Yeah, she is. She just kept—"

"We'll get there," Willy said. He eyed Alex's hair. "I think I have an inch or two on you. I'm Willy Titus."

"The barista," Kelli said with doubt.

"Exactly. Okay, Mr. Gault. You are...?"

"I'm Mr. Gault. Alex Gault. Presiding hero. I think I know more of you than any other one of you. Therefore—"

"Thank you. Now you, Miss Winston."

"Everyone knows her," Henny chuckled. "Ashley Elizabeth Winston."

"And who are you, again?" she asked.

"I'm Kenny Hinman. They call me Henny." He shrugged. "You can call me Henny, too. We came up to see to Lefty—er, I mean, Lark Fortune, my buddy."

"Yeah," Alex said, "Shouldn't you be keeping an eye on your buddy, buddy?"

"Watching him like a hawk," Sackerson nodded vigorously.

"Really?" Alex asked, "So....where is he now?"

Hinman rubbed the back of his head. He glanced at Sackerson as if expecting him to explain.

Sackerson cleared his throat, a high-pitched rooster call. "Well, you see—"

"Wait, wait," Kelli said. "You're here for Fortune? The guy we floated here?"

"That's right, Peppercorn, they go way back."

"I'm Larkin Fortune's longest running advocate," Sackerson offered.

"So, we're with Ashley. You two are with Fortune, who just happens to be the guy we brought up here." Kelli eyed the missionary. "That just leaves you as the odd man out."

"We're all here because of Krystal Price," he said. "Am I right?"

Everyone in the circle seemed to find some agreement about that.

"So, again, what's your game, Titus?" Kelli asked.

"I work here," he smiled. "Just taking Ashley for a little R&R."

. . . .

"You haven't put it all together, have you?" Sackerson asked from the side of his mouth. They had let conversation flow between the rest, and now as they all walked back toward the cycles, he and Alex hung back for their own heart-to-heart.

Alex summed it up, "We are strangers here. Both of us."

"Aliens... at least alienated by time."

"*From* time," Alex offered. "From time to time."

"Oh, that's clever. I like that." Sackerson sighed and smiled. "Truth is, my wings are clipped. I've been stuck here a long, long while."

"Henny said you ported here last night."

"Oh, I'm not talking here and there."

"You're talking *now and then*, aren't you?"

Sackerson nodded.

Alex wanted to keep him talking. So long as he was talking, even if none of it were true, Alex could suss out his motives. He could sort out this Sackerson, this Other Guy, and then decide what to do. If it came to it, if Sackerson somehow proved to be a threat, he could sic Ashley on the old man.

"So, how long have you been around here?"

"Laramie? Not even 24 hours."

"How long have you been... *in the here and now*?"

"I was younger than you when I came into Guthrie. There were a lot of us trying to make the trip. It was a one-way trip. I think I was the first survivor. I did stupid things. Ported everywhere I could hang a Hot Wire. Squandered so much! I never gave up on time travel though. Once I figured it out and had reason enough, I ported back even farther. I ended up stuck in the 1970's."

"And you haven't time traveled since?"

"Right... and never again. 'Proved to be... destabilizing to my mental faculties," Sackerson cackled. "Maybe a bad move, just aging out. In plain chronology, I'm over one hundred years old."

Alex shuddered, remembering three years he had spent in the '90's. "Wait a minute," he held an arm out in front of his companion, slowing them to put even more distance between them and the others. "You ported backward knowing you could never return? And you did that... *twice*?"

Sackerson nodded. "Wasn't much of a decision. My time was... unruly. Guthrie was already a lost cause. I had to pursue my mission even farther back."

"And you remember it?"

Sackerson frowned at him. "Remember it?"

"Your past... in the future."

"I remember everything. Even things I'd rather forget." Sackerson had a faraway look in his eye. Then he was startled, obviously, by a thought. He turned to Alex and asked, "Why are you here? When are you from?"

"That's the problem. I *don't* remember," Alex said. "Other than little trips, a decade here and there, I'm lost."

"What *do* you remember?"

"I can remember everything since I was, oh, sixteen or so. Nothing prior."

"Sixteen? Are you sure?"

"More or less," Alex wobbled his head.

"And you chose to ride it out since then? *Not* time travel."

"I did my fair share... got into some trouble. I can remember some trips, just not whatever happened when I was a kid."

The two walked along, consumed in their own thoughts. Alex was warming to this old man, the only person he had ever met who was anything like him. He found himself eager to tell more, but then he checked himself, concerned he was being Affected. He continued with some caution, "But eventually, yeah. I decided not to time travel ever again. I decided that when I decided on her," Alex smiled and gestured up the trail at Kelli. "I made her a promise."

"So, it's self-imposed?"

"If I travel, I risk losing memories, and I *like* the memories I've made this time around." He was still smiling, still watching her glide ahead. "I mean, who could give that up, man?"

"If the situation merited it, as they say, you'd travel again," Sackerson stated. "You came back here in the first place, for some reason, by choice. You'd choose that again if it was called for."

"I don't think so, Sackerson."

"I do," he said. "I did."

Chapter 51 Conquest

L ark stumbled down the stairs. They were the cold, backstage backstairs hotels hid for emergency use only. They were the same stairs Gault took Winston down just the night before. Definitely for emergency use then, and now.

He was taking them two at a time. The first run of stairs or so, he had bound down landing-to-landing. "No time to spare on stairs," he grunted, and scurried on down.

He wasn't made for this. He felt old. He felt woozy from the hooch. On another occasion, he might have played with the phrase. This time, there wasn't time—for anything.

He wasn't dressed for this, either. The Stetson was bouncing from side to side, only the chin strap keeping it on his head. His shoes kept slipping. His pants were too tight. His shirt might have torn in the armpit on his mad dash down. Ten stories, twenty-nine short runs of stairs that wound round and round, and then, he was at a cold, cinder block juncture. Inside, to the kitchen. Outside, and the fire exit door would set off an alarm, so the door's signage declared. *It hadn't last night*, Lark reasoned, and he put a hand on it to push.

He took his time only to regain his breath, but in that time, hatched a new plan.

He burst into the kitchen only to find storage and entry way. No one was there, but there was a commotion in the kitchen, farther inside. That suited Lark fine. He rummaged through the baker's racks lining the hallway and found what he wanted. Electrical tape. A thick permanent marker. Best of all, hanging on the corner post of a rack, a thick red hoodie which he ducked right into immediately.

He darted around the back rooms and had another win. A staff restroom. He bolted the door and set to it. First, he pried off the

Stetson, setting it carefully on the toilet tank. Then he scrubbed his face and dried it, and that process only brought more clarity to his plan. Then he took the marker and drew random hatch marks across his face. Lark chuckled at his reflection, then taped over his features in counter patterns. He hardly recognized himself. No facial recognition would know him out on the streets.

"Hope against hope," he said to the marked man in the mirror. He took just a beat to wonder just what the hell that really meant. He took the old cell phone from his jeans and tried it one more time. Not even a ring tone now. Begrudgingly, he tossed it in the trash can. He picked up the Stetson, thinking twice, even questioning his reflection, then shoved it in the trash, covering it with paper towels.

He wished he'd left it with Hinman, but it had been a messy exit. Henny was probably still coming around. *Little love tap with a vase was all it took.*

He darted back into the entryway. Which way was out, again? The scent of coffee lured him toward the kitchen. Things being as they were, all chaos and calamity, Lark armed himself with a screwdriver from the shelves. Brandishing it, he entered the kitchen, expecting the worst.

Several men and women dressed in white work clothes were going about their business. Two were working at a large floor mixer. Another was washing dishes. Despite his appearance, they gave him little attention. He held the screwdriver out with menace and demanded coffee.

An older woman tossed her head toward an industrial coffee maker.

It was as if men barged in the backdoor for coffee daily.

Lark tucked the screwdriver in his back pocket, found a styrofoam cup, and poured. He kept his eyes on the kitchen staff; they kept themselves busy with prep work.

"Thanks!" he said, backing out of the kitchen. As he was clearing the door, he spotted a large knife on a stainless-steel counter. He took the knife, shaking it at them, and said, "You never saw me."

It was as if they had not, actually, even noticed he was there.

That suited him fine. That was his plan. Go unnoticed. Make his way, undetected in the riotous streets, and find his way to the grain elevator. Save Krystal. Get out of town.

Lark burst through the Emergency Fire Exit and started running, but the alarm had not gone off. Luckily, there was no one in the alley. As he rounded the building onto a busy sidewalk, he spilled his coffee. People were startled by his appearance, but then, they were skittish, he understood, since their city was under attack. Everyone was in a rush, fleeing the main street ahead.

Lark pushed on. He was moving against the tide.

When he reached the street, he stopped. Port Authority trucks were, indeed, blocking off the intersections. Soldiers in gray were firing off weapons, too, but not at Laramie's citizens. They were casually leaning against their trucks and lamp posts, taking potshots at streetlights and business signage. A warning message was warbling from loudspeakers mounted on some of the trucks, commanding people to get home and stay home.

The people, however, were talking among themselves over gunfire and warnings. They carried armloads of groceries, jewelry, and dry goods. Some carried weapons improvised from lawn tools. Lark noticed teenagers spray painting anarchist symbols and "Rebels Rule," as they skipped along. An older man caught his attention and said, "Wrong way, Flannigan. We're next to the depot." He pointed to a wrist appliance read out. "Ten thirty."

He stopped and turned in a circle. The crowd surged around and past him, jostling into him, some saying "Sorry" and "Excuse me," as they passed. At the sound of thunder, their passing conversation turned to the weather. Most of them carried umbrellas.

Rioters with umbrellas.

The rioters, Lark realized, were cast members.

• • • •

"No go, buddy. We're setting up charges all around the block."

"Charges?" Lark held up his forearm to block the rain from his eyes. It had poured earlier, and it was starting again in earnest.

"Don't worry, we know what we're doing," the soldier said with a smile. "Brought in some demo team outta Georgia."

"Georgia?"

"They can drop a skyscraper in its own footprint," he nodded. "Still, you won't wanna be any closer than this barricade. Dust and debris, brother. Dust and debris." He pulled a cloth over his mouth and nose. "It'll settle fast with the storm. Gotta get the shots just right before it's all tamped down by the rain, but—"

"When? But when!"

The soldier looked down the way at his colleagues. "I dunno. Soon? You want an umbrella?"

Lark realized the umbrellas all matched. The ones the protestors, rioters, and anarchists carried were all the same as the one the soldier was offering: Port Authority gray.

"But..." Lark was still reeling from it all.

Staged. Peaceful conquest. He took the umbrella, tucked it under his arm.

"The place was a TurnCoat hideout, you know. That's why it's on the list," the soldier confided.

"The list?"

"Dude, you don't have a clue, do you?" he chuckled and showed Lark a tablet screen. Four red Xs were throbbing on the map. "You probably want to head to the depot, or..." he looked Lark over, appraising his vibe. "Maybe you'd be better at the hospital riots around noon. That's a good look for that one."

Lark shook his head. He tried to think it out. Soldiers in loafers. Prerecorded gunfire. Plans for the weather. Bombings and riots on cue...

"Where's CommCorp?" he asked.

"Everywhere," the soldier replied. "Always."

"I mean, like, *dedicated*. Who's calling the shots?"

"I dunno," the soldier shrugged. "Say, you got a cigarette?"

"No. No... hey, do me a favor. Ping somebody and tell them they'll want to get this shot, a great one for vids." Lark went into director mode, panning the distant elevator with his hands raised, framing the scene. "Get this: the dust cloud's rolling toward the camera right after the big blow up, see, and in the foreground, coming right at the camera... me. I'm the Rabble of the Plains or whatever."

The soldier was looking off at the grain elevators, nodding. "You do look a little creepy," he agreed. He held up his tablet device. "Give me your best mad bomber look. Hold up my knife, too."

Lark posed for a couple of images, then walked out into the rain through the barricade. "I'll just get some more pics, selfies, on site. It'll be great."

"Yeah, okay, man, but when you see the drones, run for it," the soldier said. He was struggling to be heard over the gunfire and rain. "They're expendables, you know, going to capture the whole thing when it blows."

Lark nodded and cast a glance at the sky. It was dark and ominous, and rain was pouring again. He hoped he'd see the drones. He hoped he'd hear them buzzing into range. Meanwhile, he had an elevator to search.

He had to find Krystal before the whole thing exploded.

Chapter 52 Surrealistic

H enny rubbed at the back of his head. It didn't help. His head still throbbed from Lefty coldcocking him. Everything seemed out of this world. "*Surrealistic*," his daughter, Gail, might say.

He was walking down a riverside trail between two beautiful women. He couldn't believe his luck. Despite the failure at the penthouse, this was becoming an adventure he'd be telling the boys at the bar about for the rest of his life.

To his left was Captain Chase. She was knockout gorgeous. She wore tight TurnCoat pants, navy blue with a white stripe up the leg. Her jacket was white with contrasting blue edging. It emphasized her wide shoulders and narrow waist. The pistol at her hip emphasized that she was no one to mess with.

To his right, Ashley Winston—*The* Ashley Winston. He had to glance at her again now and then to even believe it. She looked fiercer than ever with her ScanTats and flaring white hair. Her bomber jacket made her look like a badass supermodel.

And *they* were talking to him!

Not around him or about him.

"So, he's *not* a threat?" Captain Chase asked again to clarify.

"Well, I..." Henny wanted to sound more confident. He wanted to offer a sound judgment on the suspect at hand. Instead, he said, "I dunno. He's been good to me."

"How long have you known him?" Miss Winston's voice was cold and wispy. He liked the air in it. She sounded even better in real life than on all the vids.

Henny almost lost her question. "Known him? Well... I met him when I was in high school, I guess."

"You don't act like you know him too well," Captain Chase stated.

"It's complicated," Henny said. "Only knew him a few days, then he was gone. Now he's back, like we just left off."

The women exchanged glances across in front of him. He could see the doubt. He had to do something. Say something that would keep them interested.

"He saved my life," he offered. "Saved a lot of lives back in Guthrie."

"We watched all the vids," Winston said. "Never saw him."

"He would have planned it that way. Real off the radar type guy."

"Why?" Chase asked.

Ashley Winston smelled like leather and mint. Captain Chase smelled like patchouli and gunpowder. He was probably imagining it all, but that was how Henny was processing it. Savoring every instant of their time and attention. Every sensation.

"Why? Why's Sack sneaky?" Henny didn't really have a good answer. He had to go out on a limb. "When he first showed up, people were gunning for him. Shot up Mack's. Then they kept after him, after all of us. I think that's why he's—"

"Who?" Winston interrupted. "Who shot at him?"

"These guys in suits, like Feds, only they was—"

"They weren't Feds," she completed. "Were they?"

Now he had her attention in full, and it made him blush. He hadn't blushed in a decade. What could he tell her and not ruin the moment? What would she believe of his crazy tale?

"I heard you called them Spooks," Chase said.

Henny had to concentrate in order to not stumble on the trail. "Yeah. That's right."

Willy was out of earshot up ahead on the trail. He was out of sight around a bend. Henny wondered if the kid knew or even cared what they were talking about. He was glad to have some distance between him and them, just in case.

Henny looked from one of them to the other, still astonished but more and more confident. "Yeah, and the Spooks are back. Seen some myself just last night."

"You two!" Winston said, swatting at his shoulder with the back of her hand. "It was you guys with the trash truck."

She looked back at Sackerson, then again at him with a 'gotcha' smile.

He nodded.

"Trash—the same trash truck Alex was after?"

Henny couldn't hide his surprise from Captain Chase.

"Small world!" Chase exclaimed. Then to Ashley, she said, "So these guys got rid of everything, before Alex could get a confirmation. They're in on it?"

"No. No. No," Henny said. "Really, Sack said it was for the best. He knows what he's talking about."

Chase looked over her shoulder. "Dial it down, but keep talking, Hinman. What'd he tell you?"

"We had to get rid of them so they wouldn't bring more," Henny said. "We ported them, the whole truck, guns and all, out by the power plant. Sack said it would hide the porting if we did it out there. Nuclear radiation and all that."

They walked on, absorbing it. Finally, Ashley Winston spoke up, "How would killing those four bring more Spooks?"

"I dunno. Sack talks a lot. Maybe you should ask him."

"I'm asking you, Kenny," she said. She was warming up to him. He could feel it. Her hand on his shoulder was electrifying. This was something he'd have trouble sharing at home. Nobody'd believe him. *The* Ashley Winston had a thing for him. She was hanging on his every word.

"He said they came because it was time... and that they was drawn to the big Hot Wire like moths to a flame. He said the sooner we got rid of them, the safer we'd be, but that we should be ready for more."

"More Spooks?"

"That's right. Sack said whenever some went down, others always showed up. Said it was always like that." He shrugged. "Guess this time we're safe for a while, thanks to last night."

"I don't wanna be safe," Winston said. She and Chase were in on something Henny was missing.

"From my experience, Miss Winston, you don't want nothing to do with them."

"So, these Spooks... they're drawn to Hot Wires, and they multiply whenever some of them get offed," Chase summed up. "If TransCorp's lighting up Laramie with portals—"

"What would bring them?" Winston asked Henny. "*What would bring them all?*"

Just the thought of it startled him. Henny lost his stride and looked back at Sackerson. He and Alex were in an animated dialogue, not to be interrupted. Henny looked ahead, but the trail just went on and on.

"Well?" Chase prompted, frowning a bit like his Gail.

"Tic-Tacs," he said quietly. "They're after the Tic-Tacs."

Chapter 53 Word Travels Fast

A *waif stood waiting in the rain.* It sounded like a sentence Nathan had to say a million times from the speech pathologist. Stu hated himself for abstract thoughts, but they seeped in like mold when he was losing his grip.

He thought it was Rae standing out there in the downpour, but when Schmitty pulled up, he saw it was Nat. They wiped away the rain from their eyes, and, seeing Stu was the passenger, approached that side.

"What are you doing out here?" Stu called out.

"Eaters are coming," Nat warned. "*Here.* Lots of them."

Stu pulled Nat with him to the porch. He waved Schmitty away. "What are you talking about?"

"They think mom's been shot." Nat looked absently through the windows. It was bright and warm inside. "She's fine."

Stu shook Nat's shoulders. "Hey. You all there? What are you talking about?"

The kid seemed in shock. Shivering from the cold rain. Maybe more.

"Nat. What's going on?"

"A drone was at my window earlier. Tapping it like a cardinal. I let it in, and it was flashing a message in Morse Code."

Stu reached to hug Nat, then thought better of it. The rain hadn't washed away anything. It hadn't come off in the van, despite his efforts. He smelled like a slaughterhouse.

"This message... it said to expect them here?"

Nat nodded. "Said they were going to avenge the murder of Mrs. Wiebe."

"Word travels fast," Stu muttered.

"Said they'd meet here. Meet *you* here. Did you know?"

Stu tossed his hat on the porch swing and stripped off his coat, too. "No, I had no—I don't think it's a good idea. The Boys?"

"Mom's already working them. She's sent most all of them to the hospital."

"Why the hospital?"

"Jack in, dad. Catch up. You'll see."

"Where's mom?"

"She's up in my room, trying to use the drone like a two-way. I told her it won't work that way, that it's—"

"I'm a mess, Nat. I'm going in the mudroom and stripping down, gonna get in the shower. You keep her busy, got me?"

Nat looked at him, studied his face. "She's already seen it. We all have. Live action footage on the Interface."

"What?"

"The whole thing. CommCorp version, of course. I got a bootleg sent from the Eaters, too. It tells a different story."

"*How can everybody already...* what's the CommCorp version?"

"I'll let you see for yourself," Nat said, "After you shower."

• • • •

Nat's HeadGear was a little tight, but it wasn't a cheap model, and after just seconds of recalibrating, it was streaming smooth Interface music into Stu's good ear.

"Okay. Show me the vids, Nat. I'm ready—"

The HeadGear spun visual and sensory servos that made Stu queasy. The sound was alternating to compensate for his injury, resetting equilibrium. Suddenly Stu felt he was back on the street again, rain just starting to spit. Then he saw himself. It was like walking toward a mirror from inside a mirror. A woman was with him, then a flash of bright light and a red cloud, and Stu on screen collapsed at the same time, in the opposite direction, as the woman.

The image then was jolting and shaky. HeadGear footage. Someone filming was running toward the scene.

Sudden blackness, then the visor went clear, and the sound was off. Stu had to grab the edge of the counter to stay upright. He was in his kitchen again. Rachel and Nat were with him.

"That's your copy?"

"Yeah," Nat said.

"I'm sorry you had to see that." Stu said.

"It's better than the broadcast one," Rae said. "Seen it yet?"

"No, I... Rachel, I don't..."

"It doesn't matter, Stu. None of that matters right now."

"Dad, you got just about enough time to watch it before they start showing up, if you want to."

"Right." Stu sat on a bar stool at the counter and braced himself. "Interface vid of Lara—"

He didn't even get the opportunity to ask for the scene. The HeadGear interpreted his request and splashed it on the visor. Two gritty men, suspicious-looking men, were squinting left and right. The ticker at the bottom of the screen was running with their names and profiles, repeating again and again their affiliation with Rebels of the Plains, followers of the Eat the Rich menace that had taken over Laramie. More Rebels were on screen, well-armed, and from Stu's trained eye, running drills. Then close ups of weapons firing. A cut from the street scene. Much closer shots of the two of them, Stu and clearly Krystal Price. The muzzle flash in the distance, blood spatter—fake and hyped—dripping down the camera lens as the two bodies fell. A close up of the gore he had witnessed himself.

"You don't want to hear it," Nat said. "It's a bunch of bullshit."

"I don't need to hear it," Stu said, yanking off the HeadGear. "Message is pretty clear."

"So," Rachel said, "Our Boys have seen the Interface. They're gonna be gunning for the Eaters. Everybody's seeing that. You were *there*, though, and Schmitty said the Eaters were watching out over you when he showed up."

"That's right," Stu said. "I might've gotten picked off, too, if they hadn't surrounded me."

"Nobody got 'picked off,' Stu. Watch it again." Rachel pointed at the HeadGear. "Watch Nat's raw vid."

"I don't need to see it again."

"Nat thinks it was set off by your phone."

"What was set off by...?"

When he had answered the phone, there was an explosion. He knew that now, no mistaking that on the vid. Forensics be damned. Krystal's Implant had exploded. CommCorp made it up to be a shooting, but it was triggered by the unknown caller.

"How the hell's that work? How'd *my* phone set off a charge—"

"I'll explain it later," Nat said.

"You'd better get it together," Rachel warned. "They'll be here any minute, and they'll be wanting direction from you."

Stu shook his head. "Doesn't matter what I say." *Krystal's dead, regardless.*

"And you better be done with them before The Boys get back from the hospital run," Rachel continued. "Or things could get messy."

Chapter 54 Tourists

R ory was resourceful. He traded *just one* of the HeadGear pieces in his bag for a good many things: new clothes, bountiful food, a thick stack of local currency, a map and directions, and, of all things, a tandem bicycle.

The HeadGear had afforded them bottomless bottles and (though he was very bored with it after years) beachfront lodging. The bartering had brought them from parts of town destroyed by TransCorp's manipulations to a few blocks that had continued a tradition of tourism. Here, they had even found ice, something Rory had forgotten he even missed.

It was a fresh new day after a night of interrogation. They had swapped questions and answers deep down into a bottle of Arehucas rum, then slept it off. Now they stood in front of their cottage, arguing over the bicycle.

"I heard 'rickshaw and driver,'" Rory explained. "Last night. I swear."

"You *interpreted* this, you mean."

"What's it matter? It's wheels."

"I will not ride this," Katrina said, pulling down her sunglasses.

"C'mon. It beats walking. Lots faster." In his mind, he was calculating, arriving at a figure he was confident in. "We can get three times farther."

"It is ludicrous."

"Well... I can hunt the guy down again. Try to trade up," Rory said, though he did not look forward to more charades. "We might lose an hour or two just working that deal."

"This would be foolish. What two people can you imagine less likely to be on a pleasure ride? We do not belong on a beautiful island of such flowers and sun and—us on this bicycle for two!"

"I look like a circus ape," Rory said, crushing the front seat as he took his position. "At least you won't look this silly."

"It is not so much the way I would look," she said.

"Well...?"

"I have never been on a bicycle," Katrina confessed.

"Oh."

Rory gripped the handlebars. He swatted at the tassels at the ends of them. He ran his thumb over the bell, then could not help himself from ringing it.

He was finding that navigating the world again was difficult, but threading through conversations and customs with others—especially with Katrina—was a bigger challenge. He thought just by asking he might have hurt her feelings, or that, maybe, it hurt her just to admit she had never been bicycling.

She was circling the bike now, frowning at it. She adjusted the strap of her backpack as she passed him on a lap. Her sundress flared in the breeze. Rory was surprised to feel her hop aboard. "I will trust you," she said with some resignation. "Do not go quickly."

Rory turned back to her and said, "Just do what I do, okay?"

"How do I balance?"

"You don't think about it. Let me balance us. You just follow my lead, okay? When I stand up on it, pedaling down hard, it's gonna be my left leg. You do it, too."

"Why your left leg?" she asked.

"Took a bullet to the kneecap on the right," Rory said, again surprised at how memories returned to him.

"Let's do it," Rory said, and he put his full power into the left pedal. They surged ahead, and he settled onto his seat. "Now just keep your feet on the pedals and go through the motions. If we're going uphill, I'll need you to stroke, otherwise, have some fun."

They got off to a great start, pedaling along a winding, picturesque path. Rory couldn't believe he said that. *Just have some fun?* That was not an assassin's words. He looked back to see if it had sat poorly on her, too, but he was more surprised by the smile covering her face. The breeze was blowing back her hair, and the sun glinted on the frame of her sunglasses. She looked like a different woman.

Their plan was to pedal down shore to an old TransCorp facility Katrina had seen from the air. She had been stationed there ten years ago and knew the place to be abandoned. If squatters had not taken it over, the facility might have tools and power and other resources that could repair their HeadGear.

Functioning HeadGear might mean finding a way back to the states and eventually, as Katrina had informed him, to the trouble brewing in Laramie, Wyoming.

As Rory pedaled along, he recalled all she had told him, rolled it around in his mind. Before the HeadGear went dead, Katrina had kept up with news via dark channels on the Interface. She told him one of the big five corporations, ChompCorp, was as stupid as its name. They made blatant threats to gain ground, and when that failed, they resorted to drastic measures. They stole an airship, weaponized it, and threatened communities like Laramie.

Locals put out a plea for help, and of all who might respond, TransCorp stepped in. Katrina's retelling was venomous then. In their usual show of force, TransCorp destroyed the airship, completely vaporized it with new technology—a massive portal.

The technology was not new, however. This part of her story was steeped in rum, late at night, and even now Rory was not sure how much of it to believe. She said they had been experimenting with portals for decades. She said they had them stockpiled.

• • • •

Rory knew the sun in these parts. He had a working relationship with the sweltering heat and scorching rays that made one's head swim. During these midday hours, he typically would sleep or swim.

Katrina, however, urged him onward. She had insisted the cove was just ahead. Over a rise, curving down to the seaside, they found a cove. As she described it, there were abandoned buildings and a beachfront dock.

It was not, however, as she remembered it, and ultimately it was not the right cove. Nor was the next, nor the next.

Rory was growing weary, glazed in sweat. He wondered—but didn't dare say aloud—if her memory was misguided. He thought that maybe one of those coves they had passed might once have been the TransCorp headquarters she had known.

Finally, at the crest of yet another rise, Rory pulled over. He sipped from the canteen, then offered her a drink. She had dismounted and was shading her eyes, peering down the next hill toward the sea.

"That," she said, proud of her persistence, "was once the cove of TransCorp."

He looked past her to the little harbor. The dock had collapsed into the water, only pylons and debris suggested it had once served any purpose. Three large buildings flanked the waterfront, and of them, only one had not fallen in on itself. "Doesn't look like much," Rory said.

"The lodgings were burned down," she said, taking a swig from the canteen. "The warehouses stood against angry people but proved no match for the storms."

"How long has it been abandoned?" Rory noted power lines and pipes that made their way from the water to the warehouses. Desalination and tidal generators for power remained close to the shore, though cockeyed and wrecked.

She looked at him slyly and mounted the bike. "Let's go find out. I am not certain even that they are entirely empty."

Rory felt foolish now, dressed like a tourist in knickers and seersucker, riding a tandem bike down the hill. His swords were stored back on the beach, buried where he could find them. He had a couple of pistols in his backpack, but drawing them would not be quick or easy.

"You sure this is a good idea?" he asked over his shoulder.

"Tourists get a pass," she said.

He knew her handgun was much more ready-at-the-draw than his own.

Rory piloted the bicycle right up to the building most intact. The corrugated tin had a patina of rust about it, and the metal radiated the heat of the day. Some windows were broken out, and one door was off its hinges. It certainly didn't look occupied.

Katrina leaned the bike against the building, for it had no kickstand. Rory took this time to rummage a pistol from the tangle of HeadGear in his bag. He was not especially surprised to note that she, too, was brandishing a weapon as they approached the warehouse door.

"Try not to kill anyone," she whispered, then ducked inside and to the left, pressing her back against the wall. Rory followed, to the right.

It took a bit for his eyes to adjust. Katrina had removed her sunglasses and was blinking. Mistake number... he had not been keeping count. Temporary blindness could get one killed in an instant.

His instincts were recalibrating to potential indoor threats and scenarios. He became acutely aware that the tin wall behind him would not stop a bullet from outside. The jumble of crates and piled debris inside would be good cover for anyone inside who might have a gun aimed at them.

"I don't like this," he said.

"Maybe this will ease your mind," Katrina said, and swept her palm out across the cavernous interior.

Rory thought she looked silly. She was silly. Ridiculous. He could not stifle a chuckle, then that boiled over to full-on laughter he could not repress.

She frowned him to silence, cupped her ear for a moment, then just boldly walked into the warehouse. It was so quiet that Rory could hear her sandals crunching over debris.

"What—" he chuckled again, trying to stop it and to catch up with her. "What was that? Did you do that?"

"Don't be..." she paused as if reading his mind, "*silly*, Reed."

"You did. You... you..."

"I believe you call it an Affectation. Yes, I *affected* you. Sorry." She tossed in the apology without the least bit of sincerity. "Anyway, there is no one else here. Come along."

"What if they just lack a sense of humor?" Rory asked, finding it funny.

"Ugh," she said. "Maybe I should have chosen another Affectation."

Katrina was quickly able to find her way through the facility, narrating what it had been like, what was different. She remarked on the surprising ravages of nature in so short a time. Nature and looters, she asserted. The locals had not liked TransCorp's presence at all, and they had been ruthless in their vandalism.

Though hard to discern in the rubble, Katrina pointed out a central structure, like a pedestal, that was larger than a house. She was pleased to find a heavy door on the structure remained locked and intact.

"Here is where you come in," she said.

Rory examined it. The frame and jamb had been pried at. Someone had previously given it their all. For all their effort, only the slightest gap had been torqued from the door's metal framework.

"I dunno," he said. "What's so important in there?"

"Maybe nothing. It has been years." She tossed it off with a shrug. "Maybe you cannot get us in, anyway."

He knew a challenge when he heard one. Rory cast about for something, anything, to pry with. He found the leg of an old office chair, but it was just a chromed pipe that folded over when he flexed it. He rummaged for something more, his frustration increasing.

"The floor is concrete. The door and frame are both metal," Katrina stood looking at it, describing it, as if in telling about it she might talk it open. "It seems impossible—"

"I could pop that latch with a decent battering ram," Rory said.

"I could fly, if only I had wings," she said, suggesting how little good it did to wish for what one did not have on hand.

Rory had an idea. "Wait here," he said, and darted through the debris to the lot outside. He returned with a concrete parking stop, six feet long and easily 200 pounds.

He looked at her, proud of his find, then did not delay. He braced his feet, aimed the end of the stop at the door's locking mechanism, then swung it hard.

Nothing.

He pulled back and swung the curb stop even harder. The knob was crushed and remains of it fell to the floor. Otherwise, the door remained latched.

His third thrust with the curb stop was so fierce the building shuddered, but the door did not budge. It buckled some at the point of impact, but not enough to help.

Katrina had lost interest and circled behind the structure. She was still exploring the ample space surrounding the structure, still seeking something to pry with.

Rory cursed and pounded the end of the curb stop again and again at the door. The concrete was crumbling. His hands were bleeding. The door was not moving. He wiped the sweat from his eyes and reared back to swing the curb stop at the door like a baseball bat.

"Um, before you do that," Katrina said from the corner, "you should come around here. I believe I have a solution."

Rory tossed down the curb stop. It landed in a loud crash that stirred up dust and debris. He imagined she might have found a wooden box of dynamite, maybe, or more practically a forklift.

Rounding the corner, he saw her gesture at yet another door. Approaching, he noticed this door had not suffered the prying and abuse the other had endured. Rory took an improvised pry bar Katrina extended to him and set to work wrenching at the door crack. This door was not as airtight. It rattled and flexed with his effort.

"Wait," she said, inspired. Katrina waved him aside, turned the knob, and the door clicked open.

"Huh," Rory growled.

"What? Have you no wise quotes about doors being locked or open?"

He huffed and pushed past her.

She had not mentioned prowling through dark warehouses when they had set out for the morning. Had she, Rory would have packed a flashlight, maybe two. His old grip, his favorite bug out bag, always had several flashlights, also matches, a lantern...

"I know the HeadGear's not connecting, but can they light up or something?" Rory asked. He pulled off his backpack and dug around in it.

"Some models have forward facing—"

"Got it." He had the light on and was offering it to Katrina. He found a similar HeadGear for himself. With the bright lights on their foreheads, they penetrated the gloom like a couple of miners.

"Eureka," Katrina said, wiping her hand across a tall box.

Rory did a double take. Again, she seemed to have picked up on his thought of miners, and her exclamation was one old gold miners had used. *Eureka. I found it!*

"What is that?" he said, aiming his light at it.

The box was taller than Rory, a monolith that was otherwise three feet wide. It looked like a refrigerator box, but it was only a foot deep. She was swiping off dust and cobwebs, revealing stenciled graphics that made no sense to him. A blue doorway with an exclamation point framed within it.

"Portal," Katrina said. She cast her headlight back and forth, panning over what must have been hundreds of similar boxes. "Portals to every destination."

The two of them stood and marveled, their headlights sweeping the room.

"*If the enemy leaves a door open, you must rush in,*" Rory said, surprising himself. "That's from the Art of War."

"Rushing in might not be wise," Katrina argued, "but any one of these may be our way off of this island."

"How did you know these were here?" Rory turned to her, careful not to blind her with his light.

"I didn't. I was looking for tools and a way to power up our HeadGear. This is amazing."

"TransCorp stockpiled these? Think they have warehouses of them everywhere?"

She ignored his question and began unboxing the nearest portal.

Rory felt more hope than he could remember. This was luck he did not deserve nor expect. Laramie, Wyoming, was now just a threshold away.

Chapter 55 The Future

Ashley's jaw ached from fighting back words. She was straining to keep an Affectation from tearing out of her. So satisfying to shred the Spooks in suits, but she dare not let it loose, for she feared it would harm her friends, too.

Kelli, at her side, was equally tense, a wire about to snap.

She didn't bother looking behind her to the men with her. From his cackling, Sackerson seemed unaware of trouble. Hinman was likely cowering behind him.

She didn't risk a glance at Alex, for he would see it as a call to action.

In the distance, she could see Willy Titus zipping away on his electric bike.

This must be his revenge, she thought.

These grim men had been hiding in the neighborhood, she now knew. It had been quiet for they had made it that way, likely silencing all the residents. Permanently... at least that was her best guess.

Ashley flexed her hands, feeling them cramping.

"We're here for the time traveler," one of the identical men in identical suits said, flat and firm. "Lay down your weapons and comply."

None of them laid down their weapons.

Ashley had seen fraternal, even identical twins, but she had never seen true clones before. It was eerie, noting how they stood the same and trained their big rifles at them the same. A dozen men who might move as one, efficiently, all of one hive mind.

Alex, just behind her, was coming up on Kelli's side. He sighed in exasperation. Ashley splayed a hand to signal him back. *Maybe they did not know who the time traveler was. No need to give it away.*

"Produce the time traveler or die," another of the clones said.

"I'm buying you some time," Ashley said out of the corner of her mouth, then she strode across the gap between the two parties.

A sense of peace settled more strongly on her with every additional step.

Yes, this was the right thing to do.

The hard things were usually the right things to do.

The richest woman on earth had never had so much to give as she was gifting her friends right at this moment. She was standing in the gap. She was closing the gap. She was giving herself up for them to have another chance.

At that instant, she felt all aflutter. She choked back a startled, "Oh!"

The epiphany was so strong upon her, she nearly doubled over.

She loved and missed Rory, but beneath all that, she hated him for what he had done. She had been so angry at him. For so long now she had wanted to slap Rory Reed and confront him with the speech she'd never get to give: "Why, Rory? Why would you do that? Throwing away everything we could have had. *Throwing me away?* Throwing me through and then sealing the portal?"

She had imagined the argument a hundred times, and in every instance, he avoided giving her an answer. She would kick it up a notch in these fantasies, screaming, "I thought you loved me. How could you?"

He did love her.

She knew it now, a deep knowledge that struck her core. He had done it for them all.

Ashley risked a glance back at her friends. They were frozen in shock, just as she had been. She knew their surprise and pain. *How could you?*

Her answer, the answer there was never time to provide—not for Rory and not now in her circumstance—was simply, "How could I not?"

Chapter 56 Lucky

L ark "Lefty" Fortune argued with his mother for ten years. She thought the nickname was a horrible, thoughtless mockery of his severed right hand. She always said his nickname should be Lucky.

His father and uncle were twins, and though some thought twins skipped a generation, Lark had been a twin, as well. His brother, however, died at birth. This, then, was the never-spoken-of first argument that Lark was lucky. His luck, she claimed, followed him throughout school. Where was he, she argued, when the school bus flipped in a ditch outside of Guthrie? *Home recovering from the Chicken Pox.* What about the time everyone in the family had the stomach flu *except for him?* What about the school carnival when he won his first HeadGear? Or the time his poem won a national contest? Hadn't Lucky Fortune answered the question in Quiz Bowl that clenched his team's regional championship his junior year? He won a lottery scholarship to Purdue, though circumstances closed that door.

Those circumstances, what he considered to be his most *unlucky* life episode, had everything to do with his current nickname. His senior year his hand was severed in the meteor shower known as the Guthrie Fall.

His mom, however, even considered *that* good luck. Good fortune. Lucky. "You didn't die out there. Hot rocks raining around you like hail, but you survived. Son, you're the luckiest young man I know."

He needed that luck now. He summoned every lucky thing his mother had held as evidence, then darted under the caution tape closest to the grain elevator ruins. He jogged where he could and slowed to pick his way over debris when he stumbled.

Lucky had never realized just how large a grain elevator could be. They were familiar in every midwestern town, sometimes standing even at junctions and in country plots where no town still survived. Grain elevators like this one were poured of concrete, and this one towered 100 feet overhead. Even where it had been damaged in the TurnCoat rebellion, the elevator was majestic.

He followed the line of destruction toward where the elevator lurched open nearly to the ground, its side ravaged by TransCorp so long ago. From what he could recall of the conversation, Krystal and Stu had entered such a place. He scurried about in the open cavities of the grain elevator, slipping in the rain and rubble.

Time was not on his side. He knew that. He knew stealth took time, and he decided to forfeit that. Better to make himself known and settle a confrontation with Stu or the Rebels or some combination of them all. He called out her name. He called for help. He called and called, but no one seemed nearby.

He had a pistol in hand, one the lax Port Authority soldier had given him along with an umbrella and flashlight. He fumbled them all as he continued to explore. He darted in dark recesses of the elevator, then back out into the drizzle, then back into the next shelter. He discovered a path cleared in the rubble, as if someone had used a giant snowblower that could whisk away concrete and rebar and dirt. The path led inside yet again to a zone with plaques and signage documenting this as the last stand stronghold of Laramie's TurnCoats.

Krystal had read aloud from these, just hours before. He had heard it all on the HeadGear capture.

Lucky Lark Fortune was getting close.

And then his luck ran out.

Dust was sifting down, then gravel was raining down, then bigger debris was crashing down around him. The sound was unlike anything he had ever known, as loud as a freight train, as if he were *inside* the freight train as it rumbled and roared. He could not keep to his feet, and so he scrambled on his hands and knees.

Giant blocks of the elevator slammed down outside, obliterating the path he had just trod. He felt the blast of it hitting the earth, fought the dust cloud that billowed inside. He was blind then, crawling, seeking any shelter he could. He felt his way behind a display and hunkered there coughing, but then even here, inside, bigger and bigger chunks were collapsing in.

The elevator was suffering entropy.

It was folding in on itself, and he was at the heart of it.

He felt his way around, gagging on the dust, moaning against the rumbling and crashing that would define his end.

Finally, Lucky Lark Fortune seemed to have found a sturdier spot in the elevator. He felt around and was sure he had found a solid corner. Tornado drills had taught him that inside walls, particularly corners, were the safest place to take cover.

This was more destructive than a tornado. He sat with his back to the corner, pulled his knees up to his chin, and wrapped his arms around his shins. He made himself the smallest target he could, and he hoped for the best. The building shuddered and broke. Massive pieces pounded down, like boulders from an avalanche.

Yet here, no debris rained down on him. When he risked opening his eyes, he was happy to see that even the dust cloud was not so bad here. It was dark and dusty, but not suffocating. Yet.

The roaring thunder of explosions and collapse continued. Outside this place, he had feared his ears would rupture from it all. Here, however, the noise was lessening. The rumbling was growing faint.

He had lost the umbrella and pistol, but he was still clutching the flashlight.

He snapped it on, and though the beam of the flashlight was largely wasted on the dust it illuminated, he could see through it to the walls surrounding him. He knew their design and structure, since some of the lower levels of the Installation were created for the same purposes.

He pointed the flashlight at the middle of the room, at the grate that was always present in the middle of these rooms, just to confirm what he already knew. He was in the Lead Room Stu had commented on before the HeadGear capture went dead.

Lucky swept the flashlight around the room again, finding the foot thick door frame, then finding that doorway was completely blocked off, floor to ceiling, with rubble.

Lucky Lark Fortune had survived the inconceivable. An entire grain elevator had fallen around him, and he was unscathed. However, he was trapped in this Lead Room with walls so thick no signal nor sound would ever leave them. He was, for all intents and purposes, buried alive.

And Krystal Price had no savior outside.

Chapter 57 Spectacle

S tu sat in a rocking chair on the wrap-around porch. He'd built the house a decade ago, oriented it just so he could sit there in his golden years in his rocker and watch the sunset. Even the driveway had been carved out from the property line a quarter mile west right into the farmyard.

His whole adult life had been one of responsibility and smart decisions. His leadership carried the thirty families that had migrated here with him. They looked up to him, he looked out for them. His ranch employed them. His successes were their own.

It was the way his family had run things back home, too. Be good to your people, and they'll be good to you. His grandpa Wiebe had set the standard, and nothing—not even a nuclear bomb—could shake that up.

Stu was smoking a stogie. He'd puff on it and study the cherry of it, slowly burning. Powerful tobacco. Something his migrants brought him a box of every spring. Illegal, but then, what wasn't getting to be illegal these days?

His grandpa's shotgun, a break open lever action double barrel, lay open across his lap. The Boys, two of them with deer rifles, were watching from nearby shelters for his signal. If he snapped his gun shut and cocked it, he meant business. So long as it lay open, it was a show of force, but not a threat.

The corporations hadn't learned the value of that at all. Those assholes were about nothing but power, and they had been swinging a big bat ever since they'd come into town. They took advantage of locals scared of Chomp. They won over the Eater mob by destroying a billion dollar airship. Now, the tide was going wide, and folks were more excited about independence than allegiance to a Corp, any Corp. So this morning, they swung again. This time they weren't so clumsy. Not so widespread in the damage.

Just one girl. His girl.

Nudging the herd toward hating on the Eaters now, was it? What would be next? Turn them against each other some other way? Anything to keep folks from seeing the obvious: TransCorp was mutating to the Port Authority.

Krys had warned him.

Rachel had turned The Boys out, but the two still hid on the property, deer rifles trained on the Eaters when they rolled in. Her thinking was solid, and she joined him on the porch when the first of them, Abe himself, got out of his pickup.

"Mr. Wiebe, I'm Jeffery Burton. Thought we ought to talk."

"Come on up," Stu invited Burton to a seat on the porch swing. "Thank you for the help back there, by the way."

"Mrs. Wiebe," Burton acknowledged her with a nod. "Happy to confirm you're still among the living. Hope you don't mind we tried to capitalize on the ruse."

"Make it count, gentlemen," she said, and headed back inside.

"I'd like it if you'd stay, if you don't mind, ma'am," Burton said earnestly.

Stu raised an eyebrow, took a pull on his cigar. "Rae?"

"Don't mind if I do," she said and perched on the porch railing.

"I'm sure you've both caught up on the local news?"

"We have," Stu said. "A variety of truths to be told, eh?"

"It's what brings me," Burton said. "I fear the worse for Laramie, and for that matter, those of us of the vigilante bent, everywhere."

"So, I get you're the leader then? Head of the Eaters? How come nobody'd own that last night? Not even you."

"We shift and share leadership," Burton said. "It tends to keep us alive longer."

"We can't do anything about what's been 'cast by CommCorp," Rae said.

"So why are you here?" Stu put an edge on it.

"We're here," he gestured to the farmyard and drive, now full of ramshackle vehicles and rowdy men, "to be of assistance."

"You're here because you're in the crosshairs," Rae said.

"You're not here to help us," Stu added. "You're here for help."

"From what I've seen, you and your fellers, your Boys, haven't gotten much done. We come in, not two days ago, and brought national attention to your plight. We scared off a bully corporation and planted a flag of freedom for—"

"Aw, stow your rhetoric," Stu said. "Save it for a recruitment vid."

"We know what you want, Mr. Burton. Protection."

"Protection?" he sneered. "We outnumber you a dozen to one."

"That vid's gonna bring all kind of hate down on you. You'll all be run off the fairgrounds, probably run out of town."

"Probably run to ground, everywhere you go," Rae added.

"We don't need protection. We need vindication. We need you to get on the Interface and set the record straight." Burton wagged a long skinny finger at Stu.

"You wouldn't have brought your whole gang just for that."

"This isn't my whole troop."

"Oh, I know. I know. The campers and such are still rolling our way," Stu said. "We have our sources, too, you know. Pretty quick bug out, all things considered."

"We can put you up," Rae said. "All you all."

"A week maybe, tops," Stu clarified.

"The Boys won't take to you," Rae warned. "But if Stu says so, they'll protect you."

"We need that vid, Mr. Wiebe." Burton looked at Rae, continuing, "We do appreciate the offer of your hospitality, but we couldn't bring that kind of problems here."

"Wouldn't be the first time," Stu said. "We have the space."

"I appreciate that. I do." Burton said, "But in the same way we puttered up to your kid's window with a drone, think what this new Port Authority can do? If they so much as fly in one Hot Wire, your place could be swarmed with their troops in minutes."

"Where will you go, if not here?" Rae asked.

Burton squinted. He didn't have anywhere. Stu could see it clearly.

"Have you seen 'em? Paid any attention to them?" Stu asked. "Their 'soldiers' are worse organized than your posse. I think they're all conscripted."

"Those in town are little more than posers, you're right," Burton agreed. "But there's more coming, I'm sure."

"Why?" Rae asked, standing. It hadn't occurred to her that there might be a full-scale invasion, apparently.

"Why'm I sure? We've seen it before. From drills to off-grid land grabs."

"Doesn't make sense to me. Ought to come in strong."

"They're hyping it with this wave, and worse, they're planting ports everywhere. Like I said, even a good Hot Wire poses a threat."

"They're driving trucks through them in town," Nat said from the kitchen.

"Tanks will be next," Burton said, giving the kid a nod.

"Shut that window and mind your business," Stu said to Nat.

"Nat, go set us up to post that vid," Rae said.

"Mom, it's as easy as jacking in—"

"Just do what your momma says," Stu ordered.

Nat left the kitchen, but the window remained open.

"I'd feel better if you stayed on the property," Stu found himself saying. "You know, keep your friends close, your enemies closer?"

Burton chuckled. "We're not your enemies by any stretch, Mr. Wiebe, but if you have some back forty where we could camp for the night, that'd be appreciated."

"Rae, tell The Boys we'll have guests down at the Springs."

"There's a dozen of them there still," Rae said. "Maybe you ought to go on down with Mr. Burton and square it up."

"Down there *still*...?" Stu frowned.

"You sent them there this morning," she said, "just before..."

"Ah, you're right! I forgot all about—They've been waiting *all morning*?"

"Some. The rest are at St. Mary's."

"St. Mary's... hospital?" Burton asked.

"That's right," she replied. "We heard there was something brewing over—"

"They ain't wasting *any* time on this one!" Burton stood abruptly and tapped his temple. "Lance, who we got in town? Send them to the hospital."

"What's the problem?" Stu asked, but Burton was already off the porch and calling shots.

"Tony? Bring the RV's on out to the Wiebe's. They'll have someone around to help get 'em parked." He turned back at Stu. "Right, Mr. Wiebe?"

"What? Yeah. We'll help..." Catching up with Burton's frantic state, Stu asked, "What's the big deal about the hospital?"

"I told you they're hyping this one," Burton said. "And fast. Chasing that vid of Ms. Price will be hard to top. They'll try though. In theater it's called Spectacle. There'll be some fresh blood shed for this one."

"What makes you think it'll—"

"It's always the hospital. Clutter it, shutter it, send in Pharma to take it over. That's how they do it. Usually it takes a week, but..." Burton slid in behind the wheel of his pickup. "Got a big gas station in Laramie? Watch your Interface, that'll be next."

Stu called out questions but was drowned out by the vehicles firing up and roaring away. The Rebels of the Plains were a salty bunch of misfits, not even a poor excuse for a militia, but they weren't just the loudmouths he'd taken them for. They were driving straight at trouble. They reminded him of a younger, sloppier version of his Boys.

"Rae!" Stu shouted. "Call 'em up right now. Tell 'em what's coming. Nat—I know you're still listening—get the truck. We gotta get to town. Gotta make sure The Boys play nice with your new friends."

"I already sent word," Nat said. "And Schmidt's due any minute with the pickup."

"You're heading right back into it, Stewart Wiebe. I hope you know what you're doing."

Chapter 58 Bug Out

A lex couldn't contain himself, but Kelli held him back. "Does she know what she's doing?" Sackerson asked.

"It's them, it's them... more Spooks. Bunch a' them," Henny was mumbling.

Alex watched as they closed in on her, ordering her to comply.

"She does *not* know what she's doing," he said and drew his pistols.

Sackerson and Kelli pulled their weapons, too.

"Aim low," Alex said, and then even his thoughts were drowned out by the deafening blasts of gunfire. The *"pew" "pew"* of Kelli's plasma pistol was interspersed with the firepower of the four large caliber pistols. Hers was much smaller, but Kelli had a trained hand and virtually unlimited rounds propelled by super-heated, ionized gas.

All twelve men were downed in ten seconds, none of them had pulled off a shot. Ashley hopped from foot to foot, surveying the bodies around her, slack jawed.

"How's the Princess?" Sackerson asked, holstering his guns.

"*You shot me,*" she said, turning on them. "One of you shot me in the foot."

Alex and Kelli consumed her with hugs and laughter. He did not think he had ever heard Kelli sound so happy. "You're okay," she said over and over. "You're okay!"

Sackerson was on his knees, asking to examine her bloody foot.

Henny sat on the trail where he had stood, shaking his head in astonishment.

One of the clones made a rasping noise, trying to breathe with a punctured lung. Another was trying to drag himself away with his one good arm. Alex pried himself from the hug to complete the grim work of ending them.

"Eh," Sackerson said. "Henny, think they'll all fit in the car?"

· · · ·

"We need more time to work through this," Alex said, leaning down to talk to Sackerson. The wizard was cramped nearly to the dashboard. His chair was moved all the way forward. More room for the bodies. Any resemblance to a respectable character was gone. He had his hair tied back and his beard tied, and both had bloodstains on them. Sackerson's clothes and hands were a bloody mess.

Hinman, looking past arms and legs protruding from the back, just stared at Alex, awaiting instruction.

"You're right, Gault. We do. We *do* need more time, but Henny and I have a delivery to make. Last time, our mistake was that we did not port them properly. I'm none too sure *where* the other four and our trash truck may have ended up."

"Every second counts," Henny said, absently.

"Right you are, my helpful friend. Let's roll."

Henny started the Popper.

"We gotta catch up," Alex insisted. "You're more in the know than I—"

"Historical record," Sackerson said, "but even that's failing us now. I can tell you there's mention of local trouble at the hospital in the records. Maybe you should rally there? Maybe I can meet you, say, at the Grand Marquis later?"

"We'll be in the alley," Henny said, gathering his wits, "at sunset."

"Ohhh, that's good," Sackerson was saying to his companion as they rolled away. "Sunset. Ominous sounding! You're really catching on to this..."

• • • •

Alex needed a sojourn. Talking to another time traveler squeezed at his wanderlust. Sackerson claimed he hadn't done it in over eighty years. That would take some stamina. Alex had abstained only five years now, and he ached to act. He felt a growing and desperate need to move back in time and fix something. Anything.

Then again, his travels had been unpredictable. Inaccurate. Return time might be a matter of minutes or years—and that was the true issue. He was about to be a dad. Just the thought of missing even a minute of that stopped his clock. He couldn't break his vow to Kelli, either. Even if he could teleport back in the next breath, even if she had no idea he had traveled time and back—he couldn't do it. He'd promised her to never do it again. He'd given her his Tic-Tacs.

Those damn little travel berries.

Temporal tidbits.

If not for them, none of this would be happening.

He remembered a scheme the rancher, Stu Wiebe, pitched. Pop back to '28 and get rid of them. Wiebe would've been out of his element. He should stick to herding sheep or whatever.

Revisiting time, materializing in another time and place, that was disorienting at best, deadly—according to Sackerson—for most. It would take someone with some savvy to stick it, to port to the right place and time, even almost the right place and time. Sackerson, if he were to be believed, was good at it. He'd hit Guthrie right after the meteor fall. Even if the old man had the wherewithal, however, he was just not up to it. He was clever but frail.

The endless gunfire in this innocent little town continued. Lives were being lost because corporations were unchecked because Tic-Tacs had allowed the leviathan of TransCorp to rear its head. This perfect storm of flagrant teleportation and agitation and big news had drawn too much attention. All that had spurred those from the future to look for him back in Laramie. The threat of more clones pursuing him put everyone at risk.

He could do something about it.

Alex was fit. He felt more than capable.

Stick it.

Fix it.

Back home and unknown.

• • • •

Alex continued to roam the neighborhood with his weapon drawn. Those pursuing him could be around any corner. That creepy kid Ashley trusted could try to get the drop on him. Hell, maybe the Port Authority soldiers were already reaching out this far.

His investigation yielded absolutely nothing out of the ordinary. It was a boom town neighborhood of prefab houses and astroturf lawns. They all were unremarkably alike. His word for them was simply "nice."

Alex never liked nice. It was mind-numbing and pedestrian. As he traipsed around, through backyards and garages, past the community center and club house, he compared this planned community to the chaos of Franklin, Texas—Kelli's hometown and stomping ground.

He smelled fire and tracked it to a still-smoldering barbeque grill. It was warm to the touch.

His interest was piqued. Something here was *not* nice.

He entered a house where the door was propped open with a bowling ball bag. It looked exactly as he expected it would, but then again, it didn't. The floorplan was cookie cutter, but... there were dirty dishes in the sink. Wet laundry was in the washer.

Another house had dinner set on the table, now cold and shriveling.

These people had left in a big hurry.

His HeadGear and several jacked devices in the house lit up all at once. The montage from CommCorp streamed more rapid fire than he had seen before. It was as if the broadcast was freewheeling, spinning up the last few hours offline fast, getting to the current situation on the streets of Laramie.

Mobs. Streetfighting. Madness. Rebels of the Plains, the scourge of the earth. TransCorp executive executed. Chaos and bloodshed. More portals arriving to establish peace. Vandals. Looting. Rebels had leveled the big grain elevator. Fires. More fighting. The hospital siege and the Port Authority marching on Laramie. "Finally," the AI narration on the CommCorp vid took a breath to say, "a force for good."

Alex pulled his 'Gear and blinked. He watched it scrolling on screens in the house on continuous loop. It was propaganda and madness. It was nothing like he'd seen from his electric bike.

He donned the HeadGear again and took charge of it, dialing it back, playing full vids instead of the flashbang overview hype. He caught a glimpse of people he recognized. Sackerson and Wiebe. Some poorly shot headcam sightings of Ashley Winston. Men and women from the rebels and the ranchers and then again, Wiebe.

Alex froze the image. He read the caption and played the vid of what CommCorp was declaring as the 'shot heard round the world.' They claimed the woman with Wiebe, a TransCorp executive, had been brutally assassinated by the Rebels of the Plains, the Eaters. The vid declared it as an act of war.

Alex knew her as the White Witch, the other of the Guthrie kids. That's what Sackerson had been *not-saying* on the trail. He had not spoken openly around the missionary kid, but he and Hinman were aware of the murder and the hype. *Had they seen the vids? Had they been there? Had one of them taken the shot?*

He dismissed the idea, for it was ridiculous. He tried to, anyway, so he could dismiss the question of why this whole neighborhood had bugged out. He wasn't here to play detective. He wasn't here to get answers to anything. He was here to find them transportation.

He found nothing.

Despite the mystery of it all, despite the grim undertones, Alex could not dismiss the idea of every man, woman, and child in some giant circus parade convoy. Bicycles, cars, trucks, lawn tractors, scooters and trikes and roller skates—everybody on everything—moving out *fast*.

But why?

Chapter 59 Detente

"Over 200 portals and not a one of them set to Laramie?"

"Not one even within 500 miles of there," Katrina tossed aside a cardboard panel.

She had been opening and inspecting the crated portals all afternoon. He had been working over the tidal generators outside.

"And you? Will we have power by nightfall?"

Rory eyed the remaining light from the opened outside door. He didn't want to tell her no.

Just because he recognized generators did not mean he knew how to repair them. He had scraped all the seaweed and sediment from the vanes and paddles. He worked at the slide mechanisms, too, until it all moved freely again. When he put it back in the water, however, nothing happened right away. The generators looked like floating lounge chairs lined up for watching the sunset.

He studied them for a good half hour, but they never seemed any more industrious. It annoyed him. Alex, he realized, would have known just what to do. Alex was the mechanical one. Rory was the muscle.

He traced the cabling, making sure it was all intact, all the way back to a rack of batteries and a breaker box on the warehouse wall. That's when he had found Katrina in a multi-language rant at a clearing in the portal collection. On another day, his old self might have analyzed in which language the obscenities sounded most effective, but this afternoon, he shared her frustration.

"A big nothing," Rory said. "That's what we got."

"If we had but one of these working, we could take the rest, one by one, through it." Katrina said, "If not for TransCorp finding us out, we could sell them all."

"Then we'd be rich?"

"No, then we would be dead. TransCorp would not appreciate our piracy."

"Yeah," he said, "and even if we got away with it, the Eaters would be coming for us Rich folk then."

She snorted at the irony. "Both of us outlaws, assumed dead. Not a pound between us of honest money. What lunatics would think us rich?"

"It's like a fairytale. We're in the dragon's keep with all the gold, but we can't spend it."

"We are on the giant's cloud and cannot escape with the golden harp."

"Yeah."

"We are, as you say, screwed."

"Yeah," he chuckled. "We really are."

"More a nightmare than a fairytale."

"Why do you say that?"

"Solutions at our fingertips, yet so impossibly far away."

"Dead portals. Dead HeadGear. Dead end," Rory said. That about summed it up, he thought.

Then he thought harder. He did a self-assessment. He measured his lot in life.

Naming the processes sounded hollow to him, but doing them did feel good. In his analysis, he realized, "Things may not be so bad, Kat."

"No?" She did not believe him.

"A few days ago, I was sleeping in the sand. I hadn't had a meaningful conversation in years," Rory said. "I was killing people for years and years, butchering them on a hunch that they *might* be wealthy."

"I suppose that's—"

"And you. Stranded. Hunted. Probably getting hungry. Now we're fat n' happy."

It was an old TurnCoat phrase, the kind they'd say when they got double rations and a shot of whiskey. Contentment in all circumstances.

That seldom lasted longer than it took to say it.

"Yes," she said, "that is some perspective, but compared to the future, I do not see such good fortune."

"Kidding me? Once we get this place humming, we can go anywhere. Hock the HeadGear, and we can have anything we want."

"For how long?" Katrina countered.

"I dunno, for the moment."

"So, your good fortune is fleeting," she said. "Nothing to count when it slips through your fingers... or is pried from them by TransCorp."

"Is that what's bothering you? TransCorp?"

Katrina busied herself with peeling the protective plastic skin from the titanium portal nearest her.

"Nothing is bothering me," she said. Then she looked at him directly, "Content in every circumstance."

She switched on her HeadGear light and set it on a portal. It provided a blue grey glow to the surrounding space.

"How do you get in my head like that?" Rory asked. "Is it part of your telepathy thing? Like Ashley?"

Katrina was wadding up the plastic film now, making a ball of it. "I am nothing like my sister."

"Whoa, now that's something I don't remember. You're sisters?"

"Half-sisters," she corrected. "And it's not telepathy," she corrected again.

Rory walked around a few portals, putting some space between himself and Katrina. Here he was in the presence of a woman entitled by birthright to half of Winston Water Works. She was, in the flesh, the embodiment of The Rich. His conditioning should have kicked in. She should have been dismembered by now—yet he didn't feel his Blackbeard coming on.

And other than her confession, she didn't seem like The Rich at all. Katrina Covarrubias seemed so much like him. He leaned against a portal in the clearing where she worked and examined her more closely.

She was, at a glance, a beautiful tourist in a sundress, out of place in this trashed warehouse. She stood tall and solid. He recognized the footing, the weight on the balls of her feet, even in those ridiculous sandals. No one to mess with.

Katrina held the translucent ball of portal wrap. In the low light, it looked like a magic orb, and she, like some mystical warrior.

She *was* a warrior, one who slept standing up and endured the elements just like he did. She hadn't complained about food or water or being tired since they had met. Katrina was lithe and fierce, nothing soft about her like The Rich. He was having trouble accepting her claim of being a Winston.

"Careful. You cannot believe everything you see," she said, moving on to peel film from another portal.

"Tell me again that it is not telepathy," Rory said.

"I don't know what you're talking about."

"I was just thinking you're not what you seem, then you said as much."

"Even if I could read your mind—which I cannot—I would not."

"Why not?" This seemed familiar territory again. It felt like déjà vu.

"Your mind is like the pages of your notebook. No offense, but I am sure it is a jungle," Katrina scoffed. "This I know without telepathy."

"Yeah, but..." He intercepted her hand as she reached to peel film from the portal he leaned on. He put her palm on the side of his face, held it there, then put his free hand on her cheek. "You *can* do telepathy. You *can* enter the jungle."

He braced for her to slap him or twist his wrist. He braced, hopefully, for her to share his mind. Mind meld. Rory was sure, somehow, that she could.

"Well... this is awkward," she said, but did not move away.

"Go on. Melt into my head." He closed his eyes. "C'mon in."

She raised her eyebrows. He could feel it in the muscles of her face. Doubt. A bit of distrust. A little scoff in her breathing.

"This is stupid," she said. Then he felt her posture shift, as if she were resigning herself to his request. She sighed and he sighed with her.

· · · ·

The orb of shipping plastic hit the floor just before they did. They lay in a cocoon of cardboard and strapping tape and dust. It was dark now. In that time between standing and falling the sun had set. Their bodies were folded together, and they extracted themselves from the awkwardness.

He had been right.

In so many ways, however, he had been wrong. It was a violation to meld minds when she would not have wanted it. His every thought about Katrina was sideways if not completely perpendicular to the truth.

Rory parted his lips to apologize when she spoke.

"So much pain," she said. "How have you survived?"

"And you... you are simply irresistible," he said, summing up her situation, then damned himself for remembering the jaunty Robert Plant song. He was glad she was no longer in his mind. Maybe she didn't know the song.

"It is a curse." She rose and turned away from him.

"I'm... I'm sorry, Katrina," Rory said.

"I will take the first watch," she replied, and moved to the frame of moonlight.

Rory sat in the cardboard, his head still reeling. He felt more alone than he had over his last five years of solitude. She was quiet in general, but in stark contrast to the meld, that tsunami of communication, her silence was deafening.

In the distance, he heard her humming a tune, the Plant song, a little offbeat and out of key, but unmistakable. It made him smile.

· · · ·

He thought about it her entire shift at the watch. He should have been sleeping, but this evolving status between them proved spellbinding. He had forced something on her, invaded, and in all that he was a violator. She had no constraints on her tidal wave of emotions. She had no defenses against his opened mind.

Now she set the conditions of their detente.

They were not processing it or sharing sympathies. It would remain between them an unknown knowing, an intimacy not to be spoken of again. In other words, it had never happened.

Chapter 60 Fish in a Barrel

"Rat bastards," Stu said, kicking at shell casings. "*Machine guns?*"

"Yeah, like Cole said. They'd blink in, spray a clip, blink out."

"Picked us off like fish in a barrel."

"We couldn't hardly get a shot off. Didn't know which port they'd use next."

The crowd of Boys parted for a couple of the Eaters pushing in. Behind them, the lanky Jeff Burton, his whole side a bloody mess, lurched along with a crutch.

"They fight... unconventionally," Burton grimaced, "but predictably all the same."

Stu's Boys were waiting for him to take the reins. Some of them were obviously puzzled by Burton's words. "It's always the same *order*," Stu said, "but not always the same *way?*"

Burton nodded.

The crowd nodded sagely then, catching the drift.

The knot of them were 50 yards from the ER entrance. They were looking over a truck and portal, one of a dozen that fanned around the half-circle parking outside the hospital. The rain had let up, but it hadn't washed away the blood or bodies. A dozen dead, dropped as they'd been shot, around the ER doors. Five or six more crumpled behind the landscaping between the ER and their current location. Some of those were Stu's Boys. Others were Burton's Rebels.

"So from here, they'd pop in, pop out, randomly?"

"That's exactly it."

"Cowardly," Stu said.

"How can we fight that?" someone asked.

Burton passed his crutch to his man, Stokes. "Yesterday, I'd tell you we had their playbook and could stay a step ahead. The day before—well, we were wrong. Misguided. We thought TransCorp would level ChompCorp, and we wanted that so badly we ignored the obvious."

The way they shifted, exchanged puzzled looks, made Stu shake his head. The Boys were not following. He sighed. "They threw in with the wrong bullies."

"That's about it, yeah," Burton said.

"You've seen TransCorp do this before then?"

"Well...they're calling themselves the Port Authority, as of today, but yes. Never so sudden. Usually lots of pitching fits, getting good press... none of this," Burton gestured at the parking lot. What cars were there were shot to hell. A few of The Boys' trucks had taken some damage. "Hospital picked up the wounded already, but between us, we must have 20 casualties."

"We were holding our own with the protestors, they was shitty shots."

"But these trucks! They pulled in off the highway, and boxed us in."

"Then like all at once, they dropped off ports and was taking off."

" Soon as ports hit the ground, they were blinking blue flashes and we had real trouble."

"They didn't give a damn 'bout nobody. Shot up their own front line along with ours."

"Then, quick as a wink, they'd port away."

"Couldn't hit 'em, couldn't fight back."

"Not that fast."

"Went on like that too damn long. Ports flashing all about this half circle you see here. All along the parking lot here."

Over a dozen ports were standing at the backs of trucks. The portals were pristine. The trucks were riddled with bullet holes, destroyed. Flat tires and shattered windows. Stu took in the rest of the scene, too. The stucco of the ER entrance was pock marked and crumbling. Signage was in pieces. Bodies, mostly those of the posers hired into this mess, were pushed aside, and the survivors had been taken in for treatment.

"How many of yours inside?" Stu asked. "Able bodied."

Burton looked to one of his men. "Maybe ten."

It was grim. Stu couldn't force himself to ask about The Boys, but if even one of them had died in this skirmish, there'd be hell to pay.

"They're relentless," Burton mustered up. "Every chance they get, they're making us look like terrorists, making you and yours look like..."

"Like village idiots," Stu said. Nat had shown him some of CommCorp vid loops on the way over.

"They're throwing us in this together, Wiebe. Interface can justify anything they want to rain down on us, especially after making it look like we killed Miss Price."

"I got people trying to get the raw vids up over some channels," Stu said, pacing the line of portals. "Your people know anything about these? Can you jam them or something?"

Burton shook his head. "This is the closest we've ever been to them. We can take one on, see if we can figure what makes it tick."

"Won't have time," one of The Boys said, pointing at the sky.

"Already?" Burton asked.

A swarm of drones was getting close enough to hear, and when they came into view, they swooped in a formation like a murmuring of birds.

"They're coming in for the show, doubtless they're going to do their damnedest to make us look even worse," Burton said. He got on his Internal and began barking orders at his men.

"Tell 'em to stay clear of the ports, Burton."

"Why's that?"

Stu pointed toward the north. "I finally let The Boys have some leash," he said. "They've raided the old National Guard."

. . . .

Before Burton could raise another question, heavy equipment was rolling onto the hospital grounds. The big bellowing diesels drowned out the whining of drones. Before the trucks and trailers were completely stopped, The Boys were unchaining loaders and backhoes and all manner of heavy equipment. Some were Iraq khaki. Others were olive drab. An excavator was the first to fire up, and the operator put it to task.

Heavy, titanium clad portals that weighed as much as a car were rammed together and compacted along with the trucks that had brought them in. Portals flickered, but nothing was able to come through them. After a few minutes of thrashing and crushing, the iron and titanium mound was rendered harmless.

"What, no tanks?" Burton said when he could be heard again. He smiled at their handiwork.

"Why didn't we think of that?" an Eater marveled.

"The Boys love their theatrics," Stu said. "And their dozers."

"Won't see any of that on the vids," Nat offered.

"Speaking of..." Stu turned to some of his men and gave them the nod. They pulled shotguns from their long coats and began blasting at the drones overhead.

Burton's men joined in.

The drones and their cameras were thinned out quickly.

They pulled back to safer distances, then hummed away entirely.

"Now they got a fix on us, they're sure to pull all the stops," one of the Eaters commented, "but that sure felt good."

"What do they want, anyway?" Nat asked.

"Port Authority?" Burton asked. "To win. And they always do."

"Not this time," Stu said. He flagged the heavy equipment. "The Boys won't let that happen."

Chapter 61 Bioremediation

H enny wasn't in the mood to talk.
He wasn't in the mood to listen.

Sackerson couldn't take a hint, so Henny just turned the radio up louder.

He would have turned it up again, but he detested reaching around the foot of the dead man from the back seat. That man's shoe had been lost in all the shoving and twisting of limbs to make him fit. It struck Henny as odd that a hit man or criminal or clone—whatever this guy had been—had worn a hole in the toe of his black sock.

"I'm sure of it now, Henny. We should have ported the trash truck right on the grounds of the plant. Better radiation shielding. A mile away like that, it musta been like a beacon to those hunters in the future. They're always on the scopes for it, you know, always hoping to find a flare..."

Henny let him talk. Like many patrons of *Sharts N' Grins*, Sackerson was wired to talk it out. How many nights had Henny listened to how many schemes and frustrations? Talking that was incomprehensible over the music and laughter, words that were slurred with drunkenness. Henny only half listened, but people felt heard, and that was what mattered. So Henny smiled and nodded once in a while, looked over the limbs akimbo and shared a serious look with Sackerson sometimes, whenever he felt it was needed.

"How're we getting back to town?" Henny asked, his head clearing up a bit. "If we're ditching the car, what will we do? You can't think we'll find another Peterson. We couldn't be that lucky twice."

"We need the wheels," Sackerson frowned and nodded. "You're right about that."

• • • •

Henny grabbed the left ankle and wrist, Sackerson the right, and they tossed the twelfth clone through the portal. Sack said he would take on the dangerous task of disposing of the weapons. Henny should clean up the car.

They had argued about it some, but ultimately Henny had to admit that no, he did not know how to decouple the radio isotope accelerator or properly port a chronostatic detonator.

They'd stopped on the way, only long enough to buy a box of rags, a gallon of bleach, and a couple of gallons of water. Henny should have known then that this would be his job. Sack had said as much, that he had an aversion to bleach. He seemed to have an aversion to work, Henny thought.

He set to work yanking the blood-soaked carpet from back floorboards, grumbling and repeating all the technobabble Sackerson spewed.

Henny felt like he was working the packing house again, like he had in high school. It was as cold as the room he had hung carcasses in, as messy as the kill floor itself. At least then he had been dressed for it. Every shift he'd start in stark white coveralls and then end the day looking like someone from a horror movie.

It was a challenge to keep the crimson muck off his clothes. The effort cost him time and a backache. Henny stood and stretched, taking in a few deep, clean breaths before resuming the grizzly work. He thought it might be wise to dispose of the car's carpet as they had its occupants. He turned around to ask, noticing Sackerson was tossing the weapons wholesale through the portal.

He shrugged and returned to his work. So much blood soaked the trunk liner that it came out in matted patches like clumps of wet hair. Henny raked it up with his fingers splayed. He did not have a gag reflex. He had cleaned up worse. Once he and The Boys had gone jackrabbit hunting outside Guthrie, piling the dead ones in Henny's mom's trunk. That had been a worse clean up.

He had worked in the body shop that same summer of the Guthrie Fall, and after the Feds were done with it, he had towed the remains of Lefty's car and Stu's pickup to their shop which doubled as the city's impound. There was no cleaning those two up. Total losses. Henny had taken lots of his friends out to see what was left of them after the meteor shower destroyed them. They both looked like a car in that Las Vegas museum, the one Bonnie and Clyde had been shot up in. Lefty's had caught fire, too. Poor ol' Lefty had worked nearly full-time to buy that thing, then it was toasted just like that.

All that over a girl.

Henny wondered how Lefty was getting along with Krystal about then. Lark Fortune didn't have the sense God gave a grapefruit, but he was madly in love. He'd lost all his common sense, and if Henny wasn't such an understanding guy, he'd about lost his best friend over her, too.

Cold-cock him with a bottle!

• • • •

He had lugged all the sodden carpet and upholstery to Sackerson's Hot Wire port and chucked it through, load after load. All that, with hardly a spatter on his good coat. His shoes were another story. His hands couldn't get clean enough, no matter how much he rubbed and rinsed them.

He was giving the back seat a final going over when he heard a stranger's voice. Henny hit his head on the doorsill trying to get a look at who it was.

"I said, having a troubling time?" the man repeated.

Henny looked toward the Hot Wire, but Sack was nowhere to be seen.

"Uh... nope." Henny said. "Just cleaning up a little."

The man was of average height and build. He smiled broadly, one of those too-drunk-to-find-the-toilet smiles. He looked familiar, but Henny couldn't place the guy. He had dark hair, combed back. He was wearing loafers and jeans—and the cuffs of the jeans were rolled up revealing his socks. He had on a pink knit shirt and a striped sweater.

Henny looked around for Sack again. He looked for some idea where this guy had come from. Surely he didn't work at the plant. Not dressed like that.

"How about that ball game?" the guy asked, raising his eyebrows.

Henny tried not to show his puzzlement. What possible ball game could he be asking about? It was a conversation starter, sure, in a crowded bar on a weekend, with all the CommCorp screens running different games.

Here, in the plant parking lot, it was just daffy.

"Haven't kept up, I guess," Henny replied. He shut the passenger doors and circled around the car to close the rest. He looked over his shoulder. The Hot Wire was still suspended nearby, still glowing its aqua blue.

The man didn't comment on it.

"Nice weather we're having," he said, instead, still with the stoner grin.

Henny came around behind the car, keeping it between him and the guy. He put his hands on the trunk lid and paused. He looked over the lid at the guy. He wanted some assurance before he acted rashly.

It was funny what a change of clothes would do for a man. Henny had seen it before many times. A banker or funeral director, some suit from the city—when they dressed down at *Sharts*, they were hard to recognize. He had the same feeling with this guy, and squinted, trying to imagine him dressed differently.

The guy squinted back. His face worked strangely, as if he didn't know how to squint quite right, then he stated, "You're Kenneth Ray Hinman, right?" There was no inflection, and that gave it away.

The guy was reaching behind his back, like he was scratching some hard to reach spot up inside his sweater. That was enough of a move. Henny ducked behind the trunk lid and grabbed the big laser rifle he'd stashed there. He was about to bring it up to bear down on the Spook when gunshots blasted rapid fire. Henny peeked over the trunk as a gush of blood spewed at him. The guy flopped forward, revealing Sackerson twenty paces behind. His twin pistols were raised high.

"Where were you?" Henny exclaimed. "Waited long enough!"

He lowered the rifle back into the trunk discreetly and shut the lid before Sackerson noticed.

"I was testing you, testing him," Sack said, kicking the corpse's loafer.

"*Testing* me?"

"You have the nose for it," Sackerson smiled. "You had him figured out."

"A lot of good it woulda done me, if you weren't there!"

"But I *was* here, Henny, and you did good. They're getting crafty, aren't they? Disguises. Small talk."

Henny nodded his head. He recognized the guy now. Same face as all the others. He had made an effort not to look at their faces, not the ones in the trash truck, not the ones they'd just ported away. To focus on their faces made them seem more like people, and Sackerson insisted that they were not people, not really, just copies of a person. Clones.

He tipped his head a little, looking down on this clone's head. His hair was parted. He had combed and styled it himself, not in the same way as the ones in the elevator or the car. This clone had decided to express himself differently. He had failed, but he had tried to make conversation.

Henny felt his innards gurgle then. On instinct, he looked at the plant, trying to remember if they'd seen a restroom when they'd met Peterson just inside. He thought about the rest stop they'd been at, the boarded up one. He was feeling sick, and he was worried he'd be sick from both ends.

Sackerson had on a pair of surgical gloves. He snapped at the cuffs. "Let's chuck ol' Chuck here, and get on down the road."

Henny shook his head. *Where had those gloves come from?* Why hadn't he worn them earlier? He tossed it off. *Stranger and stranger.*

He bent over carefully. No sudden moves or he might further upset his stomach. He grasped the dead man's wrist and ankle. They were still warm.

• • • •

What was his one condition on this adventure? Not to hurt anyone. As they tossed the clone through the portal, as the flash blinded him, he blinked hard. Sackerson would say it was just cleanup.

Maintenance.

They weren't even people.

Besides, Henny hadn't hurt a single soul. He wasn't even an accomplice, really. Sack had given him some silly title, "Bioremediation Specialist." Cleaning up a crime scene, that's all. Mop up the criminals.

But this clone seemed different, like a regular guy. He was a thinking, acting, independent agent. He'd come from out of nowhere. *Was he even a clone? Was Sack twisting his head?*

Henny was starting to wonder just who the criminals were.

Chapter 62 Warning

"Really?" Kelli asked. "At a time like this?"

"It's never let me down," Ashley said. Ashley smoothed the hanky out on her lap.

Kelli leaned in, scoffed, and slumped back on their bench. "What would you ask it, anyway?"

"Doesn't work like that," Ashley said. She did not look away from it.

"Ask it if I'm having a girl or a boy."

Ashley rolled her eyes, rolled her head to look at Kelli.

"Ask it if we're gonna beat the clones... or hell, ask it what's keeping Alex."

Ashley sighed. In the last five years, the sage advice from the magic handkerchief had saved her life over and over. It had brought her and Rory together. A gift from her Grandmother, the handkerchief was the something supernatural that Ashley had no earthly explanation for. Affectations, the whole mystical magic of her Family, could be at least attributed to stimulus of different regions of the brain. Ashley had studied such things for over a decade. She had done her graduate work on the brain.

A hanky doling out advice, however, had no basis in science.

There was no point trying to explain it to Kelli again. They had gone around and around about it. Whenever the hanky had guided rightly and clearly, Kelli had been silenced. Whenever its direction had been vague, it seemed everyone sneered at Ashley's faith in it.

Sometimes, like that afternoon, it behaved as if it were nothing more than a square of cloth, and that was more frustrating than anything.

"Gotta admit," Ashley said, "Alex has been gone a while now."

"Do you think we have some time yet?" Kelli looked up and down the trail, even glanced at the hanky, as if suggesting Ashley ask it.

"Before he's back? Sure." She studied Kelli. "What is it?"

Kelli sat up straight and took a deep breath. She let it out audibly. "You won't tell him, right?"

"Won't tell him what?"

Kelli put her elbows on her knees and her head in her hands. After she collected herself, she sat up and said, "I've lost it."

Ashley sat up and put her hand on Kelli's shoulder. "The baby?"

Kelli snorted. "No. Maybe worse."

Ashley slapped her shoulder then and exclaimed, "Oh, *what could be worse?*"

"I've lost my edge."

"What are you talking about?"

"Popping off those... clones... I just..."

Ashley could tell it was tearing her up, but she didn't know what to do. She didn't even know what was wrong. She fidgeted. She stroked the hanky flat and smooth.

"It's this damn baby. Just knowing it's in there... I dunno what to do."

"You don't know what to do?" Ashley blurted. "Be happy."

Kelli sniffled. She made a pathetic chuckling sound.

"You're not happy?"

Kelli shook her head.

"You're... you're worried about the baby?"

"I don't want to be... worried. I don't want to have to think twice about every damn move I make."

"You don't want to think for two," Ashley said.

Kelli turned to Ashley and smirked, "I already do that, keeping an eye on Alex."

Ashley brushed the hair from Kelli's face and held her. She knew she was probably the only person other than Alex that Kelli would let do such a thing. It was a privileged position.

"This is just not a good time, Ashley. We have shit to do. If not here, then—you know—back on the coast."

"Maybe you need to take some time. Change it up."

"I'm not taking time away. I'm not changing a damn thing. That's what I told him, too." Kelli cleared her throat. "I'm *carrying a baby*. I'm not sick or disabled or something."

Ashley let her fume for a while, then she gave her a sharp, wake up hug.

"What's this edge you're so worried about?"

"I've never been one to think twice. I hardly even think when I fire. I don't even aim when I fire. Sometimes I just fire. You know? I go off."

"Oh, I know," Ashley smiled.

"I mean, that's what makes me good. I've always acted on impulse, first to fire. I've always been right. Snap decisions. Instinct."

"That's great, right?"

"It was." Kelli continued, "But now I'm all cluttered up. I got *other* instincts coming on, like—" she sneered. "Motherin' instincts."

"That sounds like a band," Alex said popping up behind them. "The Mothering Instincts."

"How do you do that?" Ashley asked, so startled she was standing before she knew it.

"You get used to it," Kelli said. She turned on Alex. "So? Find anything?"

He shook his head in a tight nervous jerk. "No. That's just it. Nothing. No one. They took every car, truck, and transport. We're walking. It's weird. Places aren't even locked up. Hell, some of the doors were left wide open. Folks gone in a hurry."

"The whole neighborhood?"

"Every house for blocks," he said. "It's like they took the whole evacuation thing seriously."

"Like they knew something was coming," Kelli said.

"I get the feeling everyone knows what's going on around here but us," Ashley said.

Alex was looking at the sky. It was getting dark and chilly again. "Let's pick a house, any house, and sort all this out—inside." Already the sprinkles were falling.

· · · ·

"You know what else is nagging at me?" Alex was looking through cupboards in the kitchen.

"Maybe... how the Spooks knew where to find us?"

"Exactly."

"That's easy," Ashley said. "It had to be Willy."

"Your missionary friend?" Kelli asked.

"How else could you explain him taking off like that?"

"Why here though?" Alex continued. "That's what's really got me thinking. Freaky neighborhood of a bunch of prefabs. It's like a plastic ghost town. This isn't just any rendezvous point."

"Trail was a piss poor site for a trap," Kelli added.

"Spooks *did* show up here. That wasn't just a coincidence," Alex said. "Here's another one for you... How did Henny and the wizard know to find us here?"

"Now that's a bigger boggle! Sackerson claimed it was my HeadGear, but—"

"—no one's getting signal."

"Exactly."

"What were you and Willy talking about? Maybe he brought you here to warn you of something?"

"To get your attention?"

The more they talked, the more questions she had. Ashley sat at the kitchen table and ran her palm over the placemat. This house, like the others they explored, seemed like model homes, modest and middle income. They seemed undisturbed by the recent chaos downtown. Had the residents not so suddenly ran away, Ashley would have thought the place to be ideal.

"Who *were* they?" she mused aloud, "And what did they run from?"

"Hey, Ash," Kelli prompted, pointing at the handkerchief on the table.

The pattern on it was in motion.

Ashley gently unfolded, then unwrinkled it, being very tender with it, as if any sudden motion might scare off the magic of it.

"You don't have to tell me what it says," Alex said from the living room.

"What? Why?" Kelli couldn't take her eyes off the hanky.

"We're in a ChompCorp neighborhood," Alex said. "New. HOA. All a little too perfect."

"Yeah, so?"

"What would make all the Chompers hit the road, like all at once? Not even a pet left behind."

"Not an invasion of Eaters," Kelli said. "Not the local militia."

"Nope. I'd venture that even if the old locals all turned on them at once, they'd have just stayed in their homes. Hunkered down."

"Then who?" Kelli asked. "These Port Authority thugs?"

"Nope. Not who, but what," Alex was explaining.

"*Not a-goddamn-gin!*" Ashley slapped her palm on the table. The message on the hanky was unmistakably written in multiple languages and fonts and sizes. For added effect, the hanky illustrated the warning.

Ashley held it up for them to see. The largest illustration was of a thunderhead with dozens of bolts of lightning scorching the ground below. The lightning was appearing and disappearing, simulating flashes of real lightning. Even if one could not read, the images told the whole story.

The words reinforced the artwork with a sense of urgency: *Lightning's Hand.*

Chapter 63 Good Fortune

L ark had redeeming qualities. He told himself that all the time. One Halloween he volunteered at the Scout House Haunt, and as luck and fortune would have it, he got to be the star attraction: Dracula. He did not win this role because he was the most frightening. Certainly not because he was the best actor.

He was the Dracula who popped from a closed casket when people passed by. He got the job because he had no problem spending lots of time inside the casket, the lid down, the padding hugging his legs and hips. He was awarded Dracula because he had no sense of claustrophobia.

At the moment, he could not think of any quality more redeeming than his lack of fear of tight spaces. He was buried under the rubble of a concrete grain elevator, sealed in a space known to be utterly impenetrable. This lead room, like all lead rooms, boasted foot-thick walls of lead. They were bullet proof. X-ray and gamma rays bounced off them. Even nuclear radiation was no match for a lead room. No snooping tech created by any government, nor intelligence agency, nor space agency had penetrated a lead room. They were used for absolutely the most secretive activities, most popularized by criminals.

The government agencies had a lead room implanted under the Installation back in Guthrie. Lark imagined what all it might have secreted. From aliens to space junk, Lark was certain that lead room had been at the heart of the Guthrie Fall research. By the time Krystal Price bought the facility, however, the room was largely forgotten.

When Lark moved into the complex, he rejoiced at finding the lead room. Being no big fan of the Interface nor all the deafening noise of CommCorp, he spent a lot of time in there. Ultimately, he made it his bedroom. He could sleep well at night knowing that no signal would probe his mind. No agency would be spying on his dreams.

So, once again, Dracula found his setting just perfect for his unique tolerances. He sat on a display counter, fascinated at the flashlight's beam. In this dusty hole, the shaft of light resembled a light saber. He surveyed the room with it. Just another lead room. Nothing to fear.

While he might be absolutely safe from all harm here in his concrete and lead bunker, his beloved was out there somewhere on the streets, probably running and screaming for help. Every time she came to mind, he was again on high alert, and for half an hour, he would work through potential solutions to his captivity, only to have his dreams dashed again and again.

Yes, lead was soft, but the walls were a foot thick. Even if he had something adequate for scraping away at the walls, he would be digging long after his oxygen ran out.

Yes, he might well have been in a room that was now standing tall in the debris field. However, so much overhead had collapsed that he was sure the lead room was covered in feet of concrete and dust.

Yes, that TransCorp soldier knew he was poking around the elevator just before it blew up. He might care enough to send for help. However, the explosion would not have left the soldier any hope that Lark had survived.

Lark sat thinking for an immeasurable time. The only light was that of his flashlight. The only sounds were those he made: breathing, heart beating, shuffling around in the debris. He heard his prosthetic fingers drumming absently against the flashlight. He frowned. How could that work? These fingers were not real flesh? To move them required conscious thought, he thought.

He tried not to, but his mind kept returning to a prime function of lead rooms. No screams, however tortured, could be heard outside these walls. Lead rooms were used by dark agencies and underworld operators. They were staffed with Extractors, soulless men who pried Implants from unwilling informants while they were still living.

Lark shuddered at the thought. His gaze and flashlight settled again on the drain. What secrets had burbled down that drainpipe? How many gallons of blood and tears had gone through it?

He crouched by the grate and pried it away, then put his ear to the mouth of the drainpipe. He could hear something. Thunder maybe? There was a wisp of cold air at his ear. If he could hear outside, then someone outside might hear him! He took a deep breath, coughed back the dust, drew another breath, then yelled into the hole. There was no reply. He alternated yelling and listening, thinking he must look something like a supplicant at prayer, going through the ritual again and again. Crying out to a God who did not hear him.

His throat was raw and dry. Coughing plagued him, eventually stopping the practice altogether. He slumped to lay beside the drain, hoping he might hear something yet. Maybe if someone were to come near this pipe—wherever it made its exit—then he could get their attention.

· · · ·

When he woke, it seemed late. He had to piss, and the flashlight was less bright. What would it be like when the batteries died? What would it feel like to starve here? Lark decided to always leave his waste in the same corner. If he was going to be here a while, he didn't want to be stepping in his own dung. While he peed, he held the flashlight in his mouth. He zipped with his numb, artificial fingers, a simple feat that always made him proud of the enhanced dexterity of this model.

Rivulets of urine moved from the corner, moving in the direction of the drain, though the floor was covered in dirt that absorbed it. Lark studied it with his flashlight, wondering if he had enough bodily fluids—other than blood—to ever reach from the corner to the drain. "Tears," he mused, startled at his own voice. "Cry me a river."

He returned to the drain and wished he had a long stick or wire. He wished for anything he could use to shove a message down the length of the pipe to the world outside. He wished for a mouse or a rat, even, that he might capture and strap with a message. He could train it, he thought, to take his messages out to the living.

An idea struck him then, so ludicrous and outright funny that he laughed aloud despite his hopeless situation. Maybe the crushing weight of this, his final chapter, forced the humor out.

He had been thinking of Thing, a detached hand from an old black and white horror/comedy The Addams Family. Hell with a rat carrying a message. If Thing were here, he could race through the plumbing, the fingers scurrying like five frantic feet. The disembodied hand could find someone outside. Through a ridiculous series of gestures and fingerspelling—a gag used in many episodes—Thing would convey the message. Thing would save the day!

Lark sat at the drain, smiling for long minutes. WIth his flesh hand, he imitated the scurrying motion of Thing until he perfected it. He put his hand to the gritty floor and ran his fingers as if they were grasping for traction. Then he studied his prosthetic, watched it practice the same moves. He closed his eyes and pictured it making those movements. Even though he could not feel them, he sensed resistance in the dirt. He imagined the texture of loose debris.

Then he detached the prosthetic and sat it on the floor beside him. He shined the flashlight on it and watched as he willed it to continue the scurrying motions. It made him smile.

Lark tucked his identity card in the stump of the arm. It was a redundancy. Anyone with simple tech resources could get the hand scanned and know the owner from that. So far as he knew, he was the only Lark Fortune, likely the only man in Laramie missing his right hand.

He set it carefully in the throat of the drainpipe, and willed it away. Inch by inch, it was pulling itself down the drainpipe. Eventually, he would run out of range (likely, sooner than later, due to the shielding of the lead room), but *maybe* his hand would find its way out from under their current situation.

Maybe his mother had been right.

Who else was so uniquely qualified for this situation. He was immune to claustrophobia, *and* he had a remote control hand....could anyone else have such luck?

Chapter 64 Tempting

"**I**t's useless," Katrina stated, tossing aside a computer panel. "We cannot begin to reprogram such things. TransCorp has endless resources, software and electrical engineers—those are the people who operate these, not people like us."

"Yeah, maybe," Rory said, "but I've been through a Hot Wire or two, and they're not so complicated. Maybe we can find the Hot Wire inside and, you know, go through it."

"Blindly? Without a programmed destination? What if there is no paired Hot Wire or specific destination? Where would we end up then?"

"Somewhere other than here," Rory said. "Somewhere else."

"Besides, we can't open one. We've tried."

Rory sighed. She was right. In the whole morning, they had managed to pry open control panels of only three portals. They had untangled nests of wires. To Rory, it seemed much of the wiring was only to make things appear more complicated.

A Hot Wire was simply one strand of wire, thin as a hair, that circled into a closed loop which fastened with a tiny nodule people called Tic-Tacs, for they so resembled the breath mint. Rory had heard of rogue Hot Wires and random portals, but those he had gone through were orchestrated pairs. The theory was, two matching Tic-Tacs could be any distance apart, and if people at each location made Hot Wires of them, closed the wire loop with those tiny white nodules, then a portal was created.

That was exactly the kind of Hot Wire Rory had traveled by. Alex had set them up time and again. TransCorp denied such things existed, insisting that only regulated, metered ports could possibly work reliably. They did not voice it, for they did not want even an inkling of doubt over their products, but they leaned heavily into "reliable" transportation. Their portals were calibrated scientifically. The materials of their Hot Wires were handcrafted in elite laboratories. The wire was spun from some synthetic substance only TransCorp possessed. The Tic-Tacs themselves were very rare. It was believed that TransCorp owned every last one of them.

And for whatever reason, they had encased them in titanium frames and stockpiled them like the hundreds in this warehouse at the end of nowhere.

"I tell you, Kat, somewhere inside these things, it gets simple. A wire and a Tic-Tac."

"You are not listening," she said.

Rory ran his hands over the portal again. It was well-designed. Every seam was a surgical fit. Only the control panels, which seemed like an ugly aftermarket bolt-on, could be dismantled.

He sighed and turned to her, repeating the reservations she had, one by one. "You think they're complicated. Without the control panel, they won't work at all. You're sure we'd just melt or something if we ported through a raw one, or at best, we'd end up somewhere even more awful than this."

"You cannot fix the generator, and without that, we have no power to run the control panels. We do not have power to charge even the HeadGear."

"We don't need any of that. We just need the guts of this thing, then we're out of here." He pushed and pushed, eventually getting the portal frame rocking. With just a little more effort, he was able to topple the portal completely. It crashed, forming a cloud of dust. The bottom plate of the portal was not as elegant as the rest of the machine. Rory set to work prying at its seams immediately.

· · · ·

That afternoon the heat was unbearable. In the shade and shelter of the warehouse, there was no breeze, and the air was thick and heavy with humidity. Rory was drenched in sweat. He was only wearing his cargo shorts. He had ripped a sleeve from his seersucker jacket to tie around his head as a sweatband.

Katrina had also stripped down. She was struggling with the temperature more than he was, so he insisted she spend time down at the shore, preferably in the water. She had taken a beach umbrella with her and sheltered herself from the sun with it.

What had seemed a major victory proved to give them no advantage. Yes, he had found the magical Hot Wire, he was certain, by dismantling the portal from its base. He had isolated the wire and even found something that looked like a connector serving the same purpose as a traditional Tic-Tac.

He had, in fact, dismantled four portals by late afternoon, and he had their guts dangling throughout the warehouse. Four Hot Wire lassos were hanging in series. A person could walk through one, then the next, then the next, like a croquet ball passing through wickets. Rory had done this several times, rehearsing what he was going to tell Katrina—something was missing. The Hot Wires were inert, and he did not yet know why. They were safe, and she needn't sleep on the beach to avoid some dreadful fate she had imagined.

He joined her for sunset, sitting beside her in the sand. It was a beautiful sight, and Rory was able to compartmentalize his frustration with the portals long enough to watch it set, watch the vivid colors gradually absorbed by the night.

"Tomorrow we go back to the village," Katrina said. "We will find a boat or some other way to get to a bigger island or a bigger city, and then we will pay whatever price we must to get a flight or a freighter back to the United States."

"I don't know if—"

"I *do* know. I have thought about it all day. This was a bad idea. I do not know what I was thinking."

"You were thinking outside the box. That's healthy. It wasn't a bad idea. I still think it'll work. Maybe the battery cells will be charged by morning, and we won't even need the solar or tidal generators. Maybe we'll find another circuit to fix."

"We might as well ride a rainbow or lasso a pegasus."

"That too," Rory smiled. "But really... maybe your friends will fly over with a Rainmaker, and we'll be saved."

"Flying pigs would be more likely. Ashley Winston has given up," Katrina said softly. "I do not expect her to return."

"Bah!" Rory said, standing. "If I've learned anything at all, it's that sometimes we need to put more stock in the incredible. *The unpredictable nature of man.*"

Katrina shook her head. "This is why you were sometimes called the Bulldog."

"Why is that?"

"You are... determined," she said. "You grab ahold of something and do not let go. A bulldog."

"Huh," Rory pulled his journal from his back pocket and uncurled its cover. He flipped to a page with a sketch of a bulldog. He had studied it a hundred times, thinking he might recognize his pet, maybe. "So that's like my nickname?"

"One of many," she said.

"You'll have to tell me more of 'em."

"I'd rather have you fill my head again with your empty promises, Reed. I need your optimism."

· · · ·

An hour after sunset they were still on the beach, sitting back to back. Neither of them were tired, and this afforded them a 360 degree lookout. Rory was a boulder. Katrina sat back against him. He liked this closeness, the warmth of her body against his back. In a long stretch of quiet, he became acutely aware of her breathing. She was lithe and alive and pressed against him, flesh on flesh.

Rory felt more alive than ever. Memories and sensations were rousing him. Like anyone on watch, his eye never rested, moving from the movement of a palm frond to the direction of a random sound. Stars were twinkling, vying for his attention. Rory was alive with the night. He was savoring the tang of the sea on the cool air. He drew it in deeply, feeling their backs slip a little as he did. Sweat was a lubricant between them. He was conscious that he likely reeked of sweat, and it made him uneasy. Katrina, on the other hand, smelled earthy and wild, exotic. Tempting.

"Ashley Winston will be glad to see you," Katrina stated.

"Ummm?" She had evoked the name as if it were a brand of tool, not her own half-sister. "Will she? Tell me about it."

Rory felt her back change, draw more rigid. "I would rather you tell me of our triumphant return again."

Earlier, he had predicted a tomorrow full of magic and wonder. A cruise ship sailed into the bay from a distant era. Merry travelers who had never known the Eat the Rich scourge wandered down the gangplank and all about the cove. No corporation suppressed their glee and wonderment. Crew members helped Rory load a dozen portals aboard. The titanium cargo would afford them a first class suite. They sailed into the sunset, enjoying fruity cocktails and a live band. They were going to Laramie, Wyoming, by cruise ship—somehow crossing North America, somehow at a speed that put them in the Rocky mountains in a day. Those details did not matter.

"It won't be by cruise ship," Rory said this time. "A Rainmaker will glide into the ocean and right to us."

"That is convenient."

"We won't even get our feet wet," Rory continued. "It's an airship like they ought to be, luxurious and grand. It's staffed with your winged women who recognize you as their leader and bow to your every request."

He felt her chuckle. "This is more fanciful than your cruise ship."

"The cabins are teak with brass trimmings, all spit and polish. We have a feather bed and—"

She cleared her throat.

"—and sleep 'til we reach Laramie. When we arrive, all these people in the notebook are at some sky dock on a mountain top. Alex, my long lost friend. His wife, the fighter. Astar and Zana, who you tell me are like doctors—"

"—more like parents," Katrina corrected.

"You said Zana patches us up when we're injured."

"In this story, there is no injury."

"Right," he said. It *did* feel like a fantasy, then, and he grew quiet.

"And what of Ashley? Have you thought of the reunion?"

Rory plucked at the sand, sifted it through his fingertips. He felt so acutely aware of his senses he might be able to count the grains. He thought he could count and name the stars.

Rory Reed knew everything, yet nothing at all.

"I don't know her," he admitted. "I mean, I know what she looks like. I know we have a past together... but I... I can't remember enough about her."

He turned to look at Katrina. She gave him a head nod of recognition, as if saying 'hey' to a stranger.

"Am I broken or what?"

"You have to ask?" she chided.

He looked to the heavens. He had learned to tell time by the stars. "It won't be long until our airship arrives," he said. "Fix me."

Her eyebrow went up as if she were startled by the request, as if it meant something more than it did. Rory didn't even know for sure what he meant by it. Her eyes shifted away from his to somewhere over his shoulder.

"Give me another Affec—"

"Hush." A crease in her brow as she glanced back at him. "We are not alone."

• • • •

Rory was out of practice. Threat assessment did not include damning himself for being caught unaware. It did not permit him to re-evaluate his past. Assessment was immediate. Here. Now. Three disembodied heads—no four—white hair, strange features. They might be surrounded by more. They might already be in the warehouse where he had left his weapons. Stupid. Stupid!

The heads moved into the clearing, carried by bodies clad in black from head to toe.

The four of them carried no weapons. This would be easy.

They did not put their hands in the air nor provide any other indication they came in peace. They were too distant, their features too muddled with markings—tattoos—to know their intentions.

Rory had encountered packs of deranged people in his years on shore. He had fought and slaughtered too many to count. This little group of tweakers could be yet another.

Sand. He could throw it in their eyes if they were close.

A log was nearby. It could serve as a club.

They moved closer but not directly at them, almost as if they were trying yet to sneak up on them, though they were all in plain sight.

Katrina made a girlish sound, let go a shuddering breath, and jumped to her feet.

Rory stood, too, as quickly as he could get up.

By then, Katrina was across the gap and hugging the nearest stranger.

They all came together in a quick babbling of languages.

Remembering he was there, it seemed, Katrina turned to him, smiling. She was still holding the nearest of them. "Yes," she said, only not to him. "It *is* him."

They closed on him, the five of them gliding across the sand. He could see through their heavily tattooed faces. They were all smiling like Buddha himself. One broke eye contact to look at Katrina with concern.

"Yes," Katrina said, "he is wound too tightly."

"Kat," Rory rumbled softly. "Do you know these people?"

"We are tenderlings," one said, this one an older man, in a heavy accent.

"Tender foots," another of them corrected.

"Tender feet?" said another.

"We are not of the outdoors," the old man clarified. "It's a relief to find you."

All of them sighed as if on cue.

Rory wondered if he were dreaming.

"Kat, come here," he ordered.

Again her eyebrow of surprise, but she let go of the stranger and approached him. She seemed so happy and refreshed. It was obvious she knew them, but Rory felt every nerve ping warnings.

Katrina smiled and sidled up beside him. "It is alright," she said. "They're alright."

They were coming closer yet. Rory took Katrina's hand. He would pull her to safety. They would make a break for it. They could get away, running hand-in-hand. He thought they could easily outdistance the little pack. This was his plan, since she would not want them hurt.

They stopped their advance. One of them seemed particularly surprised to see them holding hands.

"Oh," Katrina pried her hand free with an awkward chuckle. "He is just being... defensive."

"Who are they?" Rory asked. In asking this of Katrina, he realized he had not spoken *to them* at all. He wondered if she was again messing with his head like the ghosts on the beach. He turned to the four of them and asked directly, "Who are you?"

Katrina turned to stand facing him. She stood between him and them, bouncing on her toes to pull his attention from them. "Rory," she said with a radiant smile. "Rory. This is my Family. *The Family*... in your notebook."

He looked at her, then again at them. They were not related. They looked nothing like her. The four of them were not even of the same ethnicity. Sure their hair was white and wild. Sure, they all had ScanTats covering their faces, but there the resemblance ended. He squinted, but he could not see how they could be family. A cult, maybe, but family?

"This is our Family," Katrina said, as if to clarify. "Rory, this is Ashley Winston's Family, too."

Chapter 65 Sideways

Ultimately, they resorted to bicycles. It was 20 blocks to downtown, where it sounded like the fighting was most intense. Swarms of drones were hovering over the city, with the highest concentrations being over the Civic Center. CommCorp drones could only mean one thing: more footage for the Interface.

Kelli set the pace. Somehow, Alex had never known of her interest in trail biking, but it was clear now as her bicycle weaved through stalled cars and debris. He would never admit it to her, but he was having some trouble keeping up.

As Alex pedaled, he reviewed just how much of this was theatrics. Chomp attacked with a Lightning's Hand. TransCorp countered by destroying it. Chomp threatened another. TransCorp sent in an occupying force. The locals and their loyalties were easily swayed toward TransCorp, for they were sticking up for Laramie over ChompCorp demands. Then, with TransCorp morphing into the Port Authority—something he had long dreaded—it was becoming everyone for himself. The only allies in the corporate ranks were those with CommCorp, and their allegiance was skewing toward the Port Authority, at least whenever one could catch a vid on the spotty Interface connections.

Port Authority took credit for the leveling of the town's grain elevators. They claimed they were peacekeepers at the hospital standoff. Now, if rumors were to be believed, the Rebels of the Plains were going to destroy the PetroPlex. Alex saw it for what it was, another chance for the Port Authority to pose as the peacekeeping force. Meanwhile, Chomp was sending down another Lightning's Hand.

Even with that, an impending airship that would scrape over Laramie in a tumult of lightning, Alex knew that worse was on its way. So long as he stayed here, so long as the time cops sought him out here, there was the potential for even more damage. It made him want to veer his bicycle off a side street, out of town, never to return.

The two women ahead of him, however, kept him on course. He owed Ashley his allegiance and his life. He owed it to Rory to protect her from harm. And Kelli—he could not imagine a life without her. She was his moon and sun.

The rumble of heavy equipment caught their attention. A very large tractor with a bucket on front was plowing over Port Authority portals and machinery. It was taking some heavy gunfire. Bullets pocked the loader's army green paint. The cab's glass was webbed with cracks and bullet holes. One side window sloughed off. Alex wondered how the driver was surviving the fusillade of shells.

Port Authority soldiers, these in sleek gray armor, were streaming from portals that strobed rapidly. The instant they were through the port, they were firing weapons at the machinery leveling portals nearby.

A stray bullet popped the headlamp from Ashley's bicycle. "We gotta move," she said. "But where?"

It was a good question. All around them, gray troops were engaged with ragged rebels. They had biked too far into the arena for Alex's comfort. The fighting was escalating even behind them, where two backhoes were pulverizing a Port Authority troop transport.

These machines, industrial yellow models with no cabs, were driven by Stu Wiebe's cowboys. They were whooping and hollering as they worked. The treads crushed everything in their way, from soldiers to vehicles. The big buckets reached out like claws, then the entire machine would pivot hard, slamming the bucket sidelong into the troop transport again. The backhoes looked like mechanical scorpions gone mad, and the men operating them paid no attention to the gunfire erupting around them.

When the transport was crushed to their satisfaction, The Boys tapped the buckets of their machines together in a backhoe fist bump. They rounded on themselves, then headed on into the battle.

"This way," Kelli shouted, then took off down an alley. She raced from one to another, as if she knew the town. She took them through a narrow gap between buildings, then stopped abruptly rather than rolling out onto the sidewalk. "It's worse here," she said.

It dawned on Alex that they had wanted to get into the action to get word to everyone that the Lightning's Hand was coming, *yet they didn't have a plan.* There was no public address system on a road map somewhere. The Interface was still inoperative. Worse, they didn't really know how imminent the Lightning's Hand might be. If they cried wolf, then the storm did not come, people would come to disregard the threat of it. It was, after all, impossibly unlikely that ChompCorp would try such a stunt again. Who would believe them?

A spray of gunfire flecked bits of the alley's brick wall everywhere. Alex shielded his face from the bite of it. He heard the plasma pistol's rapid report and peaked to see several Port Authority Grays crumpling. Kelli shook her head, saying, "That was too close. Gun snagged in my holster."

She was not making that mistake again, now resuming her trek but navigating the bike with one hand, while the other held her gun at the ready. Alex followed her down the sidewalk, wondering at her destination. It was too loud to talk and too dangerous to pull aside and make a proper plan.

They biked into a block of hand-to-hand fighting. The roaring and slamming of machines into portals faded, replaced by sporadic pistol blasts, grunts, and screams. They had to ditch the bicycles and push ahead. When a Rebel noticed them, he or she would smile and grant passage. When soldiers were so unlucky, they fell in paroxysms of agony, gasping their last breaths. Ashley's lethal affectations were striking with precision and without mercy.

Kelli seemed to find what she was looking for—a fire station. She kicked in the door, and they went inside. "We're going to find some kind of public access, some channel, and warn people. We're going to set off the tornado siren again, too. Got it?"

Alex nodded, then set to scrambling through the offices, living spaces, and bays with her. He stopped short, sliding to a halt. Two shining red ladder trucks were parked inside. In their pristine condition, they seemed radically out of place in this war zone. He longed to drive one of them but resumed his task with Kelli.

After they found a control room, Kelli turned to them with resolve. "New plan," she announced. "We're setting this off, then you two are going up."

"Up?"

"Yeah, up." Kelli pointed skyward. "The girls should be dangling umbilicals by now. Surely they've caught wind of all this."

Alex was aghast. "No way, babe. No way I'm leaving you down here."

"They need us here," Ashley argued.

"They need you up there, more," Kelli said. "Leadership. Remember?"

"It's too dangerous," Ashley said. "What about the Lightning's Hand?"

"That's why you can't wait. Get up, get out, and get going."

"Kelli, Sweet'ums! I'm sticking this out. I am not—"

"Fine!" Ashley said. "I'll go. Alex, you stay here."

She hugged them both, then shot back down the hall, kicking the back door open to greet the battle again.

"How'd you...?" Alex began, then shook his head. "You called the cavalry. You called up an airship rescue? I'm the one with the forecast here. How'd you know this would get so sideways?"

She looked at him questioningly. "Doesn't it always?"

Alex shrugged.

"I just told the girls to keep a weather eye on Laramie, and if it all went to shit, pick us up on the highest rooftops."

• • • •

The siren and announcements were all up and running in minutes. Alex did not have a better warning, so he improvised, "The National Weather Service interrupts this battle to advise you to take cover, as a Lightning's Hand is descending on everyone in the listening area soon. Take cover. Lightning's Hand... That is all. Out."

"Think we can make our way in one of these?" Kelli asked. She knew him so well. She already opened the passenger's side door and was climbing into the fire truck.

"Oh yeah," Alex said, and sought the garage door controls.

She had started the truck by the time he mounted it, but she yielded him the driver's seat. "Take us out," she said.

"Where to?" Alex asked, buckling up.

"A couple of Rebs told me they're at the Wiebe ranch, wherever that is."

"We'll find it," he said. Alex fired up the lights and sirens. He had not been so excited to drive anything in any time.

"She's going to get scratched up, you know, but she'll serve the purpose."

He winced at the thought of the cherry red truck getting damaged, but he knew it was inevitable. He knew this fanciful moment in this dream truck with his dream girl was another of those surreal moments he always seemed to find in battle. That, he mused, flooring it, was half the fun.

The truck surged out into the fighting. Alex did his best not to run over people, imagining the bumping and lurching might be the uneven terrain of sidewalks and lampposts and general debris. One Port soldier disregarded the melee around him. He aimed his sidearm right at Alex. He had a look of determination, dedication to his cause. Before he popped off a shot, however, he was hit in crossfire and then run over. Another bump to dismiss.

Kelli was shooting out her side window with one hand, holding onto a leather strap overhead with the other. She bobbed and swung with the rhythms of the truck. She looked back over her shoulder at him and smiled wickedly. "It's almost unfair," she shouted over the sirens. Then she went back to picking off the Port Authority soldiers.

Alex was aware that their levity would be short-lived. They were joking over the impossible irony of it all. They had no chance. Port Authority troops were pouring in. The odds against them were glaringly obvious. The hand-to-hand fighting was overwhelmed with gray uniforms now, just in the few minutes they had been inside. He estimated the entire population of Laramie, including The Boys and the Rebels, numbered less than 100,000, and even a decent street army would have more infantry men.

This invasion of Port Authority soldiers was not for show. They were not just occupying, as the first wave had. These men and women were vicious soldiers. From his seat in the truck, he noted the fighting styles and disciplined attack patterns emerging. These soldiers were trained... and innumerable.

Alex coaxed the truck over bodies and debris, building up momentum. He rammed into some portals, backed up, and moved on. It was the least he could do. Even if he were able to crush every portal up and down the street, it seemed more soldiers were streaming in from ports just blocks away.

There was no winning here. That was obvious. It would be better to get out of this alive and return to settle the score another time. Alex downshifted, and the truck bolted ahead, passing block upon block of carnage. The fighting had thinned out. The ting and tang of bullets hitting their rig became more rare. The road was more clear. He was able to go thirty, then forty.

Then, some gray monstrous vehicle, racing at them from a side street, T-boned the truck. Kelli was thrown across the cab at him. The truck careened out of control, skidding on the driver's side tires. The truck's ladder swung out wide and cracked into nearby buildings. It was all happening in slow motion now. The leaning, more and more to port. Thirty, then forty-five degrees. Her limp body draped over the gearshift and a tangle of emergency medical gear. Her plasma pistol, still in her grip, was blasting randomly in the cabin.

He did not care about any of that. The truck could burst into flames, and he would not care. The only thing he attended to was his darling girl. Blood was pouring from her. Maybe a stray bullet. Maybe some glass lacerated her neck.

Before the truck had even settled, Alex was scrambling for something—anything—to stop the bleeding. He unbuckled and fought to get upright in the sideways cab. He fought to pry open a yellow plastic box that failed him. It was only fire-issue HeadGear. He twisted around and opened compartment after compartment. *This was an emergency vehicle. It had to have medical supplies!*

He popped open a cabinet with first aid materials, and he tore open gauze pads, stuffing them as tenderly as he could toward her wound. The way they were positioned, he wasn't even certain he could get to the injury, but he tried.

The truck engine and siren had died. Her pistol had quit firing. Outside, his announcement and the tornado siren vied for dominance. His cocky voice on the broad speakers wounded him. Minutes ago he had been happy-go-lucky, finding the fun even in this tragic time. Now, minutes seemed years later. Everything had happened in a heartbeat.

The fighting had grown distant. Alex took a deep, shaky breath. He swiped away his mop of hair, noting the rich red blood coating his fingers. "Baby, baby, baby doll," he chanted. "Be okay for me, baby!"

He choked up then. She was his baby. She was also *carrying* his baby. "Please, please, please!" he whispered again and again. "Please, be okay."

Chapter 66 The Juke

S tu set up shop in the second floor lobby of the hospital. He commanded a good view of Laramie. Two walls formed a corner of floor-to-ceiling windows. A couple dozen men could fit in the lobby when they needed to confer. The hospital was the first facility they had secured. To his thinking, it was the most vital. Protect the innocent, serve the injured.

One of The Boys told him it would be against conventions of war to headquarter in a medical sanctuary, but Stu didn't care. Medical neutrality had already been disrespected. A situation like this, corporations steamrolling citizens, wasn't covered by any code. Here, so far as he was concerned, rules did not apply.

They had blown up Krystal's head for a publicity stunt.

The Boys brought him bootleg vids from the Interface, ones that were not being streamed anywhere near Laramie. Those vids, like the one of Krystal's assassination, spun the story against locals and rebels. CommCorp wasn't interested in neutral news. Stu could see right through their biased delivery. Hell, he could look out the window and see it was a different story on the street.

The problem was, the rest of the world did not have his perspective.

Nat had friends with pirate broadcasts, and they were running the raw footage, gruesome as it was, of Krystal's murder. They were streaming what they could of the true battle going on, capturing the overwhelming number of Port Authority forces.

Some of his more cynical advisors reminded him that pirate broadcasts were preaching to the choir, to others in the echo chamber of conspiracy theorists and fringe folk.

So that was his lot—Stu Wiebe was a nutjob now, just like Lefty Fortune.

"You look like you swallowed a frog," Burton stated, hobbling into the lobby.

"It's the coffee," Stu said, saluting him with his cup. "Want some?"

"Hard pass."

"Any news?"

Burton wagged his head. "No good news. Grays just keep coming. Keep popping in and out on us."

"So we keep popping their portals," Stu suggested. "Close the door on 'em."

Burton settled into a chair. "They're just relentless. And the Interface is having a heyday with it."

"So I hear."

"What do you hear about the Lightning's Hand?"

Stu's chair squeaked when he adjusted his position. "I thought it was a crock until I listened to it again. I know the guy on the horn. Alex Gault."

Burton shook his head dismissively. "Never heard of him."

"If he says it's coming, we better be ready."

"Not a whiff of it on the Interface."

"More reason to expect it," Stu said.

"Maybe." Burton had more to say.

"The Boys aren't buying it, either. Folks act like it's a tornado or something, a natural storm. Something that would only happen once in a hundred years."

"You have to admit, two of those in a week? That's pretty damn unlikely."

"If it's a big win for ChompCorp, it might never make the news. Wouldn't make the Port Authority look like they're in charge. Might shake up alliances something awful."

"If you really think it's coming, you're taking it well. Detached."

Stu rubbed his face. "I'm trying."

"We can't de-port another one."

"Not going to borrow a Hot Wire from the Port Authority?"

They both chuckled. It was all gallows humor. Gallows posturing. Gallows effort. If the Port Authority didn't run them over, Chomp's Lightning's Hand would. *Be strong or be gone*, his grandpa used to say. Stu feared it was looking more like strong *and* gone.

"Have you looked at the numbers?" Stu asked.

"We're making *reports* now?"

"Downstairs, they take headcounts. They're still acting like a hospital, like they're going to turn claims in to Pharma or something. Just over 200 people have been in, sixty of them checked in."

"So, the rest checked out... like... fatalities?"

"Forty fatalities, the rest released, but nobody's got anywhere to go... lot of them in the cafeteria."

"I saw that. Saw the school buses, too. That was smart."

The Boys had all the buses in the district circled around the hospital's grounds, layers deep. It was both a defensive wall and a shelter if the hospital ran over or defenses had to fall back.

"Fuel's getting scarce. We had to tow about half of them in." Stu cleared his throat. "You were right about the gas. We still have men at the PetroPlex trying to shore it up."

"And it's all on the news, right?"

"We've been getting creative with Comm's drones. We're making the whole town a no-fly zone."

"I heard them saying 'hunting season's open on drones,'" Burton smirked. "I have to hand it to your men, they're resilient."

"Indefatigable," Stu added. He could play at this game.

"Nonplussed."

"Oh, they're plussed enough. They're outright agitated, but..." Stu shrugged, "Whaddya gonna do?"

"What *are* you going to do?"

"We'll be at it 'til the last man's standing."

Burton was uncomfortable with that.

"You fellas don't have to be here, you know," Stu said. "Nobody'd hold it against you if you got out while you can."

"You and your Boys could leave, for that matter. I hear you're immigrants."

The point was made. Neither party was here for Laramie. They were here to make a stand. Burton was right, too. They *were* still immigrants. Even after decades in town, the Wiebe clan wasn't rooted.

"So we all tuck tail. Laramie gets ground to pulp somewhere between the Grays and the lightning, and the corps just look all the better, come out all-the-stronger for it."

"That's one ending," Burton said. "Not a very happy one."

They sat in it, neither saying a word, but both imagining the other ending.

• • • •

A kid Stu barely recognized burst in. "They're retreating."

"What?" Burton came up out of his chair, nearly losing his footing.

It was Nat's old buddy from Scouts. Stu was struggling to pull up his name. "Burley? What are you—"

"The soldiers, Mr. Wiebe. They're dragging their dead with them, piling in the portals. Shipping out."

Stu walked to the windows and looked out them. Portal flashes had been going all day long with more soldiers coming into town. When The Boys destroyed portals, the Grays ported in *more* portals. The flashing continued, but if Burley was right...

"They quit firing," Burton said, confirming the story on his Internal. He looked at Stu with a question behind it. "Could be a full retreat."

"Get to Schmitty," Stu told the kid. "Tell him to keep at the portals. Crush every last one of them."

"Yessir!" the Burley boy said, turned on his heel and left.

"If we had an army of kids like that..." Burton mused.

"Still wouldn't be enough."

"*Retreating...* What do you make of that?"

"Could be a juke."

"Why would they need to? They have the numbers, the media, soon-enough the will of the people."

"They think like a corporation. Efficiency. They're running analytics somewhere and maybe they decided to change it up."

Burton nodded. "Then what's next? What's more efficient?"

"How quickly could we make a map, you know, of the ports they've propped up around town?"

"Probably a pretty good one by dark, if we use our drones. Faster, if the Interface cooperated. We could call it all in from the field—"

"But then they'd hear every word," Stu said. He really was sounding like Lefty now.

"We can make a code. I got a cipher guy."

Stu thought of Nat. "My cipher's a wiz. Let's get them together and get this going."

"If the Grays are just rebooting, the problems remain, possibly new ones, too."

"Doubtless."

"Who are the savviest men you have?" Burton asked. "Mine are old TurnCoats... and they dealt with TransCorp first-hand. Maybe we round some up here in the calm before the storm."

"A couple locals might be good for that. My Boys... not so much. I'll ask about. Where do want them, and when?"

"Right here and soon." Burton nodded to the windows. The overcast sky was darkening.

It could be just another storm surge.

Or it could be the storm front on the edge of a low-flying, ground-arcing airship.

"Maybe they pulled out just to wait that out," Stu offered.

Chapter 67 Believe

Ashley didn't think twice. When the elevator doors opened, her Affectation was already radiating across the roof. The Perch was abandoned, but for one man who stood on the far side, balanced on the parapets decorating the edge.

"Gnnnuh," he writhed. William Titus was teetering, his eyes wide with fear. "Fallnnnrh."

She had questions first. She relieved the cramping enough for him to fall forward, onto the roof in a clatter of patio furniture. Ashley approached, keeping his juices flowing, keeping the pain as high as he might bare. The cramping would feel like his muscles were tearing themselves apart, and in her mood, she might not stop that from happening.

In this state, however, he wasn't much good to her. His nostril was bubbling blood in a puddle of rainwater. His teeth were raking at the flooring. Willy had looked better.

With an exaggerated sigh, she released her stranglehold on him. He flopped free of it, a torpid fish out of water. He gasped for breath for a bit, his eyes were still glazed over. Maybe, Ashley thought, it had been a little much.

She crouched next to him and studied him closely. As he regained his senses, his eyes pulled her into focus, and the calm choir boy expression gradually gelled into place. He found strength enough to fold and sit up, leaning his back against the brick border of The Perch. His hair was a mess. His pink shirt was wet, blotched with rain and blood and sweat.

"You left me behind," she began in measured tones. "You took off when those... those agents showed up."

Lark had called them Spooks. Alex, Time Cops. Sackerson, Clones. No one seemed to know who the hell they were, but in their matching black suits and sunglasses, they looked enough like federal agents that she thought it was good enough, at least for an opener.

"Shift change," he said. His teeth were red with a glaze of blood.

"Don't make this harder," she said, and let the sensation of waking limbs tingle in his extremities. That terrible 'pins and needles' feeling was an easy one for her to simulate, and she smiled wickedly as the paresthesia pricked at him.

Willy clenched his mouth and eyes shut, enduring the wave of tingling until it subsided. "See?" he said when he could. "You've really come into your own."

"If you don't cooperate, you might just get to experience *lots* of my gifts." She held up her hand with menace. Affectations had nothing to do with gestures, but they did let new initiates know she was wielding something potent.

"When I see guns, I get out of the situation. I'm not stupid."

"Why didn't they stop you?"

"They weren't interested. Really. I walked right through them with my hands above my head."

"The Lord as your shepherd, right?"

"My hand to God," he said with a smile.

"Why didn't you stick around to help?"

"Help? What could I do?" He shrugged. "I could hear the gunfire. I don't have a gun, Miss Winston. What could I do?"

"How do you know about this?" She looked at her Affectation hand puppet.

"Signs and wonders," Willy said. "Miracles and gifts and portents."

"Yeah, yeah. If you know so much, why didn't you say so on the bench?"

"We were interrupted."

"So? Tell me now. And tell me fast. I got a cloud to catch."

• • • •

An hour had passed. They sat side by side in the pouring rain, their backs to the brick. It was a cold, dark Wyoming rain, but Ashley didn't feel the chill. The handkerchief was plastered to her thigh, sopping wet, but the message on it was clear—Believe.

Prior to their conversation, Ashley had limited her acceptance of the supernatural to hankies and time travelers, and both strained her grounding in the sciences. That rag had an undeniable prescience. It was truly mystical. Alex and those who sought to catch him through time—that was harder yet to accept. Teleportation was growing commonplace, but she could recall when it, too, would have been relegated to science fiction or the supernatural.

"I can't begin to know what it's like," he said. "Despite your science, you can't teach it to me. We don't believe anyone can learn it. Your gifts are just that—gifts."

Her *gift* had nearly killed him with muscle contractions and cramps.

"I'll never be part of your Family," he said. "I'll never be closer to God than I am to you right now."

"What?"

"Your gifts are my first proof that God is still in the business of miracles."

"Wait. Wait." She frowned, pulling on all her memories of the Bible. "What's that about faith, about promises and things hoped for—stuff you can't see?"

"Oh, I could counter," he smiled, "but for what purpose? I'm a doubting Thomas, especially after what happened to mom... but then Garden enlightened me. We believe in God because of your Family who walks closer to God."

What had Rory always called such talk? Cult babble? She was having a very hard time obeying the handkerchief.

She cleared her throat, blew some rain from her face. "Willy... Hey. What if we're just wired differently? Like psychics or savants or whatever. The Family... I'm not so sure anyone's walking any closer to God."

"Doubt is the first phase of faith," he said, cocking his head in obeisance to the phrase.

Yep, cult babble.

"So, somewhere in there's going to be some talk about sacrifice, I'm sure, and somewhere around all that is your vengeance speech again, right?"

"We give to receive," he said it so simply, as if he were reciting a math fact.

Ashley got to her feet, and stuffed the sodden hanky in her belt. She offered a hand to Willy, helping him up. The rain was right on cue, and the umbilical would be by soon.

He did not release her hand, but squeezed it. "Since I cannot learn Affectations, and I cannot fight them, either, I can only manage them, second hand. I want the power of God, but I'll settle for owning an Angel to do my bidding."

A flash of lightning backlit him in radiance.

Ashley was about to drop him with another Affectation, but something in his demeanor made her too curious. "Own an Angel?"

His missionary smile was back. It didn't melt in the rain. Thunder rumbled like a deep chuckle from hell itself. "You will serve me, Ashley, and together we'll serve God. I'll be the conduit. You'll be the instrument. Oh! Oh, oh, oh—wait now. Don't Affect me again, or something *terrible* will happen to someone you love."

"You're trying to blackmail me?" She clutched at his hand now. If she couldn't Affect him, maybe she'd just break some bones in his hand, snap his wrist. She had to keep him talking, figure out what he was saying. "Too bad, pal. The only person I love died five years ago."

Willy pried his hand free—easy in the slick of the rain—then he grew smug. "Be that as it may, *pal*, his daughter, Calissa, is alive and well at Boise State. And—STOP—don't do it! Don't Affect me or you'll endanger her."

The lightning illuminated a giant black snake whipping behind him in the sky. Ten blocks. Five seconds. Answers would wait. She huffed out air, again and again, blowing the rain from her face. She was hyperventilating. Summoning strength. She Affected herself. She released all control over common sense and reservation, all sense of self-preservation, in both Willy and herself. It was the only way she could hope to pull this off.

Timing was everything.

He turned to see what she was fixed on, and that was her cue. She pushed off a patio chair, springing skyward. The umbilical swatted Willy into her. She snapped her legs open, then squeezed him with her knees as they fell from heaven.

The very last rung of the umbilical flashed by.

Ashley gritted her teeth for the pain.

She latched onto the umbilical rung with both hands.

Her shoulders—every joint from her fingers to her ribs—screamed with her. Willy screamed with her. The umbilical drooped, then sprung up. It whipped one way, then swung wildly the other. Ashley clenched the rung with all her strength. The pipe was wet. It was twice as thick as her wrist. She didn't know that she could hold on. Willy's weight wrenched at her, tugging her downward. The umbilical gave some, then fought back, jerking them upward again.

Ashley felt her fingers slipping. She dug in as if they were claws, as if the pipe were clay. A shrill scream escaped her as she struggled for a better grip, but she was giving out.

Despite her Affectation, self-preservation was seeping back into her. It had to supercharge her hands or she would die. Her common sense told the fix: drop him. *Kick free and live!* She felt her legs releasing him. He was grappling for his life, holding onto her left leg.

She kicked at him—if he fell, she lived.

She kicked again. If he died, what of Calissa?

Her kicking lacked conviction and power. All of her true energy was in her hands, and that was almost gone.

The umbilical was pulling harder. The ship was ascending. Ashley wished she could see it. As her fingers were slipping, the strength of her grip fading, she craned her head back for even a glimpse of her precious airship. It was all she owned of her father and all she could do in his memory.

Keep flying.

Water for the world.

"Sorry, Poppy," she cried, and the last of her grip slipped away.

· · · ·

Lightning strobed the faces of her loved ones. Calissa, Rory's beautiful daughter. Carl, her sidekick from the lab. Catman. Grandmother. A staccato ripple of Family in their ScanTats and grins. Alex. Kelli.

Every face was happy to see her. Welcoming her. Cheering her.

Reunited with them all—dead and alive—she felt a stronger love than she had ever known.

And then Rory.

And then Poppy.

Both men so happy for her.

Then it was Zana Amin, the benevolent husband.

All of them in rapid-fire succession.

Then a freeze-frame on Astar Amin, Zana's wife!

She too was smiling at Ashley.

She was smiling *down* at Ashley.

Astar's face was doused in rain, and she was upside down, smiling. The veins bulged in her forehead, but she was smiling.

Astar's arms and hands reached out for Ashley.

"Come child," Astar called over the storm. "Believe."

Ashley was a toddler, full of love and faith and happily extended her arms overhead. She reached for Astar, felt the woman's meaty hands grasp her wrists. Astar was still smiling, now nodding her head in reassurance. Then she was spinning with Ashley, as if Astar were twirling in circles, and Ashley was whirling out from her like a baby, only their hands holding them from the centrifugal pull.

"Yes!" Astar said, seeing something in Ashley's expression.

Astar Amin *was there*, dangling from the umbilical, holding Ashley by the wrists.

It wasn't possible. Astar was a thick, matronly woman in her seventies. She was an antique dealer in Springfield, Texas. She had never been on Ashley's airships. She didn't seem the athletic type.

Yet here she was, pulling Ashley to her. Somehow, Astar was retracted inside the umbilical. Inside the jaunty tube, they gasped for air and laughed together. The wind was fierce inside the umbilical, alternatively forcing them farther inside and then sucking them out again. Ashley switched her grip to the rungs and planted one foot on the opposite wall of the tube. She sighed. Several of the airship crew were crowded above Astar. They had held Astar's ankles. They had pulled the two of them inside.

Three of them.

Willy was still clutching her ankle. He was whimpering, a keening, haunting sound. Ashley wanted to kick him free and watch him fall back into the storm. She *did* kick him, just to get his attention. She yelled down, "We're okay. Grab a rung and climb."

"Let us get inside, yes." It was Zana! "These two will need medical attention. Prepare the tankroom." Though out of sight in the dark blend of others above her in the tube, even the distant sound of his voice made her smile.

Chapter 68 Reunion

Henny swore the car still smelled "meaty," but Sackerson waved the thought away.

"How can you even smell that over the cinders of our Mesozoic ancestors?"

"What?"

"Gas, brother. Petroleum. This old Popper is burning through the fuel."

Henny shook his head. Sometimes Sack was an environmental extremist. Other times he was revving engines just to hear them roar. He could switch in an instant.

This instant.

"Henny, you remember car shows?"

"Yeah."

"Drag runs? Burn outs in the streets. Cruisin' main?"

Henny never had his own car as a kid, but he'd ridden shotgun often enough. He told Sackerson a story about the first time he rode in a car that broke 100 mph. It felt like they were breaking the sound barrier.

"Ohhhh yeah. Good times." Sack revved up the little generator engine in the hybrid-gone-bad. "I've always found it a guilty pleasure. Back in the '70s, I owned my share of muscle cars. I had an outbuilding full of them, bought them up cheap back then, you know."

"Oh yeah?" Henny was not really paying much attention. It was sounding like another of Sackerson's long yarns that made no sense.

"Yeah. Some people collected matchbox cars; I collected muscle cars."

"What happened to them?"

"Spooks."

"Really?" Henny looked over at him. "The Spooks stole your muscle cars?"

Sackerson nodded. Even in the dashboard lights, he looked sincerely sad.

"Well... go on. What happened?"

"Spooks have taken everything from me." Sackerson tipped his head to the windshield. "Now they're coming back."

Henny looked toward Laramie. Last night at this distance, street lamps and vehicle lights had shined and twinkled like a patch of stars on the prairie. Tonight the twinkling had turned to strobing, bright and blue even from miles out. Much farther out West, a thunderstorm echoed the flashes on a distant horizon.

"That's from Spooks?"

Sack shook his head, just a fraction, as if even he was not sure.

"Sack?"

"Never enough time," he sighed. "Even when I've had lifetimes, it's never enough. It's like it gets all... wrinkled, and when you need it most, you're out."

Usually, Henny would roll his eyes and mutter "here we go," but there was something somber in Sackerson's prelude. He decided to wait the old man out.

"This... that ahead... it's all accelerated. Ever been through something and said to yourself, 'I don't remember it happening so fast last time'?" Before Henny could untangle that, Sack continued. "You're on a vacation, then you're coming home, thinking, 'Over, already?' Or you're presented the check after a fantastic evening with your whole family, and now... it's time to pay up."

Henny wanted to interrupt and ask Sackerson about the flashing that they were driving toward headlong. He recognized port flash, but he had never seen it so vivid, so constant. Were that many Spooks invading Laramie?

"See, Henny? It's time to pay up. Prematurely. Despite my best efforts. My life's work... it came, anyway." He pulled down on his beard thoughtfully and continued in a strange, low voice. "It came without needles. It came without bobbins. It came without ghosties, or monsters, or goblins."

"What?"

"Ah, my heart's about to burst, young Kenny Hinman. It's grown three sizes at least. We have a gift to bring yon stressed out town, friend. I want you to see something. Like a short before the main feature. An exhibition before the main match."

"Sack," Henny had to ask, "are you okay?"

"I'm okay, and you're okay, but the rest of this... well, you'll find it unsettling."

They were tearing through the outskirts of the dilapidated 'skirt town. Sack was dodging abandoned cars and debris in the street. In the hours they had been at the power plant, Laramie had gone to weeds. The farther they raced into town, the more bizarre it became.

Portals were mashed into heaps, sometimes in the middle of intersections, sometimes up against buildings. Some of them blinked as if crying for attention. Large portals were coming into view ahead, and these were surrounded by troops in silhouette.

Seeing them, Sackerson cranked the wheel. Their little Popper chugged harder as it rounded into a side street. Sack brought it back to highway speeds on the narrow road. He didn't make much effort in avoiding roadside rubble. Henny was sure they were going to careen out of control into the brick buildings that lined the road so tightly.

"Anyway," Sack continued, as if they were chatting over a cup of coffee, "what we are seeing here is the desecration of a good attempt at civilization. Oh, it could have been done better. Eventually people will put the environment in the equation, and we'll live in harmony with it, like Hobbits or what have you."

He pressed the brakes at an intersection, looked in all directions, then flipped a U turn. In a block, he diverted the car down an even less-developed street. When they scrabbled across some railroad tracks, he shook his head in recognition and asked, "Where was I?"

"Desecration of civilization," Henny said.

"Yeah. Right. Here's the thing," he said, turning attention to Henny, even as the car was rocketing along, "I think civilization is like parenting. Nobody knows what they're doing. We all get a little of it right, and it all works out."

"Sack—"

"But there's those among us who think they have it right. They'll be damned if anybody else is going to do it any other way." He turned back to the windshield, much to Henny's relief. "That's about right," Sack reflected, "*they will be damned.*"

Sack was looking out the top of the windshield, paying attention to rooftops, it seemed, more than the road in front of them.

"Want me to drive?" Henny finally asked.

"What? Naw, you just sit back and take this all in. Who knows, Henny, you may be the eventual historian of this monumental—"

They hit something, and it crunched under the car.

Henny hit his head on the ceiling.

Sackerson fought the wheel.

"Deer," Sack explained, though Henny knew better. It had been a Port Authority soldier. He could see the corpse in the rearview.

"*That* was not a clone," Henny said firmly. "You said we wouldn't hurt anyone."

"I said, if you'll recall the conditions of our travels, that *you* wouldn't hurt anyone."

"Stop the car, Sack."

"We're about there, old pal. Just—"

"I said, stop." Henny used his 'clear the bar' voice.

Hailstones were dinging at the hood and roof, and Sack did not stop driving. "You may want to duck," he said, flooring it.

Something cracked the windshield.

Someone throwing rocks at them?

One of their headlights popped out.

Then Henny heard the gunshots. Lots of gunshots.

As they dashed through an intersection, a mass of Port Authority Grays were firing on them. Henny ducked, but he wanted to see for himself. His side window exploded, and he hunkered down. He could hear thunking all over the car.

"Safety glass," Sackerson said, brushing bits of glass off Henny's head and shoulders. "Misnomer if you ask me."

"What is going on?" Henny hollered.

"They're behind us now. You can sit back up."

The cold wind from the shattered window helped slap him back to his senses. They were on the edge of an industrial park, down in the old shipping area where freight trains had once been so busy. Henny knew these parts of a town. It didn't matter if it was Laramie or Guthrie.

Sackerson slowed to a stop. The old Popper sputtered and died. In the dim light of their single headlight, Henny saw an enormous pile of rubble that extended far off into the dark. Beyond that, and behind them some ways, the portal flashes and gunfire continued.

Sackerson pulled up a sleeve to consult an appliance he wore at his elbow. He nodded at it, reassured, and said, "This should be in the neighborhood."

Henny had seen Sack's old, oversized wrist watch several times. The dial was bigger than a silver dollar, and it had several knobs and bangles on it. Altogether it looked like he had the lid of a jar strapped to his wrist.

This device, however, was sleek and conformed to his arm. It was a discrete digital appliance Henny had never seen before. It looked to him to be of Stetson quality.

Sack tugged down his sleeve and pried at the door handle. He gave the door his shoulder. Then he stopped and turned back to Henny.

"I was going to save this, but, well, you never know. Kenny, you've been good to me, and I appreciate it."

"Thanks, Sack... I appreciate you, too?"

"I want you to keep all this in your head, especially this."

"This... this what?"

Sackerson's beard twisted at his mouth. *Was he having trouble finding his words?*

The old man cleared his throat, that high rooster sound again. He seemed to have himself collected when he said, "Think about this, Henny: mankind."

"O-kay. What about it?"

"You'd think it would be, you know, a statement about civilization, like someone just said, 'Hey, let's always remind ourselves to be kind. Let's call ourselves, mankind.'" Sack smiled. "Could have been 'man-friendly' or 'man-love,' I guess, but that gets a little—"

"I don't think words work like that, Sack."

"But talk about your misnomers. Whew. Man *kind*? I mean—" he chuckled. "Really?"

Henny didn't know what to say. As usual, he didn't know where this was going. Sack still had one hand on the door lever, as if this speech was pre-empting the battle in town and whatever mission they were on.

"I've had a lot of time to think about it. I wonder if it's really being mis-pronounced. Like, what if it's Mank-ind?"

"Mank-ind?" Henny repeated.

"Yeah. Mank, you know, like gross... manky?"

"You're saying this word for all humanity is sayin' we're... manky?"

"That's a better fit, you ask me. *Mank. End.* Like *ass-end.* Like God or somebody's passing judgment on all this, and says, "Mank. The End. That's all there is to them. Manky."

"You really feel that way? About mankind?"

"Nah," Sack said, popping the door open. "If I did, I would have given all this up years ago."

Henny got out and stood, waiting for Sackerson's next move. It seemed it should be something monumental after his rash of testifying.

"Come along, Hinman. We have a very woeful moment in our very near future."

Henny sighed. He longed for the rambling, slurred stories of the drunks at *Sharts N' Grins.* Their stories were equally confusing, but at least they did not include him directly in their telling. Once again, Henny felt Sack was making it up as they went along, as if he was creating their reality as he told it.

They trudged along at the edge of the crushed concrete pile. Sack was intent on his every footfall. Sometimes, he would stop and get his bearings from the buildings nearby, then continue walking.

Explosions in the distance drowned out the gunfire sometimes. When the sprinkles began again, Henny thought some of those explosions might be thunder. The storm he had noted out West should be far away yet. He commented on it, but Sack silenced him. "Really, the weather at a time like this?"

"Time... like what?"

Sackerson pointed at the ground. "Reunion!"

Henny had to do a double take.

Crawling slowly through the clods of concrete, leaving a snail trail in the dust behind it, was a mechanical hand.

Chapter 69 Blitzkrieg

S tu was dog tired, but he couldn't sleep. He didn't even try.
Everything he could delegate had been delegated, but there
was still too much to do. Much of what he was doing overnight was
the work no one should have to do: planning worst-case scenarios,
writing condolences, drafting triage policies.

Other work might have looked like fretting around, but to
him, it was vigilance. He walked the halls of the hospital regularly,
looking in on the injured, consoling the families. He walked the
grounds, through the lines of school buses and sentries. He crossed
the improvised courtyard, stark black and white in the floodlights
they'd set up.

Every step of the way, Stu Wiebe felt more responsible.
Somehow, he had brought this on them. The toxic cocktail of too
many Boys and too much testosterone had attracted the Eaters.
Altogether, The Boys and the Eaters had given Chomp a
focus—Laramie. Now, Chomp was to be the Port Authority's
whipping boy and Laramie an example to the rest of the world.

The lightning storm had been nothing but a storm. It came
and went like weather did. Rumors sprouted that something was
hanging out of that storm, but since nothing came of it, no one
cared. There were worse things to worry about.

Port flashes had stopped with the storm and did not continue
after it passed. It was as if they had been drowned out. Stu let
himself entertain the idea that maybe, just maybe, the Port
Authority was moving on.

Enough lives had been lost.

Enough damage had been done.

Their point had been made and broadcast without mercy.

• • • •

The Walkie on his belt squelched and Cort Bradley reminded him of the midnight meeting. Stu poured himself and a nurse another cup of coffee, and he said his goodbyes. The hospital was nearing capacity, he had learned, and their only hope of supplies would be those they might normally get ported on site. There wasn't going to be any plasma, bandages, nor antibiotics coming in by medical portals, but Stu didn't have the heart to tell her.

The meeting was in his "office." The corner lobby windows reflected the lights and people in the room after dark. At least a dozen men and women crowded around a makeshift table and map of the city.

In all the corporate "wisdom" since they came out from behind the guise of government, the dumbest thing they ever did—in Stu's opinion—was the Land Rush. It was a ChompCorp stunt that had created a false economy, but a big boon for Wyoming towns like Laramie. Seemingly overnight, it had doubled in size. With the people came businesses and buildings and a boomer culture that had come in hot and blown itself away. The map reflected that, even in the design of the streets and city planning. All the new stuff looked out of place around the edges of town. Out of place, and now, except for the ChompCorp community, largely abandoned. Reports were that even that neighborhood had been suddenly evacuated when the Grays came to town.

Boom gone bust. Just like Oklahoma.

The map was covered with green houses and red hotels from board games.

"Is that accurate?" Stu asked, crouching down to see it from eye level.

"Green ones are about all dozed," one of The Boys said.

"Red ones are too damn big to mess with."

"And besides, they're sticking around to guard them."

"What?" That got Burton's attention.

"Hardly any Grays about town, except at these big ports."

"All of the larger ports, and *only* the larger ports?"

The men hem-hawed around, but someone finally spoke up. "We didn't count soldiers. Nobody told us to do that. We just tried to spot all the ports and mark them."

"Just over 300 portals still standing, almost all of them big as a double door garage."

"How did we miss that—all of them spread out like that, like, in a pattern?"

"Doesn't matter now. What can we do about it?"

"Dad," Nat said, edging up to Stu's shoulder.

"Yeah?"

"The Interface is back online, and in the bowels of it, there's images like this."

"Probably several," Burton confirmed. "Drills."

"What if this isn't a drill?" Stu asked. He looked from Burton to Nat and didn't like what he saw. "Well... spill it."

"They did practice runs with big trucks dropping refrigerators off of them," Nat said. "There's two stories of it."

"Outside Vegas," one of the Eaters nodded. "I was there."

Burton nodded to the man to continue. "It was so strange. Middle of a Sunday afternoon. They'd been propping up ports for weeks. Had to be a hundred or more. All a'sudden, ker-pow!"

"Deployment rigs, bumper to bumper, rolling out of the ports, fast. They shot out and took the streets like they were on auto pilot, and once they were all out and rolling fast, that's when it got weird."

"The sides rolled down on these big trailer trucks and they pushed off fridges. Brand new fridges."

"Refrigerators?"

"They didn't land so well. Most of them were smashed up. Ruined."

"Scratch and dent."

"Fall off the truck bargains."

"Port Authority left them all. Most of the trucks just rolled back to their portals, flashed away."

"The rest of the Grays worked all night at loading the big ports, then they all rolled out of one last one. Left if behind, like a reminder... it's still there."

"Why haven't we heard about this? On the news or something?"

"It's not the news they'd think we'd need," Nat said. "So it gets buried."

"And you think that was a drill for something?"

"I do. I think refrigerators are of a similar mass as the standard ports." Burton said.

"So, they're going to give away ports, just dump them out on every street corner?"

It reminded Stu of something Krystal had said about putting a port in every garage.

"Or they're going to drop ports like that and come out 'em, guns blazing. All at a time. Blitzkrieg style."

"So what was today? That wasn't nothing."

"I think that was rehearsal," Burton said. "The way we figure it, they're gonna level this whole damn town yet tonight. It'll make a statement for the morning news."

• • • •

No one was ready for it when it started. Every portal in Laramie winked on and in the next instant, Port Authority trucks were roaring into town. Stu watched it from his window, watched it taking shape exactly like they described it in Las Vegas. This time, like Burton predicted, *portals* were pouring off the trucks. He understood now why they were built so solidly—to withstand such abuse. Of the hundreds littering the streets in his view, many were tipped on a side or toppled flat on their backs. On impact, the portals all glowed, ready for action.

As far as he could see, the portals were stationed in haphazard radiance. They looked like oversized luminaries lining the streets.

The Boys fortified the hospital grounds and the PetroPlex, parking semis and heavy equipment densely in front of big portals. They ran out of time before they were able to shore up much else.

Time ran out completely when the Grays started flashing in by the thousands, city-wide. These soldiers shot on sight. There was no sense of decorum nor military code. They just fired at will.

A stray bullet or two cracked webbing in Stu's window glass.

It was too dark to use binoculars, the ports and gunfire too bright to use night vision scopes. Stu and the men in his lobby had to rely on the erratic images covering the HomeRoom display. The Eaters' drones and helmet cams captured the destruction.

Port Authority weaponry was overpowering. While the Rebels of the Plains and The Boys were limited to rifles and pistols, a haphazard arsenal of their own collections, the Grays were firing advanced automatic weapons, rail guns, hand cannons, shoulder-fired missile launchers...

Several of the drone cameras flared white at once. A repercussion rattled the windows of the hospital. They were using bigger bombs now, destroying the city's infrastructure.

None of the defensive forces could hold. Local men and women were lying dead in the streets, trampled by more and more soldiers advancing. Someone's helmet cam was focusing on the dead.

"Hit that guy's mic," Burton commanded.

"Merciless. Even when we give up, they gun us down. Everyone they see. Dragging people out of houses... group of teenagers were just throwing bricks at 'em. Dead." His narrative was interrupted with explosions and the outbursts of those with him. "Extermination. That's what it is."

Burton nodded, and the HomeRoom was again muted. Outside rumble and gunfire continued. Constant rat-a-tat of weapons punctured the thunder.

Thunder.

Stu turned back to the window. He looked out West, shielding his eyes from the bursts of light and flames throughout Laramie. The night sky was roiling purple lightning, low to the ground.

"Get word to everyone you find," Stu commanded. "Gault was right. It's coming in."

They all struggled to see for themselves, then fell quiet. Nothing but this could be more shocking than the carnage of the invading troops. This, however, was no flyover warning storm like TransCorp had ported away. This was a horizon-to-horizon monstrosity, flaring lighting, raging toward town directly. This Lightning's Hand would truly leave nothing in its wake but scorched earth and ashes. It would finish the job the Port Authority had started.

Stu had a sick sense of satisfaction. *The Grays would fry.*

"Take cover but block their retreat as best we can," Stu said. Everyone sprang from their awestruck reverie and looked to him. "We got minutes, tops. Head them off at their ports. Let the storm do the rest."

Chapter 70 Healers

With the Family, Rory remembered feelings more than facts, and that alone made him uneasy. Facts were coming to him about all things otherwise. Most of the notes he carried were emerging from his haze. He found the concept of killing the Rich to be repulsive now, and he struggled not to spiral into depths of depression over the actions of his past.

But the Family was not coming clear to him. Even with them sitting in his camp, even with them attempting small talk, he was wary of them. When he felt even the brush of an Affectation, Rory would stiffen and glare at them. He had Katrina translate his order: *Affect me and I will a) know it and b) hurt you.* When it was relayed to the Family, their smiles and snickers were impossible to mask, even behind their ScanTats. That they found humor in his threat made him even more angry. He tried to choke it back but realized then they were probably reading his mind anyway—and that made him feel even more naked and vulnerable.

Rory was not a man who liked to be vulnerable.

Long into the night, Katrina and the Family chattered away in various languages, catching up. Once in a while, she would realize he was left out of their conversation and backtrack, relating back to him in English passages of their stories, punchlines of their jokes. She would ask questions he was reluctant to answer. Finally, Rory retreated to the warehouse and curled up on a pile of cardboard. He intended to sleep.

• • • •

"Daddy?"

Rory rolled over to face her. She was backlit by the moon, framed in the warehouse doorway. He caught his breath.

"Daddy!" she said, and rushed to him.

"Cal?"

"I've missed you," she cried, sitting with him on the cardboard.

"Come in for it," Rory smiled, and pulled her close. He felt a sense of peace come over himself, a calm he did not even know was missing. He hugged her tightly, and she hugged back.

"Smowurh," she said, as best she could, smashed against his chest. Calissa pushed back, caught a breath, and said, "You could use a shower!"

He laughed with her. He didn't release her entirely, for a part of him feared she'd float away like a dream. "You're a dream," he said, taking in her features. She had his hair, wavy and dark and more auburn than black, even in the moonlight. She was of a small but sturdy build, his daughter for certain. Rory choked on his words, "Best dream I ever had."

"I'm no dream, Dad. I'm here." Calissa sat back, crossed her legs under her.

"But... how?"

She smiled and looked over her shoulder at the doorway. "I came with them, with the Family."

Rory frowned. "But... why didn't you—"

"They thought it would be better. Little bit at a time," she smiled.

He studied her, head to toe. His little girl, all grown up... and safe... and with him now half a world from home. She had on a t-shirt from her college, shorts and black patent shoes. He was no fashion expert, but the shoes looked oddly out of place. He was about to comment on them, when he realized it must have been a trick of light. She was barefoot, like the rest of them.

Calissa. She was everything to him. She had been through everything with him. He had lost her once before, when Combs

took her. He had been lost to her, these last few years. "How long
has it been, kid?"

"Five years," she said, sobering up a bit. "I've missed you!"

"So... fill me in. How's college? How've you been, you know,
without me?"

Calissa sat back and rested on her elbow. "School. Work. Pretty
boring, really. What about you? They tell me they found you on the
shore? What happened?"

He recoiled inside, thinking of the last time he had to admit
anything of his past to her. It was when he had confirmed that he
was, in fact, an assassin. An Extractor. He was so worried she would
never forgive him for hiding it from her.

"What is it, Daddy?" She said with concern, putting a hand on
his forearm.

"Ah, nothing. It's nothing. The whole thing's nothing. It's just a
wash. Five years I can never get back."

"I want to know. Tell me about it. We thought you died at sea."

He nodded and thought again that maybe he *had* died at sea.
He had been reborn, then resorted to crimes and deeds more
bloody and wicked than anything he had done as an Extractor.
"I got to use my survival skills, that's for sure," Rory joked.
"Everything we learned in Girl Scouts, too. And then some."

Calissa didn't say anything, just encouraged him to tell more.
At first, he told her stories of the good life on the beach. Sand
castles. Beach combing. Meeting people. He told her of some of the
most incredible shorelines he had all to himself. She sat listening in
rapt attention.

"But what about you, Cal? What have I missed? Really?"

"I studied Ultraviolet Spectroscopy."

"Right. Rainbows."

"Edge of the atmosphere type stuff, yeah. I graduated, and
guess what? I got on at Winston." She beamed. "I work for 3dub!"

Rory squinted, thinking. Had he arranged something for her through Ashley? Was there some legacy plan in place, should anything happen to him?

"Yeah, it's a little shaky, what with the problems with the brand, but I love it." She talked about her job, about a man she met—careful here to not rile him up. She adjusted her seat, then turned the conversation back to him.

He was pouring out all kinds of stories now, still dodging the gruesome business of ridding the world of the Rich. He felt more at peace and more whole with every story. It was all coming back to him as he spoke with her. Rory couldn't keep from smiling, and she smiled with him.

"You seem really happy here," Calissa said, after a while. "What is it about this place?"

"This warehouse?" he glanced around, incredulous. "There's nothing about this place, Cal. I can't wait to get out of here."

"Not here... I mean, the islands. *Tropical islands*. It's so pretty. You look so good here. I've never seen you so relaxed."

They had traveled extensively throughout the states as she grew up. He had taken her on some pretty extreme backpacking adventures, he recalled now, and smiled at the thought. Wasn't she just seven, maybe ten, when they were repelling in a canyon?

"Maybe we shouldn't rush to go anywhere, Dad. Maybe we should take some time here together."

"Time... here?" He felt a little dazed by that, about sticking around. He was no longer on his mission against the Rich. He did, however, have something driving him, some sense of urgency to leave here.

"Yeah," she smiled. "We can go back to town, settle down for a while."

"What about your job?"

"Leave of absence."

"What about them?" he gestured toward the Family and Katrina, somewhere outside.

"I dunno." She looked their way, then looked back at him, a new idea coming to her. "We could give them all the slip, Dad. Just you and me. We could find another way out of here and—"

Rory so wanted to communicate with her, with *only* his Calissa, and so he resorted to their most private and primitive morse code conversation via the Clench in his jaw. His message was simple: *I wish we could talk again, out of earshot.*

Calissa continued with her fantasy of escaping the Family and holing up in the nearest village. She did not bat an eye at his morse code message.

He tried again: *I need you to help me with Ashley.*

Then aloud, he said, in contrast, "We'd just go it alone, let the world turn?"

"That's right," she beamed.

She wasn't listening with her inner ear. She wasn't attending to her Clench. She was not herself, then. That much was coming clear.

I was going to kill Ashley, but now I think I'm meant to save her, Rory tapped on his Clench. *I need you to help me save her.*

Still, nothing registered with her. She was not his Calissa.

"We can have the Family look out for us, and we can just hunker down for a season. Get all fat and happy, like your friends say," the not-quite-Calissa said.

"Why would you do this?" Rory groaned, getting to his feet. "Why torture me like this?"

"Daddy?" Calissa asked. "What did I do?"

"It's what you didn't do, whoever you are." Rory trod off into the darkness, far from the imposter and the Family that had fueled the deception. He remembered now that this was Katrina's greatest gift, that of being a chameleon. "Why, Katrina? Why?" He rumbled in the black of the warehouse, moving through the portals.

"We are only helping with the healing, Rory Reed," she said. Though she had not moved from the cardboard pile, her words were with him. "I am so sorry. We are trying everything we can to..."

She was continuing, but he wasn't hearing it.

He was reading off a Morse Code message clacking in his jawbone, interpreting a sensation he had not felt in all these too quiet years. The Clench code was unmistakable, and he knew it to be true:

"Daddy? Is that really you?"

Chapter 71 Self-actualization

Thunder. That was all he could make out.

Lark pressed his ear to the pipe fitting and listened attentively. He wanted to hear it if anyone found his hand, for maybe he could somehow point them in his direction.

He lay on the floor in the gravel and debris for hours.

Then he felt a tremor. The air pressure from the pipe changed, pulling air from his chamber. He didn't know what to make of it, but he welcomed the change.

Another tremor. Then it was a constant tremor.

The floor of the Lead Room vibrated.

The whole space reverberated with a loud boom. Dust was again thick in the air.

Lark sat up and panned the flashlight. What was happening?

Again, a resounding boom shook him to his core. The room quaked, then settled.

This was not thunder.

He got to his feet, worried the whole room might collapse.

Again—this time he sensed it was the wall behind him. He turned as it happened again, and this time, if his eyes were not deceiving him, *the wall moved.*

Lark watched that wall closely. A few seconds passed, and then another powerful thud shook him. This time he could see the wall move, and with it, the ceiling. Was the pounding coming from something outside? Had they found him?

He tried calling out, but his voice was hoarse and the dust choked him. Besides, he realized, the slamming was now almost constant. Nothing out there could have heard him over all that noise.

A great low rasping sound then frightened him. It was a wall moving. A gap at where the ceiling met that wall sucked out the dust cloud. He could see a brighter darkness through the crack. *Outside!*

In a brief reprieve from the pounding, he strained to understand what was happening. Lark heard voices, but there was thunder and gunfire and the sound of a revving diesel engine to contend with. He couldn't catch the words altogether, only snippets.

"...knock the whole thing in!"

"...could do better?"

A rumble of thunder cracked the sky.

"Get the teeth in the crack and pry," one of the voices was yelling. He knew that voice from somewhere.

"Grand idea!" the other shouted. The engine revved again, and Lark watched a black shadow obscure the sliver of night sky. It was easily six feet wide, some metal hulking thing that rammed at the crack, poked and prodded—iron versus lead—forcing itself inside.

Huge metal teeth, each a hand-span across, a row of them mounted to something—a bucket! He knew it then. This was a bucket from some piece of heavy equipment. Lark called out as loudly as he could, "I'm here. I'm in here!"

The engine was at high RPM, the power of the machine was being tested. He could hear it in the groan and grating of the wall against the bucket's teeth. He could feel the struggle even in the floor of the Lead Room.

Lark retreated to the far corner. Even here he felt the prying and the strain.

The roof wasn't going up. It seemed the bucket sensed it just when Lark did, for it changed its angle of attack, and the machine outside again bellowed.

"That's it. That's it," someone outside coaxed. "It's working, Sack. You got it. Keep pulling."

Sack? Sackerson? And the voice cheering him on—*was that Henny*?

Before Lark had time to question it more, the bucket's teeth advanced into the room and then pulled down the far wall in a heaving motion. The machine outside died. Loud thunder, however, continued in its place.

Flashlights blinded him. The two advanced over the fallen wall and into the Lead Room.

"Laaaaark? Are you in here?"

"Lefty! Hey, call off your claw, eh?"

Lark had not thought of his prosthetic. He had been willing it to crawl, but then in all the chaos of the Lead Room attack, he hadn't realized what his hands had been doing. His fist was clenched. Henny shined a light on his prosthetic. It was clutching Henny's coat.

Brightness strobed with the storm outside. Lark blinked at the blinding flash of his HeadGear. The Visor Henny wore lit up abruptly, highlighting his worried features. Henny handed the prosthetic back to Lark. "Want me to fit it?"

"Not right—"

A blast of thunder more deafening than any Lark had ever known cut him off. Sackerson darted to the opening and looked around. When he looked overhead, he flinched and rushed back toward them. "Shelter!"

"What's that?" Lark yelled back.

"We gotta hunker down. In here. Nowhere to go."

The rain was back and coming down in a wall of water and wind. It whipped inside the Lead room, a mist of it spraying Lark against the back wall. Henny and Sackerson crowded into the safest corner with him.

"Lightning's Hand!" Henny explained.

Lark saw images in his heads-up display of the devastating effects of such storms. He remembered what he had heard of them on the Interface. He worried again about Krystal. He pictured her, out in the storm, struggling with her parasol against the storm.

The Stetson was intuitive. The display and vids switched immediately to a scene from that morning, overcast but not yet the storm pouring out there now. The view was erratic, but between two or three points of view—headcams—it came to center on Krystal Price. The ticker at the bottom of the CommCorp display identified her just as something happened to her.

"Wha—?" Lark reached his hands out to touch her. He clouted the HeadGear to get it to reset or rewind or do *something*. "Henny," he called out blindly. His view was only that bloody mess on the Interface, displayed again and again in vivid detail. "Make this damn thing—Henny! *What is this?*"

He felt them trying to remove the device, and he fought to keep it on as best he could with his one hand. He twisted left and right to free himself from them.

"Lark!" Sackerson called to him. "I didn't want you to find out like this!"

"I didn't know he'd have it on him," Henny was explaining to Sackerson. "I didn't think he'd still have power. I didn't expect us to get signal!"

"What happened to Krystal?" Lark ranted, but it was lost in the crash of the storm. "*Is she okay?* Is she going to be okay?"

He had to find out for himself. She was out there in this lightning storm!

"Get back here," Henny was saying, wrenching at him, pulling him back toward the corner.

"Find her!" Lark was screaming. "I gotta find her!"

He took a swing at Henny, then resorted to swinging his prosthetic like a bat. He switched it up then, and held hands with his plastic hand, the grip tight and reassuring in the strangest of ways. At this rate, he could fend them both off and get away.

It was Lark Fortune against the world.

He felt the club collide against Sackerson's shoulder, Henny's forearm. They kept trying to grasp him, to secure and subdue him.

Lark felt invigorated by the lightning storm. It sparked a power in him to be the hero he was made to be. He swung until he was free of the two who cowered in the Lead Room corner. He was striding out into the fire and torrent of storm.

Then he was on the ground, and they were pulling at his feet. Henny had tackled him! He kicked at them, seeing their bloodied faces in strobing, stop-action emotions. Fear. Anger. Pain.

Lark scrambled to stand and run out through the opening they had made, to take the escape they had provided. The rain and wind threw him back, but he pressed on. He gasped for air and shielded his face with his good arm.

He was going to find her and save her and to hell with them both! What were they trying to do with that fabricated footage? Drive him mad?

Lark was running then, stumbling over rubble and stone. It was all so slick and wet. He struggled to stay on his feet. *He had to.* He had to put distance between him and those two.

In a whip of wind, the rain sheets parted and Lark saw them coming out of the black jaw of the Lead Room. Then, in more strobing, they moved erratically toward him. A wild-haired skeleton and a thick, squat henchman, both of them moving like rickety ghouls.

Lark fell, got back on his feet, and tried to run backward.

A blast of energy and light walloped the backhoe, a bolt of lighting coursing over it, encasing it in celestial power. It knocked all three of them off their feet. Lark was struggling to see—to see anything!

He was being dragged then, and he fought it. Hinman and Sackerson were not messing around this time. They were pulling his arms out of the sockets.

More lightning struck not thirty yards distant. Several more white-hot streaks hit the ground nearby. Deafening blasts of thunder clapped right after.

Then they were in the Lead Room again. Rain wasn't drowning him. Wind wasn't sucking at his every breath. They might be out of the lightning's reach.

Sackerson tossed him into Henny, and they fell toward the safe corner. In black and white snapshots, Sack was standing tall. He fished in his pocket. He mounted something to the wall, then something else.

Lark could hear his cackle between blasts of thunder.

Sack glanced back at Lark, and in that instant, that thunderbolt of recognition, Lark knew himself.

Chapter 72 Hypervolemic Shock

A lex knew a lot about blood loss.

When she started turning blue in the lips and fingertips, he turned over and over inside. She was getting colder as her body was in full retreat—keep the vital organs alive as long as possible, and sacrifice extremities. Hypovolemic shock.

"So cold," she whispered, and he died a little inside.

At least she was with him, aware and communicating.

He didn't even remember the details, but they'd ended up in the hospital. When Wiebe recognized them—and the situation—he made sure they had a room to themselves. It was close to the nurses' station. It was a room that still had power. They had the best monitoring and care left in Laramie.

Stu Wiebe had checked in on them, but Alex knew the look of a man who had a war to look to. Wiebe was with them, but then again, he was strategizing, most likely agonizing for the hundreds at his command.

They gave her pint after pint of precious blood. The nurses, like the rancher, put up a good front when they visited, but they, too, were frazzled and overburdened and already giving up on Kelli Jo Chase.

The generator also had provided light and heat, and electric blankets were draped over her to help with her body temp. As other resources in the complex went dead, hospital staff discretely passed through their room, running extension cords and cables from their room to others. They did not make eye contact as they worked, not disturbing the man and wife in their agony.

Alex thought they were selling her short. He told a nurse as much, an innocent young girl who was just there to bring her water. "She's been through worse," he explained to the girl. "You'll see. She bounces back."

"Yessir," the nurse said.

"I mean it. You should have seen her when she got a knife in the gut. Most people woulda keeled right—"

"Alex," Kelli interrupted. She muttered something then that took his attention.

The nurse, he noted, made a break for it.

"Come back and see us in the morning," he shouted after her. "We can all eat breakfast together."

"Alex," she said again, raising her hand under layers of blankets. "I didn't want to be a Hallmark movie."

"What?" he struggled to chuckle. He smiled as best as he could.

"Maudlin."

"Honey, your education is showing. We don't talk like that in war zones, remember?"

She sighed and licked her lips. He brought the water bottle to her, placed the straw at her mouth. She drank and settled back into her pillow.

"The dying pregnant woman has to choose," she had to regroup, take a breath, to continue, "and I don't wanna choose."

"Choose what, darlin'?"

"In the movies... she always chooses the baby's life over hers." Kelli swallowed hard and tears welled in her eyes. Her mouth puckered some as she fought with something. Pain. A problem. Alex longed to help her. He offered her more water, but she turned her head.

"I'm so selfish," she cried, not in her whispery voice but one that made her wince in pain. "I don't want to die, Alex."

"Die?" he scoffed, but choked on the word. "You're not gonna—"

"I want to be with you, forever."

Alex set down the water bottle and took in the room through his tears. The blinds were askew, for furniture and equipment was barricaded against the windows. Paperwork from medical charts was strewn all over the floor. Tablets and appliances had been discarded, one lie broken on a counter nearby. Empty blood bags, sharps and other trash overflowed the little bedside trashcan.

He saw it. Just what he was looking for on a tray of fruit. Some thoughtful locals had brought them fruit and cheese. Though it had gone untouched—his appetite was gone—it provided him with the visual aid he needed.

Alex snatched a strawberry and held it a few inches in front of her face. "See this? Do you see this, Kelli?"

She nodded.

"That's the baby right now. They said you were maybe 8 weeks, tops, right? We walked it back. Couldn't be any older."

Her shoulder moved a little under the blanket. She looked at him. "So?"

"So it's not a question," he popped the strawberry in his mouth. "No bigger than a strawberry. There is no issue here."

He chewed and swallowed. His demonstration had no effect on her.

A loud explosion rattled the window. She raised an eyebrow at it. "I want up," she said.

"You gonna suit up and kick ass? Is that your plan, punkin?"

"I'm not going to be a burden." She gritted her teeth and tried to sit up but failed. "Just shoot me if I'm burdensome."

"Deal," Alex said, humoring her. "Or I could just slit your throat if you want me to save a bullet."

She nodded in firm agreement. "Or just leave me here with the rest of them and skip time. Get the hell out of here."

Before he could even utter a response, the last of the power supply popped off. Battery powered alarms throughout the hospital squawked warnings. Alex dismantled the one on her bedside immediately.

"Generators are fried," someone observed from the hall.

Lightning flashed brighter now and more frequently. Thunder and rain kept at the windows. Alex could hear hospital staff scurrying around, giving worried orders to one another. They were doing their damnedest to save lives without any resources now. Meager light from HeadGear. No other power. Not even running water. They were doing what they could to help those they could still help.

No one was coming to their room.

"I'm so cold," she whimpered in the dark.

Alex let down the side rail and carefully curled up around her. He tucked the blankets in around them both. His heat would be her heat. He would keep her alive with nothing but sheer will power if he had to.

He had a lot of that.

．．．．

Wiebe was back. He took it on himself to pry a chair from the barricade and was slumped down in it. He was quiet for a long time. Alex wondered if he might just tip his hat over his eyes and sleep.

The ravages of the Lightning's Hand continued. It was the worst one Alex had ever heard of, though not the first one he had endured. He wished they had a room in the basement, away from the storm, but he knew that was where they kept the bodies, a makeshift morgue.

Kelli wasn't talking much, and Wiebe had put a cramp on his small talk. There was only so much he felt comfortable talking about with the cowboy in their room. The nurse had advised him to keep Kelli conscious, and he did, but she had run out of things to say.

Zana had explained stages of shock to him once, and neither of them agreed with the human body's prioritization. Sure, it made sense to regroup around the vital organs, to keep the core warm. That was simply brilliant design. Not considering the brain one of those vital organs, however, seemed a fault of the system. All that was in the abstract. Now that his bride was going through the stages, Alex longed to fix the system.

Keep her talking, that was the mission. He asked her the names of the girls on the airship, and with some struggle, she recounted over a dozen of them. He had her naming the streets of Franklin. He could get one or two word answers from her, and they checked out with his memory of the town. She seemed to perk up with talk of Franklin, so he spoke of the town as she had rebuilt it, the new library, the child care center, the rehab center. She was mayor and chief enforcer of the little burg, and he could see the pride in her eyes as he described her town.

"Sounds like a great place," Wiebe said, stirring.

"Shithole," Kelli said, attempting a smile. "But it's mine."

"It's come a long ways in the last five years," Alex said. "You know the story?"

Wiebe shook his head.

"Franklin, Texas, was hit by a Lightning's Hand *and* a tornado in the same night."

"Skirt town," Kelli offered. "Tough."

"Yeah, Chomp really had them on the skids down there. They'd sold out. All the land was corn production. All the people were sharecroppers."

Wiebe nodded.

"You're doing the right thing, fighting them," Alex said. "People will notice."

"Franklin came back from... this?" The rancher was gazing toward the windows. The lightning animated his craggy features.

"Yes," Kelli said. She drew a breath to tell him more, but a claxon sounded from every device, everywhere, all at once.

Wiebe sat up. "What the hell? How's that possible?"

The power was out. The Interface was down. Alex had only one explanation.

"WE'RE HERE FOR THE TIME TRAVELER. DELIVER HIM OR DIE," the simulcast was slightly staggered from device to device. It sounded as if dozens of mechanical men were making the same request all around them.

Wiebe lumbered out of his chair. He drew out a revolver. He was looking it over, checking the load. His eyes sparkled in the dark.

Alex would have been doing the same, tooling up, but he was cuddling his beloved.

She spat profanities.

"Guess this is it, then," Wiebe said.

"I need some time." Alex pointed his chin at Kelli, clarifying, "*We* need a minute."

"I hear they don't negotiate."

"So?" Alex asked flatly. "Turning me over to them?"

The pause before Wiebe's answer was telling. This was not an easy decision for him, either way. He looked a long while at Kelli.

"Deliver him or die," Stu quoted, a mockery of the clone's flat voice. He straightened, and turned toward the door. "I'd rather die."

"Where are you going?" Alex asked.

"I'm gonna find your time traveling friends and welcome them to Wyoming."

Chapter 73 Truth

A shley was a hot mess. She was back aboard an airship, and that always made her spirits soar. She was reunited with the Amins, Zana and Astar, who she considered her adopted parents. She was safe in the skies, miles from the war-torn town below... and from there, her mind was mixed. Alex and Kelli were down there. People needed her help in Laramie. She wanted to dive down and make everything right. Avenge the underprivileged. Fight for the locals.

She also wanted to return to the coastline and hunt Blackbeard.

More an imperative than any of that: find and save Calissa Reed.

They were in the Tankroom, the bay where vast reserves of Aether were stored for flight. Ashley had played hide and seek in such places when she was a girl. She had been a stow-away on daring airship test flights. More recently, she had been part of an interrogation in the Tankroom of another ship, the *Arcus*. In that setting she had been doubly deceived, by Steve Spexarth and Katrina Covarrubias.

She would not make such a mistake again.

She studied Willy and the people surrounding them. Three of the girls were there, arms crossed, stern expressions—backup security. Astar and Zana had been tending to her, and were now at work on Willy. They had taped closed a gash in his cheek, applied something to his split lip, and wrapped the fingers of one hand. His face was bruised. His shirt was bloodied. He did not stir, despite their attention.

Astar never approved of administering the Aether as they had. It was an accepted anesthetic for such field operations, Zana argued, and one with a proven track record in a similar situation.

On this point, he waggled his eyebrows at Ashley. "Even such precautions did not protect you then, did they, Princess?"

Astar wasn't hearing it. She clearly did not like the restraints they had used on him, strapping him to a bench with ratchet straps! She had Zana loosen them twice. "Gassing him and tying him down! He is a man of God, not some fiend."

"The two are not exclusive," Zana chided.

Zana's careful ministrations of Aether went beyond the medicinal; Aether was also good at loosening one's tongue. Questioning Katrina Covarrubias had been frequent and deep, and Ashley was interested in what Zana might learn from Willy in the same way.

"A few restraints will be the least of his problems," Ashley said, turning her full attention to them. "He's holding Calissa hostage."

Astar's expression contorted with concern and worry. Her eyes widened and she moved her mouth to speak, but only muttered in her native tongue. She took a deep breath as Zana stroked her shoulder. "This man...?" she asked through gritted teeth. "He has done something to our baby?"

Ashley nodded.

Zana's arm wrapped around Astar, and he pulled her away from Willy, just as her body was recovering from the shock. She thrust him away. She dived at Willy, her fingers reaching for him, clawing at him.

Ashley readied an Affectation, one that might do them all some good, but Zana whispered something to her, and Astar subsided.

"Let us hear from him," Zana suggested. "I will fashion a drip kit and—"

Astar dived forward and grabbed Willy's bad hand, savagely unwrapping it. She pried back on his little finger until it snapped. He gasped and struggled with his straps, his eyes darting. He found his voice and cried out, but Astar was already pulling his ring finger back, yelling at him, "Stop your crying, and tell us where she is!"

"Astar, darling. This is no way—"

"Za-na! If I want your advice I will ask for it." Astar added another finger to her mighty hold, bending them back mercilessly.

The three girls in wingsuits stepped back. They were not ready for this. Ashley shrugged at them, then loomed over her prey. "Willy, we want Calissa," she said. "If you ever hope to play piano, hell, even scratch your balls, you'd better start talking."

"Yyyyyyyyyyaaaaaaaaaagggh," Willy cried out. "Don't know! Don't have her!"

Zana leaned in, his smiling face joining the triptych. "With Aether and Ashley, we can divine your every secret. Do not make us manipulate you."

"I don't have her. Really!"

Ashley nodded, and Astar snapped Willy's ring finger to the back of his wrist.

Willy screamed and cried. One of the wingsuit girls wretched and turned away.

"That on the roof was in a panic. You can't imagine what I can do when I put my mind to it." Ashley held up her hand with menace.

"Alright!" Willy whimpered. "I'll tell you everything."

Zana nodded. Astar reluctantly released the mangled hand, tossing it back on his chest. "Your truth had best ring true," Zana said.

"The truth shall set you free," Ashley said. She thought it sounded Biblical, and she hoped it would set Willy aright. However, it backfired. He turned his attention from his hand, and the smiling missionary returned to his features.

"We share a truth, Ashley. It is the white hot truth of ven—"

Ashley slapped him.

"Get the juice," she snapped at Zana. "Let's get this over with."

"But Ashley," Willy said, emotionally wounded. "We have to stick together in this. We have our legacies to repair."

"Oh, shut up!" she shouted.

Willy was gagging, his tongue sticking out, his whole face contorting with the heaves. He tried to plead with her but had little control.

Zana nodded, then turned to retrieve some supplies.

Ashley let the Affectation of gagging wane.

"I can continue with his fingers," Astar offered.

"Like Job, I can endure for my cause," Willy said. "Pain will only—"

He stopped when Ashley gestured to Affect him. "Think twice before blathering," she warned. "There's no end to the hurt I can bring."

Willy slumped back on his bench.

Astar cranked the ratchet straps tighter. She was grumbling with each crank.

"The last person we worked on together was incapacitated for weeks," Ashley said. It was a fact, but the cause and effect did not entirely play out as she implied. "I wouldn't want to be you about now."

The ship was moving erratically. The rhythms of its transpiration seemed abbreviated. Its motions were a-stutter. The wing-suited guards were holding onto anything they could find. Astar sat down at Willy's side. Ashley took a knee on his other side.

Ashley put her lips to Willy's ear. "If you don't comply under Aether, I'll dismiss the others. With them gone, I won't have to worry about spill-over, about Affecting *anyone* but you."

His eyes were bulging in her direction.

Zana dropped something in the distance. She knew what he was up to, creating fear by acting clumsy. "How very careless of me," he was muttering, fumbling around to gather his supplies. "The lilting makes me not so steady."

He returned to their station with an armload of materials, including some clear hoses, a large syringe, and gauze tape. Under his arm was a tubular canister. Zana noticed it was the object of Willy's attention. "Oh that. It is the Aether, boy. Straight from the tanks."

"We will drip it, though," Ashley said with mock assurance. "Straight up, it would really fry your brain."

"Temporarily, of course," Zana said. "Only for a few days."

"Listen, listen, really!" Willy pleaded again. "You don't have to. You don't have to do any of this."

"Perhaps now we *want* to," Astar said. "Anyone who would bring harm to our Calissa—"

"That's just it. I didn't. I... I... never touched her," Willy said. "You gotta believe me!"

Zana was screwing a fitting to his canister, pausing to let just a puff of gas out under pressure. "The Romans found alcohol, ethyl alcohol, to be a good sedative and as such, good at relieving inhibitions, Mr. Titus. Our Aether is a kindred substance."

"In vino veritas," Astar said. "In wine there is truth."

"In *whine*, there is truth," Ashley chuckled bitterly.

"I promise you, Ashley. I was bluffing. Just bluffing! I didn't think you'd help me otherwise."

"*You said Boise State.* You admitted as much. You *do* know where she is."

"Yeah, but I didn't touch her. Didn't so much as snap a capture. Honest."

"You would be better off to sully her fleet like the corporations than to threaten her Calissa," Zana said.

"I get it. I get it," Willy said. "Listen, I'm sorry about the whole—it was stupid. I know that now. I just... I can't bring them down alone, and I thought it was the only way you'd help."

"Ask better," Ashley said, pacing.

"I gotta pursue my truth. I'm on a mission from God," Willy said, lifting his head from the bench to fix his attention on her. "If you're merciful, if you forgive me, forget me. I'll go it alone, sure. I'm sorry I said all that. I'm sorry I even bothered you."

He'd endured broken fingers and Affectations, and he was being threatened with much worse. Zana might have seemed a bungling old man, and that could have struck even greater fear into him. *Aether managed by that old geezer?* Astar was intent on snapping more fingers. Ashley occasionally gestured the threat of yet another Affectation. Still, he had not changed his story. He had divulged nothing new. He was true to his mission, whether it was from God or madness.

The ship's typical undulations were more pronounced. Ashley could hardly think. She stumbled to the nearest brass bell, flipping open the voice tube. "What the ever-loving hell?"

"It's the storm, miss," her helmsman returned. "We're still down in its wake, like you asked."

The girls had determined the Lightning's Hand was once an Altostratus, the *Altosaxon*, which had previously sailed in a route over Britain. The crew aboard their ship refused to engage in flashpot comms with them. When the *Altosaxon* went into a dive, they speculated that it might even have been flying unmanned. Ashley hoped so. She hoped none of her former crewmen would do such a thing to her ship then die so disgraced.

On its current course, the ship would crash land east of Laramie, likely in the mountains, and no one remaining aboard or below would survive the impact. She wished that the ship would land gracefully, but whoever had weaponized it had no concern for life or property.

ChompCorp was only interested in profit.

She envisioned a time when she might come calling on their board of directors, first Chomp, then TransCorp... the new Port Authority as they called themselves now. She wondered if the Parkers were still in command.

Her thoughts returned to Rory Reed. When would she head back to sea to continue her mission? What would happen if she ever found him?

"We'll have first light soon, at altitude," the helmsman in the voice tube offered.

"Flash the others," Ashley said, standing. "We'll take formation out West and come in hard at dawn."

"What ever are you thinking?" Astar asked. "You just got here. You're finally safe here."

"I am," Ashley said, "but they're not safe down there."

"That is not your fight," Zana said. He glanced back at Willy. "You have bigger problems."

"Willy here? I believe him. Just for the record, send a ship to Idaho." Ashley wheeled on them and continued, "He might be a bit of a freak, but he has the right idea. We're not drifting off to let them spin this up their way. We're not going to let these guys pound an example out of Laramie."

"We're going to stick it to them," one of the girls said. She was from the area, and she had spoken of her interest in this mission on their way to Wyoming. She screwed up her face then, however, and asked, "Just how 'we going to do that, Miss Winston?"

"With finesse," she said. "Now get your sisters suited up."

Chapter 74 Omelets

Henny wanted nothing more than to call his wife, but the HeadGear was in and out, and the storm was deafening. He sat slumped in a corner of the Lead Room with Lark while Sackerson rigged his Hot Wire and watched the storm. Neither of them was talking.

If a bartender had an addiction, it was surely conversation. He could say it was all for sake of the customer, but deep inside, Henny knew he needed to talk, too. He needed it at times like this when nothing much made sense. It had helped him to talk it out when they'd had a miscarriage, when he'd gone bankrupt, when the bar burnt down, when Peg ended up pregnant, when a patron had offed himself... Over the bar, deep in a bottle, you could talk about anything.

He checked himself. How could he ever talk about this with the bar's dark denizens? In brighter days, "dark denizens" was one of Lefty's turns of phrase. When Lefty *was* talking now, it was pickled babble about Sack, and most of that was drowned out in the thunder. Nobody back at *Sharts* would doubt Lefty Fortune had shorted out.

They'd have a lot harder time, though, with the rest of it. *Sure, Henny, you were right in the thick of it at Laramie,* they'd scoff. *You hid out in a Lead Room through a Lightning's Hand, eh? Hung out with a time traveler. Went through a Hot Wire?*

He smiled again, reflecting on the best part of this big adventure—the women he'd met. Kelli Chase, that tough as nails legend from Franklin. Ashley Winston, wild as they came and even more beautiful in person. And Krystal Price, the hometown hero... he'd hardly had a conversation with her since they were kids, and now she was gone again—this time forever.

"I think I got it, Hinman," Sackerson said, offering to help him to his feet. "Ready to travel?"

"I dunno, Sack. You think it's safe?" Just as he said it, a triple strike of lightning rippled outside.

"Safe?" Sackerson said, pulling Lark up. "If you wanted safe, you would have stayed home."

Henny shrugged. At this point, Sack was starting to make sense. Somewhere in his addled mind, he knew that couldn't be good.

• • • •

The Hot Wire flash was blinding as always. He was the first one through, and he crashed into a table, hit his head on something. Sackerson and Lark were stumbling into him from behind. As his eyes adjusted, Henny realized it wasn't just the portflash. They'd entered somewhere only dimly lit. Emergency lighting far down a hall provided only a glow through some distant double doors.

The usual bleach smell was paired with something he'd had nothing to do with since high school biology. Antiseptic? Formaldehyde? "Where're we at?"

"Don't think too much about it," Sackerson said, edging around him. "This way."

The storm wasn't gone, but it sounded farther away. They hadn't ported far, just like Sack had promised. This trip hadn't even upset his stomach. Henny followed Sack and the shambling silhouette of Lefty Fortune. They headed through the double doors and toward the emergency light.

It was a dark hallway cluttered with covered tables. Gurneys.

The floor was white tile.

The smell was now more recognizably that of a hospital.

The tables were covered with bodies, covered with sheets. Some sheets were soaked in dark stains.

"Sackerson?" Henny wasn't liking this at all.

"Ah, when I put the Wire here, I had no idea they'd be stacking corpses in the basement. C'mon. We're almost back to the land of the living."

"Land of the lost," Lefty said. "We're living in the land of the lost."

"Great show, wrong millennia," Sackerson said, putting an arm around Lefty. "You're not quite yourself, are you, pal?"

They passed under the emergency light and into a stairwell. Somewhere above, another light beckoned. One flight up, Sackerson was struck with an idea, and he pivoted Lefty around, his arm still encompassing him, to face Henny.

"Fellas, I know I've said this more than once, but you should expect a little... resistance ahead. Folks are jittery, and rightly so. We're from out of town, you know, and that makes locals trigger happy. Just let me lead, okay?"

Lefty, his dance partner, snorted and shook off Sack's embrace. "Lotta good that's done anyone."

"Oh, perking up to join the party? And just in time, too! Well... come on then."

"Sack, maybe..." Henny couldn't believe he was saying this. "Maybe I ought to lead."

"You?" Sack grinned at the thought of it.

"Yeah," he said, swallowing. "I'm... you know... affable."

Sackerson cackled. Lefty rolled his eyes and leaned against the stairwell waiting for Sack to compose himself.

"You're a little... shocking," Henny continued. Sackerson looked like a horror movie homeless guy who'd been out in a lightning storm too long.

"By all means," Sack swept him along. "Lead on, Kenny Hinman."

Henny pulled his pistol from his greatcoat. He didn't even know if it was loaded. He couldn't remember if he'd put in the shells. The weight of it was comforting, but he stuffed it back in his pocket. He still clutched the grip of it as he pushed open the door on the main floor landing.

Chapter 75 Cordite

S tu spun and fired before he'd even seen them clearly. It was enough to know they weren't hospital, weren't Pharma, weren't The Boys. Catching sight of the wizard Sackerson gave him an instant of satisfaction. He'd nipped the Spooks. Cut them off at the pass. He was going to press them back into the stairwell with a barrage of fire—

Kenny Hinman fell back into the other two, Sackerson and... Lark Fortune?
Stu let his gun hand down.

"What'd you do that for?" Sackerson spat at him.

Several others were in the space now. Everyone seemed so alarmed. Guns and curses were bristling.

"Cordite," Henny groaned.

"What?" Lark said, crouching down to be with him.

"Kelli Chase smells like patchouli and gunpowder," he said. "I know that's not right. I know it's cordite, but that don't have the same ring to it."

"Sackerson?" Lark cried out. "*Do something.*"

"That wasn't supposed to happen," Sackerson sighed. "Not in any timeline."

Chapter 76 Gut Shot

H enny woke on a hospital bed, relieved to find it was not in the basement. This room was lit by flashes from outside, by a couple of HeadGear displays glowing across the room, and by the flashlight a doctor was shining in his eyes.

"He's good," the doctor said. "Coming around."

He was coming around. He was squinting past the flashlight at others in the room. Alex Gault was leaning in, a look of dire concern on his face. Several of Stu's ranch hands were crowded in the room, looking wary. Closer up, Lefty and Sack stood at the foot of his bed. They, at least, seemed happy to see him.

Henny didn't have his coat on. He was wearing a hospital gown, and through it, he felt bandages. He touched at it gingerly, then looked up at the doctor. "Gut shot?"

"Not as bad as that," the doctor smiled, pocketing his pen light. "A lucky through and through. Didn't hit a bowel or bone."

"I've been gut shot," Henny smiled, then winced at the pain as he sat up.

"Oh, you'll have some stories to tell now, won't you, Henny?" Sackerson smiled, squeezing Henny's foot through the blankets.

"Imagine the class reunion. I was gut shot by Stu Wiebe!"

"That would be something," Lefty muttered.

"We'd be grateful if you left Stu out of the story," one of the ranchers said.

"Stu's not... he's not been hisself." This cowboy took off his hat and bowed his head with his plea. "Can you see it in you to forget about this?"

"He's just got a lot on his mind."

"Accident, ya see?"

Henny pressed back into his pillow, shaking his head, trying to sort it all out. This story would be legendary back in Guthrie. How could he *not* tell it?

One turn of his head went wide to the other bed in the room. He was shocked to see Captain Chase down. Alex Gault was cuddled up with her.

"What happened to you?" Henny asked.

When she didn't reply, he asked Gault, "What happened to her?"

The doctor rattled off something about a vehicle accident, about an artery lacerated. "It's all too close to her carotid for my liking. Damn lucky her ligaments aren't cut. Missed her larynx, too."

"She's lost blood," Alex said, glum. "It's touch and go."

"Damn!" Henny said, shaking his head.

"While you were out, Henny, I had my say with Mr. Gault here," Sackerson said. "We're good now, right?"

"Golden," Gault said.

Sackerson brushed his hands together. "Okay then. That's that. Put your clothes on, Henny. We're off."

"Off... where?" He asked. One nurse was helping him to his feet, steering him toward the bathroom. Another was gathering up his things.

"Lark?" Sackerson cued him up. "Tell the man."

"To the land of pure imagination," Lefty said, loopy as hell.

Sackerson leaned in on Alex and Kelli. As if finishing a previous conversation, he said, "You'll know when it's time."

The old man reached into the folds of his robe and produced a baby rattle, which he shook, marveling at the sound. "For the kid inside," Sackerson said, folding Gault's hand around it.

Henny shook his head in confusion, then let the nurse lead him away. In the adjoining bathroom, he struggled out of his gown and into his street clothes. He couldn't fasten his pants. The bandages were thick at his waist. He huffed around with it entirely too long, worrying what he was missing. He only caught remnants of their back-and-forth.

"I'm not up to this," Gault said. "Do it yourself."

"It would kill me," Sackerson said, "but if you fail, then I'll die trying."

Henny came back out of the bathroom, gently buckling his belt over the gauze padding. The nurse had to help him with his shoes. His stomach wound wouldn't let him bend over. "Sack," he panted, "I don't think I can."

"What? Sure you can."

"It's gonna hurt. I can feel it coming."

"The shock has worn off," the nurse announced, "but the meds could relieve him of some pain if he would just get back into—"

"We are on a mission," Sackerson said curtly.

"Yeah, but don't you think I could sit this one out?"

"What? That's ridiculous! I need you now more than ever."

"Take me," some scrawny local kid interjected.

Sack gave him the once over. "You look just like your dad, little Wiebe."

Henny glanced at him. *Stu had a kid?*

"I have a crew, or I'd take you up on that." Sack patted Lefty's shoulder, helped Henny to his feet. He had an arm draped around each of them. "*Time's out of mind.* Show us to the door, would you?"

"I'm going with you," the kid said.

"Like hell," Stu Wiebe grumbled, his mass blocking the doorway. "These three aren't worth the shit off my boots."

The ranch hands drew to attention. One stepped in the gap between Stu and the others. "Now boss—"

"Schmitty!"

"Excuse me?" Sackerson said. "How rude!"

"You are a lunatic," Stu said.

"And you!" He pointed at Lefty next. "You're a loser, always have been."

"Now, that's not—" Henny began.

"You!" Stu whipped out his pistol, and his men pulled up weapons, too. "You're the reason all this is happening again."

"I'm the what?"

"Throwing in with the likes of him. Sackerson. You're in with the Spooks."

"What are you doing, Stu? We're the good guys," Sack said. "Well, you all are the good guys, fighting the corporate empire and all, but we're—"

"I thought I was through with you thirty years ago!" Stu said, cocking his pistol.

"Now c'mon, Stu," one of his men said.

Stu wheeled on his man and ripped out a rant. "These are the guys! Torched Horse Thief Canyon. Cost us everything!"

"You know better," Henny said. "Think on it."

"You betrayed me, Kenny!" Stu held up his pistol in his palm. He was reared back to crack Kenny Hinman in the skull.

Henny didn't budge. He folded his arms over his belly.

"He did no such thing," Lark said. "He was working the other side."

"Counter agent-like," Sackerson nodded.

Stu was quivering with rage. He glanced from man to man. Fierce. Threatening.

"Dad?"

• • • •

Henny wasn't sure if it was the meds or his imagination. He couldn't quite trust what he was seeing. Down the hall, on the other side of the double doors, Stu Wiebe was in a loud conversation with Nat Wiebe. Schmitty went with them to arbitrate, but he had been sent back in the first exchange between the two.

The doors had windows, but even if Henny had pressed his nose to one, it wasn't easy to see what was going on beyond. Sometimes Stu would pace through a shaft of light from the emergency lamp. Other times his voice would carry. In one exchange, Nat had fired back at a similar volume.

Schmitty stood closest to those doors and served now as the color commentator for the others gathered in the hallway. "They're arguing about how the other embarrasses them. Both of 'em tossing it out there."

Nat had just said something conversational but muted. The tone alone made Henny's shoulders tense up.

"...don't get it." Stu was countering. "Best friend... how will I ever know what side he's on?"

There were more muted arguments. Schmitty's head turned left and right, following along. "Nat's on him about trust. Stu's not having it."

The two were having a shouting match of profanities. This much of their argument was clear enough through the doors.

"I wouldn't wanna be him 'bout now," one of Stu's men said.

Schmitty opened the door to poke his head into their space. Whatever he told them earned him another tirade of profanities. He shut the door and put his back to it.

"Fired again?" one of The Boys asked.

"Yeah," Schmitty said. "But at least I said my piece. Ain't right talking to Nat like that."

"He'll be over it by morning," another said.

"I know," Schmitty replied. "Tomorrow's a brand new day."

He sighed and threaded through the group in the hallway. "I'm gonna find a cot 'round here and catch my 40 winks."

Henny assumed the position at the doors. The conversation inside had settled out to dull murmurings. Stu was no longer pacing, but he leaned against a vending machine in the half-light of the hall. He looked so old, so tired. Henny let out a sigh. They'd all become old men since their last tussle. He glanced at Lark. The years, this loss of his Krystal Price—it was weighing on him heavily.

Sackerson caught his attention and gave him a questioning thumbs up.

Henny nodded but then turned his attention back through the window. Stu and Nat were hugging. It was a private moment. Henny tried to dart from the window before Stu saw him.

"Hinman!" he heard from beyond. "C'mere."

Henny looked over the shadowed people in the room. No one was going to save him. Hell, the way he read the room, nobody trusted him.

He swung the door open, but before he could even step through the threshold, Stu spoke up. "I'm sorry I shot you."

"Yeah... well..."

"And I'm sorry I didn't trust you." He cleared his throat, glanced at Nat, and continued, "There's no way you threw in with the Spooks."

"That's right," Henny said. *Affirm and restate,* the bartender's code. "No way in hell."

"I'm a little edgy's all. This is a lot to take on, y'know?"

"And it's a lot like before," Henny added.

"And it's just getting worse."

· · · ·

"To the basement," Sack commanded, and Nat led the charge. Henny noticed Stu and his Boys close on their heels. A nurse up ahead opened double doors that led out into a wide hall bordered with the wounded awaiting treatment. They passed by in a ripple of gray HeadGear illumination.

Back in the morgue downstairs, Sackerson approached his glowing portal with uncharacteristic concern. He studied it a bit, then turned on the gathering crowd behind him. "Was there something, um... odd... here recently?"

"The announcement," one man said.

Then all of them were babbling about a warning and demand for a time traveler. Henny knew the warning. He knew they were after Sack. Again.

"Ah," Sackerson said. "Sounds like we've brought enough attention your way. I *can* fix this, at least, in a jiffy."

"Fix... what?" Stu asked.

"I've heard them call me the Wizard lately, Stuart, and that is not an insult, not at all. Now *Mr. Wizard*, that's a little derogatory, like I'm pedaling some 1950's schlock—which I am *not*, I tell you. Your science is as antiquated as—"

"Sack," Henny said, tugging his sleeve.

Sackerson continued. "A true wizard commands real magic, if you believe such things. Alchemy. Sorcery. Alacazam!"

"Sack. We're in a hurry."

"Right, right," Sack said with exasperation, yet despite Henny's pleading, he continued, "So whether I'm a wizard of the pinball variety, or whether I'm wielding magic that's no more than a slight of hand, the point is, *a good wizard gets it done*, pulls it off... pulls a fast one, as my mom used to say."

"What the hell are you saying?" Stu asked.

"We're going, and we're going to screw things up royally to make them right a while. All the while, erh... *in* a while, anyway, you'll think differently—especially you, Stu—but *you will get it.*

You'll all catch on eventually, and by then, even the future will have played out its merry tune."

"Henny?" Stu asked. "You're on team Sackerson....what's he—"

"I dunno, man. I guess he's saying to wait for it."

"Lark?" Stu prompted again.

"Omelets," Lark said, tossing it off with a gesture.

"Exactly that," Sackerson was beaming. "Let's go break some eggs, guys."

"Back through that?" Henny asked anxiously.

"Yes, yes... but the rest of you, stick around. It's about to get interesting here."

At that, Sack pulled Lefty through the portal. Henny looked back at the cluster of cowboys and nurses, locals and rebels, who had crowded into the dark of the morgue.

"I'd like to think he knows what he's doing," Henny said with a shrug, then followed Sackerson into the blinding bright port flash with blind faith.

Chapter 77 Attenuation

"**A**h, there you are again. Welcome to the party, Lark!"

All Lark could see was blinding white. He sensed he was in a room, in some kind of enclosed space, but his eyes didn't register up from down. He couldn't see walls, nor floor, nor ceiling. Just white. Where was the storm? The fighting?

He was standing in a white void.

"Lark, over here."

He turned around and there they were: Henny, Sackerson—and some kid... *Stu's kid?*

"Hey," the kid said. "I'm Nat Wiebe."

Lark's eyes ached from all the white.

There was something else, too, or rather a strange lack of something. It felt as if gravity were nothing but the force of an invisible fan, a crude fake gravity that wasn't quite right.

"Quite the contrast? Maybe a little much, eh?" Sackerson said, approaching him.

"It's like a Clean Room?"

"Good. Good start. I call it The Attenuation." Sack spread his arms wide and smiled at the pronouncement. "I know, a little dramatic maybe."

"He says it's the absence of everything," Henny offered. Lark could hear Henny's doubt in every word he spoke. He looked past Sackerson at Henny. Damn, but the guy looked out of place with no context.

He guessed they all did.

"I think he said it was the management of inputs or something like that."

"Good little Wiebe," Sack said. "So, we're all right. In The Attenuation, I've crafted a space where I've used a big equalizer to control inputs like light, sound, sensation—really everything

548

but gravity... and I'm working on that. I started working on this chamber when porting got to be too much. I'm sharing this space now, and the coordinates to it, so you kids can have a spa day, if you need it."

He handed each of them a large coin.

"Spa day?" Henny asked. "Why would we need—"

"Trust me, if you port much, you're going to need it," Sack said. "It's like sunglasses or noise suppressing headphones or... an isolation chamber."

"Is that why Ashley Winston's into isolation chambers?" Nat asked.

"Hmmm. No. I don't think so, but... no. Anyway, the differences are that this is a balanced environment, not one to deprive but to sequester. You won't know the difference or at least not the effect of it, between attenuation and isolation, and we don't have time, I suppose, to really dig into Beer-Lambert—though, *can you imagine*? Dudes over a hundred years ago thinking about this stuff?"

"Sackerson!" Henny snapped. "Why are we here? I get this is a rest stop, but, c'mon. Why bother? It's not like we're going to be porting around a lot. Why would we?"

"Why *wouldn't* you, Henny?"

"Dad said it'd kill you. I think it ruined him," Lark said. Something about this space had alerted him, heightened his senses by denying them so much. His mind returned to the vids of Krystal again, and he opened his eyes wider in this white space, trying not to see her in Jackson Pollock blood spatter.

"Lark's onto something, and by the look of him, he's enduring something, too. I find when I get time in here, my mind opens. Feels like when your sinuses open up, doesn't it, Lark, or your bowels, you know, after you've been plugged up? Well, anyway, he's going to experience it more than you two, for obvious reasons."

"Obvious reasons?" Henny asked.

"You're saying it's good to come here," Nat asked, "'for a sense of balance?"

Sackerson jumped on the more interesting question. "Yeah. If people were going to port as a daily practice, they'd need spaces like this, don't you think? People of means would have ones like mine, one that's specifically dialed into me."

"You *made* this place?" Nat asked.

"Stay tuned, friend. I've been busy for the last generation," Sackerson cackled, but his laugh lacked its usual ring. Lark was coming to notice everything sounded as if it were coming in from far away.

Lark heard something from Henny. A groan? Was it his injury?

"We're going to be in so much trouble," Henny groaned. Pointing at Nat, he continued, "Why are you here, again?"

Nat smiled broadly. "Beats Laramie," he said. "Besides, I wanted to go where the action is."

"Technically," Sackerson said, unable to resist, "The Attenuation is a lack—"

"Sack!" Henny interrupted. "Let's just get on with—with *whatever*, and get Nat back home before I get blamed for kidnapping."

"Right. Right. Okay, well, after today, things will be set into motion." Sack stood a little taller, as if realizing something, and he continued in a more profound tone of voice. "Today will live in infamy... or *famy*... I suppose it depends on your point of view."

Lark forced himself to push Krystal to the back of his mind. He forced himself to listen to Sackerson, though he expected the usual binge of bullshit.

"We are about to be disruptors, so to speak. Really, we're just going to turn it on, the big disruption, but it takes a village, so..."

"Disruption?" Nat picked up on it. The kid was sharp.

When Sackerson started using words like that, it was seldom a good thing.

"I think calling it The Disruption sounds too negative." He gave Nat a nod, then continued, "For the launch, for now, it will be easier with your help. Besides, you get to be part of history. Of course, no one will know you had a hand in it, and Henny, sorry pal, this is something nobody's ever going to believe back at the bar—"

"Sack, you're spinning off again. Just lay it out, man. I want to get back home."

"*All this time*, Henny, all this and adventure, too, and you wanna go home?" Sackerson was astonished. "Really? Why can't you be more like Nat?"

Henny glowered at him.

Nat was glowing.

Lark was shaking his head.

"Anyhow," Sack turned to Lark and Nat, "instead of seeing it as sabotage, I think of it as a gift. It's my *greatest* gift to mankind, as they say. So, Disruption is out. For this season, let's call it *Christmas Day*!"

"Christmas Day?" Lark asked. It felt funny in his mouth, like times he had known a name for something new or could pronounce something foreign with surprising ease.

"Like it?" Sackerson beamed. "You know, after the wrapping paper?"

"Wrapping...?"

"Sack. What's this all about? Disruption. Christmas Day. Whatever. Why do you need us? What's the plan?"

"Gentlemen, what's brought down every cocksure kingdom and charismatic leader?"

"Oh, here we go!" Henny groaned.

Lark wanted to play out the riddle. He was feeling good in this room, like his head was clearing, just like Sack had said.

"Sin," Nat offered.

Sackerson looked him over with a little pout. "Did Stu teach you that? Is that really your answer?"

"Pride," Lark said. It was one of the big seven, he reasoned.

"You guys are so judgmental," Sack said with some surprise. "You sound like that Titus kid!"

Henny shrugged. "Who cares?"

"Apathy," Sack nodded, interpreting Henny's question as a contribution. "A more honest contender, but no... What rains on every parade is simply this—an undermining of faith. When the people lose their faith, they lose their way. Without vision, the people perish. That's in about every religion you can wave a censer at—"

"Sackerson!" Lark found himself joining Henny in the reprimand.

"Right. Right... so my gift is exactly that—doubt. We're going to undermine what otherwise will dominate the future. I hope it's gonna be enough. Christmas Day comes but once a year. There's no way to really know if I got the balance right on the future."

"If you disrupt the future, what's that do to you and your timeline and all the things you know about the future?"

"Ah, now that's the *true* you, isn't it? I wish we had more time together, wee Wiebe." Sack said, then continued. "Undermining the Port Authority through establishing doubt. Lifting the rug just enough to give folks a peek and trip them up. We're disrupting teleportation so that people might never really buy in from now on. That's what we're up to fellas. I have to say, that's the first time I've said it all aloud. Sounds pretty cool, doesn't it?"

"Undermine the Port Authority?"

"That's right, Larkin. And here's how: I've created a bit of a blip, a rent in the curtain, a chink in the ol' armor... once a year, every year, there'll be a disruption. Christmas day!"

"On Christmas day?" Nat asked.

"That would be sweet, wouldn't it... but no, we can't wait. We have to drop it in today, like now. On this Day of Disruption, see, nobody can count on portals working right."

He waited for a response, and when it was lagging, he continued, "Don't you see? Well, can't you *imagine* it, anyway? Do some *extrapolation, boys*. Ports now are just coming into vogue, but if they replace all kinds of transportation, pretty much every kinda get-along you can take... and then you find you can't really trust them once a year, then... see? Undermined!"

"Why won't everybody just not go porting on this Christmas Day thing?" Henny shrugged.

"See, again Hinman, you have spent your whole life being undervalued. That, sir, is the crux, isn't it? It took me another ten years to solve for X. That is to say, you're right, and I knew it. I had to *randomize* when Christmas Day will come."

"So it *could* land on Christmas?"

"Yes, yes, it could, I guess. That would be an irony." Sackerson smiled at Nat, but did not miss a beat. "So you see? You'll never know. Patrons of ports will be risk takers, every single time. About when they get numb to the threat—bam! Christmas Day."

"If you could scramble the way ports work once a year, why not just scramble them all the way?" Lark asked. "I think I'd just be done with the damn things."

"What do you take me for? That would be catastrophic failure, a collapse of the system. I don't want *that*, and neither would you. We just want to inject some doubt. A little mayhem. Undermine consumer confidence enough that people won't make a religion out of teleportation."

"But why? If it's so bad, why not get rid of it, altogether?" Henny asked.

"Because it's really not so bad. You'll see."

"I saw," Henny said. "I saw all them troops pile into town."

"The same tech could be used for emergency response teams, the redistribution of refugees or food, or... well, see for yourself! Let's spark this up and go play."

Chapter 78 Safe Travels

The world could have stopped turning. It could all go up in smoke. None of it was important so long as Calissa continued to correspond with him.

Rory swapped impatient exchanges with her over their Clenches long into the night. His jaw ached, but he was so overjoyed it did not matter. He had long forgotten Katrina's ruse. Now that he was reunited with his daughter, Rory harbored no ill will toward anyone. Nothing could distract him from the clicking in his jaw, the words of his beloved Calissa.

"I can't wait to see you again," she said.

"We leave at dawn, whether by boat or by plane," Rory told her. "Heading to the states."

"Meet in New York."

"Too dangerous," he warned. "Meet me in Wyoming."

"Laramie, Wyoming, I am sure."

"Yes. Ashley is there."

"Interface. Reports are not good. Laramie is a battlefield."

Rory did not have a comment coming to him. It was dangerous there. He would be putting Calissa in danger to meet her there. Still. He knew Ashley was there, fighting for her airships and her corporation. Ashley Winston never shied away from the tempest.

"You could ask her to meet you anywhere. She will come. I will join her."

They continued messaging, catching up on years of lost time. Rory's heart swelled. He could not stop smiling. He flopped back in a hammock and watched the morning tide. He was filled with joy. Soon he would be reunited with his daughter, Calissa, and with Ashley, too. He relaxed into it, as if he were again floating on his back in the ocean, and for a blissful little while, he slept.

. . . .

"Rory! Come quick!" Katrina shouted from the warehouse door. "In here!"

He struggled up from the hammock and rushed after her. When he breached the threshold, he stopped dead in his tracks. The entire warehouse interior was aglow with blue flaring lights. The portals were coming online.

Rory joined Katrina at the nearest portal. "What does it mean?"

"I do not know," she said. "They have all come on."

Sometimes, like at that moment, the obvious seemed profound. Rory nodded his head, dumbfounded. After all their effort and frustration, all the desperation and struggle, the ports were working. Not just any one portal   *every* portal. Even the wires he had pulled from their frames glowed where they were suspended.

It was a bright and glorious sight.

"You know what this means?"

"You will be leaving us," Katrina said.

"We can all leave this—"

He stopped when he noted someone darted out of a portal across the room. He cocked his head and tried to get a better look.

"Who are they?" one of the Family asked, joining them at the door.

Several more people were flashing into the warehouse space. Others entered by one port, then flashed away through another. One ported into the room through a port very near them. It was an older man who seemed equally surprised to see them. He asked something in a language even Katrina did not know.

She tried speaking with him in several other tongues. Finally, they struck up a conversation, halting and fractured, depending as much on gestures as words.

"He is from the far north," she said. She gestured in an arching curve. He nodded.

"How did he, you know, come through the portal?"

Before she could get the answer clearly from him, others were moving into their space, passing between them, rushing past them for the outside door. One woman in a housecoat stopped and smiled at Rory. In a British accent, she asked him for the time of day.

"It's... well... it's early." He didn't know quite what to say.

"How did you get here?" Katrina asked, abruptly.

"Through the port, 'course. E'ryone's using 'em... and for free!"

A well-dressed man, overhearing, joined in, "I was on my way in to work, from my home port, but the damn things are tossing us off. I was just in the Alps, now I'm... wherever this is!"

Rory was amazed at the range of people and their reactions. Some, like the executive, were irritated. Others were fascinated with porting. Most were even *more* fascinated to find themselves on a beautiful island when they stepped outside.

Rory and Katrina walked among them, seeing the island again through the eyes of the new arrivals. They asked questions of every traveler who would talk with them, but the sum total of their findings left them little to work with.

"Porting is everywhere."

"Deregulated. Random."

"It's as if they had them warehoused for just such an instance," Katrina offered.

"I don't think so," Rory said, looking back at the flood of people pushing their way outside. "It's too messy."

Hundreds of people were milling around between the outbuildings now. They were shouting out their place names, calling out names of loved ones, waving for people they thought they recognized. Some were distraught, and they just held themselves and drifted to lean against trees and buildings.

"I'm going to take one," Rory said. "I'm going to port back home."

"They say it is unpredictable."

"I know. They're saying it's a nightmare. One minute you're home, then you port into who knows where. How do you prepare for that?"

"You don't. You do not go," Katrina said. "We can find another way."

"We don't know that," Rory said. "This, crazy as it is, works."

"It works? How does it work? You don't know what will happen if you step through one of these. What if you step through to your death, Rory Reed?"

"What if I step into Laramie, straight away?"

"That may be the same thing."

Rory nodded.

They were standing well-away from the crowd and out of the general directions of their migration toward the beach or road. He looked at Katrina, but she looked away, as if she were studying someone in the distance.

He took advantage of this lull in their conversation to continue his conversation with Calissa on the Clench. She reported it was happening there, too, masses of people at every TransCorp portal. There was no explanation for it on the Interface, very little coverage of it.

"It's out of control," Rory stated, first via Clench, then aloud. "They're not talking about it because they can't explain it."

"*Who* can't explain it?" Katrina asked.

"The Port Authority's lost their authority," he said.

Calissa told him she was going dark, but she arranged a time to resume their Clench conversation. It was wise he knew. He respected her caution. Rory wondered if he had taught her to be so very careful. Two hours. He set his diver's watch.

The little group of Family had joined them on a rocky rise away from the crowd. Katrina was engaging them variously in multi-lingual babble. He caught passages now and then between her and the one who favored English, the youngest of the Family here, a woman who called herself Serenity.

"We are better equipped for that," she said.

Katrina was shaking her head at the comments from all the Family at once.

Rory was watching the transaction from the corner of his eye. If they did not want to include him in their conversation, he wanted to know why. He feigned distraction, rummaging in his bag for binoculars he then used to watch the crowd.

"I do not know that his mind is so much better," another of the Family muttered.

"The dude's, what, a week old," Serenity said. "You've done good work, but—really?"

"Together we can continue our good work, but should we let this teleportation separate us from him?"

Katrina began in a foreign tongue, then switched to address the latest comment in English. "Even with all of us giving our best, he will not be ready, but..." He assumed she was looking his way, likely assessing him to confirm. "He will not be dissuaded."

"He could be," one of the men said very quietly.

Just try it. Rory felt his shoulders flex. His neck was tight. He popped his neck, then resumed scanning the crowd with the binoculars.

People were most recently arriving better prepared for travel. Some of the first were caught off guard, carrying a half-eaten sandwich or wearing only their under garments. Those had been the curious who simply stepped through a portal like it were any other doorway. He assumed them to be people of means—who else would have a portal in their private quarters. Others were using ports like the executive, and these had the look of commuter class workers about them.

The latest arrivals, however, were often wearing backpacks or sporting weapons. They had donned their HeadGear and were confident it would immediately inform them of this new location they had come into. To their frustration, it was obvious, the HeadGear was not so reliable here in the islands in the middle of this strange mix. These HeadGear-dependent arrivals were growing to be the most anxious.He followed some with his field glasses. They would arrive jacked into their devices, then find their 'Gear defunct, then return to port away.

Katrina had returned to stand beside him. He knew this even without putting down the binocs. The days they had spent so closely together had affected him, roused something in him. She was in his head and on his mind more than anyone he could recall.

She was Affecting him, and he knew it. Whether intentional or, as she claimed, as a byproduct of who she was—she Affected him constantly. It was stirring.

"You could be incapacitated," Katrina said, offering it as a statement more than a threat.

"I suppose I *could*," Rory said, finally turning to them. "I wouldn't go easy."

Katrina gave that a nod, glanced over her shoulder with an "I told you so" look on her face. The Family members seemed less than convinced.

"You do not see it as a danger? You do not realize you could... revert?"

Rory smirked. "I know you guys are holding me together, somehow. I can feel it, and I'm grateful. It's just that this is an *opportunity*, all these portals, and I—"

"What's the rush?" Serenity asked.

Another Family member responded in his own language.

"Kofi is right," Katrina said. She then looked Rory in the eyes, "Love is his rush."

"I just have to get back."

"To Ashley Winston?" one of the Family said.

"To her, and his daughter," Katrina ran a finger along his jawbone. He thought he felt the Clench tingle. "To all of them, I am sure."

"Kat's told us what you were doing here," Serenity said, stepping in. "What if you go through a port or two and just lose it? If we're not there to, you know, do some anger management..."

One of the men offered, "We go, too."

The other Family members protested. He could hear it in the tone, regardless of the language.

"She says it is too dangerous," Katrina interpreted. "We might become separated by the portals."

Another flurry of multilingual argument erupted, then Katrina pulled the focus back to Rory. "The general consensus comes to this, Rory. What difference might a day make? This... phenomena... who knows what is the cause of it or how it will go? Couldn't you give us just another day to soothe your—"

"That's just it," he said. "We don't know. We don't know how long it lasts or who's behind it or—I won't miss my chance."

"What if you port right into TransCorp headquarters or some fancy soiree and pop a cap? What if you go berserkers again?" Serenity was taking a direct approach. She reminded him some of Calissa, a little of Ashley.

"What if you again decide the Rich should die? Are you ready to live with that?"

"I'll leave my weapons."

Katrina smirked.

She was right. He didn't need swords to cause damage. Everything was a weapon.

"Okay, let's try it like he said," Rory pointed at the Family member. "*Let's all go*. Cradle me with love or whatever. Keep me calm."

He thought of the Don't Mess with My Head club... and the irony of this, where he was asking for their support and interference.

"The harm to you could be worse. The shock of such porting might be too jarring. We might be separated from you. Leave you to compensate on your own. Or, we might try too hard to help you. Think of it. What if we were to port right into a battle, then in our efforts to help you, we might ruin you."

"I'm already ruined, Katrina," Rory said. He zipped his bag and slung it over his shoulder. "Let's go find that port dialed in for Yuma again."

"That won't even be close to—"

"It's *closer*," Rory said. "C'mon. We're wasting time."

Chapter 79 Memento Mori

S tu doubled the guard on Alex Gault's door. He doubled the guard on the entire wing. Everyone was on edge, unsure how an announcement like that could even be transmitted. Every device, everywhere.

He would have asked Nat about it, but the kid had dived through Sackerson's portal. It took all Stu had not to give chase. Gone, just like that.

"Don't feel obligated to hang around for our sake," Gault said. "If I were you, I'd snuggle up with my wife while there's still time."

"Nat..." Stu said, but didn't know where to go with it.

"Probably not a safer place to be than with Sackerson," Gault said. "You can count on that."

"It's safer with me," Stu grumbled. "Right here."

Kelli stirred. "For some of us, it's not safe anywhere."

"That's right, kitten. Not anywhere. Not any time." Gault sounded more defeated than Stu knew him to be. He had reason. He was being hunted. His wife was mortally wounded.

Earlier, he'd said he blamed himself for the whole of the Corp War and for the death of his best friend. Stu hadn't tracked that last bit, but Gault had moved on to other topics while Kelli was under the knife, and now that he was reunited with her, Alex was preoccupied.

Snuggle up with the wife! Stu scoffed at that. Then again—he watched the Gaults talking and cuddling—he missed her. She was still mad about Krystal Price, even if she'd buried it. She would be hopping mad about Nat porting around, too. That was part of her nature, and as he sat watching the Gaults, he realized again it was a part of her he couldn't bear to be without.

He flagged one of The Boys to go out to the ranch and bring her in.

He sent another on an errand to get Rachel's favorite cinnamon rolls.

"Where's your time cops?" Stu finally asked.

"Ah, maybe they're bluffing," Gault said, a faint glimmer of his cavalier nature.

"Maybe they're lost," Kelli said with a half-smile.

It had been an hour and change, and still no sign of the Spooks. In his encounters with them, they always seemed a step ahead. *Not so much this time.*

"I think they're fishing," Stu offered. "I don't think they have any idea where you are."

"Why is that?"

"The Boys say that announcement went out on everything, everywhere. Not just in the hospital or this room."

"Maybe it was for effect," Alex offered. "Freak everyone out."

"Maybe."

It hadn't lasted. Stu's reports told him it hadn't even caused a momentary ceasefire. The Port Authority troops were relentless, and the later into their drive, the more vicious they were becoming. It was as if they had left their most efficient warriors until last. Stu wondered if they were coming up on the last of all this.

He pulled his Walkie and excused himself to the hallway. He nodded at the guards, paced the hall as he tried to scare up Nat. Where the hell had Henny taken his kid?

Stu spoke with Patrick and Fry and checked in with others. Fry was at the hotel, where it never seemed to calm down. Patrick was at the ranch, reporting that Rachel was on her way with escorts.

He sighed. At least that was going right, maybe.

Another report was setting his teeth on edge. They'd gotten a transmission through all the Interface noise, one that seemed legitimate. They said it was from the airships, circling high above. Help, they claimed, was on the way.

What could they do? Swoop down and burn the ashes of the town?

The Boys on door duty had spent a lot of time standing around out there, and they had a lot to say. Things had gone to shit all over, they claimed. Wouldn't recognize much out there after the Lightning's Hand and the battle. There were so many Grays in town after the storm it wasn't even funny. He swapped strategy with the men, drawing strength from their undying support.

Stu called up another checkpoint. Rachel was almost there.

He knocked, then entered Gault's room, only to find the bed empty. "Guys!" he yelled over his shoulder, and the guards were at his heels.

Stu had his pistol out and scanned the room with it. One of The Boys shined his flashlight into the darker corners.

Movement. The bathroom door was shut, but there was light and movement inside. Stu leaned against the door frame and tapped the door with his gun. "Gault?"

"Yeah," Alex's voice. "We're suiting up."

Stu sighed. He nodded his men back to their post.

Suiting up? How had Kelli even gotten out of bed?

The IV hose was knotted off, draped over the corner of the bed. A trail of gauze and tape led toward the bathroom. Damn, but she was a tough one.

Stu took his post back at his chair, sitting as nonchalantly as he could. He adjusted his position, took out an Interface appliance, and acted interested in that when they opened the bathroom door.

Kelli Chase Gault was backlit by the emergency light in the bathroom. She stood like a gunfighter. Her leathers were zipped and tight. Her plasma pistol hung low and ready at her hip. She was steeled up for battle.

Then she moved.

She sidestepped to let her husband past her, and in that, she teetered. Gault caught her and escorted her back to the bed. He glanced at Stu, then continued doing his best to make her comfortable. "She said she was going down fighting."

"I am," she groaned. "But they better hurry up."

"Poppycock," Gault said. "We have all day. Probably ought to check out room service, don't you think, Wiebe?"

Stu was a little slow on the hint, but he got up and mumbled something about getting them some coffee at any rate.

"Black for me," Gault said, "But Kelli likes the sugar... and two creamers."

It was ludicrous, and everyone knew it. There wasn't any food to serve, and the coffee only came black and cold.

Stu let the door close behind him.

"Sir?" one of the guards asked.

"Get them some coffee. Find them some food. Anything," Stu commanded. He trod off down the hall, marveling at the Gaults. She was gritty, even when she could hardly stand. He was always quippy, but Stu was starting to get it. That cocksure comedy was how Alex Gault was getting through all this.

All Stu had was anger.

• • • •

Stu sat on a kitchen chair in the alley. Cigarette butts were crushed on the ground around him. An ashtray full of sand was toppled beside him. Hospital folk loved their smokes. This rickety little weigh station was how they handled it, all the life and death at their fingertips. They teased death one puff at a time. Every smoke break was a memento mori.

Yeah, everybody's going to bite it, he thought. Sooner or later.

Hell, he'd nearly killed Henny!

Nat had taught him the whole concept of memento mori, the philosophy of mortality, the thought that being conscious of one's imminent death might lead to better living.

Stu chuckled at himself. *Getting all sentimental and reflective when his town was ash and battle.* Spooks from the future were on the way to do more damage. Meanwhile, his Boys and the Rebels were fodder for the Port Authority. Those gray invaders fought dirty, ducking in and out of ports, pouring in from God knew where with reinforcements.

He wasn't going to win this one.

His "leadership" had done nothing but feed more meat to the grinder. Everything had careened out of control. Even his own son—child—had been sucked in and away by it all. Even Nat was lost to him. Out porting around with those clowns!

God forgive me—

His Walkie told him Rae was in the building.

Stu wiped his eyes and blew his nose. He stood tall and faced the doors she'd come barreling through to berate him. He deserved it.

He got another report while he was waiting. In these days of crazy, this one beat all. "I'm tellin' you like it is, boss. *Just random people*. Not just the Grays. Only these ain't fighting. They're taking cover."

"And the Grays?"

"They're all in a panic. They've been hot shots, porting out and back just two ports down, just popping up like magic, right? Not now. Now they just port out and that's it. They lost their supply chain, too. It's like their whole strategy's trashed."

"These people coming in, are they okay?"

"We're trying, Stu." It was another voice, Schmitty. "Damn Grays use them like bait. Use them like human shields. Hell, sometimes they're just gunning them down as they come in."

Rachel was coming through the door.

Stu held his hand out, palmed her back.

"Do what you can for them," he said.

Rachel was frowning, as he expected, but she was frowning at his Walkie. He didn't know how much she had heard. "Ask if there's kids."

Stu did, pulling her close as he radioed the question.

They held each other while Schmitty spoke of women and children.

"Where?" Rae asked, taking the Walkie. "Where's the most of them?"

Another voice chimed in, "They're all over, ma'am, but we took back the school and we've been trying to protect 'em there... but it's no use."

"Let's go," she said, and pulled Stu by the hand. "We'll talk in the truck."

Chapter 80 Winston's Fighting Squirrels

Her quarters had been undisturbed. No one had so much as sat on her cot. Ashley passed up a meal in favor of a nap, and that nap swallowed her whole. She passed out on top of her covers, fully-clothed. She had not even removed her boots.

The thunder woke her, and in those first moments of waking, she pieced together that they were now running low and slow, and that could only mean it was morning. Morning!

She strode from her bunk toward the Tank Room, tossing her hair to shake away the last cobwebs of sleep. How long had it been since she'd slept so soundly?

Girls passing her in the narrow halls were happy to see her. Fist bumps and hugs were exchanged along the way. God, but they were a loyal crew, happy to serve, even though by now they had been briefed on what they were about to dive into.

Ashley stopped one of them, Tiffany, and asked about a peculiar patch on her jumpsuit. It was a yellow circle, the size of a palm, and in that circle, a caricature of a winking, furry female face. It smiled from Tiffany's chest in a frisky challenge.

"Miss Astar brought 'em up for us all. Armbands and patches and sashes and such." Tiffany pointed to the red border text. "*Winston's Fighting Squirrels.* See?"

Ashley smiled and shook her head in wonder.

"Look familiar?" another of the girls, Brittney, asked.

The ship was rocking down through its own stormfront. Thunder was a constant just outside the teak and brass fuselage. Both girls were giggling, showing off their patches in the golden light of the hall. The moment seemed all the more surreal when Ashley considered their certain future, but it was charming and sweet, all the same.

"It's you, Miss Winston," Tiffany said.

"I asked Astar for the pattern," Brittney said. "I'm gonna get a tattoo of it, right here over my heart."

More of the girls were crowding the hall, so happy to see her among them. It had to be close to launch, she knew, for they were already going through pre-flight routines with one another.

Kelli would have had her on the Interface, shouting brave words to all aboard all the Nebulosus vessels streaming down together. It would be important for her to command these crews, all of them, and the strength of her voice deserved to be heard below, too. Anyone on the channel was welcomed to listen in.

Ashley knew it was important. She knew her place by now, much as she wanted to jump from the Spear with her sisters. She would take to the HeadGear and cheer on the Fighting Squirrels with all she had within her.

But first, she needed a moment with William Titus.

• • • •

When she unscrewed the wheel to the airtight door of the Tank Room, she met with resistance. She pulled at it, and the suction was telling, no more than that of a mag door, but present. The Tank Room was depressurizing.

"Willy?"

Ashley strode into the room, scanning. The exhaust duct was opening slowly and the Nebulosus was yawning. She was slowed in her descent but still dropping. The floor tilted gradually toward the tail.

As the duct opened wider, light from outside revealed an unlikely pair: Zana Amin, and behind him, Willy Titus.

Ashley's eyes adjusted quickly in her panic, and she spied Astar sprawled by the bench, unconscious. An Affectation was welling up, but Ashley didn't know how to release it. The two men were dangerously close to the edge already. The exhaust was whipping at their clothing and hair.

Zana couldn't speak. A length of clear hose was choking him off. His hands were splayed in his familiar "don't panic" gesture she had seen from him so often.

"Don't throw him over," Ashley said, loud enough to be heard over the exhaust, over the groaning of the ship.

Thunder answered before Willy could. He waited on the bellowing bass, so much louder with the tail open. He smiled then, tossed his head toward the duct and said, "God speaks for me."

"Listen, I don't know what you want, what you're doing, but just don't! Willy, they've done nothing wrong. Only what I asked them. Please."

One hand was keeping the tubing tight on Zana. Willy held the mangled hand up as if arguing her point. She noticed then that a parachute was dangling by a strap in the crook of his elbow. "The old woman took her job seriously," he said, glancing over at her. "She'll be fine though. Bumped her head."

Zana tried to protest, tried to pry the tubing free to speak, but Willy jerked it like a leash. They stumbled a little in their struggle. Willy's foot was inches from the edge.

"Whatever you want, Willy," Ashley said. "Anything. Just don't hurt Zana."

She could not Affect just Willy. Zana was elderly, but not feeble. She didn't trust herself to control her gift. It didn't work like that when her adrenaline was so high.

Willy was so confident. He knew she couldn't zap him. It made her all the more angry. She looked for something she could throw at him. Tangle him in a ratchet strap that was sliding slowly past her toward the ship's tail. Zana's little Aether tank was rolling around with the airship's breathing. A pipe could be a spear. *Everything's a weapon*, Rory had taught her.

She was a weapon. Zana was a weapon. The ship itself, a weapon.

Ashley eyed the chute at Willy's hip. Early daylight behind them revealed it to be a military surplus model stocked aboard airships for emergencies. It was not the sleek, lightweight canopy the girls used. She was doing the math, converting kilograms to pounds. Guessing their altitude.

Lightning streaked behind the men, bleaching the Tank Room and blinding them all. Thunder chased it, abrupt and deafening.

Ashley bolted toward them. 30 feet. The tilt of the ship, the angle of attack, the rage within her—she was sure she could hit them hard enough. The three of them could fight over the parachute on the way down.

"Stop!" Zana coughed. He shifted his weight, cocked a knee, and spun free from his captor.

Ashley was unable to stop.

Zana knew it. A geriatric gymnast, he grabbed at the cowling of the exhaust and pulled himself up and out of the way. His legs were there for her. He was trying to snatch her up, but it was all happening too fast.

Ashley hit Willy. Violent wind tossed the two of them up and away from the airship. She immediately grappled for the chute.

Willy was catching on, and fought her for it.

Seconds.

Falling.

Rain again was drenching them and the fight became slippery. At one time she dug her nails into him to keep from getting tossed away.

He had one arm in the chute. The emergency chime on the altimeter was sounding, competing with the rumble of the turbulence.

If neither of them wore the chute when it deployed, it would be jerked from both of them, and their landing would be fast and final.

She screamed deep in her throat. Save this man she hated!

He had the advantage, and she helped wrench his other arm into the other strap. They both worked at the buckles. His bad hand was worthless. She clutched him with one hand and together, they managed to get the chest buckles latched seconds before everything snapped and the chute unfurled.

More lightning and thunder.

They were surrounded by it.

The Nebulosus would have to pull up or even it would become a Lightning's Hand. Ashley willed it with all her soul. She couldn't have another of her Poppy's ships go bad.

She scaled Willy's body until they were face to face. He had that stupid look on his face again, that smile, the one she had come to most detest. Willy put his mouth to her ear and shouted, "Luke 12:2."

"What?"

"For there is nothing covered, that shall not he revealed; neither hid, that shall not be known. Therefore whatsoever ye have spoken in darkness shall be heard in the light."

"Oh shut the fuck up!" she shouted and knocked him unconcious with a headbutt.

She had had enough cult babble.

She longed for her man and his quotations. What would he say at a time like this, skydiving in a lightning storm, being shot at from the ground, risking it all in an antique parachute not at all designed for two?

He would say, "Ride the lightning."

Chapter 81 Self-preservation

L ark had experienced enough porting decades ago. It was unnatural. An abomination. It had fried his dad, and he had no reason to believe things would turn out any differently for him.

Then again, who cared? Krys was dead, and the only way to get any kind of revenge, it seemed, was to follow Sack's lead. If the old man claimed this would bring down TransCorp, then Lark was all about it. He volunteered to be first in line.

Henny fixed Lark's hand back into position as best he could under the circumstances. "Keep your sleeve down, buttoned. If you feel it coming loose, it's 'cause the poor thing's gummed up."

"Yeah," Lark flexed his bionic fingers. "It's had a tough time of it."

Sack was poised at the portal, peering into the glow. Nat was at his side, pecking him with questions that Lark had no interest in. He didn't care about the mechanics of it all. He cared only about throwing the wrench in the works.

Henny was aloof in the void.

"Four of us can cover a lot of ground, which is great since this is going to be a manual process... of sorts." He never took his eyes from the portal as he spoke, as if he were speaking into it. "Wherever you go, every port you pass through, you're scrambling their system."

"So, when we go through a portal, it becomes part of the mix up?"

"Yeah. Fact is—" Sackerson dug in his robe sleeve and extracted a plump leather bag. "If you even toss one of these through a port, it's part of the show. And since you're random already, by virtue of lugging these around, there's no telling where you'll go next." He cackled. "Gawd, this is going to be fun!"

He grabbed a handful of the pebbles from his bag and poured them in Nat's outstretched hands. "That's prolly thirty or so. If each of us pops thirty ports, plus the ones we teleport through, we'll take out over 100 of them in no time."

Henny filled his pockets with the pebbles Sackerson gave him. "They're not going to, like, blow up or something, all concentrated like this?"

"I've been carting around this bag full of them, porting dozens of times, without a scratch. Have a little faith, Henny. I won't get you blown up."

Henny's attention went to his wound.

"I had nothing to do with that," Sackerson said.

"I don't see how tossing rocks in portals is going to do anything," Lark said at last, unable to contain himself.

"Of course you don't. You doubt. You're the Ying to my Yang. Without you counterbalancing—"

"They're not rocks at all. They're like the whole attenuation thing, right Sackerson?" Nat asked.

Sackerson smiled at the kid again. "Close enough. Yeah. They're like little black holes, making swiss cheese from the cosmic constructs these things are counting on."

Henny sighed.

Lark was tired of it, too. Either the pebbles worked or they didn't.

"They suck up the coordinates, muting the portals they pass through. After this one pass, however, I'm in! The system, every single port on the planet, will be infected and confused over time. It'll be great!"

"But it only lasts a while?" Lark asked for clarification.

"That's right, 24 hours. That takes some processing power. I wish I could tell you all about it, but... you're in a hurry. So... c'mon, let's get on with it."

"We come back here in an hour, you said... but how?" Henny asked.

"I'll pull you all in. Just don't stray from a port too far. When you see a blue one, take it. *Only the blue ones.* That's a good rule of thumb."

"Why the blue ones?" Nat asked.

"One of the blue ones will bring you back here," Sack said with a smile. "But only at the one hour mark. Otherwise, we'd have a welcoming party here we won't want. This port's staying offline except for our movement through it."

Lark looked at Henny who looked a whole new brand of confused.

"Okay then, like my hero, John Chapman, let's sew some seeds."

"John Chapman?" Nat asked.

"Johnny Appleseed," Lark answered. It seemed a strange analogy. How and why did both he and Sack know the idiosyncrasies of a folk like Johnny Appleseed? What parallels was he tripping over? Lark reached for the thread of it, but Sackerson was on with more instructions.

"Walk through when you're ready, but be ready for anything. Remember, you only need to pass through and you've done the damage. Don't dilly dally. And watch for a blue port."

Lark held his jacket pocket full of pebbles tightly. He stepped up to the portal, so close he could feel an electricity about it. He closed his eyes, and on Sackerson's mark, stepped through.

• • • •

He was standing in an ankle-deep stream of ice cold water. Warm wind tousled his hair. The loamy green landscape greeted him. So earthly and alive, such a contrast from the

Attenuation chamber. He looked all about, finding the titanium portal standing behind him to be very out of place in this landscape of woods.

A portal in a forest?

He shrugged. Not finding another nearby, he shook the loam off his shoes and stepped back into the portal again.

· · · ·

C haos on a crowded hot street in bright sun. It was humid and smelled of spice and sweat. He was pushed away from his port of entry by the masses of people streaming past. He was in a market square, somewhere, by his best guess, in the middle east. Everyone was chanting something Lark did not know. They were so enthusiastic he found it contagious. He hopped into the midst of them, doing his best to imitate their chant.

He was trying to not stand out, but there was more to this than simply that. All these people, all intent on the same something, was so powerful he could not resist it. The crowd was moving at a trot, thousands and thousands milling around counterclockwise. They were circling a huge monolith.

Lark noted more and more were pouring in from portals that made a ring around the courtyard. Portals stood edge to edge, and they were all flashing as people teleported in to join the mix.

Lark set about tossing pebbles in each portal he was pressed past. The ports did not explode, or change color, or behave any differently at all. As he danced with the crowd, he didn't mind if he missed a toss or two. He didn't mind if a pebble might miss its mark, or if he might be missing a cue for a blue portal. None of that really mattered compared to the giddy dance.

More than once, he paused and backed upstream to hold back the current long enough to help someone back to their feet from being trampled. More than once, he wondered if he had lapped his first portal in this swirling mass.

Lark didn't really care if he went porting around like Sack had suggested. He guessed he was bringing down more ports in this one place than he might in a whole day of travel, let alone the hour they were allotted.

He didn't really care even so much about that, thinking that the pebbles weren't doing anything at all. He was almost able to let go of his bitterness toward TransCorp, even, as he circled the yard. This movement, his moving with all these others, seemed to matter more.

Then he started noticing irregularities like himself. People of *all sorts* were porting into the square, most of them frustrated with their HeadGear, trying to talk their way home in frantic JackChat. Housewives and hunters, bankers and children. All these people were stopping up the circulating crowd. They were not joining the dance. They stood squinting, most of them shading their eyes from the intense sun. Many of them were shouting questions at those passing them by. Some fighting was breaking out where the recent arrivals were trying to get answers.

The pebbles, then, *were* working. The hundreds of ports circling this space were now just allowing in random people from all over the globe, people with other destinations than this in mind.

As the conflicting crowds became more and more aggressive, Lark decided it was time to go. He worked his way around to the edge, then pushed past someone entering a port so that he could duck out.

· · · ·

Cold and dark. It felt like the middle of the night. Lark pulled his jacket tight around himself and shivered. Where was he? Anywhere, USA, or so it appeared. A winding street in a neighborhood of homes all the same. A place not badly upended yet by the corporations, perhaps.

He walked the neighborhood of manicured lawns, pristine sidewalks, identical homes. It was strangely both beautiful in its uniformity and yet upsetting, too. All the homes were dark inside. It truly must have been the wee hours of the morning, Lark guessed.

He looked back the way he had come, and saw the portal still glowing there, right in the middle of a cul de sac. Again, there seemed no more explanation for it there than he could think of for the one in the forest. No one was using it.

Maybe, he thought, this was the model of teleportation. A neighborhood portal. People could walk from their homes to port to work or school or shopping. He was thinking that over as he continued his walk in search of another port to infect.

Another man could have questioned the port crippling project. Any other man might have second thoughts given the circumstances... but again, Lark Fortune saw himself as just the right man for the job. Even if the other three gave out, he would take their pebbles and continue. He was resolute in this mission, as if his every constitutional had been training for this long walk from port to port, as if this were his pilgrimage and the end of TransCorp's hold on him was his Mecca.

If he had any doubt he was doing the right thing, it evaporated when he entered a gated community of huge homes. How had such a place been preserved these last years of chaos? How had they afforded the security to keep the Eaters away, and where was that security now? Lark's curiosity and skepticism jangled his nerves.

Looters and the lost were streaming into the gates and out from them, too. Many people Lark brushed by in the dark were wide-eyed with panic. Several were crying out for loved ones. Many were babbling JackChat, agonizing that they were lost. Several were chanting the ravings of the Eaters of the Rich, a familiar chorus.

He followed some into a home that was lit up brightly. It looked like a house party from the curb, but inside, it was pandemonium. Some were admiring the decor while others were destroying it. Others yet were flipping cushions and looking behind paintings and upending furniture as if in search of something.

Lark knew what they were seeking, that special something that separated the rich from the rest. "You won't find it," Lark chuckled to himself. "It's not in a safe or in plain sight. It's just in them, the lucky ones."

"What are you carrying on about, man?" a grubby woman asked, pushing him aside.

"I'm saying, you're not going to find it here."

People rolled their eyes at him and went about their business.

In an upstairs room, a converted bedroom perhaps, Lark found a knot of people around a portal. In the mouth of it, a man in silk pajamas struck a defensive pose, wielding a shotgun. "I mean it," he said again and again. "Back!"

Lark recognized him. A mid-level TransCorp executive. He was on some of the Interface vids Lark had taken recent interest in. He wasn't a board member, but he might as well have been.

"Aren't you missing something?" Lark asked, pushing through the crowd. He snatched up a photograph in a garish gold frame from the nightstand. "Where's your family?"

Though the crowd pushed back, eventually Lark was at the front, staring down the barrel of the rich man's shotgun. It was a very nice shotgun, all polished wood and blued barrel.

When Lark asked again, the man's crazed features lapsed for an instant into caring, then back again into an expression of doubt and defense. "My port," he growled. "You—you all get out of here!"

Lark casually tossed a pebble past the man. "You no more own that port than you do the rest of this stuff," he said. "Or us."

"I seen his wife and kids take the port downstairs."

"Two ports?" someone asked, angered to the point of an animal growl.

"Fat cats don't take the stairs!" someone else chided. "They port around the house."

The crowd groaned. It was, Lark agreed, the epitome of laziness, selfishness, greed. Others would never be able to afford to port, not even for medical emergencies, and yet this family had two ports in their house! Take the port instead of the stairs.

Random people began flashing in from the port and pushing past the rich man. He was so shocked by this that his shotgun bellowed up into the air, raining ceiling debris down on Lark and those around him.

It was a good time to get out of there.

Lark pushed past the TransCorp man and on into the port with nothing but disdain.

• • • •

H e didn't know how long it had been, but he was waking up on the floor of the Lead room... again. He felt like he'd traveled *back* in time, like it was the moment *before* they left for the hospital—all over again.

The storm was blasting. Lighting was continuously arcing across the heavens and scorching the earth. Sackerson and Henny were yelling at each other now. The storm's energy had electrified them, burnt away pretenses between them.

Lark sat up. He had never seen Henny so angry.

"Self-preservation!" Henny yelled. "How's that—"

A clap of thunder drowned him out, but Lark was able to follow Henny's gesture to the point in question—a Hot Wire portal was rippling blue plasma on the Lead Room wall.

Sackerson had mounted yet another portal.

"Ah!" Sackerson noticed Lark's surprise. "I'm *damaged goods,* Kenny, but Lark here—Lucky Lark Fortune's still got a chance."

Lark stirred and tried to get up. "What? What are you..."

Henny was shaking his head. "He'll get over her. He'll be fine." Henny was pleading. "Give the guy a break, Sack. He just saw—"

"*I know what he saw!*" Sackerson snarled at him. "I see it every day of my life!"

"I'll get him back to—" Henny finally noticed Lark was coming around. He chuckled theatrically, "Lark! You feeling better?."

"What... what's happening? Where's the Wiebe kid?"

"He took the wrong port, just like you. I said blue portals. Blue! Do you know how hard it was to find you?"

"No, I..."

"He's gonna be fine. Look at him."

"No," Sackerson said, "he's going to be *great*! He's going to live out his greatest childhood dreams in a whole 'nuther place and time."

Henny tried to get in between them, but Sackerson tossed him aside. Henny, the linebacker, the bouncer, was nothing for this scrawny old man. Before Lark could react, Sackerson was on him, grabbing him, lifting him high off the ground, taking him toward the portal.

"What are you doing?!" Lark was screaming, striking at Sackerson with all his might. "What are you—"

Sackerson slammed him into the wall of the Lead Room right beside the glowing portal. Lark hit so hard his teeth chipped. The back of his head throbbed. He fought to catch his breath.

Sackerson was nose to nose with him. Expressions were changing on his face with every flash of lightning.

"Stop fighting it," Sack screeched. "You stupid, stupid ass!"

He pounded Lark into the wall with each word. "I'm. Doing. This. For. *You*."

Then he was crying.

Old Sackerson was pulling air hard and wailing with the storm.

"Long John Silver," Sack yelled and slammed him into the wall again.

"Cap'n Hook," Sack continued.

Lark felt himself pulled back, slammed again.

"Jack Sparrow!" Another slam.

"SACK," Henny said. Beyond Sackerson's wild hair, Lark could just make out Kenny Ray Hinman pointing a snub-nosed .38 at them. "Let him go. Now!"

"*Adventure is yours!*" Sackerson declared. "*Live our lives large!*"

A blast rang out. Lark knew it to be from the pistol.

In the same flash of lightning—or muzzle flash—or port flash—he felt Sackerson pull back for one last slam against the wall. Except this time when he was pushed, Lark did not hit the wall at all.

He was weightless, and all went blue, then white, and then away.

Chapter 82 Wild Dog Unleashed

The Yuma port deposited the group of them in the Arctic. That port sent them to somewhere none of them recognized, but they all knew it to be deep in a jungle.

"Why are there ports in places like this?" Rory asked.

"They may have once been dealt to the people here, like once beads and baubles were traded for their lands," a Family member offered.

"We were placing them strategically. These were the deals I brokered often," Katrina explained.

"Strategically?" Rory swatted at an insect. What strategy was there in putting a portal in the middle of nowhere?

"They are roughly in a network, a portal placed every one thousand miles in any direction."

"And stockpiles of them yet to deploy?"

She turned to look at her Family members splashing in the muck. "I told you, I was not familiar with the stockpiles... but they seem..."

"A bit much, maybe?"

"Yes," she agreed.

"How are you feeling?" Serenity asked, returning to them. She was clearly not interested in staying around this location. She shook mud from her shoes. She was already sweating. Still, she had his interests in mind. "If you're, you know, getting port sick, we could stay here a while."

Even her voice betrayed her. Yes, she was offering, but it was obvious to Rory that she really wanted to move on.

He felt a little punchy, and the extremes in weather weren't helping, but he knew he could carry on. He felt he had to.

"Gather up," he shouted, and the straying members of the Family returned to all clasp hands together and parade yet again into the portal.

"Wait," one of them said. "What is missing?"

Rory looked at each of them in turn. Most of them seemed equally puzzled. The old man of the Family continued, "The others. Here there are no others. Only us. Why?"

"Maybe we ported way off grid or something. Hell, I don't know."

"Maybe," Serenity said. "Maybe we're at the end of it. Gawd, I hope we're not stuck here!"

"I do not know," Katrina said. "But perhaps some portals are different than others?"

"We should practice safety," a Family member said.

"How?" Rory asked. "Just how are we going to do this any more safely?"

"One by one," the old man replied.

"We might all go different places."

"We may never see each other again."

"I say one by one," the old man said again. "Go our separate ways but with the same mission."

"And what is that?" another Family member asked. "Save the Princess?"

"Of course," the old man smiled.

"If it is as simple as crossing one port after another until we arrive, the odds of one of us getting there more quickly would, indeed, be much better," another woman in the Family said.

"We must watch over Rory," Katrina said. "I will port with him."

"Me too," Serenity said. "The two of us can manage."

Kofi said something to Katrina.

"He says he will go with you, too," she interpreted. "Kofi will follow love."

Despite the protests of the others, Rory clasped Katrina and Kofi by the hand, and along with Serenity, they again stepped through the portal.

• • • •

"Someone's idea of a joke?" Rory yelled over the roar of the waterfall. They had ported into a recess behind a massive waterfall. Everything was wet. The mist was thick and cold.

"I cannot explain this one," Katrina said.

"Let's go," Rory tugged, and pulled them through the portal again.

• • • •

They were in a portico of a sandy red brick building. The portal was built into a doorframe they had just passed through. Here, several others were frantic on their HeadGear, JackChat in every direction. Everyone was pushing and shoving, every last one was eager to get out to the broad plaza and street ahead. To the north, a pointed black building, to the south a large rounded auditorium. Rory read signs. They were on campus of the University of Wyoming, standing in the shelter of a new building that was not yet complete.

Even here there was gunfire. They seemed to have ported right into the action this time. Huge gray transports were parked up and down the block, three deep across the roadway, up into the parking lots and landscaping. He knew in an instant that this was a stronghold.

To his right was an architectural feature they had repurposed into a big portal. It was heavily guarded with soldiers in gray uniforms. Rory pushed his team back into the shelter of the portico. He did his best to keep them from being seen, but others wandered out from the portal to the open courtyard beyond. Some were shot on sight randomly. Others ran for shelter. A few dived right past Rory back into the portal they had just exited.

Distant gunfire popped constantly. It was accentuated with larger explosions. Some force was closing a loop around this place.

Kofi and Serenity did not heed his warnings. They were paces ahead, passing under another archway, and before Rory could get them to stop, they disappeared in the familiar port flash. When his eyes adjusted, he looked at Katrina, questioningly.

"I do not wish to follow," she said. "It seems... different."

He nodded. They agreed to dig in here, as long as they could, to get their bearings. The University of Wyoming was in Laramie. They had made it! Rory was smiling broadly despite the carnage just yards away. *They were very close now.*

"Rory!" Katrina pointed up.

The sky was peppered with hundreds of base jumpers... hang gliders? The way they maneuvered, like flocks of birds, was familiar. They reminded him of the winged women who had haunted him. As they descended, small rectangular chutes were deployed, steerable airfoils that gave them the most controlled landing they were going to get. Rory had been a paratrooper himself, but he never attempted landing in a city. Too many obstacles presented themselves. Electric lines. Fences. Irregular landing surfaces. Narrow streets...

As they dropped, they looked more and more familiar. Slight of frame. Gymnastic daredevils of the sky. *They really were the winged women from the airships!*

Rory roared and dashed out into the open.

Katrina was about to Affect him, he realized, and he spared a smile back in her direction. "No, no. I'm not going to *hurt* anyone!" He said. "One of them's Ashley!"

"How can you know that?" Katrina asked, rushing to keep up with him.

He smiled broadly. "I dunno. I just know!" He bellowed her name again and again. He ran along the street, looking skyward more than ahead of himself. "Ashley! Ashley Winston, I love you!"

Gunshots rang out closely. He stopped and ducked behind a wrecked vehicle. Ahead, men in gray uniforms were firing—not at him, but at the winged women. They were picking them off like birds.

Katrina was with him, unholstering her weapons. They did not waste words between them. She snarled at the troops and gave Rory a nod. He had a scimitar drawn from its scabbard and a pistol in his other hand.

The Affectation she had been straining to hold snapped, and he was a wild dog unleashed.

He and Katrina stormed recklessly toward the soldiers, both of them firing and screaming.

Chapter 83 Worth the World

Alex brought her a bouquet of flowers he had found in the hallway rubble. The first wing to sustain damage from the Port Authority, it had been considered unsustainable, uninhabitable, and that was where he liked to pace—the faraway places. These flowers might never have even been delivered to their intended recipient. Alex tossed away the card, but kept the silly balloon attached for good measure.

"They're beautiful," Kelli said. "How did you—"

She knew better than to ask. In their years together, if nothing else, he had been full of surprises.

Alex shrugged. "Believe it or not, deliveries are still spot on."

"Not," she choked with a chuckle.

He joined her in bed again. She tossed the flowers aside to give him a big hug. It obviously hurt, but she pulled him in for a long kiss. She was combing back his hair, smiling at it. "You need a haircut," she said.

"You too. At least a shampoo and style," he said, gently pulling her hair back from her face.

Outside, an explosion set off alarms. Some dust showered down from the bathroom ceiling.

"This place is going to hell," Kelli said.

"First the room service, now this."

She took a deep breath that made her clear her throat. "Sackerson said it's all up to you."

"Nah, I think you must have—"

"I heard him." She bit her lips together. She was fighting pain, physical and otherwise. This was the conversation he didn't want to have. It hurt to even broach it.

"I thought you were out," Alex said. "Resting."

"I never rest," she said.

There was no laughter. Not even a chuckle between them. The humor wasn't working now. They had gone too far toward the truth.

Alex didn't know how to talk about it. He felt the knot in his chest getting tighter and tighter. An elephant could have been crushing his chest, and it would not have felt worse. She knew too much. Sackerson's plan—Wiebe's for that matter—would force his hand. He would forfeit all he knew and loved here. Kelli. Ashley. Calissa. Rory.

Leaving now would mean closure. Only he and Ashley had held out hope that Rory was still alive. To go would mean he would never really know the fate of his best friend. Alex didn't know if he could deal. Remorse and sorrow were heavy with him and his looming decision.

"You took my Tic Tacs," she said at last.

He had. She'd kept them all this time in the shoulder pocket of her bomber jacket. Alex was struggling to formulate an explanation when she continued.

"I *want* you to have them. I want you to *use* them." She was fighting back a girlish cry now, her mouth all puckered up.

"Kelli, I...."

"I'm not going to last," she gasped. "There's nothing left for you here."

"That's ridicu—"

"You know I'm right. You gotta go do what you do. Use the Tic Tacs and go save the world."

He swallowed hard. He had to be strong for her.

"If you can go back and fix this, like Sack said—the world will be a better place, right?"

"I can never come back to right here, right now... I might never see you again."

"Maybe. Maybe you'll find me back in Franklin, running the bar."

He laughed. "Maybe. But maybe it's a different world then. You might be someone's housewife. We might never meet under different circumstances."

"Housewife?"

"If I leave you here, you might die. It could be years before I can follow through on Sack's big scheme. Time's different when you travel."

"It's not a conversation, really, is it?" She drew another pained breath. "I'm not worth the world."

"You are to me."

They sat quietly holding hands. He didn't know if she was thinking up another argument or just resting. He didn't care. He was cherishing the feel of her chest rising and falling.

"Doctors are better in the future," he said at last.

"I should hope so," Kelli replied. "Feels like they stitched me up with piano wire... and I'm leaking."

Alex laid back with her in the bed. He looked at the canopy over them, an oxygen tent that was folded up and held in place with velcro strips. He had rigged the canopy during one of her naps. It had a special border now.

"Better stylists, too," he said, reaching above and behind him for a cord that dangled from above.

"Again with the hair," she said.

She seemed to be catching onto his thoughts then. Her body stiffened. Maybe it was a spasm of pain.

"Wait, you mean..."

"Yeah," he said, pulling the cord that sparked up the Hot Wire overhead. "Let's check out tomorrow, together."

"I'm more a retro girl," she said, hugging him. "We could save the world if we take Sack's plan."

"Either way," Alex said, "Time to go."

The white-blue Hot Wire descended from the canopy, and they were gone.

Chapter 84 Love and War

Ashley did not like the scene they were falling into. Under the best of conditions, the parachute wasn't maneuverable. She struggled, too, with Willy's deadweight. She recognized the criss-cross sidewalks of the quad at the university, the open park called the Prexy Pasture, but overshot it in her careening descent.

Ashley managed to land in the cemetery, not a lot of fighting nearby. She hoped she had made it down undetected.

Willy was rousing, and she dragged him to the nearest headstone and secured him with the rigging from their parachute. "Don't go anywhere," she said, donning her leather pilot's cap. The HeadGear instantly lit up, not messing around.

Ashley watched both the feeds from her squirrels' helmet cams and from CommCorp Interface. The footage was not from the same point of view, and the story being told was once again one of opposites.

Ashley's girls were being picked off by gunmen below. She could see for herself when one of the girls' cameras filmed another nearby taking a hit. Blood spatter, sometimes a shriek. The corresponding camera feed would jolt, then be a limp transmission of the girl's bloodied body and her feet dangling limp. It made Ashley furious.

Some of the squirrels caught vids of the shooters, rooftop snipers pumping fists in the air with every hit. Ashley tried to commit these locations in a stream of commands to the ships above. *Targets for the next wave.*

She crouched next to a headstone, both for balance and cover. Still, no one had noticed their arrival. She spied Willy through the HeadGear's transparent display. He was alert now, his expression questioning.

"Thanks to your tour yesterday, I kinda know where we're at. East of campus."

The CommCorp story showed the wing suited women on a devilish and unprecedented aerial attack. Yes, a few of her girls were dropping grenades and small bombs, but most were surfing the sky until they had to deploy chutes, then lacing their way to a landing among the buildings. None of Ashley's girls were returning fire from above. She shut off the commentary from CommCorp when she tired of hearing about airborne anarchists and surprise attacks.

The composite of the helmet cams did give her good intel that she related to Stu Wiebe's people on the ground. It allowed them to pinpoint some Port Authority strongholds and portal clusters. In the half hour of her girls' first wave, enough data was relayed to wipe out two dozen portals and two base camps.

"You should release me," Willy said.

"Not on your life," she replied. "When I'm done here, I'm going to mine you for all you're worth. You keep on with the threats on the Family and all your vengeance talk. Talk all you want here; the dead are good listeners."

"Ashley, really. Please. It's cold." He was soaked with rain. Everything was soaked with rain. Her ships had brought it in, and it was a cold rain. Willy could fend for himself, she resolved.

She pressed on toward the nearest action. Southeast, toward the stadium, the gunfight sounded fierce.

She studied the squirrels' HeadGear montages, picking some to pin in her heads-up display as she darted through the headstones. Most of her girls were back in the thick of town. She noted storefronts and streets. Here, she was in a more open country. She relayed that to the ships, too, hoping the girls might land out here in the wider open landscape and not end up struggling with buildings and power lines.

The audio feeds from the girls kept Ashley's spirits up. Even as bullets cracked past them, her girls were chipper. Even when a comrade was hit, the girls vowed revenge. When they started landing, the huffing and yelling caused Ashley to mute audio. It was tough going in the rubble and rain. It was a suicide mission, but her girls fought valiantly.

Most of them used bow and arrow, but a number of them, like Ashley herself, favored rapiers for their light weight and immediacy. Watching them drop behind enemy lines and decimate the Grays gave Ashley an adrenaline rush.

The helmet cams caught some great vids of Laramie's locals defending their town. As she focused in on this, once all the first wave was aground, she realized Stu Wiebe's ranch hands were as bold as her own warriors. These men and women were closely followed by the Rebels, a ragtag bunch engaged in guerrilla warfare. This was Franklin all over again. This time the Fighting Squirrels might make a difference, too.

One man among these feral ground fighters caught Ashley's attention. He did not cower or sway from his objective. The camera was following him, a jouncing vid from a girl running in this man's wake. Another of her girls was running beside him, her mane of black hair furled out behind her. They looked familiar.

Ashley let the rest of the war wage.

The second wave of winged warriors, her squirrels, were now deploying on her location. Ashley rifled through several vids, collating several angles, listening in from several feeds. The gunfire was deafening. The shrieks of her girls in combat was frightening. The bellow of the large man just ahead was nightmarish.

He was swinging a broad-bladed sword, tossing it back and forth from one hand to the other, sometimes using his free hand to punch or maim a man as he passed. He was quick but brutish. He was an armed animal with no reservation nor remorse.

She knew his fighting style. She had been in his wake for years. It was the madman from the coast, Blackbeard. Up close on vids, however, he was a frothing mad man she knew and loved and had long been told was dead—Rory Reed.

She made her way toward their location as discreetly as she could in a side street. She was fortunate not to be taking fire here. Navigating by display was a challenge, but trying to composite perspectives while she ran was very disorienting. She kept one screen in her forefront, that of the warrior himself.

The vid feed showed Rory jump, spring on the roof of a car, and dive into a thicket of Grays. The black round roof of the auditorium was in the background, not a block away. She was running toward the image on her display, then witnessing it herself through the visor and beyond.

Ashley cross drew her rapiers from over her shoulders and joined in the battle, catching many of the Grays from behind. Some of the girls had caught up and were flanking her. Some others focused on a large caliber cannon encampment, jumping over sandbag embankments and attacking those within.

She pulled up her goggles and kept pressing forward, trying to keep him in sight, but Rory was whirling and lashing like no man she had ever seen in battle before. She closed in, thirty, then ten feet away, then she stopped running and yelled his name.

He twisted, swinging his big sword down from overhead. She brought up her blades and crossed them an instant before the edge of the scimitar reached her. There was a clash of metal, but he had let up, that much was obvious, or his strength and weapon would have shorn her rapiers into pieces and hewn her in half.

The astonishment on his face instantly turned to uproarious joy.

The girls closest at hand struck a formation around them. One of the women was the raven-haired girl who had fought alongside him on the vids. "Kat?"

"Be careful," Katrina Covarrubias warned, striking at another enemy. "He is uncontained. I cannot—"

Rory nudged her aside and grasped Ashley by the shoulders. He seemed so much larger than before, larger than life, a warrior from some Greek pantheon. She suffered an instant of fear. He might crush her between his hands and toss her aside.

Then he *did* get a strong grip on her and lifted her by the shoulders. He held her at his level, face to face with him at arm's length, and in a hoarse and mighty voice said simply, "Ashley!"

Another bullet buzzed between them. They both looked in the direction it had been fired from, then back at each other.

Her feet were dangling off the ground, but she didn't care. An old battle injury, a broken collarbone courtesy of Katrina herself, ached in his powerful grip, but it did not matter.

"Kiss me, you big oaf!" Ashley shouted.

And he did.

Chapter 85 Larkin Wayne Fortune

The blast had been deafening.

Henny's hand tingled around the pistol grip.

"What have you done?" Nat Wiebe asked, astonished.

What had he done?

What had happened to Lark?

It had all happened in an instant.

Sackerson stumbled away from the portal. He leaned his back against another wall, did a chair squat against it, then slid to sit down, a dazed expression on his face.

"Where's Lark?" Henny shrieked. He wanted answers, no Sackerson psychobabble. He pointed the pistol at the old man again. "What'd you do to him?"

Sackerson tapped the back of his head gently against the wall. *Was he jarring loose a reply? Trying to stay awake?*

"Well?"

"If that was the right Tic Tac, he's in the seventeenth century, the Caribbean," Sackerson admitted.

"What?" Henny stepped toward the port and looked at the swirling blue white glow. He wished it was a window to wherever Lark was now. The port's brightness illuminated Nat Wiebe stepping away from them, tracing along the far wall. Fearful. Good.

"Ha." Sackerson coughed a pained chuckle. "'Wish I could go with him, but I'd never survive time porting again... and...'" he raised his hand to show Henny. In this light, it was wet and black. Dripping blood. "You got me, pal. I'm no longer fit for travel, time or otherwise."

Henny saw the broad dark smudge that trailed down the wall behind Sackerson now. He dropped the .38 and took a knee by Sackerson.

"Go get help, okay kid?" Henny said over his shoulder to Wiebe's kid.

"Don't kill him," Nat pleaded. "I'll get somebody, but you gotta promise."

"I promise," Henny said, nodding at Nat. He felt he was promising something to his girls when they were young. *Parent promises*—he didn't have time to think about it.

He reached out to touch Sackerson, but he couldn't quite do it. Why touch him, to see if he was real?

The old man pulled aside his beard and pointed at his chest with his eyes. "If I were guessing, I'd say you clipped an artery."

"Sack... I'm sorry. I... I didn't mean to." The words sounded as childish as Nat asking for a promise. What was happening here? *Didn't mean to?*

Sackerson's hand fell to his lap, and his head was tapping the wall again. He was looking Henny in the eyes, and at this unlikely moment, Sackerson was smiling. Even more unusual for the old man, he didn't say anything.

"Does it hurt?" Henny asked, brushing aside the beard himself, spying the bullet hole burned in Sackerson's robe, a frayed black star. Again, he realized he was saying the most stupid things! *Of course it hurt.*

Sack grinned. His teeth were slick with blood. "It hurts a little," he tried to laugh. "Thankful for shock."

"Gawd, Sack. I dunno why I... I dunno... I'm sorry."

Henny noticed the blood pooling at the waist of Sack's robes, soaking up the front of his tunic now.

"It's cold, just like they say," Sack said, closing his eyes. "Death is cold." He said it like it was a lesson now learned. *Confirmed. Death is cold.*

"Can I... can I make you more comfortable, or..."

"Comfortable. I'm here with my best friend through thick and thin," Sack said, his eyes still closed. Henny wondered at that statement. *Best friend?* Was it from a nursery rhyme?

Sack was tapping the back of his head against the wall again, and Henny now knew it was to keep himself awake. Sack's eyes flashed open. He sat up a bit. He spat blood off and away, like a saloon cowboy. "Hinman," he said with resolve. "I've not told you everything, and I won't." He winced, then continued, "But I will tell you this. You're the best friend I ever had."

"Sack... I think you're..."

"When we were kids, you saved me, saved all of us. I was there and grown, too, and you were the only one who trusted me." Sackerson nodded, end of statement. Then he added with a wrinkle in his brow, "That matters, you know?"

"Sack, I don't think a friend would—"

"What? Friends don't let friends shoot—" he fell into a messy, bloody coughing fit at his own joke. He spit again and collected himself.

"What's keeping that Wiebe kid?" Henny cried out.

Sackerson put his bloody hand on Henny's forearm and gripped it. "Listen. You did what you thought was right. Protecting me... from me."

Henny sighed. He was getting justification for shooting a man from the very man he had shot. Nothing was making sense anymore. He'd never shot at anyone before. He'd never drawn the gun, not even at the cowboy in the hospital. He couldn't hit the broad side of a barn, and now he'd cracked off a shot through Sackerson's heart?

Henny was sick at himself. How could he live with himself?

If Wiebe didn't get back soon, Henny would have to admit he'd killed Sackerson.

Protecting me... from me. Sackerson was fading, getting loopy. *More loopy.*

"Sit," Sack said, tipping his head to the side.

Henny sat beside him. They sat quietly for so long, Henny wondered if this was it—was he going to just sit it out while Sackerson died at his side?

Sackerson drew in a raspy, bubbly breath, very slowly. A last breath?

"I am 116. Had a good life. Got to share a bit of it with you, twice now. Watched you—" he broke off in a more severe coughing fit. This one had to hurt. He whined as he recovered a few short breaths, then sat back, again still as the dead.

Sack smiled. "Paroxysm," he said. "It's a pretty word but," he cleared his throat, "but let me tell you, hurts like a bitch."

Henny didn't know what to say. He'd nursed many a person through lost loves. He'd heard out dozens of grieving spouses. A couple of patrons had treated *Sharts* like Hospice toward the end, coming in and drinking every night, reminiscing.

He'd never sat out dying with someone quite like this.

"You don't look a day over a 'hunnert," he said at last.

"Thanks," Sack coughed. "I might be wrong in my diagnosis. Might've clipped a lung, too."

It was grim, but Henny continued his attempt at rising to Sackerson's good spirits. "Stop bubbling and get on with your babbling, man."

Sackerson nodded, pounding the back of his head on the wall. Once. Twice. He was doing his best to stay lucid. Henny was sure of it now.

"Christmas Day screwed the Port Authority... confused the Spooks... shrouded that, too," he nodded at the glowing portal. "Important. All that chaos, *ports gone wild*, let me... erh... *let Lark...* leave here free and clear. Gault, too, if he followed through."

Henny shrugged. It was all too much.

"See? We won!" Sackerson gagged and spat away more blood. "Not the war, but a big battle. Port Authority gets the shaft. Now they won't build up like in my time."

"Well, there's that, I guess." Henny played along with filler, like he'd do at the bar. "There *is* that."

"*It's so sloppy here.* Maybe people won't be able to turn away. Maybe they'll see the PA for what it is—gang of thugs. Bullies. Brutes."

"I get it," Henny said, patting Sackerson's hand.

"Thanks to you, we get closure, too," Sack grunted. "You saved the world again."

Henny frowned hard. He turned to look at Sack for clarification.

Sack turned his head and said, "I die here, and they give up looking for Lark and Gault and call it a day."

"Who?"

"Spooks," he said as if it were obvious. He took Henny's hand and held it tightly. "Now you got a story to tell back home, huh?"

"Yeah. Sure."

Henny waited. He sat quietly, trying to ignore the bubbled breathing as it slowed. He waited as Sackerson's grip eased off, thinking of the times he'd had Lark grasp his hand just like this, strength testing his prosthetic.

Sack tapped his head at the wall one more time. "Famous last words?"

"Yeah, sure," Henny said. "Whadda ya got?"

"*Always tip generously,*" Sackerson said.

"Really, that's it?" Henny nudged the old man a little with his elbow. Surely there was more. To have lived a hundred years, to have traveled time and saved the world... and this was it?

Sackerson nodded, satisfied, and slumped some more against the wall. He was leaning on Henny. He was going to die that way.

"Kenny?" he heard Sack say.

"Yeah?"

"What's my name? My real name."

"Larkin Wayne Fortune." It defied all logic and reason. Time travel would always give him a headache, Henny resolved, but he said it, and he didn't know if it was more a point of fact, or a confession he'd known all along, or a concession to a dying old man.

"That's right, pal."

Chapter 86 Make a Difference

B usses parted long enough for Stu to drive through the improvised gate, then they pulled back into interlocking positions. He gunned it, dodging bodies and debris piled on the street.

"That," Rae said, licking the icing from her fingers, "was a good idea."

"The cinnamon rolls?"

"The bus barricade." She watched it recede in the big rear view. "But the rolls are good, too."

"Which school?" Stu asked, realizing he hadn't been told. He reached for the mic clipped on the dashboard, but Rachel snatched it up first.

"They're looking for you. They already popped Krystal, and I heard they got the Rebel's leader, that Jeff Burton, too." She shook her head. "Let me do the talking."

In no time, she had secured directions, and they were rolling toward Snowy Range Academy. What should have been a five minute drive was complicated by wrecked cars, piles of portals, and—much as Stu hated seeing it—piles of bodies, the Grays and the locals jumbled together.

"About time you called for me, Stu," Rachel said around a mouthful of roll. "Everybody, and I mean every last reb and hired hand—they all left to join the fight."

"I'm sorry. Had a lot on my mind."

"I stayed put, just like you said," she continued. "This is better. We can get through this together."

"I didn't want you to get—"

"Oh, I know. Always watching out for me when I can kick ass and take names with the best of them." She shook her head. "Our child is out there, I hear. You let 'em jump in one of those damn ports, didn't you?"

"Nat gets an idea in mind and there's no stopping them." Stu gripped the wheel, still furious that Nat had gotten away like that.

"I know," she said in a surprisingly understanding tone. "And I hope you know they just wanna be like you. Wants to make a difference."

Stu looked around outside his truck as they eased along. *A lot of difference he'd made!*

He had seen the results of a Lightning's Hand. His own truck had been totalled by one. This level of wreckage and ruin, however, was beyond his imagination. Street signs had been stripped of paint. Entire homes and businesses had been pummeled to dust or burned beyond recognition. Every flat surface, roadways, rooftops and yards—all of it was ash and ruin. Highway 80 was choked off by hundreds of cars and trucks that had been pounded down trying to leave Laramie. Not a one of them had any glass left in it. They were charred and pock marked to the point he couldn't tell one model from the next.

"They say Nat's safe with Sackerson."

"The wizard? Where? Where's Nat gonna be safe with that lunatic?"

So she *had* met Sackerson, Stu thought. She had the same misgivings he did.

Shots rang out from the drugstore and were returned from a broken building across the street from it. Stu forged ahead. His attention was on the road, but Rae's warning made him twitchy. Any movement on a side street caught his eye. Usually, it was just someone picking something up, but he spotted more in gray uniforms, still slinking around, than he expected.

Garfield was blocked off. The Grays had made a stand here. He could tell by the piles of crushed portals and heaps of bodies near them. He downshifted and took the sidewalk, shearing off street signs and bike racks as he passed.

Rae spoke over the raking metal and grinding noises of the truck plowing through. "Damn foolishness, but I know you meant well. I know you always do, Stu."

"Yeah," he said. He glanced over, a bit puzzled.

"I know, right?" she smiled. "I want you to know that I get it. I get you."

"Do you?" he asked, jostling the truck back onto the road.

"And I love you for it. For who you are."

"You're supposed to be reaming me for losing Nat," he grumbled. "What'd you do with my wife?"

"Stuart, the last time this happened, you were a kid. You had to rebuild on your own." She let it sink in while he stopped to study the next situation they were facing.

He sensed she expected him to say something. "Mmm-hmmm," he managed.

"I want you to know, I'm with you this time. You're not alone. I'm gonna help you through whatever we get into."

A stray bullet pinged off the grill guard. It motivated him to keep rolling. Around and through. Get to the school. Help the kids.

"How's the place? What's left of it?" He was revving the diesel, listening to the motor. It didn't sound like a bullet had caused any damage.

"Lightning missed the ranch," she said. "Got a lot hotter here, though."

Between the battle and the storm, Laramie had been laid to waste. How had anyone—anything—survived it? It was shot to hell. Little fires continued to burn here and there. Refugees were rummaging through the ruins seeking their loved ones. It smelled of smoke and sulfur.

Laramie was hell.

Ahead on Garfield, they had to detour around a skirmish at Boulder street—he knew the intersection though he wouldn't otherwise have recognized it. His CPA had officed there. Now the Grays had taken it, and barricaded up. His Boys were surrounding it, taking shots at it. Stu blew his air horns as they went by, waving in encouragement.

"What part of lie low do you not understand?" Rae asked.

The windshield snapped a spider web crack. They were taking fire again.

Stu floored it, whipping off on an obscure side street, then went barreling over the highway. Then they were at the school's parking lot. Again, had he not known the place, he wouldn't have taken it for a school at all. The entire front of the building had been razed, and every surface of the school and every vehicle piled around it—everything in sight—was singed and dimpled and a broken mess.

Rae radioed in. The reply offered curt directions, "Come 'round the southeast, on around back and in the service bay. We got ya in sight."

Stu popped the curb and slogged down a gully alongside the remains of the building. The farther he went, the better the school looked to have survived the onslaught. Out back, it had taken damage from the Lightning's Hand, but little else. Here, there were no bodies piled up, but a dozen local parents were crouched behind cars and makeshift shelters, their guns trained on Stu's truck.

"Hands where I can see 'em," someone shouted.

"It's Wiebe," another person called out. "They're good."

Stu edged the truck inside the service bay. Several trucks and a bus were fitted with makeshift armor. Stu was flagged to a spot just inside the door, and like the others, backed his truck into position.

A pack of the Rebels of the Plains were coming right at him. They were carrying something, three to a side—pall bearers, Stu thought.

When they got close, the men in front stood aside and the pall bearers lifted the head of a pallet, lowered the foot of it. There, secured to the stretcher, was the thin, grizzled Jeff Burton. His men held him upright, face-to-face with Stu.

"It's worse than it looks," Burton said with a sardonic tone. "Doc says I took it in the spine this time. C6 vertebrae." He smiled with half his face, the rest looked paralyzed. "Otherwise, I'd shake your hand."

"Shake my hand? Why the hell—"

"Your Boys knocked out the ports. You shored up the hospital. Damn, man, what more could you do?"

Stu looked around the service bay at the gathering crowd. Everyone looked haggard and hurt. Several were limping or helped along by someone. They were dirty and ragged and had that hang dog look of defeat on them.

Could have done a lot more.

Stu cleared his throat to say something, even though nothing was coming up that was worth a damn. Rae stood against his side, patted his chest and said, "He's a little frazzled. We all are. I can tell you though, we're mighty proud of your folks, bringin' in our kids."

"They ain't just ours," someone said. "These kids are from all over the planet."

"Poppin' up in those portals like they was playin' at it."

"How many?" Stu asked.

"We don't know for sure," Burton said. He looked to the side with just his eyes, and one of his men stepped up. "Dempsy, how many do you figure?"

"We have over six hundred inside," he said.

"Damn," Stu mused.

"Now that's something to be proud of," Rae said.

"That church fella, from the dinner the other night? Thompson, right?" Burton asked. "He's got a bunch a women and elderly in the church basement, they say. One of the civic groups, Lions or Knights or whatever, they're bunked up at the armory with a mess of people."

Someone rushed up to the circle and pushed through. She was mousy and lean, dressed in Land's End camping gear, head to toe. "We have another bunch," she said, breathless.

"This is principal—"

"I know," Stu said. "Hi, Dixie."

"Mr. Wiebe," she acknowledged. They'd put Nat here, at Snowy Range, back when he was Nathan, back when he was first recognized as off-the-charts with the smarts. The school had meant a lot to him, and it was the first time Stu ever joined Rae in teacher conferences, fundraisers, and the band booster club. Dixie Lawler had seen something special in their kid. Good parenting, she'd said. If the ranch hadn't been so demanding, she would have had him on the school board.

She turned back to Burton. "There's a big parade of kids coming in from the subdivision, just walking up the streets together like a little army," she said.

"From the Plastics?"

"All on their own?"

"They have a leader," the principal replied. Her survey of the crowd seemed to settle on the Wiebes. "Come see for yourself."

• • • •

ChompCorp was big in the boom years of Laramie, and with their support, an entire subdivision was set up in weeks. The roadways were the most time consuming. Then pre-fab composite houses were airlifted in by the hundreds. They were identical modular units that raised a lot of curiosity from the locals. The ChompCorp community was not gated nor secured, but the residents kept to themselves. The mystery of it all, since they all worked for Chomp, was heightened when they developed their own entertainment lanes and banking.

The kids, however, were mainstreamed with the rest of Laramie's youth. Since the neighborhood was in Snowy Range Academy's backyard, they all went there. The kids seemed like any other kids, but they dressed alike and some said looked a lot alike.

Between such characteristics and the prefab houses, everyone started calling them the Plastics.

Stu rode shotgun with Rae on his lap. They were in a big troop transport vehicle that rambled and pushed through everything in making its way to the Plastics. The transport was heavily armored, and thus the lead vehicle in their convoy. Visibility was limited to slits through the metal covering the windshield. Rae was peering through the slit, eager to see what the principal had described.

The transport driver was Lyle Ladner, an old bus driver Stu knew from the cafe. He was adept at turning the large machine in tight maneuvers, not minding if he raked the side along a pile of cars or cracked off a utility pole along the way. He obviously loved the power of it.

"Stop!" Rae shouted. "Lyle, stop the truck."

She turned behind to the open cargo area. She craned her neck to spot Mrs. Lawler. "Is that them?"

The principal made her way to the window slits and beamed back at Rae and Stu. "Yeah. Go see."

Stu pried open the door and he and Rae spilled out. Already a dozen rebels had weapons out, watching the houses surrounding them. Coming right up the road, just as the principal had said, was a mass of children. Someone had taken the initiative to round them up and herd them in the right direction.

Stu tipped up his hat, not certain of what he saw.

Hundreds and hundreds of children, none of them over shoulder height, were marching down the street boldly. They were singing a hauntingly familiar song that Stu couldn't quite sync with—until he spied the leader of the march.

Nat Wiebe, formerly Nathan Wiebe, formerly of the Boy Scouts, was marching with a drum major mace keeping the rhythm, keeping all those kids in order. Buoying their spirits in song, they led them in an old scout march, *Marching to Pretoria*.

Nat led them past the transport, smiling at their parents as they passed.

Burton's men parted and let the assembly through. They were shouting directions to Nat and the leading edge of the marching children. There were several hundred too many to fit on the meager transports from the school. They were making their way in an orderly show of force. No one would have it any other way. As they passed, parents and rebels and all present could not help but smile and cheer.

"Well," Rachel said, her hands on her hips. "What do you make of that?"

"They could have marched right into an ambush," a nearby rebel said.

"They sure wasn't stealthy about it. Lucky, if you ask me," another said.

"Making an awful bold move."

"Yeah," Stu agreed. "Really making a statement."

Burton's attendants approached with the pallet and again stood Jeff Burton up to speak with Stu. "That's your boy?"

"That is indeed my child, yeah. Nat."

"Crazy as the old man, huh?"

"Yeah," Stu smiled. "Crazy brave."

Chapter 87 Something Blue

Rory Reed had served with honor and yet had done, sometimes, some dishonorable deeds. He had fought with all his heart, only to have it crushed by corporate power that seemed it could never be contained.

Again in Laramie, Wyoming, he had taken up his weapons and done his damnedest to protect his love and honor what was right. Trudging down the ashen street, carrying Ashley in his arms, he smiled. This would be chalked up in the win column.

"Reed! Reed!" someone ahead was flagging him.

Rory blinked hard, trying to clear his vision and to better understand what he was seeing. A very well-dressed man was picking his way over rubble, struggling to keep his shoes from getting scuffed. Rory tried remembering the man's name. Long locks of hair in a stylish wave, gold-rimmed glasses glistening brilliantly in the sun.

He shook Ashley a little and nudged her head up. She wasn't down yet, not even dozing, just lolling in his cradling arms. He needed her now, though, he guessed. This guy looked to be of her class and world.

Her body jolted in recognition. "Kyle?"

"Whew, am I glad to find you two!"

"Kyle, what are you doing here?"

"Working entirely too hard. This is billable, Ashley. Billable!" He pulled out a silk pocket corner and dabbed his forehead. It wasn't forty degrees and the sun was mostly in the clouds. His actions were charades.

"Attorney!" Rory thought aloud. "Kyle... Dupree. How's law and order?"

"It's a damn sight better than... than this!" he said. "Ash, you okay?"

"Never better," she sighed, wriggling from Rory's arms. She pecked a kiss on Kyle's lips.

He blanched.

Rory chuckled.

"They want you to talk on the Interface, to tell the true story of what happened here," Kyle said to Rory. Turning then to Ashley, he continued, "I advise against it. For both of you."

"Laramie's going through your attorney to get to me?"

She shook her head and shrugged.

"Not like that, no. I caught wind of it and caught the first functioning port to town. Rory, it's good to have you back." He looked again at Ashley and added, "Good for our girl, more than you'll ever know."

"So what do you advise?" Ashley inserted.

She wanted to keep Dupree from saying something. It piqued Rory's curiosity.

"I'd say stay the hell away from Laramie, Wyoming, but it's a bit late for that." He pulled a flexible tablet from inside his suit and presented them with the screen. On it, in hyper-saturated colors, was a looping vid of the two of them jumping over barriers. Their weapons were raised high. Their faces were in earnest battle cries.

"What. The. Hell?" Rory said.

"I thought CommCorp was with the Port Authority," Ashley said. "What's the sudden turn about?"

"It's making great ratings. I'm sure there's someone somewhere making t-shirts and posters of it. You two are famous."

"It's not even our battle!" Rory said.

"Look," Kyle smiled his courtroom best. "Ashley's uber famous. She could be running alongside a pot bellied pig and the people wouldn't care. They see their Princess all over again. *The rebel is returned*, they're saying. It doesn't hurt that you're the biggest badass on the battlefield, either, Reed. Altogether, you're a celebrity circus, just the two of you."

"Great," Rory grumbled.

"I'm here to manage your image."

"Manage my—"

"Your collective image, see."

"Oh Kyle. Not again."

"Look. He's back. It's a miracle. You said so yourself!" Kyle was smiling broadly. "We have to cashier this moment. Right now."

"Kyle!" Again, Ashley tried to dial him down, with no effect.

Rory took a half-step back when Dupree was pulling something else from his jacket. He held it out to Rory, opening the little box in the handoff.

Rory looked at the glimmering, gaudy diamond ring for the longest time.

His mind was fixed on only that.

"Kyle, he's just cooling down from the most grueling..." she went on and on, but Rory was thinking about the ring. He'd never have that kind of money. He'd never even know where to find a ring worthy of Ashley Elizabeth Winston of Winston Water Works. And a ring, a diamond ring... it could only mean one thing! Was he proposing?

Was Kyle proposing that he propose?

"I have the perfect bead on things," he said framing his view with his hands. He tapped his gold-framed glasses with their built-in HeadGear. "The ol' goggles are catching it all."

Rory shook off his daze. His hands were stiff and clumsy from the battle, scuffed and bloodied, but he managed to pinch the ring from the box. He tossed the box away and took a knee in front of Ashley. "I lost my mind without you. I was... lost. I saw you in the sun and moon and didn't even know it was you, but I knew you and I loved you and... and I missed you something awful."

He reached for the ragged journal he had carried all along. He flipped to a page with a drawing of her, a photorealistic, accurate portrait of her. "This is all I had, not even your name. All I had was your memory. I don't want to just remember you anymore. I want to be with you, Ashley. I wanna be together always."

"That's it, that's great!" Kyle was saying. He was moving around them, intent on capturing it all. "Now ask her!"

"Ashley, whaddya say? Will you marry me?"

"I dunno..." She pulled off her leather aviator's cap and shook loose her platinum mane. It unfurled around her with the wild abandon that was her spirit. She took a knee herself and clasped his hands in hers. Tiny hands on bear's paws.

"Do you think you can handle me?" she asked. "You think we could grow old together?"

"Yes..." he said, "and no. I doubt we'll live to a ripe old age. But I wanna kick it with you while we can."

"It's a package deal," a woman's voice said from behind him. "If you take on Daddy, you're taking on me, too."

"Oh, yeah. I forgot to mention my ward, your daughter, the lovely miss—"

Rory spun around, nearly knocking Kyle over as he darted to grab up Calissa in a hug he'd long forgotten. "Baby girl?"

"Daddy?" she smiled through her tears. "You getting married again?"

"I dunno," he said, putting her down. He turned back to Ashley. "Am I?"

The ring was already on her finger. He marveled at the mystery of her. Richest woman alive but still the pickpocket thief of his heart. She was admiring the ring's sparkle in the sun.

"Well?" Rory rumbled.

"Hmmmm," Ashley said. She rummaged through her inner pockets and pulled out a handkerchief. She shook it out to its full size and studied it like a map.

"Are you kidding me?" Kyle asked.

"Will you marry me, or are you gonna torture me first?"

"I will," she said. "The hanky says so."

She held it up to them. Rory had forgotten the magic, moving threads, as if it were sewing a new pattern whenever it shared a message. It swirled to a stop, and Rory read aloud, *"It's time."*

• • • •

Dupree found a port that would take them, he claimed, directly back to Springfield. It was in the remains of the Laramie Civic Center. Oddly, a runner of red carpet went right up to it. Someone had gone to some effort to sweep it off.

Calissa, Katrina, Kyle, and some locals were assembling there to see them off. They hadn't even showered yet. Off to Springfield, then off to the courthouse, where Kyle had arranged CommCorp's brightest team.

"Come along," Rory pleaded with Calissa. "We've hardly had a chance to talk."

"I'm here," she said, subtly swiping her jawline. "And I'll be along soon. I'm still trying to stay under the radar, you know."

"What about you?" Rory asked Katrina.

She shifted her weight to her other foot, then back. "I will find the Family," she said. "We'll come by the Estate, sometime soon."

"Reception will be in a week," Kyle said loudly, waving his arms. "Give these two some time for a honeymoon. Give us all some time to catch our breath."

A large man moved their way from the crowd of locals. He looked like a cowpuncher right out of the movies, his duster battered and dirty, his hat in his hand. "Don't mind my sayin' so," he rattled, "I'd like to host you here."

Kyle chuckled and stepped toward the man.

Rory pushed him aside.

"Stuart Wiebe," the cattleman said, extending his hand.

"Rory Reed."

"You're Ashley Winston," Wiebe stated.

"I am," she said, extending her hand for a shake.

"Your girls took a lotta lead. I'm sorry for that, but grateful for the help."

"Well..." Ashley squirmed a little. "You know..." she looked around at all the devastation.

They all knew.

Wiebe grimaced at some movement from behind, someone poking him to speak. "So anyway... Ahem... thank you both. Thanks to all for the help around here," he said.

Rory didn't know what to say. Kyle was stepping up to take back over when Wiebe continued. "So... we got a great parson, friend of mine. He could do the honors. You could stay at the ranch. We got a special cabin down at the ford that's—"

The woman behind Wiebe stepped around him. "It's a real nice place," she said. "And there's not a camera nowhere."

"Thank you," Rory said. "That's the—"

"That's nice. We're grateful," Kyle said quickly. "They really do need to get back, however, so we're—"

"Ash?" Rory asked.

She nodded. She turned to Kyle, "Thanks for the nudge, Skipper. Sticking around for the cake?"

"But Ashley..."

Rory could tell Dupree knew when it was a lost cause. He seemed more intent on having them together than having them rush home.

"Maybe," Wiebe stepped closer to Rory. "Maybe you'd like it here. Maybe you'd want to stay on for a while? Help us rebuild?"

It seemed familiar. It seemed right.

It also seemed a little suspicious. "What makes you think we'd be inclined?"

Wiebe chuckled. "Friends of yours told me all about your work in Franklin."

"Friends?"

"Alex? Kelli?" Ashley asked. "They're still here?"

"Back at the hospital," Wiebe smiled. "And they're not going anywhere for a week or so. Recuperating, to be sure."

Rory didn't wait to hear more. "Hospital?" he asked the nearest local.

"We'll drive you," Wiebe offered. "It's just a few blocks."

. . . .

It was the longest few blocks Rory had ever known. They were all crammed in the ample cabin of Wiebe's big pickup: Rory, Ashley, Katrina, Calissa, and the Wiebes. There was a good deal of chatter and excitement. Along the way he quizzed Ashley on his friends. Yes, they were married. No, they didn't have kids. No, she had no idea they'd been hurt. She admitted to having been a little distracted.

His best friend! Alex Gault, Ashley reminded him, was his high school buddy, his college roomie, his brother in arms in the TurnCoats.

He couldn't wait to see him!

The hospital was as battered and beaten as every other building in town, but Rory didn't care. He pushed down the hall right behind the Wiebes. He threw open the door to their room and threw open his arms to announce his return.

The room was empty.

"What the?" Wiebe asked.

An orderly came from the bathroom with a handful of towels. She shrugged and said, "Gone when I came on, and that was a couple hours ago. Checked themselves out I guess?"

Ashley was studying the bed, fingering a crusty black wire that crumbled to her touch. That seemed familiar to Rory, too, but he couldn't place it.

Then he saw something even more familiar, and maybe even more out of place than a crusty black wire in a clean hospital room. On the bedside table was a blue yo-yo and a note. Rory squinted his eyes, pulling at the thread of memory. All he could think of, all he could say was, "something blue."

He snatched up the yo-yo, plucked the note from it, and read aloud:

"Don't stop believing."

Chapter 88 Love and a Baby Rattle

H enny had been shot by a Wyoming cowboy. Gut shot, and lived to tell about it.

He'd fought alongside TurnCoats and Rebels against the Port Authority Grays and survived it all!

He had known a man who'd traveled time. Ralph Waldo Sackerson, that was his given name (at least the name Henny had given him). He was a God damn, real life, time traveler!

He'd survived the fury of a Lightning's Hand.

If that wasn't too hard to swallow, he'd had conversations with Ashely Elizabeth Winston herself and Captain Kelli Price, too.

Those Spooks some said still came around? He'd been in a gunfight with some. Bad odds, 3 to 1, and yet—this was his overall theme—goodness still prevailed.

He looked up among the junk on the walls at a special little box, glassed in. Nobody would know that it mattered, just a scrap of a letter jacket with the yellow "B" sewn on. It was a story in itself.

One day a curious looking person strode into *Sharts*, tall and graceful, confident and cool. He ordered a water, no ice, and sipped it like it was $1,000 gin. He had some fancy package, and he set it on the counter, face down.

"Nice place," he observed.

"Thanks." When there was no further reply, Henny continued, "I'm Kenny Hinman, folks call me Henny."

"It's me. Nat Wiebe."

The kid had grown up and grown into a slender gentleman. Henny was shocked.

"Dad was shaken pretty bad by what happened in Laramie. He always meant to come here and visit with you, but he was pretty busy until... well, he passed."

"Sorry to hear about that."

"He got on with most things in life. Accepted some big changes. Accepted me..." Nat's lips rippled tight.

Henny polished a glass. The bartender's crutch. Almost anything could be waited out in the time it took to polish up a glass.

"Anyway... he always had one regret, he told me. Said there was one apology he never got to make."

"Ah, bygones are bygone," Henny said.

"He wanted you to have this, Henny." He flipped over the box, revealing the yellow letter from Bluejackets. It was just like the big yellow B on the letter jacket hanging in his closet upstairs. Complete with the little brass football pinned to it. "Dad said a quarterback's nothing without his center."

"He said that, huh," Henny said, swallowing hard. "And he told you to tell me... is that right?"

"That's right."

"Always had to have the last word, the bastard," Henny chuckled.

· · · ·

He'd retell that story, some of it. He'd brag up Stu Wiebe, the best quarterback to ever come out of Oklahoma, robbed of his senior year. He'd tell stories of the Installation, too, picking up where Lark had left off, adding color and flavor as it fit.

His favorite stories were ones he only told his granddaughters, fanciful stories of a pirate he claimed to know. All the stories about Captain Hook? They were true, Henny would say. He knew Captain Hook personally. Good-natured guy. Drank right here at *Sharts*. Loved the peanuts. The girls would giggle and punch him in the arm.

There were stories he never spoke of again. Not even to Darla. He'd done the grizzly work of cleaning up after over a dozen dead men. He'd lied to his friends and family and damn near died from going undercover—and that was when he was a boy! The story he kept closest to the vest was that he'd shot a man and then sat with him in his warm, pooling blood and watched him die.

The one story he was absolutely sworn to never tell, however, was one that fascinated and boggled him most of all. It was a time traveling tale that he would always wonder about.

Shae Ward, Guthrie PD, retired, had hired him for her daughter's wedding reception, and over a few too many drinks, she was talking it up. She missed Rob. She missed the force. She was gonna miss the girls, too, but there was nothing to be done about any of it. They talked about family a while. She asked how Peg and Gail were doing.

Eventually, for no good reason, Henny asked about her folks.

Shae tipped her glass to him. "Now *that's* a story."

Henny leaned on his elbows. "Let's hear it."

"Me and Robbie," she sighed, "we had it about right. Hell, he was the best thing for me to ever come a long. I miss him bad."

Henny nodded.

"They say when you marry, you do try one of two things—subconsciously of course. You either try to get a partner and make a match as good as your parents, or you find fault in your parents and try to do better for yourself. Ever heard that?"

"I don't know if I have..." he said.

"I knew all through growing up there wasn't any better. My mom and pop loved on each other like they'd invented it. They started with nothing, and I mean nothing. All they had between them was love and a baby rattle."

"That sounds like a song," Henny said.

"It sounds like a storybook, doesn't it... and it was. They had a bungalow with a picket fence, a beagle, and me. That's all they needed, they always said."

"That's real sweet," Henny said. He started clearing the table, still listening. "You're talking in the past tense. When did you lose them?"

"Feels like forever ago. It was before I met Rob. Mom passed from heart trouble. Pop dropped right after, in the same year." She took a drink and continued, "She wore the pants in the family, but he let her. I never seen any man love a woman like he did Momma."

"That sounds like a good home to come up in."

"It was, and it wasn't."

Henny waited her out. He stopped fussing with the table and nodded when she looked up at him. He'd never seen Shae Ward have a hard time saying anything before.

"Down at the station, we used to reclaim dogs—abused dogs, you know—and some of them were the strangest animals. They'd be free in the yard, but they'd stand there and whine like they wanted to bolt. Like they wanted to go do something or be somewhere else... but they wouldn't never make a break for it."

"Uh-huh. Kinda like that elephant rope thing?" Henny said.

"The what?"

"Elephants would get their spirits broke a little at a time. At first, trainers would use log chains and trees to stake them out. Then when they got used to it, tow ropes and tent spikes. Get used to that, they could go all the way down to string and a paperweight. Finally, they'd just set them loose and know they wasn't going anywheres. Tamed."

Shae squinted, processing, then she nodded curtly. "Yeah, just like that."

"Your folks were like that? Made you feel funny as a kid?"

"It made me feel like maybe I was missing out on something, like an inside joke or something just over the horizon I'd never know. You know?"

Henny nodded. He was wondering how much she maybe *did* know.

"Pop subscribed to papers from all over the world. Had stacks of them, and he'd pour over them every morning like he had to, like a job. When things went all digital, he was hours on screen, same thing. He was looking for something. Well... I got snoopy. Real snoopy," she continued. She finished her drink in a swallow, tapped the butt of her glass on the table for more. "I think that's why I became a cop, 'tell you the truth. I just had to know."

"And what did you find out?" He asked, taking a drink himself.

"They were from the future."

Henny spit his drink out. He apologized. He mopped the table and offered her a clean towel from his waistband.

"They were on a mission. I found her uniform, blue and white. Leather. They were in some military thing or some damn thing, and they both got hurt bad enough to rethink it all."

Henny didn't have any words. Only questions.

"Dad was wounded pretty bad. I saw that for myself when we were down at Turner Falls. Went swimming, and he forgot himself. Took his shirt off. I was only maybe ten or so, but his whole side was buggered up with scar tissue."

"And your momma..." Henny didn't want to jump to conclusions, but he had a big idea. "Shae, did your momma have a bad scar, right here on her neck?"

Shae Ward sat back and looked at him like he was an alien. "How could you know that?"

"I figure they kept an eye out for the Guthrie Fall, same as I woulda, then probably the CorpWars," Henny said, "They coulda got involved again, but they made a choice to live in peace and raise their little girl."

He was flush with the alcohol and caught himself. He'd said way too much and only hoped she was drunk enough it might not matter in the morning. He topped her glass and tried frantically to be busy about something.

"Whatever they *weren't* doing, it tore them up," Shae nodded. "Oh, there was lots of love to be sure. I never felt a loss of that. I never wanted for anything... but I always felt bad for mom and pop."

"Don't feel bad," Henny said. She'd let his misstep pass, but now, here he was doling out advice? He found himself stepping from behind the table, unable to stop himself. "Sometimes we make choices. Being a parent... settling down... it's important."

"I think they were cut out for more. I think they would like to have been heroes."

"Parenting's heroic enough, though. Am I right?" He gestured around them at the venue trashed by the wedding party.

"It is," she mused. She stood with him surveying the damage. Cups and cake and spilled drinks and chairs tipped over. Henny had seen it all before.

They made small talk about the venue and the charges, and he reminded her again he was waiving his fees for bartending. It was early in the morning, and they were the only two still around. Henny escorted her outside and looked all around before asking her his zinger: "Shae... whatever came of that baby rattle of yours?"

"That ol' thing? Why, it doesn't even rattle anymore," she chuckled. "The only time I ever saw my parents fight was over that."

"Why?"

"Momma was mad as a hornet when she found out he'd tried gluing it back together. Sloppy job, I guess. She accused pop of breaking it open—*using* it somehow when he promised her he wouldn't."

"*Using* it? Henny asked, as much to himself as to her.

"Like a grown man would have any use for a baby rattle!" She shook her head. "Like I said, Henny, they were hard to figure, but they loved hard, too."

"I'm sure they did," he confirmed, and pointed her in the direction of her hotel room. "You have a good night now, Ms. Ward."

As soon as she was out of earshot, Henny pumped his fist in the air and shouted, "I knew it!"

They'd gone back to when? The '90's? They'd made good for themselves. It was perfect. Alex Gault had used the last of the Tic-Tacs ol' Sackerson had sneaked him in that rattle.

Henny didn't yet know where or when that wild-haired stranger had strayed, but just the thought of him out there—somewhere and sometime—stretched his imagination and smile across his face.

Chapter 89 Anything

D rums.
　　Alex woke to a steady pounding, a sound he'd never heard before. He knew it had to be hundreds of drums outside the drab canvas tent he woke in. It was a barracks of sorts, and a number of people were sleeping on blankets and cots throughout.

Kelli was not one of them.

A round man with a cherub face noticed him and stepped near, his palms outstretched. "Calm, man. Calm."

"What?"

"CALM... you're at CALM, brother. They brought you in to sleep it off. You're safe here, friend."

"I... I don't understand." Alex sat up, finding himself stripped naked, nothing in his possession but Sackerson's baby rattle on a string around his neck.

"Yeah," the man said. "Found that with you. Nothing else."

"Where's my wife?"

"Just outside."

"Outside?" Alex struggled to his feet.

"I'm StayPuff," the man said, running his hand over his abdomen. "You know, like the marshmallow."

"StayPuff, eh? I'm Alex. She's... outside *where*?"

"She's in a bus. Better climate control." He gestured around the tent. "Also, more sanitary than these digs. Wounds like hers can get infected easily."

Alex glanced around for his clothes, snatched up a sheet from his cot and wrapped in it on his way out of the tent.

"I'm a doctor," StayPuff offered. "I can tell you we're doing what's best for her."

"Doctor of what?" Alex grumbled. He emerged from the tent into the cool of night. Mountain air tinged with the smell of something delicious cooking, something herbal, wood fires.

Dr. StayPuff was smiling at his side. "See? Bus village. You're in our CALM."

"Which bus?"

"Take it easy, friend."

"Friend? What are you, a quaker? Where the hell is she? Where are we?"

"A couple of greeters found you both at the main gate. Welcome home!" StayPuff said, holding his arms wide.

Alex did not accept the hug. He headed for the nearest bus. In the moon's glow everything looked stark and blue. Old school buses, rigged with roof racks, had canopies off both sides. He was heading toward one with a large red cross painted on it.

"Hello friend," a woman said as he neared the open door.

"Where's my wife?"

StayPuff was catching up to join the conversation. "He... he's with the gate girl," he puffed.

The woman's eyes flashed with surprise, then she assumed her peaceful demeanor again. "Oh yes, she's in the camper."

"Did the blood come in?"

"Yes, doctor," she said. "Plenty."

"This way," Dr. StayPuff said, pointing Alex along.

As they took off, Alex asked, "So you really *are* a doctor?"

"Proctologist, but yes," he replied.

"She's already been back on her feet," the woman offered as they were walking away.

"Really?" StayPuff asked. "Are you sure?"

"Best healers in the world, right here," she said.

It was a short, brisk walk to the campers. Dozens of old Winnebago campers were in a line along the side of the gravel drive. Alex was more aware of his surroundings. They were in the mountains. Far from a town. The incessant drumming was at his back. The moon, not full but bright, was directly overhead. Middle of the night?

"Just where is *here*?" Alex asked.

"You're at the National Gathering of the Rainbow Family of Living Light. Overland Reservoir, in colorful Colorado. And this? This camper is our ICU."

"Kelli!" Alex shouted, pushing toward the door.

"You really must chill out," StayPuff said. "And not just for the injured."

Alex looked beyond them at the many people who had stopped to stare. Dozens of people, hippie people he would call them, seemed uneasy at his shouting.

"It's okay, it's just..." he said, "my wife..."

The crowd moved on toward the drumming.

"Have you come to relieve me," asked the young girl in the captain's chair. She wore a crisp nurse's white cap but the rest of her wardrobe was tie-dyed. She was barefoot.

"Elpis, I'm bringing you our friend here. Something of an alarmist."

She said to Alex, "I think I'll call you Buzz."

"Your name is Elvis?" Alex muttered, momentarily distracted by that.

"Elpis," she corrected. "I'm the spirit of hope."

"It's her gift—well other than healing. *Naming*. In some cultures, names are infused with power, you know. To know a name is to..."

Alex wasn't listening. He was scanning the cavity of the RV. Makeshift beds lined the walls. Every bed was occupied, and every patient had an attendant. It didn't smell like a hospital. It smelled like a flower shop. The floor was ankle deep in petals.

"Kelli!" Alex pleaded in a stage whisper. "You here?"

Movement far down the line. She sat up and smiled.

Alex blew by Elpis, weaving through the cots.

"He *is* stirred up," she said.

"*By love*," a patient said, and several of them sighed a sweet "ahhhh."

He was at her side, hugging her gently. Yellow sprigs of flowers were woven into her hair. She was wearing a gauzy thin blouse, wide at the neck. Embroidered flowers trimmed the collar and cuffs.

"It's a peasant blouse," Kelli said, noticing his attention to it. "I've gone native."

"You're... you're okay?"

"I like your toga," she said.

"Ah, Bunnyhop, I'm so—"

"Her name's Willow," Elpis said. "And be careful of the—"

"I know," Alex growled.

"It's okay," Kelli said. "She's a nurse."

"Phhhpfft... *nurse*? She's too young to be a nurse. You need a doctor, real medical attention."

"Back in Babylon, I'm a phlebotomist, but here I'm—"

"Where the hell are we?" Alex asked again, then more quietly added, looking Kelli in the eye, "And *when*?"

• • • •

Kelli said they were free to roam the grounds. The work the healers had done on her seemed nothing short of miraculous. She felt little pain, which Alex attributed to the herbal remedies. She had boundless energy, which he thought a byproduct of her time traveling, perhaps, the way an astronaut experienced different gravity. This, too, he thought, could be drug induced. He was more curious than skeptical. Whatever had happened in the hours he had been unconscious was a delicious mystery; the gift of healing was one he could never repay.

Kelli told him they were in the early stages of an encampment that would swell to thousands of people in the days ahead. This was the transition, the buildup from the seed camp to the full-on Rainbow Gathering. She said they were found at the trailhead, at the gate that had not yet even been marked. Their arrival was seen as a portent: mysterious strangers stepping in from death's door, showing up at camp under a lunar eclipse.

"They're all about peace here," she said.

"Peace, love, and *weed*," Alex returned, cracking his first smile in their new world.

"Apparently Bush and Yeltsin just signed an agreement on nuclear disarmament," Kelli said. "They laugh about it. Call it a *joint* agreement."

They passed through a large open meadow where the majority of campers seemed to be assembled. This was the place the drumming was centered, Alex discovered. They had formed a very large circle and played around the clock.

When they skirted the meadow, they were met with smiles and greetings as if they had known these people all their lives. Everyone seemed to have a dog, and all the dogs were as friendly as their owners.

On the far side of the meadow, they resumed their conversation, here, where the drumming wasn't so very loud.

"Looks like we got a spirit animal," Kelli said, picking up a cat that was walking with them.

"Kelli, you'll tell me when you need to rest, right? We can go back anytime you're ready."

She pulled a deep breath of the night air. "I don't ever want to go back. Or forward. Or whatever. I like it here... and now. 1992."

"I meant back to the CALM camper."

"I know. I know..." she mused. "I just want to walk to the ends of the earth with you."

It had to be the 'medication,' Alex reasoned. For one, she was allergic to cats, and for another, she never waxed on like this. Not that he minded. She could be blissed out forever more, so long as she was on the mend.

"I don't want to go back," she continued. "This is perfect."

A passerby greeted them in some foreign tongue, hugged them each in turn and then moved on.

On a long path with no one in sight, where the trees hung heavy and dark over the path, she slowed and spoke a bit more like Captain Chase. "Sackerson couldn't have planned it better for us. Tuned us into this campground where we can be whoever we want. A clean break, he said. Even your time cops lost our trail with his Christmas Day. Just like he promised me."

"It's definitely off the radar," Alex agreed, though he was not so confident.

"We can start over here, assume identities, live our lives our way without you being afraid of being hunted." She squeezed his hand. "Ever again."

"Yeah, okay, but..." he smiled at her. "Buzz and Willow? Really?"

"Elpin and her naming? Yeah, I know... maybe a little eccentric, but you know what? She knew I was pregnant. She's already named the baby. She knows it's going to be a girl. Named her Shaelyn."

"You're kidding."

"Nope. Totally knew it from the moment they carried me through camp. One girl said she had her first born child at a Rainbow Gathering. She was sorry we wouldn't have the same experience. It sounded... well... magical."

She had such a twinkle in her eyes.

"I guess we can find a midwife wherever we—"

"A doula," Kelli corrected.

"Okay, sure. As you wish, my Buttercup." He bowed to her. "Anything you want, darlin.'"

"Anything?" She stopped and turned to face him.

"Anything," he said.

She tossed the cat aside and pulled him off into the shadows. Before he could argue her frail condition, she planted a convincing and passionate kiss on him. He forgot his reservations and lowered her to the soft forest floor.

He appreciated her broom skirt and his toga, thinking he could get used to such easy access. Then he didn't think about anything but Kelli for a good long while.

• • • •

The lunar eclipse didn't amount to much. It was a little overcast, too, but Alex lay beside her, trying to watch for falling stars up there beyond the branches. She slept safe and sound while he studied the night sky. Someday, the meteor shower would come again, bombarding Guthrie, and with it, the mystery might recycle.

He idly shook the rattle on his necklace. There might be something he could do about it, when the time came... or he might find that time and solve the problem before it even started.

She snuggled against him, and he pulled his sheet over them to ward away the cool night air. Buzz and Willow might not save the world, might not even *change* the world, but they were no longer on the run, and he no longer felt the obligations that had so weighed him down for so very long. They just might grow old together. He sighed and mused that they had time enough, at last.

Epilogue

Willy Titus was chilled and soaked to the bone. His gums were bleeding, maybe his lips too, from the hours he had spent gnawing at his restraints. Teeth were no match for parachute webbing. His back ached from being pressed against even the slightest filigree on the gravestone he was tied to.

At least the rain had lightened up.

Ashley had forgotten him.

He had read all the markers he could see from his position. His nearest neighbor had died eighty some years ago. The oldest inscription was illegible, having been washed and weathered away. A few epitaphs gave him inspiration:

"He has kept the faith." Even though it had led him to this sullen, sodden situation. Even though he had borne ridicule and rejection. He had, indeed, been faithful.

"Faith—to suffer, to die, and to rise again." Even if it killed him, Willy vowed to rise again, and this time, without mercy.

His favorite, at least within his line of sight was one between just him and Ashley Winston: "God could not have made earthly ties so strong to break them in eternity." He knew they would be reunited, and united, they would be unstoppable.

Willy sang from an old camp song, "Neither height, nor depth, nor principality, things present or things to come..." Then his tone changed, and he completed the verse with his own twist, "Though the devil hate us, he can never separate us... *Ashley*... from the wonderful love of God."

"You sing for shit, kid," a man said, approaching from behind.

Willy craned his neck, found a new pain in doing so. "Oh, hey."

The man circled around to get a good look at him. He wore a frumpy raincoat and a big brimmed fedora. He had a crooked smile. He was chewing something, like a big chaw of tobacco.

Something was wrong with his mouth, too. Scar tissue or something Willy couldn't quite make out. The guy needed a shave.

"You're with Garden?" he cocked his head, favoring one eye that seemed larger than the other. He was studying the logo on Willy's shirt.

"Yeah." Willy collected himself. "Yes, yes I am. Can you help a brother out? I'm a little... tied up here."

"What's your name, kid?"

"William Titus."

"Titus, like the Roman emperor." The man stepped closer, crouched with the aid of a cane. He was very intent.

"Titus, like Paul's amanuensis, I like to think." Willy smiled. "And who are you?"

The man bounced a little in his crouch, and a switchblade knife snapped open in his free hand. "Name's Combs. Stanley Combs."

As quickly as that, he swung the knife across Willy's restraints. They fell away like confetti.

He flicked his wrist, pocketed the knife, then stood. "I dunno what an amanasis is, but I'm looking for recruits."

He gripped his cane more tightly, then extended his other hand to help Willy to his feet. He helped brush away the cords, and Willy stepped free of the parachute trappings, altogether.

"Gypsies done you wrong, boy. Ashley Winston in particular."

"How would you... gypsies?" Willy felt a little dizzy as he regained his footing. "How would you know about Ashley doing—"

"Implants," Combs said, pointing at his eye. "I can tap into her Internals."

"You can see what she sees?"

"You can, too. Like being in her mind's eye."

Willy didn't need to think long about that. He wanted to be closer to her. He wanted to see what she might see. This man was offering that?

"Count me in," Willy said, shaking the man's hand. "But... how do we—"

Combs spit tobacco on a nearby headstone. "Have a little faith in me."

• • • •

Find your way to the author's website at MarkLandonJarvis.com[1] for newsletters, blogs, bargains and more. *You know you want to.*

1. https://www.marklandonjarvis.com/

Don't miss out!

Visit the website below and you can sign up to receive emails whenever Mark Landon Jarvis publishes a new book. There's no charge and no obligation.

https://books2read.com/r/B-A-QYDU-VFLLC

BOOKS 2 READ

Connecting independent readers to independent writers.

Also by Mark Landon Jarvis

Endless Tempest
Lost and Found

Standalone
Lightning's Hand
Bewildered

About the Author

Born when the world was black and white, when a phone was simply something one talked on, Mark Landon Jarvis appreciates modern technology and yet abhors its abuses. Most of his speculative work is from this vantage point of concerned enthusiasm.

Jarvis is from the rural Midwest. He lives on a hobby farm with his wife and four teens, along with seven goats, five dogs, four pigs, and a flock of chickens. He is a college professor and Spam connoisseur.